WILLIAM WORDSWORTH was born in Cockermouth, in Cumberland, in 1770. He lived to become Poet Laureate to the young Queen Victoria in 1843, seven years before his death in 1850. Wordsworth travelled through France during the turbulent period of the Revolution, where he met Annette Vallon, who became the mother of his first child, Caroline. After his return to England, he published *An Evening Walk* and *Descriptive Sketches* in 1793, continued to frequent radical circles, but experienced severe psychological turmoil later recalled in his great autobiographical poem, *The Prelude*. Once reunited with his sister, Dorothy, Wordsworth began a period of poetic composition which was greatly enhanced by the close friendship with Coleridge. *Lyrical Ballads*, a joint enterprise, was published anonymously in 1798, and an enlarged edition in two volumes was published under Wordsworth's name in 1800, with further additions in 1802. Wordsworth visited Germany before settling in the Lake District, which became his home for the rest of his life. He married Mary Hutchinson in 1802.

SAMUEL TAYLOR COLERIDGE was born in Ottery St Mary, in Devon, in 1772. He was a supporter of the French Revolution and worked as a political lecturer and journalist, publishing his first collection of *Poems* in 1796. With the poet Robert Southey he planned to establish an egalitarian society in America, and married Sara Fricker, sister of Southey's wife Edith. He moved to Somerset where he met Wordsworth and worked with him to produce *Lyrical Ballads*. After travel in Germany, in 1800 he moved to the Lakes to be nearer Wordsworth. He was afflicted by poor health, opium addiction and domestic unhappiness for much of his life. In 1817 he published *Biographia Literaria*, a personal account of his critical and philosophical opinions, which was to prove enormously influential. A slim volume of earlier, unpublished poems, including 'Kubla Khan' and 'Christabel', was brought out in 1816, followed by the more substantial *Sibylline Leaves* in 1817. Coleridge died in 1834.

FIONA STAFFORD is Professor of English at the University of Oxford. Her books include *Reading Romantic Poetry* (Oxford: Wiley Blackwell, 2012) and *Local Attachments: The Province of Poetry* (Oxford, 2010), and editions of Jane Austen's *Emma* (Penguin, 2003) and *Pride and Prejudice* (Oxford World's Classics, 2004).

OXFORD WORLD'S CLASSICS

*For over 100 years Oxford World's Classics have brought
readers closer to the world's great literature. Now with over 700
titles—from the 4,000-year-old myths of Mesopotamia to the
twentieth century's greatest novels—the series makes available
lesser-known as well as celebrated writing.*

*The pocket-sized hardbacks of the early years contained
introductions by Virginia Woolf, T. S. Eliot, Graham Greene,
and other literary figures which enriched the experience of reading.
Today the series is recognized for its fine scholarship and
reliability in texts that span world literature, drama and poetry,
religion, philosophy, and politics. Each edition includes perceptive
commentary and essential background information to meet the
changing needs of readers.*

OXFORD WORLD'S CLASSICS

WILLIAM WORDSWORTH and
SAMUEL TAYLOR COLERIDGE

Lyrical Ballads
1798 and 1802

Edited with an Introduction and Notes by
FIONA STAFFORD

OXFORD
UNIVERSITY PRESS

OXFORD

UNIVERSITY PRESS

Great Clarendon Street, Oxford OX2 6DP
United Kingdom

Oxford University Press is a department of the University of Oxford.
It furthers the University's objective of excellence in research, scholarship,
and education by publishing worldwide. Oxford is a registered trade mark of
Oxford University Press in the UK and in certain other countries

First published as an Oxford World's Classics paperback 2013

Impression: 16

British Library Cataloguing in Publication Data

Dataav ailable

ISBN978-0-19-960196-7

Printed in Great Britain by
Clays Ltd, Elcograf S.p.A.

ACKNOWLEDGEMENTS

SPECIAL thanks are due to Jeff Cowton and the staff of the Jerwood Centre and the Wordsworth Trust for invaluable assistance of various kinds, and for enabling access to the rich resources of the collection in Grasmere. I would also like to thank the staff of the Bodleian, the British Library, the English Faculty Library, and Somerville College Library. Those in the Academic Office at Somerville have also been cheerfully helpful in responding to various practical requests. For introducing me to Wordsworth and Coleridge, I am indebted to Kelvin Everest and Martin Stannard, and for deepening my knowledge and understanding of both poets and the period in which they worked, I owe long-standing debts to Paul Hamilton, Tony Nuttall, Roy Park, and Jonathan Wordsworth. The preparation of this edition has been greatly helped by discussions with students and colleagues over a number of years. Particular thanks are due to Ben Brice, Tim Fulford, Stephen Gill, Richard Gravil, Nicholas Halmi, Andrew McNeillie, Lucy Newlyn, Meiko O'Halloran, Craig Sharp, Neil Vickers, Damian Walford Davies, and Rachael Sparkes. Judith Luna has been the ideal editor throughout—prompt in her insightful responses, and immensely tactful in her prompts.

CONTENTS

LYRICAL BALLADS, WITH PASTORAL AND OTHER POEMS, 1802

VOL. I

VOL. II

ABBREVIATIONS

ANY editor of *Lyrical Ballads* is indebted to the remarkable work of the most distinguished Wordsworth and Coleridge scholars. The list of works below includes the books that have been most helpful in the preparation of this volume and to which the editorial material refers most frequently. Additional studies and critical works are cited in the notes and in the Select Bibliography.

BL	Samuel Taylor Coleridge, *Biographia Literaria*, ed. James Engell and Walter J. Bate, 2 vols. (Princeton, 1983).
Butler and Green	William Wordsworth, *Lyrical Ballads and Other Poems*, ed. James Butler and Karen Green (Ithaca, NY, and London, 1989).
CL	*The Letters of Samuel Taylor Coleridge*, ed. E. L. Griggs, 6 vols. (Oxford, 1956).
CP	Samuel Taylor Coleridge, *Poetical Works*, ed. J. C. C. Mays, 3 vols. (Princeton, 2001).
EY	*The Letters of William and Dorothy Wordsworth: The Early Years, 1787–1805*, ed. Ernest De Selincourt, rev. Chester L. Shaver (Oxford, 1967).
Gamer and Porter	*Lyrical Ballads, 1798 and 1800*, ed. Michael Gamer and D. Porter (Toronto, 2008).
Gill	*William Wordsworth*, ed. Stephen Gill (Oxford, 2010).
GJ	Dorothy Wordsworth, *The Grasmere Journals*, ed. Pamela Woof (Oxford, 1991).
Guide	William Wordsworth, *Guide to the Lakes*, ed. Ernest De Selincourt, with introd. Stephen Gill (London, 2004).
Hazlitt	*The Works of William Hazlitt*, ed. P. P. Howe, 21 vols. (London, 1930–4).
Herd	David Herd, *Ancient and Modern Scottish Songs*, 2 vols. (1776; Edinburgh and London, 1973).
IF	*The Fenwick Notes of William Wordsworth*, ed. Jared Curtis (London, 1993).
Jacobus	Mary Jacobus, *Tradition and Experiment in Wordsworth's Lyrical Ballads 1798* (Oxford, 1975).
Johnson	Samuel Johnson, *A Dictionary of the English Language* (London, 1755).
Journals	Dorothy Wordsworth, *Journals*, ed. Ernest De Selincourt, 2 vols. (London, 1941).
LY	*The Letters of William and Dorothy Wordsworth: The Later Years, 1821–1853*, ed. Ernest De Selincourt, rev. Alan G. Hill, 4 vols. (Oxford, 1978–88).
Mason	*Lyrical Ballads*, ed. Michael Mason (London, 1992).

McCracken   David McCracken, *Wordsworth and the Lake District* (Oxford, 1984).

MY   *The Letters of William and Dorothy Wordsworth: The Middle Years, 1806–1820*, ed. Ernest De Selincourt, rev. Mary Moorman and Alan Hill, 2 vols. (Oxford, 1969–70).

Newlyn   Lucy Newlyn, *Coleridge, Wordsworth and the Language of Allusion*, 2nd edn. (Oxford, 2001).

Notebook   *The Notebooks of Samuel Taylor Coleridge*, ed. Kathleen Coburn, 10 vols. (1957–2002).

Percy   Thomas Percy, *Reliques of Ancient English Poetry*, ed. H. B. Wheatley, 3 vols. (London, 1885).

Prose   *The Prose Works of William Wordsworth*, ed. W. J. B. Owen and Jane Worthington Smyser, 3 vols. (Oxford, 1974).

Reed   Mark L. Reed, *Chronology of the Early Years 1770–1779*; *The Middle Years, 1800–1815*, 2 vols. (Cambridge, Mass., 1967, 1975).

Ritson   Joseph Ritson, *Scottish Songs*, 2 vols. (London, 1794).

WH   T. W. Thompson, *Wordsworth's Hawkshead*, ed. Robert Woof (London, 1970).

Woof   *William Wordsworth: The Critical Heritage*, i. *1793–1820*, ed. Robert Woof (London and New York, 2001).

Wu   Wu, Duncan, *Wordsworth's Reading*, 2 vols. (Cambridge, 1993–5).

INTRODUCTION

ANYONE glancing over the opening page of *Lyrical Ballads* in 1798 might well have been rather put off. Instead of enticing readers with the promise of great art, deep wisdom, exciting or heart-rending tales, the Advertisement offered a caveat—these poems were 'experiments' and unlikely to suit everyone's taste. Prospective purchasers were even warned that should they 'persist in reading this book to its conclusion', they would have to 'struggle with feelings of strangeness and awkwardness'. This could hardly be further removed from today's glossy superlatives. That a book published in 1798 should seem less instantly eye-catching than a modern volume is not surprising, given the steady advances in book design and sales techniques in the years intervening, but the literary world of the later eighteenth century was already a jostling marketplace, with booksellers eager to meet the demand that came with improved literacy, social aspiration, and increased leisure among the middle classes. In an age when collections of poetry were increasingly prefaced by brief lives and frontispiece portraits, however, *Lyrical Ballads* entered the world without so much as a hint about the identity, education, or background of the man behind the work. The 'author' even concealed the fact that 'he' was really 'they'. Was this merely commercial ineptitude? Or reluctance to treat poetry as a consumer item, dependent on the whims of unknown readers? Or was the Advertisement the perfect threshold to a volume that was meant to surprise, challenge, and perplex those who dared to continue? The opening portrayal of the bewildered reader looking around 'for poetry' is very hard to resist.

Scholarly research has uncovered a great deal about the composition of *Lyrical Ballads*, but there is still something to be said for approaching the collection with its original readers in mind, who were picking up a slim, anonymous volume of new poems. Many modern readers have been conditioned to read the collection in relation to its famous Preface, often treated as a manifesto not only for its authors, but for the entire Romantic movement. The substantial essay was not written until 1800, however, and so those encountering the first edition of *Lyrical Ballads* in 1798 had only the anonymous Advertisement by way of preparation. Here, very few poems attracted special mention— 'Goody Blake and Harry Gill', 'The Thorn', 'Expostulation and Reply', and 'The Rime of the Ancyent Marinere'—and there was little guidance as to meaning. What it did suggest, among the tongue-in-cheek warnings about style, was that the poems were nevertheless 'a natural delineation of human passions, human characters and human incidents'. Four years later in 1802, the third edition of *Lyrical Ballads* would be introduced with an eloquent account of the poet as 'a Man speaking to men', but even in the first, anonymous edition, the emphasis was on the human dimensions of the poems.

For those willing to respond sympathetically came the invitation to 'consent to be pleased in spite of that most dreadful enemy to our pleasures, our own pre-established codes of decision' (p. 3). In other words, *Lyrical Ballads* was intended primarily to please, but the poems would only succeed with those prepared to abandon their prejudices and allow themselves to be moved by the unexpected. The speaker in 'Expostulation and Reply' observes that 'we can feed this mind of ours | In a wise passiveness' (ll. 23–4), and so the brief, apparently humorous, reference to the poem in the Advertisement was also a gentle pointer towards open-mindedness as the condition for mental growth. When the collection was reorganized for the second edition in 1800, 'Expostulation and Reply' and its companion, 'The Tables turned', were moved to prime position at the start of Volume I. Those who bought the expanded, two-volume *Lyrical Ballads* were thus advised to stop reading—'Close up these barren leaves'—by the time they reached the second poem. In this larger edition, however, the extensive—and evidently serious—new Preface provided a considerable counterweight to the quiet wit of the poems themselves. In the original 1798 volume, the joke in 'The Tables turned' seemed lighter and, since the short lyric was positioned towards the end of the collection, remained imperceptible until readers had been very persistent.

With nothing but a warning to abandon all preconceptions, then, the first readers of *Lyrical Ballads* were plunged into the opening poem—'The Rime of the Ancyent Marinere'. And what could be more disconcerting than this? The 'Argument' promises 'strange things' in a voyage to the remotest parts of the earth, while the central figure is identified only by his occupation and age. And if the comment that the poem imitated 'the *style* as well as . . . the spirit of the elder poets' (p. 4) meant that its old-fashioned diction was not wholly unexpected, nothing prepared readers for the sudden appearance of the Mariner, with his 'long grey beard' and 'glittering eye', nor the predicament of the Wedding-Guest, who remains in his power, baffled and terrified, throughout. Eighteenth-century readers were more accustomed than modern audiences to traditional ballads, which had been enjoying a major revival through the printed collections of Allan Ramsay, Thomas Percy, David Herd, and Joseph Ritson,[1] but none of the familiar folk narratives or old songs was quite like this. The 'Rime' may open with a wedding, but it is no love story. It tells of a voyage, but there is no obvious objective: no king's command, no princess to be escorted, no wrong to be righted, no quest to be accomplished, no land to be discovered, no treasure to be found. And yet, as the tale continues, the reader, like the Wedding-Guest, 'cannot chuse but hear' (l. 22). It may be the Mariner's bright eye that overpowers the Wedding-Guest, but readers are entranced by the sound of his words:

> Listen Stranger! Storm and Wind,
>   A Wind and Tempest strong!
> For days and weeks it play'd us freaks—
>   Like Chaff we drove along. (ll. 45–8)

Throughout, the poem works aurally and visually. The chaff-like ship, the 'mast-high', emerald-green ice, or the 'broad and burning face' of the sun, peering out through prison bars, all make an indelible impression on the imagination, but equally powerful are the accompanying sounds, 'With heavy thump, a lifeless lump', or the deathly silence, without 'breath ne motion'. Perhaps most striking of all, though, is the strong rhythm and insistent rhymes that propel the poem through the long sea miles and 151 stanzas:

> The Ice was here, the Ice was there,
>   The Ice was all around:
> It crack'd and growl'd, and roar'd and howl'd—
>   Like noises of a swound. (ll. 57–60)

We accept the strangeness of the acoustics largely because of the satisfying metre and internal rhyme—'It crack'd and growl'd, and roar'd and howl'd': the rightness of the sound enables the animation of the towering icebergs and intensifies the pervasive sense of apprehension. The rhyme gives momentum to the verse, even as the words suggest painfully slow progress through a terrifying frostscape. Like the Wedding-Guest, the Mariner has been trapped by forces greater than

---

[1] On the ballad revival, Nick Groom, *The Making of Percy's Reliques* (Oxford, 1999); Maureen Maclane, *Balladeering, Minstrelsy and the Making of British Romantic Poetry* (Cambridge, 2008); Patricia Fumerton and Anita Guerrini (eds.), *Ballads and Broadsides in Britain, 1500–1800* (Farnham, 2010). See also Jacobus for the popularity of Bürger's ballads and reprints of William Taylor's English translations of 1796.

himself, and the reader experiences a similar powerlessness as the poem slows and speeds on its way.

Although the poem appears to adopt a simple, ballad form, its stanzas vary in length and pattern, often reflecting the twists and turns of the narrative. Unexpected metrical disruptions contribute directly to the overall uncertainty and, as the breeze drops, for example, so does the jaunty third-line rhyme: 'And we did speak only to break | The silence of the Sea' (ll. 105–6). The visual resemblance of 'speak' and 'break' recalls the full rhymes of the previous stanza, but it is as if the verse is registering its own fault-lines, for in the ensuing stanzas, the third lines are distinguished by the absence of their internal chime. In what is perhaps the best-known stanza of the entire poem, the third line not only lacks a rhyme, but seems so drained of energy that it fails even to muster new words:

> Water, water, every where
> And all the boards did shrink;
> Water, water, every where,
> Ne any drop to drink. (ll. 115–18)

When, at the end of this section, the rhyme is restored, its impact is all the more powerful: 'Instead of a Cross the Albatross | About my neck was hung' (ll. 138–9). The unfamiliar spellings also draw attention to the sight and sound of the words, as when the famished sailors, 'With throat unslack'd, with black lips bak'd' (l. 149), both invite and discourage an internal rhyme. For a modern readership, thirst would demand a throat 'unslaked' rather than 'unslack'd', a suggestion strengthened by the rhyme with 'bak'd'. However, pressure from the 'black' lips works to render the throat 'unslack'd' and the line more awkward and prolonged—as befits the desperation being conveyed. 'Unslack'd' or 'unslak'd'? In later versions of the poem, the ambiguity was resolved as the word was revised to 'unslaked', but the first readers of *Lyrical Ballads* had the disconcerting—and exciting—experience of two possibilities simultaneously. Since the origin of the verb 'slake' relates to loosen, relax, or slacken, the line in 'The Ancyent Marinere' was effectively recalling the earlier meaning and in doing so, revitalizing commonplace language and restoring a metaphor long dimmed by familiar usage.

In the later eighteenth century, the language of the older poets was increasingly admired for its natural energy and figurative character. To imitate the spirit of past masters also meant being true to their original genius—so an enterprise that might risk descending into pastiche could, in fact, be highly innovative. A ballad was no longer traditional once its form had been stretched to embrace the travel account, natural history, true adventure, ghost story, imaginary voyage, spiritual autobiography, confession, Gothic drama, conversion narrative, and even medical case-study. The timelessness of the encounter between the Wedding-Guest and Mariner, with its unspecified location and uncertain conclusion, gave readers the freedom to make what they would of the tale. Why does the Mariner act as he does? Is what follows the consequence of his crime, or a random sequence of events, wrestled into order by a traumatized victim? The poem conveys a deep sense of guilt, but offers little by way of explanation.[2] If some lines invite religious readings, much of the detail suggests the influence of modern scientific exploration. Traditional ballads carried stories that had been repeated over centuries, with different meanings for successive generations and so, too, 'The Rime of the Ancyent Marinere' came laden with unpredictable possibility. *Lyrical Ballads* opened with a poem that was at once traditional and experimental.

Since 'The Rime' ran to fifty pages of the first edition, with its small pages and spacious page layout, its original readers may well have experienced something of a shock when it finally came to an end. If they turned the page expecting a further narrative in brisk ballad stanzas, they were in for another surprise, for here was 'a dramatic fragment' in blank verse, offering a dialogue between two women. It was a 'Tale', but no more a ballad than what came next: 'Lines left upon a Seat in a Yew-tree'. After this there was more blank verse in 'The Nightingale', but instead of being a retrospective on solitude, this was a 'Conversational Poem', and a very recent one, judging by the subtitle: 'written in April, 1798'. Presumably these were some of the 'Few Other Poems' advertised on the title page? Most of what followed was stanzaic: some ballad-like, some lyrical, some Spenserian, and some almost resembling nursery rhymes. For readers expecting traditional ballads, 'The Mad Mother' might have recalled the 'Lament of Lady Anne Bothwell' and 'The Thorn', 'The Cruel Mother', both widely familiar from popular folk collections. Lyrics such as 'Lines written in early spring' also had something in common with Scottish songs featuring the arrival of spring, which eighteenth-century editors often included alongside older ballads. Those who had thrilled to recently published translations of German Gothic ballads might also have noticed in 'The Thorn' a similarity to Gottfried Bürger's

---

[2] Coleridge added the marginal glosses to the poem in 1817 (see App. 1).

'The Lass of Fair Wone', or to Leonora's ghostly night-ride in 'The Idiot Boy'. No previous ballad, however, had dared to take as its subject matter the feelings of a mother so desperate to help a sick friend that she despatched her mentally impaired child on horseback at night to fetch the doctor, nor to treat a tale of this kind with such high-spirited good humour. The comic portrayal of Susan Gale's illness, Johnny's disability, or Betty Foy's mounting panic can make us laugh *and* wince, while simultaneously inviting participation in the very real emotions that drive the poem. As the Advertisement warned, most of the pieces were 'absolute inventions' or 'personal observations' and any assumptions based on earlier reading were to be set aside.

Whatever the title, *Lyrical Ballads*, may have suggested, the recommendation to abandon 'pre-established codes' was reiterated throughout. In 'The Nightingale', age-old literary conventions were explicitly overturned, as the eloquent speaker invites his readers to reconsider the traditional association of nightingales with melancholy, through listening directly to the birds. The baby's laughter at the nightingale's 'skirmish and capricious passagings, | And murmurs musical and swift jug jug' (ll. 59–60) demonstrates the wisdom of 'The Tables turned', that 'One impulse from a vernal wood' teaches more 'Than all the sages can' (ll. 21–4). The underlying seriousness is almost lost amidst the immediate celebration of love and nature—and the running joke about the perils of reading. Such powerful evocation of first-hand experience is nevertheless part of the wider emphasis on reconsidering inherited truths and tired language. Here nothing is to be taken for granted and 'wise passiveness' is really a means to independent thought. *Lyrical Ballads* gives pleasure by evoking emotion: grief, sorrow, joy, laughter, indignation, and resignation; but it also makes readers think—and rethink.

Even the seemingly simplest poems had the capacity to wrong-foot readers. In 'We are Seven', the limitations of the opening voice are quickly revealed, as conventional thinking about mortality is challenged by the larger, imaginative understanding of one whose ideas have yet to be conditioned by her elders. In 'Simon Lee', the surprise is delivered by an older figure, whose experience punctures both the speaker's assumed superiority and the reader's comfortable sense of poetic norms. The lively rhythm and simple opening images evoke a traditional hunting song, making its subsequent revelation of the physical facts of illness, poverty, and old age all the more distressing. Rather than joining in any jolly chorus about running with the hounds or hallooing down the hillside, we are left to make what we can of

Simon's tale, by the subdued voice of a narrator prompted to mourning by 'the gratitude of men'. 'Old Man travelling' is equally unsettling, not on account of the physical facts of ageing, which are presented much more calmly, but because of the direct speech that suddenly overturns the earlier, third-person, perspective. At first, everything seems to lead naturally from the subtitle, 'Animal Tranquillity and Decay' towards a state of 'perfect peace'. Conversation with someone so composed that even the wild birds are unafraid seems oddly intrusive, and yet, when he is at last invited to speak, his words challenge everything that has seemed so settled. Far from being a distant figure, quite beyond feeling or social interaction, the intensely human quality of the old man floods the poem, leaving the voice of the observer entirely submerged.

This is a volume in which nothing is quite as it seems, where what appears to be the guiding voice of a poem is repeatedly exposed as unreliable or in need of redirection. From the very first poem, readers were disconcerted and dislocated, and the mysterious voyage led into poems set all over England and Wales, and even North America. Some characters in *Lyrical Ballads* are named, but most of the speakers are identified only by their situation or state of mind—a Forsaken Indian Woman, the Mad Mother, the Female Vagrant. One of the few directions offered in the Advertisement is to read 'The Thorn' not as the words of the author, but of a 'loquacious narrator' whose character 'will sufficiently shew itself' (p. 4). What may initially appear to be a sensational ballad about abandonment, infanticide, and insanity might be better understood as a dramatic monologue, an exploration of storytelling, or perhaps of the workings of superstition on suggestible minds. Like 'The Thorn', many of the poems seem to direct attention to a particular figure, but increasingly reveal more about the speaker than the ostensible subject. Often, startling moments of clarity occur when the most unlikely figures command attention, making readers reassess almost everything hitherto taken for granted. For many poetry readers of the 1790s, the idea that the homeless, the uneducated, the abandoned, the poor, the very old or very young should not only matter, but have things to *teach* those whose lives were rather more secure, was decidedly unsettling. In the decade of the French Revolution, the suffering of those unprotected by wealth and rank was evident everywhere, but so too were the measures designed to contain any internal threat to national stability. To find new poems expressing not so much pity as sympathetic admiration and even reverence for those whose lives had fallen outside the pale of respectability was to encounter revolutionary voices, whose meaning went beyond matters of literary style. This was perhaps another reason for the anonymity of the collection.

The early warnings of 'strangeness and awkwardness' related not solely to antique spellings or unadorned language, then, but to the whole reading experience. By the end of the volume, readers had witnessed such a range of human passions, human characters, and human incidents that they could no longer have any confident expectation about what the next poem might bring, nor what response it might elicit. The irony of the Advertisement's quip about the persistent reader struggling onwards only became fully apparent, however, at the end of the volume, for the final poem, 'Lines written a few miles above Tintern Abbey', with its famous setting, fluid blank verse, and emphasis on returning to the familiar, was probably the least likely to seem strange or awkward and the most likely to satisfy those in search of poetry. As another of the 'Few Other Poems', its very existence was a hidden surprise. What was really unexpected, though, was the range, tone, and sheer beauty of the closing poem. In any other volume, 'Lines written a few miles above Tintern Abbey' would probably have been the title poem, but here it was, lying almost like a postscript to the collection.

If many of the preceding poems had been table-turners, the final, blank verse performance seemed to shift the entire volume into a different mode. The contrast between the ambling anapaests of 'The Convict' and the confident, self-authenticating rhythm of the poem that follows could hardly be more marked. It is as if the last, tentative, word of 'The Convict'—'again'—has been caught up and transformed into a kind of refrain:

> Five years have passed; five summers, with the length
> Of five long winters! and again I hear
> These waters, rolling from their mountain-springs
> With a sweet inland murmur.—Once again
> Do I behold these steep and lofty cliffs,
> Which on a wild secluded scene impress
> Thoughts of more deep seclusion; and connect
> The landscape with the quiet of the sky. (ll. 1–8)

The unassuming 'again' appears only four times in the first fifteen lines of the poem, but because it is surrounded by so many repeating words and phrases, every detail seems to be uniting in an overall celebration of continuity and recurrence. The speaker is returning to a place of perpetual renewal, where everything is connected and everything replenished, and where the sense of gratitude flows as surely as the rolling waters. As the poem moves on, the feeling of being part of 'something far more deeply interfused' (l. 97) is voiced in the hymn-like celebration of that which 'impels | All thinking things, all objects of all thought, | And rolls through all things (ll. 101–3). The poem meanders from individual experience to embrace an all-encompassing affirmation of spirituality, but already in the opening lines, a sense of connection is emerging through the description of the landscape.

For the first readers of *Lyrical Ballads*, the title of the poem would probably have raised expectations of a loco-descriptive poem, centring on Tintern Abbey. The site was a very popular tourist destination in the 1790s, made famous by books such as Thomas Whatley's *Modern Gardening*, William Gilpin's *Observations on the Wye*, and the fashionable discussions of picturesque landscape by Richard Payne Knight and Uvedale Price, who both owned estates in the Wye Valley. As with all the poems in *Lyrical Ballads*, however, preconceptions were not a reliable guide, and although by this stage in the volume readers were probably no longer looking round for poetry, they might still seek in vain for Tintern Abbey. The famous ruin never appears in the poem and despite the specificity of the title, with its precise date, 13 July 1798, the actual setting 'a few miles above' Tintern is rather less easy to identify. The Banks of the Wye run for many miles and any clues about the poem's location are oddly inconclusive; even the early footnote does little more than echo the vagueness of the title: 'The river is not affected by the tides a few miles above Tintern' (p. 87). Although this can be taken as an explanation for the 'sweet'—or unsalty—murmur of the waters, it also serves to emphasize the elusiveness of the scene. For such a confident poem, 'Lines written a few miles above Tintern Abbey' is decidedly tentative in its development, constantly suggesting what is by what is not. The steady accumulation of negatives ('not', 'neither', 'nor', 'no more') throughout nevertheless produces an extraordinarily positive effect overall. Even in the opening passage, where the speaker's delight in seeing the landscape again is so vividly conveyed, the description is perpetually qualified, as if the immediate response is not quite full enough. The 'orchard tufts', which 'lose themselves' among the woods seem almost deliberately hiding from view, while the hedgerows are 'hardly hedgerows' and the wreaths of smoke are rising 'with uncertain notice'. The smoke may indicate 'vagrant dwellers' in the woods, or a hermit at his cave, but by now we are in the realms of speculation, not sight, led on by the poet's imagination, or perhaps his memory of the earlier visit. Though the scene is so vivid, it is oddly difficult to visualize in any fixed, photographic way, and even the river, though audible, may or may not be visible. Can the speaker 'behold' the Wye now, or is he recalling it from before? The fluidity of memory is evident throughout the poem, but it also shows that the present is in motion, because even immediate impressions are coloured by earlier experience—the eye and ear half-create as well as perceiving.

Although the opening lines, with the dominant present tense, emphasize the now-ness of the speaker's experience, traces of earlier experience are also evident, quietly contributing to the complicated sense of connection and rediscovery. Eighteenth-century readers would have been quick to recognize the language of the picturesque in the 'steep and lofty cliffs', but there is no attempt here to seize a tiny portion of the whole for a manageable view. The poem, if anything, seems to reject the fashionable emphasis on turning the world into a series of pleasing pictures and to reveal instead the human significance of the place. The Wye Valley means somewhere 'Felt in the blood, and felt along the heart' (l. 29) and the poem seeks to convey depth as well as surface. The opening section is filled with words that carry literary as well as geographical meanings—the '*lines* | Of sportive wood', the '*pastoral* farms', the '*plots* of cottage-ground', the 'wild, secluded *scene*' (my italics). This is a landscape filled with hidden stories, somewhere that means everything to those who live there and yet remains open to those who come and go—vagrants can also be 'dwellers' in this place of connection, where all is deeply interfused.

Beneath the immediate satisfaction of the senses, the poem overflows with things felt, if not fully articulated, and the numerous half-glimpsed literary allusions all contribute to the larger sense. The curious footnote referring readers to an 'admirable line of Young' which cannot quite be recollected, succeeds in both introducing and distancing other poems. As the poem describes the 'blessed mood', when even the blood-flow is 'almost suspended' and we 'become a living soul', its language evokes the original moment of life, as presented in *Paradise Lost* with the creation of Adam and Eve. It is as if physical revisiting is a kind of rebirth, enabling divine connection and poetic renewal. And yet, the allusions are so much part of the personal experience as to be scarcely perceptible, and certainly far from essential to the enjoyment of the poem. Are they there, or not there? Remembered or unremembered? Echoes may sound very differently in different ears, and may not sound at all. But that sense of catching something, of perceiving what is only half-visible and perhaps half-created by the perceiver, is a brilliant rhetorical strategy for conveying the central experience of revisiting. The poem captures the complicated sensation of seeing something that has been seen before, may be remembered in parts, but never in full. The blend of earlier writings with new lines creates a momentary sense of familiarity which is then submerged almost at once beneath the dazzling surface. For at the forefront of the poem is a strong, distinctive voice, expressing personal enthusiasm for the here and now: a passionate response to a real place and a present moment overwhelming the past.

Connection with the past is nevertheless the premise of this returning poem, which sits firmly at the end of *Lyrical Ballads*, looking back and yet directing readers towards the future. Wherever the experience takes place, it is not in isolation and unlike the last visit, five years before, the poet returns to the Wye with a beloved companion, 'My dear, dear Sister!' (l. 122). The landscape that has lived in his mind, prompted his reaffirmation as a created and creative being, has now become even 'more dear' for her sake: just as it has sustained him through periods of absence and deprivation, so he imagines his companion being similarly supported in the years ahead. Where earlier eighteenth-century poets peopled their odes with personified figures of abstract virtue— Peace, Hope, Simplicity—'Lines written a few miles above Tintern Abbey' ends with a real woman in a real place. Thankfulness rolls through everything, and although its sources remain largely hidden from view, the feeling is evident to anyone who is prepared to read the poem with sympathy. The promise of a 'natural delineation of human passions' is more than fulfilled by the closing poem of the volume, which celebrates both 'nature and the language of the sense' as

> The anchor of my purest thoughts, the nurse,
> The guide, the guardian of my heart, and soul
> Of all my moral being. (ll. 110–12)

This is not just a reiteration of the advice offered in 'The Tables turned', but an expression of faith made all the more powerful by the poem's emphasis on real, personal experience. Of all the statements in this apparently modest volume, none is more startling than this.

Wordsworth, Coleridge, and the Beginnings of Lyrical Ballads

That *Lyrical Ballads* should end on a note of gratitude for shared experience is only too appropriate, for it was the joint enterprise of two brilliant young men, whose creative collision proved life-changing to both. The 'dear, dear Sister' celebrated on the Banks of the Wye, in 'The Nightingale', and in 'Lines written at a small distance from my House', was also a crucial element in this highly volatile, interactive company. William Wordsworth and Samuel Taylor Coleridge first met briefly in Bristol in 1795, but many months were to pass before they became properly acquainted. In September 1795, William and his sister, Dorothy, now reunited after years of separation, moved into a house belonging to friends in Racedown, Dorset. In December of the following year, Samuel Taylor Coleridge and his wife, Sara, with their baby son, Hartley, arrived in neighbouring Somersetshire to rent a cottage in the small village of Nether Stowey. The two men had been well aware of each other for some years. As a student in Cambridge when Wordsworth's *An Evening Walk* and *Descriptive Sketches* were published in 1793, Coleridge had been very struck by their distinctive language, at once 'peculiar and strong, but at times knotty and con-torted, as by its own impatient strength' (*BL* i. 77). Though two years his junior, Coleridge had also registered positively on Wordsworth's mental horizon, as a prizewinning student poet and then a published writer and lecturer, committed to humanitarian causes. Coleridge's first book, *Poems on Various Subjects*, published in April 1796, included 'Lines written at Shurton Bars', with its allusion to *An Evening Walk* and note on Wordsworth as a Poet 'unrivalled among the writers of the present day in manly sentiment, novel imagery, and vivid colour-ing' (*CP* I. i. 236).[3] Wordsworth, in turn, borrowed lines from 'The Complaint of Ninathoma' for his own 'Address to the Ocean', and published the poem in the *Weekly Entertainer* with a similar note acknowledging his debt to Mr Coleridge. The two writers were, in a sense, working together even before they really knew each other at all.

Aspiring poets are usually highly sensitive to their contemporaries and to the prevailing literary climate, but Wordsworth and Coleridge also shared political opinions, intellectual interests, and educational experiences. Both had been students at Cambridge, both had been enthusiastic supporters of the French Revolution, and both became involved in radical circles after they left. Like other British radicals of the day, they then had to come to terms with the violent, unpredictable course of events across the Channel, with the French declaration of

---

[3] For Wordsworth and Coleridge's mutual discovery and for the biographical con-texts of *Lyrical Ballads*, see Stephen Gill's definitive biography, *William Wordsworth: A Life* (Oxford, 1989).

war, and with their own government's subsequent repression of any-
thing deemed seditious. The outcry against intellectuals such as Joseph
Priestley, whose house, laboratory, and library were sacked on Bastille
Day in 1791, or the public arrests and high-profile Treason Trials of
political writers such as John Thelwall, rendered any expression of
sympathy for Liberty, Equality, or Fraternity very dangerous indeed.[4]
Since Britain had long since prided herself as the home of Liberty,
however, many of her citizens, deeply troubled by such reactions to the
French Revolution, felt that the need to defend human rights was more
urgent than ever. At the same time, the declaration of war in February
1793 meant that those who had welcomed the storming of the Bastille
as the dawn of a new age were now faced with the prospect of violent
invasion by their Continental brothers. In October 1797, a French
battalion landed on the coast of Pembrokeshire and, though rapidly
defeated, made the new military threat to British Liberty very real.
Only months later, news that France had invaded Switzerland, the
small mountainous country and home of modern republicanism, was
chastening even to the most committed radical. For young men gripped
by a compulsion to write and a burning desire to make their world a
better place, the national mood of anxiety and the atmosphere of
repression were at once stimulating and frustrating. It is not surpris-
ing, then, that when Wordsworth and Coleridge met again in 1797,
they felt a deep bond of mutual admiration.

Coleridge arrived at Racedown in the first week of June and stayed
for the rest of the month. On the first day, he listened to Wordsworth's
new poem, *The Ruined Cottage*, and, after tea, read out the opening acts
of his own play, *Osorio*. The following morning, Wordsworth
responded with his tragedy, *The Borderers*. The effect of Coleridge's
arrival is best caught in a surviving letter by Dorothy Wordsworth,
who wrote: 'He is a wonderful man. His conversation teems with soul,
mind, and spirit. Then he is so benevolent, so good tempered and
cheerful, and, like William, interests himself so much about every
trifle. At first I thought him very plain, that is, for about three minutes'
(*EY*, 188–9). Coleridge was equally impressed by Wordsworth's
'exquisite Sister', whose eye was 'watchful in minutest observation
of nature' and whose taste was 'a perfect electrometer' (*CL* i. 330–1).
As for Wordsworth himself, Coleridge tried to explain to his publisher,
Joseph Cottle, 'I feel myself a *little man by his* side: & yet do not think

[4] Nicholas Roe, *Wordsworth and Coleridge: The Radical Years* (Oxford, 1988);
Kenneth Johnston, *The Hidden Wordsworth* (New York, 1998); Gill, *Wordsworth: A Life*.

myself the less man, than I formerly thought myself.' Far from being intimidating, Coleridge's sense that his new friend was 'the greatest Man he ever knew' (*CL* i 325) was enormously empowering. That each man should wholeheartedly admire and be admired by the other was a positive affirmation of their lives and work to date—and a massive encouragement to future endeavours.

Within days of Coleridge's extended visit to Racedown, the Wordsworths were in Nether Stowey, continuing the creative conversation and in search of a new home. They moved into Alfoxden House, only about 4 miles from Coleridge's cottage, in July and for the next few months were almost constantly in each other's company, talking and walking in the Quantock Hills, reading and discussing books, and entertaining a stream of visitors. It may have been the visit from John Thelwall that prompted the arrival of Mr Walsh, a government spy, who sent reports on the suspicious group of 'disaffected Englishmen' to the Home Office. Alfoxden House also provided a home for Basil Montagu, the 5-year-old son of one of Wordsworth's friends, who was under their care until he was old enough for school. For a group already concerned with theories of mental development and the social implications of educational practice, both little Basil and baby Hartley were sources of endless intellectual fascination, as well as the more commonly experienced emotions associated with parenting and childcare. As the same group had also been deeply affected by the loss of their own parents in childhood and subsequent separation from siblings, the recreation of a family atmosphere was also satisfying a much more profound need. Wordsworth, especially, was haunted by memories of Revolutionary France and painful thoughts of his French lover, Annette Vallon, and their young daughter, Caroline, whom he had never even cradled because the war which forced him back to England made subsequent Channel crossings impossible. To be part of a loving, sympathetic circle now was to feel blessed indeed. These new-found, highly charged emotional and intellectual relationships seemed to be fostered by the surrounding hills and woodlands, where streams ran as rapidly and variously as their thoughts. The place seemed made for poetry. When William Hazlitt visited Alfoxden, he was struck by the harmony between the poets and their place, as he listened to Coleridge reciting one of Wordsworth's poems 'on the trunk of an old ash-tree that stretched along the ground'. Hazlitt saw Coleridge being drawn to the 'traditional superstitions of the place', while Wordsworth's genius 'sprung out of the ground like a flower, or unfolded itself from a green spray, on which the goldfinch sang' (Woof, 42).

It was only when they began to make bracing winter tours, exploring the Exmoor coast-path towards the Valley of Stones, however, that *Lyrical Ballads* really came into being. The earliest reference to 'The Rime of the Ancyent Marinere' is in a letter written by Dorothy Wordsworth in November 1797, which describes their latest evening walk of 8 miles, with 'William and Coleridge employing themselves in laying the plan of a ballad, to be published with some pieces of William's' (*EY*, 194). Some years later, both Wordsworth and Coleridge would single out the composition of 'The Rime' as the genesis of *Lyrical Ballads*, even though their retrospective accounts differed considerably. As he reviewed his long writing career in 1843, Wordsworth explained to his friend Isabella Fenwick that 'The Rime of the Ancyent Marinere' was conceived as a collaborative project during the walking tour to Watchet, largely to pay for the trip. Wordsworth recalled furnishing some ideas and even a few lines of the poem, but as the effort of joint composition began to reveal some fundamental creative differences, he had rapidly concluded that the best thing was to 'separate from an undertaking upon which I could only have been a clog' (*IF*, 3). Coleridge's surviving recollections are rather more formal, being part of his elaborate literary memoir, *Biographia Literaria*, published in 1817. Here, the origins of *Lyrical Ballads* formed the start of the second volume, following extensive philosophical analysis of the imagination. Unsurprisingly in this context, Coleridge made no reference to 'The Ancyent Marinere' as a holiday enterprise, presenting it rather as part of a larger project, carefully planned according to serious poetic principles. In Coleridge's account, a division of labour was agreed from the start, his own task being to focus on 'persons and characters supernatural, or at least romantic; yet so as to transfer from our inward nature a human interest and semblance of truth sufficient to procure for these shadows of imagination that willing suspension of disbelief for the moment, which constitutes poetic faith' (*BL* ii. 6). To complement the supernatural poetry, Wordsworth's aim was to

give the charm of novelty to things of every day, and to excite a feeling analogous to the supernatural, by awakening the mind's attention from the lethargy of custom, and directing it to the loveliness and wonders of the world before us; an inexhaustible treasure, but for which in consequence of the film of familiarity and selfish solicitude, we have eyes, yet see not, ears that hear not, and hearts that neither feel nor understand (*BL* ii. 7)

And with these principles as a guide, Coleridge recalled: 'I wrote the "Ancient Mariner".'

For both Coleridge and Wordsworth, 'The Ancyent Marinere' represented the beginning of a working partnership, which first became public in October 1798, with the appearance of *Lyrical Ballads*. Their insistence on anonymity, in opposition to the publisher's advice, was partly pragmatic—as Coleridge commented, 'Wordsworth's name is nothing, to a large number of persons, mine *stinks*' (*CL* i. 412)—but also consistent with principles developed in tandem with composition of the poems. For although a few pieces had been written earlier and some were adapted from longer works, most of the poems published in 1798 had been written in the months preceding. The final contents were still being decided only weeks before publication, with 'The Nightingale' replacing 'Lewti', which had already appeared under Coleridge's name in the *Morning Post*. Wordsworth's grandest poem appeared at the very end because the others were already in the press when he returned from his walking tour of the Wye in July with 'Lines written a few miles above Tintern Abbey' in his hands. Such openness to change was nevertheless part of the very character of *Lyrical Ballads*, which had grown so rapidly through the spring of 1798, gathering strength from the invigorating conversations about poetry, its nature, style, subjects, and purpose.

While evidently coloured by the intervening years and changing relationship with Wordsworth, Coleridge's emphasis in *Biographia Literaria* on the 'two cardinal points of poetry' demonstrated in *Lyrical Ballads* remains instructive. Poetry, according to Coleridge, should have 'the power of exciting the sympathy of the reader by a faithful adherence to the truth of nature, and the power of giving the interest of novelty by the modifying colours of the imagination' (*BL* ii. 5), and if *Lyrical Ballads* is read in the light of this ideal, some of the more surprising subjects become easier to understand. The intense focus on human suffering, the revelation of profound feeling in unexpected quarters, were part of a new understanding of the nature of poetry—which was to find emotional significance in subjects either too familiar to be seen truly, or too unfamiliar to offer any immediate bond of connection. The essential 'novelty' of poetry arose from the fresh perception and treatment of things, rather than being inherent in the things themselves. This is why the volume might initially appear to offer familiar poetic kinds or subjects and yet deliver such a startling reading experience. As the Advertisement made plain, these poems were 'experiments'.

To make the supernatural entirely believable, or to transform the ordinary into something equally compelling, required extraordinary imaginative and technical powers. Whether these twin aims were originally so clearly separated is open to question, however. For although the supernatural elements are most obvious in 'The Ancyent Marinere', the poem can be—and has often been—read psychologically or symbolically. Conversely, Wordsworth's 'Goody Blake and Harry Gill' or 'The Thorn' may offer themselves as 'supernatural' or Gothic poems. For many readers, the greatest 'supernatural' presence in *Lyrical Ballads* is God, whose power can be felt with equal force in 'The Ancyent Marinere' and 'Tintern Abbey' and who might also be found showering the 'blessings' of 'the first mild day of March', presiding over 'evening darkness' on the Thames, or protecting the transfigured Idiot Boy. Wordsworth may have been intent on exciting 'feelings analogous to the supernatural' in his focus on the 'every day', but, as Coleridge's biblical echoes emphasize, in redeeming those who have 'eyes, yet see not, ears that hear not, and hearts that neither feel nor understand', his poetry was also inherently spiritual.[5] Nor were Coleridge's contributions to the volume exclusively concerned with otherworldliness; apart from 'The Rime', the poems that most closely fitted the 'supernatural' specification—'Christabel' and 'Kubla Khan'— were not included. Those that did appear—'The Nightingale', 'The Foster Mother's Tale', 'The Dungeon'—were all as concerned with the 'loveliness and wonders of the world before us' as Wordsworth's contributions. In the months when the two friends were working together, they were sharing ideas and books: Wordsworth's borrowed copy of Erasmus Darwin's scientific study *Zoonomia*, which provided the psychological case-study behind 'Goody Blake and Harry Gill', was just as interesting to Coleridge as he worked on poems dealing with curses, dreams, mesmeric power, and infant development. When *Lyrical Ballads* was offered to Cottle in the spring of 1798, Coleridge was more concerned with its overall unity than with making distinctions: 'We deem that the volumes offered to you are to a certain degree *one work*, in *kind tho' not in degree*, as an Ode is one work—& that our different poems are as stanzas, good relatively rather than absolutely' (*CL* i. 412).

Whatever the authors' later views, the volume published in 1798 was presented very much as '*one work*'. Its internal variety may therefore be seen not in terms of contradiction or incompatibility, but rather as an essential aspect of its overall originality. Don Paterson has commented admiringly on Robert Burns's ability to accommodate 'humorous and

---

[5] Jeremiah 5: 21; 6: 10.

grave registers within the same poem', contrasting this with our own 'less emotionally sophisticated times', when different moods have tended to be assigned different genres.[6] In Paterson's reading, the complexity of Burns's tone is crucial to his 'project of showing the whole man'—a comment that may also illuminate the mixed style of another volume published only two years after Burns's death. *Lyrical Ballads*, with its emphasis on the varied situations and perspectives of men and women, children and parents, old and young, rich and poor, distant and local, healthy and sick, seems to strive, overall, towards a representation of complete human experience, shifting register to accommodate the extraordinary range and subtlety of associated emotions. In this collection, too, laughter and tears are often provoked by the same poem, the reading experience more easily felt than described.

When the volume was published in London, in October 1798, reactions were, unsurprisingly, mixed. Although Sara Coleridge had concluded by the following March that 'The Lyrical Ballads are laughed at and disliked by all with very few excepted' (Woof, 58), the surviving critical notices and private letters of the period tell a different story. The notice in the *New Annual Register*, for example, considered the ballads to be 'distinguished by great simplicity and tenderness' and the other poems, 'highly beautiful and pleasing', while the *Anti-Jacobin Review* declared that *Lyrical Ballads* had 'genius, taste, elegance, wit, and imagery of the most beautiful kind' (Woof, 70, 84). Some comments were designed for particular audiences: the *Naval Chronicle*'s general approval of 'these admirable Poems' included specific enthusiasm for 'The Ancyent Marinere', with its obvious appeal to a maritime readership (Woof, 82). Daniel Stuart, who edited both the *Morning Post* and *The Courier*, was so taken with the volume that he reprinted several of the poems in successive issues, finally observing in June 1800 that he would continue 'if the volume of Lyrical Ballads were not already in the hands of everyone who has a taste for Poetry' (Woof, 86). Not everyone was so impressed, however, and some were clearly discomfited. Charles Burney, writing in the *Monthly Review* in June 1799, found the poems too 'gloomy' and was troubled by the 'tenderness for criminals' evident in 'The Dungeon' and 'The Convict', the anti-war sentiments of 'The Female Vagrant' and 'Old Man travelling', and the 'real anarchy' threatened by 'Goody Blake and Harry Gill' (Woof, 76–8). Political and social comment of this kind was all the more alarming in a collection marked by 'so much genius and originality'; and the

---

[6] Robert Burns, *Poems Selected by Don Paterson* (London, 2001), p. xvi.

review concluded with the hope that the author might soon turn his attentions towards 'more elevated subjects'.

Of all the poems in the volume, it was 'The Rime of the Ancyent Marinere' that most perplexed its first readers. Burney regarded it as 'the strangest story of a cock and a bull that we ever saw on paper . . . a rhapsody of unintelligible wildness and incoherence', though not without 'poetical touches of an exquisite kind' (Woof, 75). The review in the *British Critic* was similarly guarded, weighing its 'many excellencies' against its 'many faults', but concluding that it ultimately failed 'from not being quite intelligible' (Woof, 79). The *Analytical Review* was less measured, finding not the expected simplicity of an English ballad but rather 'the extravagance of a mad german poet' (Woof, 68). It was Coleridge's brother-in-law, Robert Southey, however, who made the most damning comments in the *Critical Review*, dismissing 'The Rime' as 'a Dutch attempt at German sublimity'. Though as struck by the 'originality' of the poem as anyone, Southey thought the long narrative 'absurd or unintelligible' and offered distinctly double-edged praise of the many stanzas, 'laboriously beautiful' (Woof, 67). Despite this public denunciation, however, *Lyrical Ballads* was one of the very few books he took with him when he set off on the long sea voyage to Portugal in April 1800. Francis Jeffrey, too, who launched the first edition of the *Edinburgh Review* with a scathing attack on Wordsworth and Coleridge, had confessed to being 'enchanted' with the little volume that first appeared in 1798 (Woof, 58). This apparent inconsistency may have arisen from the differences between the anonymous first edition and the enlarged collections of 1800 and 1802, but it also points to the inherently unsettling nature of *Lyrical Ballads* and its capacity to force its readers into continual reassessment. George Crabbe, for example, was initially only 'a cool admirer' of the poems but, as his son recalled, 'there were few modern works which he opened so frequently—and he soon felt and acknowledged, with the public, that in that simplicity was veiled genius of the greatest magnitude'.[7] Many early reflections indicate similar shifts in response—not between readers or generations, but between readings. The delayed effect of the poems can be seen in the reaction of Alexander Carlyle, who admitted that his expectations of 'The Idiot Boy' had been far from sanguine: 'I was alarmed at the term as well as the subject, and suspected that it would not please, but disgust' (Woof, 115). But, as he read on, he began

---

[7] G. Crabbe, *The Life of George Crabbe by His Son*, ed. Edmund Blunden (London, 1947), 148.

to realize that the poet had 'done more to move the human heart to tenderness for the most unfortunate of our species, than has ever been done before'. Carlyle's experience first of discomposure and suspicion, followed by gradually awakening sympathy, and eventually profound feelings of emotion and deep admiration for the poet and his subject is an early example of the extraordinary power of *Lyrical Ballads*. The modest volume may have been laughed at and disliked by some readers—or even many readers—at first; but in time, it worked its way into the hearts of numerous admirers, whose understanding of 'poetry' would never be the same again.

Germany, Grasmere, and the Enlargement of Lyrical Ballads

As *Lyrical Ballads* was making its way into the hands and hearts of readers in the autumn of 1798, its authors were on their way to Germany. Coleridge, in particular, who had never been abroad, was eager to visit the Continent and to encounter the exciting intellectual circles of contemporary Germany. The Wordsworths, who had to give up the lease on Alfoxden House, needed somewhere to go, had some interest in learning German, but above all, were keen to continue sharing Coleridge's enthusiasms, opinions, and experiences. Germany was the homeland of so many modern writers and thinkers—Herder, Goethe, Schiller, Klopstock, Bürger, Lessing, Blumenbach, Eichhorn, Kant. As such, it exerted a magnetic force on ambitious young poets, landlocked by the war with France: the author of 'The Ancyent Marinere' was at last able to make a voyage of his own. To sail from Yarmouth, on the east coast of England, across the sea to the German port of Hamburg in 1798, was to gain a new perspective on Britain's place in the world as well as their own.

The trip turned out to be (as so often the case with exciting if not very practical plans) a rather mixed experience. As the temperatures fell and the prices rose, Coleridge and the Wordsworths ended up in different destinations. Dorothy observed rather ruefully in December, 'Coleridge is very happily situated at Ratzeburg for learning the language . . . We are not so fortunately situated' (*EY*, 247). Though far from his wife and small son, and soon stricken with the news that his second baby had died, Coleridge nevertheless found the challenges of the German language, literature, and philosophy enormously invigorating. His letters to friends veered between anguished meditation on the death of his child and accounts of his own experiences: 'I am very busy, very busy indeed!—I attend several Professors, & am getting many kinds of knowledge; but I stick to my Lessing—The Subject more and more interests me' (*CL* i. 480). He was at once acutely homesick and yet intellectually at home. Instead of writing poetry, Coleridge was more absorbed in German translation and grappling with new ideas about the mind and metaphysics. 'Christabel' remained unfinished, 'Kubla Khan' lay unpublished, as Coleridge read and talked, talked and read, scribbling down notes, plans, and brilliant letters capturing his impressions of German life and landscapes.

For the Wordsworths, on the other hand, Germany was not sufficiently unlike England to offer the imaginative rewards they had anticipated, but it was strange enough to accentuate their own sense of difference. Cut off from friends and familiar landscapes, William seems to have turned inward, for it was in Goslar, the small town on the edge of the Hartz mountains, that he began to compose the first passages of blank verse that would eventually grow into his great autobiographical poem, *The Prelude*. One of his problems was the shortage of books. At Racedown and Alfoxden, he had had a large library to hand, with further resources available from Bristol. In Germany, things were very different; and although they were now able to read Bürger's ballads in the original, and even to find odd English volumes such as Percy's *Reliques*, there was nothing to match the rich supply of poetry, travels, science, and politics they had been devouring in England. Lack of books did not, however, mean lack of activity—as Wordsworth commented wryly in December, 'As I have had no books I have been obliged to write in self-defence' (*EY*, 236). In the same letter, he sent Coleridge copies of new lyrics, 'She dwelt among th'untrodden ways' and 'Strange fits of passion', together with early versions of 'Nutting', and the 'Stolen Boat', which would later form such a memorable part of *The Prelude*. A second volume of *Lyrical Ballads* was in the making, even though the poems that were emerging in the cold winter months at Goslar seemed very different in kind from those composed a few months earlier in Somerset.

In the foothills of the Hartz mountains, troubling childhood memories, meditations on loss and death, feelings of guilt, fear, or anxiety erupted in poems whose rhythms were nevertheless so subtle and assured that the overall effect was of an almost other-worldly beauty. Wordsworth was finding words for things 'half-hidden from the eye'; once embodied in his lines, they possessed a haunting quality, resistant to paraphrase or rational explanation. The figure of Matthew, 'with his bough of wilding in his hand', takes its dwelling place in the mind, without any need to account for its existence. Critics may speculate on the identity of 'Lucy', or psychoanalyse the speaker of 'Nutting', or provide philosophical foundations for 'A Slumber did my Spirit Seal', but, in the midst of elaborate extrapolations, these elusive poems often seem to be slipping quietly away. 'Nutting' may begin with an apparently vivid, down-to-earth boyhood memory, but there is nothing ordinary about the 'merciless ravage' of the patient hazels, nor the force of the 'silent trees and the intruding sky', which bear witness to what has taken place. 'There was a Boy' draws similarly on childhood experience, but the nameless child, who stands alone at dusk by the glimmering lake, hooting to the owls, vanishes so suddenly that the entire scene is transformed into something far beyond the mundane and literal. These are poems that leave the reader mute, like the speaker in the poem, reflecting perhaps on what 'would enter unawares' into the mind, the 'uncertain heaven', and 'the steady lake'.

In the West Country the previous summer, Wordsworth had responded spontaneously to the local people, to the books he read, to conversations and country walks, but now he was drawn more and more to the recollected landscape of his childhood. After a decade of travelling, powerful images of the English Lakes and his own youthful experiences were rising unignorably from within. The poet who had stood beside the Wye, feeling the imaginative force of revisiting, was now ready to see that he already possessed immense supplies of creative nourishment, laid down unconsciously in childhood.

In Germany, homesick and frozen, Wordsworth was beginning to live on the 'spots of time' that now re-emerged in his mind and, as he did so, to understand what kind of poetry he should be writing. Now that he could read Bürger's poems in the original, he decided that much of the appeal was mere sensationalism: 'when I have laid the book down, I do not think about him' (*EY*, 234). Very different were the works of other modern poets such as Cowper and Burns, who drew on everyday life, but, by representing the feelings of unremarkable people and things with utter conviction, succeeded in creating poems of lasting power. Genuine poetry, Wordsworth now realized, possessed the 'life and charm of recognition' and so originality had more to do with embodying lasting truths than with superficial novelty. Unlike Bürger's transitory satisfactions, Wordsworth had come to value poems whose characters possessed 'manners connected with the permanent objects of nature and partaking of the simplicity of those objects. Such pictures must interest when the original shall cease to exist' (*EY*, 255). For Wordsworth, returning home meant moving back to the English Lakes and back to the native traditions of poetry. In December 1799,

William and Dorothy Wordsworth were making their permanent home in Grasmere.

On the cold journey across the Pennines, they passed 'Hart-leap Well', where the legend of the exhausted, dying deer, panting towards its birthplace, spoke powerfully to Wordsworth. Back in the north of England, the region of his birth and boyhood, he was once again open to the immediate encounter, to the stories hidden among the rocks and stones. Here life was truly connected with the permanent objects of nature, whose distinctive forms preserved unwritten memories and prompted deeper feelings in those who could understand. In such places, there was no need for shallow thrills, or blood-freezing tales, because of the abundant inspiration for poems that might satisfy 'thinking hearts' ('Hart-leap Well', l. 100). Once settled in Grasmere, he realized that the quiet vale was overflowing with food for future thought. A mile or so from Town End, where he and Dorothy rented their small, damp cottage, was Greenhead Gill. As Wordsworth walked beside the stream, he remembered stories from his boyhood, and imagined an elderly shepherd, trudging up the steep fell to build a shelter for his flock from the grey Lakeland stone. From Michael's hillside, he could look towards Easedale or Langdale, and imagine Dungeon Ghyll Force shooting down, with deep black pools where unwary sheep might drown. Everywhere he turned, the straggling stones and racing streams prompted ideas and stories. Each revelation was remarkable and, together, they contributed to a larger sense of human experience inseparably bound up with the landscape. As the Priest in 'The Brothers' explains, a small Lakeland valley was witness to countless events and their human consequences, from an unseasonal snowstorm, fatal to unsuspecting sheep and shepherds, to a christening, new job, or domestic refurbishment (ll. 152–61). The closeness of the small community meant that every event, ordinary or extraordinary, was shared by old and young, by one generation and the next. Whether cause for joy or sorrow, fear or relief, the experiences of the rural world were worthy of recollection.

The poems Wordsworth wrote on his return to Grasmere caught something of the random variety of local experience and the overriding sense of interconnection. Michael's heart-contracting sheepfold found a strange, comical counterpart in 'the hillock of misshapen stones' on the island at Rydal, abandoned when its aspirational owner realized his island was more accessible than he had assumed. Sir William's desire for an island 'Pleasure-house' recalls both the melancholy hall in 'Hart-leap Well' and St Herbert's quiet hermitage on

Derwent-Water—a disconcerting twinning of dreams. And all are linked to the Island house at Grasmere, where the poet comes and finds 'Creations lovely as the work of sleep, | Fair sights, and visions of romantic joy' (ll. 28–9). The poet is at once discoverer and recipient, moved to gratitude by everything he encounters, surprised into fellowship with unlikely rural architects and travellers. Wordsworth was feeding deep on his rediscovered landscape and although the resulting poems could hardly be more different in tone, they are part of a whole, linked by connections half-hidden and not fully understood.

The 'Poet' approaches the Island at Grasmere in a 'Pinnace', which underlines his own literariness and sense of difference from those who might have built the 'homely Pile' (ll. 13–17). Grateful awareness of the Lake District community also meant assessing the relationship of the returning son, an educated observer and would-be recorder, with those who had never left. Admiration for Michael is expressed by a speaker conscious that strangers might not notice the heap of stones above Greenhead Gill, while the limitations of tourists are memorably summarized by the Priest in 'The Brothers'. These are poems that register differences of perspective and recognize the need for mediation between the resident and visitor, both of whom might fail to see quite what was there. In 'Poems on the Naming of Places', Wordsworth caught the peculiar situation of the returning native, by expressing his deep delight in the local landscape and acknowledging the dangers of misreading what seems familiar. The first of these lovely poems captures the intensity of Wordsworth's response to Grasmere:

> Up the brook
> I roam'd in the confusion of my heart,
> Alive to all things and forgetting all. (ll. 17–19)

The impulse to create a personal place within these overwhelmingly beautiful, communal surroundings emerges in the private naming of Emma's Dell, Joanna's Rock, or Mary's Nook. Through careful description of distinctive natural details, birch, yew, holly, and bright green thorn, or the catalogue of real hills, Silver-How, Loughrigg, Fairfield, Wordsworth found a way of conveying the most private feelings with utter conviction. No matter whether Joanna *did* laugh at this particular spot, setting off the echoing brotherhood of ancient mountains—what matters is the poem's capacity to recreate the subtle emotion of a moment that might now assume a life of its own. Despite the celebrations of such individual interactions with the landscape, Wordsworth also knew that the very eyes most primed to see things freshly might also be most inclined to misjudgement. The fourth, and longest, poem of the sequence is an admonition, in which the joyful speaker is made to reconsider his spontaneous response to a particular spot. He and his companions have been delighting in the quiet lake on a hot September day, when they spot a man fishing on the far shore. Their immediate reaction is well meaning enough, as they wonder why he is not helping with the harvest in a season when work is so plentiful. As he turns, however, they see

> a Man worn down
> By sickness, gaunt and lean, with sunken cheeks
> And wasted limbs (ll. 64–6)

This is someone who, like Simon Lee, has no means of support now that his physical strength is wasted. He is fishing because he needs food, and the lake that delights the poet with its 'dead calm' is to this poor man a 'dead unfeeling lake | That knew not of his wants' (ll. 71–2). That Wordsworth recognized the partiality of his own natural perspective meant that he was also able to reveal not only the unexpected dimensions of the place he had chosen to live, but also the need for constant revisiting. His poetry arose from powerful first-hand experience, but it was just as dependent on reflection and reconsideration.

Wordsworth was deeply moved by what he saw and heard and felt, and began to find a language fit for recapturing his experience and conveying it to those who might be willing to watch and receive. The blank verse of 'Nutting' and 'There was a Boy' was fluid enough to accommodate both the delicate, personal emotions of the 'Naming of Places' and the profound, dignified sadness of 'Michael'. 'Hart-leap Well' adopted simple quatrains, reminiscent of a medieval ballad, but the elongated pentameter imbued even the energetic opening with a reflective quality. Wordsworth was experimenting with form and metre as well as subject, and some of the simplest tales, such as 'The Idle Shepherd-Boys', were set in the most complicated stanzas. Return to a pastoral world—where people's livelihoods depended on sheep and wool—meant returning to a kind of poetry as ancient as literature itself, but self-conscious recovery involved sophisticated, highly literate poetry. Often Wordsworth drew on the oldest traditions to find forms for his fresh discoveries. The natural variety of the Lake District meant that the bright yellow broom bushes, which sprang up as easily as weeds, could be found beside vast, slow-growing native oaks, but when Wordsworth composed 'The Oak and the Broom' he was also drawing on Aesop's *Fables* and *The Shepheardes Calendar*. In 'The Brothers', Wordsworth developed the Virgilian dialogue of the *Eclogues* into a new kind of pastoral, capable of encompassing both the acute psychological insights of modernity and the perennial values of a community where orphans are the responsibility of all. The new poems took seed during Wordsworth's heady rediscovery of Grasmere and were rooted in real places, but they were also sustained by the books he had absorbed over many years and continued to revisit just as eagerly.

Back in England, Wordsworth was now able to read the reviews of *Lyrical Ballads* and to reflect on the way in which the joint volume had been received. Southey's unkind assessment was especially galling and even though the first edition had sold out, prompting demand for a second, Wordsworth's faith in the power of his poems to speak directly to readers had been shaken (*EY*, 283). As he began to prepare a new, enlarged edition, he was less inclined to leave the poems to make their own way in the world, anonymous and unprefaced. Wordsworth and Coleridge had spent many months discussing their poetic principles, but it was evident from the early reviews that the original Advertisement had not given everyone quite the help they needed in approaching the volume. The new edition offered an opportunity to explain the choice of subject, language, and style, perhaps pre-empting any more crass objections or hasty, unimaginative readings. If the language of 'The Ancyent Marinere' had really deterred readers, it would have to be modernized and moved to a rather less prominent position. Wordsworth had written enough in recent months to supply a second volume, but although Coleridge was now preoccupied with political journalism and German translations, he might still contribute some new poems, and even complete 'Christabel' for the new collection. Since his return from Germany, he had been mostly in London and the West Country, pulled in different directions by conflicting enthusiasms, loyalties, and necessities: he had collaborated with Southey, written extensively for the *Morning Post*, and composed a lengthy verse translation of Schiller's *Wallenstein*. New work on *Lyrical Ballads*, though, would bring him to the Lakes.

When Coleridge visited Dove Cottage in April 1800, he wrote to tell Southey that Wordsworth was publishing 'a second Volume of Lyrical Ballads, & Pastorals' (*CL* i. 585). The pastorals were part of his new life among the rural residents of Cumberland and Westmoreland, which Coleridge admired but could not fully share. In the end, the only new poem of his to become part of *Lyrical Ballads* was 'Love', which he had written after what would prove a life-changing visit to the Yorkshire home of the Wordsworths' friends, the Hutchinsons. Coleridge threw himself into *Lyrical Ballads* again nevertheless, taking copies of Wordsworth's new Lake District poems down to Bristol and making revisions to what would now become 'The Ancient Mariner, A Poet's Reverie'. In late June, he made his way north again, with Sara and Hartley, to make a home in Keswick and help Wordsworth prepare poems for the press. Coleridge spurred Wordsworth into work on the Preface, which he later described as 'half a child of my own Brain' (*CL* ii. 830)—a telling metaphor for their working partnership. The rest of the new, two-volume edition was, however, almost entirely the work of his friend and so, when its authorship was finally revealed to the public in January 1801, the title page read 'W. Wordsworth'.

In the Preface, Wordsworth was determined to explain the aims of *Lyrical Ballads* and, in so doing, offer a new understanding of poetry itself. Its purpose, he announced, was 'to produce excitement in co-existence with an over-balance of pleasure' (p. 109); it was, in other words, aimed at the feelings of readers and worked by awakening their emotions through well-chosen language and poetic forms. The poems, accordingly, focused on people in situations conducive to the most powerful emotion, though Wordsworth, anxious to avoid sensationalism, insisted that it was the feeling that gave 'importance to the action and situation, and not the action and situation to the feeling' (p. 99). Metre was crucial to the proper embodiment of emotion and to sustaining pleasure in situations otherwise excessively painful. There was something in the order of metre, reassuring as a healthy pulse, that meant even the most distressing feelings could be both shared and observed. The rhythms of verse also intensified the delight of the reading experience, deepening participation in the experiences being represented or working in gentle opposition to create comedy or reflective distances.

Poetry was 'the spontaneous overflow of powerful feelings', but in order for the feelings to be recreated in the mind and subsequently in poetry, they had to be 'recollected in tranquillity' (pp. 98, 111)—as Wordsworth had found again and again, in the Wye, in Germany, in Grasmere. As he grappled with the nature of poetry, Wordsworth, encouraged by Coleridge and his new philosophical interests, was offering profound insight into the creative process and beginning to reveal the complicated psychology of the writer. These were questions that would preoccupy him for years to come, receiving much fuller treatment in *The Prelude*, which he began in 1799, completed as a 'Poem to Coleridge' in 1805, but continued to revise for much of his life. Already, as they worked together again on *Lyrical Ballads*, Coleridge was becoming convinced that Wordsworth's powers should not be issuing in short lyrics, but rather harnessed towards creating the great philosophical poem of the age.

For Wordsworth, the significance of *Lyrical Ballads* was not primarily a question of the poet's internal drama, however. Since his arrival in Grasmere, he had found abundant support for a belief in rural life as the best condition for discovering essential truths. As he explained to John Wilson, an early admirer of *Lyrical Ballads*, the unchanging aspects of human nature were most evident in the 'simplest lives', where 'false refinements, wayward and artificial desires, false criticisms' were unknown. The great obstacle to educated writers was a tendency to suppose that 'human nature and the persons they associate with are one and the same thing' (Appendix 4, p. 318), but Wordsworth had come to realize that it was among those who were *not* continually discussing the latest books, theories, investments, current affairs, or politics that the human condition was most visible. To strip away distracting surfaces was to reveal deeper feelings and truths, and hence the choices in *Lyrical Ballads*:

Low and rustic life was generally chosen because in that situation the essential passions of the heart find a better soil in which they can attain their maturity, are less under restraint, and speak a plainer and more emphatic language; because in that situation our elementary feelings exist in a state of greater simplicity and consequently may be more accurately contemplated and more forcibly communicated; because the manners of rural life germinate from those elementary feelings; and from the necessary character of rural occupations are more easily comprehended; and are more durable; and lastly, because in that situation the passions of men are incorporated with the beautiful and permanent forms of nature.[8]

Despite the ideals being presented, Wordsworth's own sentence is neither simple in style nor modest in scope. The polysyllabic elaboration of poetic purposes is in telling contrast with the brevity of 'The Tables turned' or 'We are Seven' and sent a clear signal that the volume was aimed at the most sophisticated even as it celebrated the least. Conversations with Coleridge, reflection in Germany, return to Grasmere and life among a rooted community had all helped to clarify Wordsworth's understanding of *Lyrical Ballads*, but if complex thoughts had culminated in an ideal of simplicity, the Preface was there

---

[8] In 1802, this key passage was modified slightly, with the revision of 'situation' to 'condition'.

to reveal the underlying profundity. The poems now being published were no longer being presented lightly as an experiment in literary taste, but rather as works with deep moral purpose and aspirations to permanence.

The seriousness of the new Preface was not merely a result of irritation over reviews of the first edition. The return to England in 1799 had coincided with one of the darkest phases of international experience, as the thrilling revolutionary energies of the French turned into expansive, imperialist ambitions, while at home, food shortages, high prices, and the endless demand for new recruits drove ordinary families to despair. These were indeed days 'of dereliction and despair', as Wordsworth put it in the 1799 version of *The Prelude*. The first *Lyrical Ballads* had registered the poverty, fear, hunger, and displacement associated with the long, brutal war, in its focus on bereft and suffering figures. In the second edition, Wordsworth addressed the problems directly in his Preface, deploring the effects of 'the great national events which are daily taking place, and the increasing accumulation of men in cities, where the uniformity of their occupations produces a craving for extraordinary incident which the rapid communication of intelligence hourly gratifies'. With the technical advances of the eighteenth century, Wordsworth and his contemporaries were witnessing the development of an economy based on mass production, with long hours of factory labour as the working norm for much of the population. The profound shift from a predominantly rural to urban, industrial society was accentuated by the unpredictable course of the war, as anxieties about the British campaign and the immediate future of the nation intensified the larger sense of change. In such an atmosphere, the hunger for news and diversions of every sort was not at all surprising, but from Wordsworth's perspective, instant gratification of such fears and desires was far from healthy. What may strike modern readers as a somewhat excessive diatribe against 'frantic novels, sickly and stupid German Tragedies, and deluges of idle and extravagant stories in verse' (pp. 99–100) makes more sense once the difficult and alarming context of Britain in 1800 is taken into account. In *Lyrical Ballads*, Wordsworth was struggling to save the people of Britain from what he saw as an irreversible catastrophe, and was dismayed by the idea that much contemporary literature was contributing to the downward slide. But what could—and should—a poet do in the face of national decline and international conflict? To opt for a small village in one of the remotest corners of England might suggest retreat from public engagement, but in the Preface to *Lyrical Ballads*, Wordsworth was stating his faith in the power of poetry to open minds and hearts to a better understanding of the world and, therefore, to the possibility of a better world.

One Human Heart

That Wordsworth's moral and literary aims were also political is evident from the letter he sent to the leading Whig statesman, Charles James Fox, with the new edition of *Lyrical Ballads*. Here he wrote even more plainly of the disastrous human costs of industrialization in 'every part of the country', arguing that the consequent destruction of families and close-knit communities was having long-term effects on the very foundations of British society. In poems such as 'Michael' and 'The Brothers', Wordsworth was presenting exemplary figures and attitudes, from which everyone, including the lawmakers, landowners, and captains of industry, could learn before it was too late. As he warned Fox, 'If it is true, as I believe, that this spirit is rapidly disappearing, no greater curse can befal a land' (Appendix 2, p. 308). In the original *Lyrical Ballads*, curses featured as part of the psychological, supernatural, and social concerns of the individual poems, but the enlarged, two-volume collection was being brandished as a prophylactic to protect the entire nation against perdition. Fox wrote back politely, but expressed a preference for 'Harry Gill, We are Seven, the Mad Mother, and the Idiot', because he thought blank verse inappropriate 'for subjects which are to be treated of with simplicity' (Woof, 106). Though pleased to receive a reply, Wordsworth can hardly have felt that his Preface had quite succeeded.

On the other hand, there were those who had read, understood, and deemed it unhelpful: Charles Lamb admired the arguments, but thought the Preface should have been published as a separate essay, because it had associated 'a *diminishing* idea with the poems which follow'.[9] For Lamb, Wordsworth was at his best when writing beautiful, emotive poetry rather than in his lengthy analyses of its purposes. He responded very positively to the more elusive lyrics and to the striking celebrations of the Lakes, which provoked an outpouring of corresponding local attachment to his own home territory in London. These were imaginative responses to imaginative poetry, not critical engagements with the literary principles set out in the Preface. But the didacticism of the Preface even seemed to be affecting his enjoyment of

---

[9] *The Letters of Charles and Mary Lamb*, i. *1796–1801*, ed. Edwin J. Marrs Jr. (Ithaca, NY, and London, 1975), 267.

the poems, particularly 'The Old Cumberland Beggar': 'the instructions conveyed in it are too direct and like a lecture: they don't slide into the mind of the reader, while he is imagining no such matter. An intelligent reader finds a sort of insult in being told, I will teach you how to think on this subject'. Wordsworth was faced with a problem: reactions to the original *Lyrical Ballads* had suggested serious misunderstandings, but now that he had explained more, he seemed in danger of alienating those most sensitive to the poems.

Nor was this the only cause for concern—the new edition of *Lyrical Ballads* had appeared with a number of minor printing errors and without fourteen lines of the key poem, 'Michael'. These problems could be corrected easily enough, but they raised new questions about the very nature of modern poetry. Where ballads had traditionally circulated by word of mouth, the printed poem was part of the uniform, industrial processes that Wordsworth denounced in his Preface. The realization that no one was immune to the world of 'getting and spending' would prompt a series of anguished political sonnets in the following year, which deplored the disappearance of 'Plain living and High thinking' in modern Britain and called for a return of true Liberty. The exemplary figures of *Lyrical Ballads*, whose unadorned lives and language revealed what really mattered, seemed ever more important to the nation. That they spoke directly to the poet himself was also becoming increasingly apparent. In the early months of 1802, as Wordsworth worked on the third edition of *Lyrical Ballads*, he recognized that creative spirits were prone to sudden depression and even despair. The recently published life of Burns by James Currie had offered so compelling an account of genius prematurely wrecked, that any faith in the redemptive power of poetry must be tested. Coleridge was by now suffering from an acute combination of physical and emotional problems, and so the spectre of blighted poets such as Burns, Chatterton, and Cowper all rose to darken Wordsworth's horizons. In response to Coleridge's stricken verse letter to Sara Hutchinson, which would later become 'Dejection: An Ode', Wordsworth grappled with the vulnerability of the poet and the search for hope in a bleak universe. 'Resolution and Independence' portrays a temperamental young poet confronted by one who has lost everything and yet still commands admiration because of his inner strength and quiet faith. It is a poem that seems to return to *Lyrical Ballads*, seeking strength from Matthew, Michael, or the Old Man travelling, whose wise passiveness gave them qualities capable of stopping the self-involved speaker-poet in full flow.

By 1802, Wordsworth had come to understand that being a 'poet' was not a question of getting published and receiving favourable reviews, but of possessing a certain cast of mind and a heart open to the astonishing revelations of an ordinary day. In the 1800 Preface to *Lyrical Ballads*, he had dealt perceptively with the creative process, as part of his defence of unprepossessing subjects and simple language, but when he returned to the essay in 1802, the question that now demanded an answer was this: 'What is a Poet?' His response drew on thoughts that had been crystallizing ever since the last manuscript had gone to press:

He is a man speaking to men: a man, it is true, endued with more lively sensibil- ity, more enthusiasm and tenderness, who has a greater knowledge of human nature, and a more comprehensive soul, than are supposed to be common among mankind; a man pleased with his own passions and volitions, and who rejoices more than other men in the spirit of life that is in him; delighting to contemplate similar volitions and passions as manifested in the goings-on of the Universe, and habitually impelled to create them where he does not find them. (pp. 103–4)

The poet was not just an exceptional individual, however, but an essen- tial part of the social fabric, vitally connected to others and the world which they shared. Wordsworth's unprepossessing figures were the ones who could unlock the great secret of the world—that 'We have all of us one human heart'. In his freedom to move among the natural world and those who lived more insulated lives, the unlikely Cumberland beggar has more in common with Wordsworth's ideal than all those successful writers who published in the London magazines. As Wordsworth warmed to his theme, the things that preoccupied him most deeply came bursting out, enlarging the Preface with a visionary dimension:

[The Poet] is the rock of defence of human nature; an upholder and preserver, carrying every where with him relationship and love. In spite of the difference of soil and climate, of language and manners, of laws and customs, in spite of things gone silently out of mind and things violently destroyed, the Poet binds together by passion and knowledge the vast empire of human society, as it is spread over the whole earth, and over all time. (pp. 106–7)

This was no self-portrait. Wordsworth is talking here of Poetry in the grandest and widest sense—as a redemptive force in a world that is constantly subject to loss and violent destruction. 'The Poet' is not an individual author, but stands for something larger; he is not confined to any single valley, city, or nation or any particular historical moment, but rather has the capacity to reach out to people in all places and ages. It is a very startling claim, but one that had grown from months and years of deep meditation on the nature of human beings, their relationships to each other and to the world.

Wordsworth's anxieties about the state of the nation had not abated, but nor had his intuitive faith that hope lay all around, if only people learned to see what was before their eyes. He was continually learning from the natural world, from the yellow celandine that pushed its way up through the frost so unerringly, from the cuckoo whose unique call was an annual renewal, from the rainbow that shot across a rainy sky, catching the heart off guard. He learned, too, from his sister's acute sensitivity to what could be seen on their daily walks, and from his brother, John, who, despite years away at sea, still felt for the hills of his native countryside as powerfully as his siblings. John was 'a silent poet': not a man speaking to men, but one with a 'watchful heart' and 'an eye practised like a blind man's touch'.[10] To be a poet, it seemed, was to be receptive to everyday blessings and to nurture similar sympathies in others. And for Wordsworth himself, the great task was to compose poetry adequate to the larger vision. The poet who wrote powerful poems had a vital role to play in the world, wherever he might be situated physically, for the very technology that threatened the spiritual welfare of society could be the medium for its salvation. Once published, poetry could not only embody human nature but also awaken ideas and sympathies in others, and therefore had a claim to be 'the breath and finer spirit of all knowledge'. Whatever was accumulated materially or intellectually, Wordsworth now knew that it amounted to nothing in comparison with what might survive in well-chosen words: 'Poetry is the first and last of all knowledge—it is as immortal as the heart of man' (p. 107). And what better justification for *Lyrical Ballads* could there be?

---

[10] 'When first I journeyed hither', ll. 88–91.

NOTE ON THE TEXT

THIS edition is based on early printed editions of *Lyrical Ballads*. It includes the first, anonymous edition of 1798, printed in Bristol, and the third edition of 1802, which was published in two volumes under Wordsworth's name. In order to preserve the integrity of the early editions, Wordsworth's notes have been retained in their original situations, whether in the form of footnotes, endnotes, or introductory remarks. Original spellings and punctuation have also been retained. Editorial notes can easily be distinguished from Wordsworth's notes because they are gathered together at the end of the volume and indicated by a degree mark. The edition is designed to allow readers to compare the first and third editions, and so any additions and revisions by the poets after 1802 have not been incorporated, though Coleridge's important marginal glosses to 'The Ancient Mariner', which he added in 1817, are reproduced in Appendix 1. The typographical errors in the first edition (to which the volume's first readers were alerted by a small errata slip) have been silently corrected in accordance with the poets' directions.

SELECT BIBLIOGRAPHY

For essential resources, see the list of Abbreviations. Additional sources and suggestions for further reading are listed below.

Biography

Gill, Stephen, *William Wordsworth: A Life* (Oxford, 1989).
Holmes, Richard, *Coleridge: Early Visions* (London, 1989).

General Studies, with relevance to Lyrical Ballads

Austin, Frances, *The Language of Wordsworth and Coleridge* (Basingstoke, 1989).
Averill, James, *Wordsworth and the Poetry of Human Suffering* (Ithaca, NY, 1980).
Baron, Michael, *Language and Relationship in Wordsworth's Writing* (Harlow, 1995).
Bate, Jonathan, *Romantic Ecology* (London and New York, 1991).
Beer, John, *Coleridge the Visionary* (London, 1959).
Bewell, Alan, *Wordsworth and the Enlightenment* (New Haven and London, 1989).
Bialostosky, Donald, *Making Tales: The Poetics of Wordsworth's Narrative Experiments* (Chicago, 1984).
Blank, Kim, *Wordsworth and Feeling* (Cranbury, NJ, 1995).
Bromwich, David, *Disowned by Memory* (Chicago, 1998).
Butler, James, 'Tourist or Native Son: Wordsworth's Homecomings of 1799–1800', *Nineteenth-Century Literature*, 51/1 (1996), 1–15.
Curran, Stuart, *Poetic Form and British Romanticism* (Oxford, 1986).
Duff, David, *Romanticism and the Uses of Genre* (Oxford, 2009).
Eilenberg, Susan, *Strange Power of Speech: Wordsworth, Coleridge and Literary Possession* (Oxford, 1992).
Fairer, David, *Organising Poetry: The Coleridge Circle, 1790–1798* (Oxford, 2009).
Fraistat, Neil, *The Poem and the Book* (Chapel Hill, NC, 1985).
Fry, Paul, *Wordsworth and the Poetry of What we Are* (New Haven, 2008).
Fulford, Tim, *Romantic Indians* (Oxford, 2006).
Gamer, Michael, *Romanticism and the Gothic* (Cambridge, 2000).
Gill, Stephen (ed.), *William Wordsworth, The Salisbury Plain Poems* (Ithaca, NY and London, 1975).
—— (ed.) *The Cambridge Companion to William Wordsworth* (Cambridge, 2003).
——*Wordsworth's Revisitings* (Oxford, 2011).
Gilpin, George (ed.), *Critical Essays on William Wordsworth* (Boston, 1990).
Gravil, Richard, *Wordsworth's Bardic Vocation* (Basingstoke, 2003).
Harrison, Gary, *Wordsworth's Vagrant Muse: Poetry, Poverty and Power* (Cambridge, 1994).

Hilles, F. W., and Bloom, H. (eds.), *From Sensibility to Romanticism* (New York, 1965).

Leadbetter, Gregory, *Coleridge and the Daemonic Imagination* (New York, 2011).

Leask, Nigel, ' "The Shadow Line": James Currie's "Life of Burns" and British Romanticism', in Claire Lamont and Michael Rossington (eds.), *Romanticism's Debatable Lands* (Basingstoke, 2005).

McCracken, David, *Wordsworth and The Lake District* (Oxford, 1985).

Mcfarland, Thomas, *Romanticism and the Forms of Ruin* (Princeton, 1981).

——*William Wordsworth: Intensity and Achievement* (Oxford, 1992).

Levinson, Marjorie, *Wordsworth's Great Period Poems* (Cambridge, 1986).

Manning, Peter, *Reading Romantics: Text and Context* (Oxford, 1990).

Matlak, Richard, *The Poetry of Relationship: The Wordsworths and Coleridge, 1797–1800* (New York, 1997).

Newlyn, Lucy, *Coleridge, Wordsworth and the Language of Allusion*, 2nd edn. (Oxford, 2001).

——(ed.) *The Cambridge Companion to Coleridge* (Cambridge, 2002).

O'Donnell, Brennan, *The Passion of Meter* (Kent, OH, 1995).

Owen, W. J. B., *Wordsworth as Critic* (Toronto, 1969).

Patterson, Annabel, *Pastoral and Ideology: Virgil to Valéry* (Oxford, 1988).

Pirie, David, *William Wordsworth: The Poetry of Grandeur and of Tenderness* (New York and London, 1982).

Roe, Nicholas, *Wordsworth and Coleridge: The Radical Years* (Oxford, 1988).

——*The Politics of Nature* (London, 1992).

——(ed.), *Samuel Taylor Coleridge and the Sciences of Life* (Oxford, 2001).

——(ed.), *English Romantic Writers in the West Country* (Basingstoke, 2010).

Sheats, Paul, *The Making of Wordsworth's Poetry, 1785–1798* (Cambridge, Mass., 1973).

Stafford, Fiona, *Local Attachments: The Province of Poetry* (Oxford, 2010).

Wolfson, Susan, *The Questioning Presence: Wordsworth, Keats and the Interrogative Mode in Romantic Poetry* (Ithaca, NY, 1986).

Wordsworth, J. F., *The Borders of Vision* (Oxford, 1982).

Selected Critical Studies of Lyrical Ballads

Averill, James, 'The Shape of *Lyrical Ballads*', *Philological Quarterly*, 60 (1981), 387–407.

Barfoot, C., *'A Natural Delineation of the Passions': The Historical Moment of Lyrical Ballads* (Amsterdam, 2001).

Butler, James, 'Poetry 1798–1807: *Lyrical Ballads* and *Poems, in Two Volumes*', in Gill (ed.), *Cambridge Companion to Wordsworth*, 38–54.

Campbell, Patrick, *Wordsworth and Coleridge: Lyrical Ballads* (Basingstoke, 1990).

Cronin, Richard (ed.), *1798: The Year of the Lyrical Ballads* (Basingstoke, 1998).

Duff, David, 'Paratextual Dilemmas: Wordsworth's "The Brothers" and the Problems of Generic Labelling', *Romanticism*, 6/2 (2000), 234–61.

Foakes, R. A., 'Beyond the Visible World': Wordsworth and Coleridge in *Lyrical Ballads*', *Romanticism*, 5 (1999), 58–69.

Foxon, D., 'The Printing of *Lyrical Ballads*, 1798', *The Library*, 5th ser. 9 (1954), 221–41.

Glen, Heather, *Vision and Disenchantment: Blake's Songs and Wordsworth's Lyrical Ballads* (Cambridge, 1983).

Jacobus, Mary, *Tradition and Experiment in Wordsworth's 1798 Lyrical Ballads* (Oxford, 1975).

Jones, A. R., and Tydeman, W. (eds.), *Wordsworth: Lyrical Ballads* (London and Basingstoke, 1972).

Jordan, John E., *Why the Lyrical Ballads?* (Berkeley, Los Angeles, and London, 1976).

Parrish, Stephen, *The Art of the Lyrical Ballads* (Cambridge, Mass., 1973).

Perry S., and Trott, N. (eds.), *1800: New Lyrical Ballads* (Basingstoke, 2000).

Prickett, Stephen, *Wordsworth and Coleridge: The Lyrical Ballads* (London, 1975).

Reed, Mark L., 'Wordsworth, Coleridge and the "Plan" of *Lyrical Ballads*', *University of Toronto Quarterly*, 34 (1965), 238–53.

Stafford, Fiona, 'Plain Living and Ungarnish'd Stories: Wordsworth and the Survival of Pastoral', *Review of English Studies*, ns 59 (2008), 118–33.

Selected Critical Studies of 'The Ancient Mariner'

Empson, William, 'The Ancient Mariner', *Critical Quarterly*, 6 (1964), 298–319.

Fry, Paul (ed.), *The Rime of the Ancient Mariner* (Boston and New York, 1999).

Fulmer, Brian, 'The Ancient Mariner and the Wandering Jew', *Studies in Philology*, 66 (1969), 797–815.

House, Humphrey, *Coleridge: The Clark Lectures* (London, 1953).

Hughes, Ted, Introduction to *A Choice of Coleridge's Verse* (London, 1996).

Jones, A. R., and Tydeman, W. (eds.), *The Ancient Mariner and Other Poems* (London and Basingstoke, 1973).

Kitson, Peter, 'Coleridge, the French Revolution and "The Ancient Mariner": Collective Guilt and Individual Salvation', *Yearbook of English Studies*, 19 (1989), 197–207.

Lowes, John Livingston, *The Road to Xanadu*, 2nd edn. (London, 1927).

McGann, Jerome, 'The Meaning of the Ancient Mariner', *Critical Inquiry*, 8 (1981), 35–67.

Perry, S., 'Kubla Khan, Christabel and The Ancient Mariner', in Duncan Wu (ed.), *A Companion to Romanticism* (Oxford, 1995).

Selected Critical Studies of 'Lines Written a few miles above Tintern Abbey'

Fertel, R., 'The Wye's "Sweet Inland Murmur"', *The Wordsworth Circle*, 16/3 (1985), 134–5.

Johnston, Kenneth, 'The Politics of Tintern Abbey', *The Wordsworth Circle*, 14/1 (1983), 6–14.

Lake, Crystal, 'The Life of Things at Tintern Abbey', *Review of English Studies*, ns 63 (2012), 444–65.

Mitchell, Julian, *The Wye Tour and Its Artists* (Woonton, Almley: Logaston Press, 2010).

Rzepka, Charles, 'Pictures of the Mind: Iron and Charcoal, "Ouzy" Tides and "Vagrant Dwellers" at Tintern Abbey, 1798', Studies in *Romanticism*, 42 (2003), 155–86.

Walford Davis, Damian, 'Romantic Hydrography: Tide and Transit in "Tintern Abbey"', in Roe (ed.), *English Romantic Writers in the West Country*, 218–36.

Woof, Robert, and Hebron, Stephen (eds.), *Towards Tintern Abbey: A Bicentenary Celebration of Lyrical Ballads* (Grasmere, 1998).

Further Reading in Oxford World's Classics

Coleridge, Samuel Taylor, *The Major Works*, ed. H. J. Jackson.

Wordsworth, Dorothy, *The Grasmere and Alfoxden Journals*, ed. Pamela Woof.

Wordsworth, William, *The Major Works*, ed. Stephen Gill.

A CHRONOLOGY OF
WILLIAM WORDSWORTH AND
SAMUEL TAYLOR COLERIDGE

1770 WW born 7 April, at Cockermouth, Cumbria.

1771 Dorothy Wordsworth born 25 December, at Cockermouth.

1772 STC born 21 October, at Ottery St Mary, Devon. John Wordsworth born in Cockermouth.

1776 American Declaration of Independence, 4 July. War with Britain begins.

1778 Ann Wordsworth, mother of WW and Dorothy, dies. Dorothy is taken in by their relations, the Threlkelds, in Halifax, Yorkshire.

1779 WW becomes a boarder with Hugh and Ann Tyson in Coltfoot, and attends Hawkshead Grammar School.

1780 Gordon Riots in London.

1781 Death of STC's father.

1782 STC goes to Christ's Hospital school in London.

1783 John Wordsworth, father of WW and Dorothy, dies 30 December. America becomes an independent republic, ending the war with Britain.

1785 William Cowper's *The Task* published.

1786 Robert Burns's *Poems, Chiefly in the Scottish Dialect* published.

1787 WW publishes 'Sonnet, On Seeing Helen Maria Williams weep at a Tale of Distress' in the *European Magazine* in March and goes up to St John's College, Cambridge, in October.

1789 Storming of the Bastille, 14 July. March on Versailles and French royal family taken to Paris. Richard Price delivers 'A Discourse on the Love of Our Country' on the anniversary of the Glorious Revolution, 4 November.

1790 WW spends his summer walking through France and Switzerland with Cambridge friend Robert Jones. Suspension of habeas corpus. Edmund Burke publishes *Reflections on the Revolution in France*.

1791 STC enters Jesus College, Cambridge. WW in London until November, when he returns to France and witnesses scenes of revolutionary fervour and violence. Joseph Priestley's house sacked by anti-radical mob in Birmingham. Mary Wollstonecraft publishes *A Vindication of the Rights of Men*. Thomas Paine publishes *Rights of Man*, part I.

1792 WW has a relationship with Annette Vallon and their daughter, Caroline, is born in December. WW returns to England. Thomas Paine's

The Rights of Man, part II, published. Mary Wollstonecraft publishes A Vindication of the Rights of Woman. France declares war on Austria.

1793 Execution of King Louis XVI in January and Queen Marie Antoinette in October. France declares war on Britain in February. Reign of Terror begins in France. September Massacres in Paris. WW sees the British navy mustering on the south coast, crosses Salisbury Plain on foot, which inspires a long eponymous poem, and visits the Wye Valley on his way to North Wales to see Robert Jones. WW publishes An Evening Walk and Descriptive Sketches, and writes, but does not publish, a radical essay, Letter to the Bishop of Llandaff. STC publishes his first poem and enlists in the dragoons under the name Silas Tomkyn Comberbache. William Godwin publishes An Enquiry Concerning Political Justice.

1794 STC returns to Cambridge. He meets Robert Southey in the summer and they make plans for an ideal community, or Pantisocracy, in America and become engaged to the Fricker sisters. STC leaves Cambridge in December, and publishes his 'Sonnets on Eminent Characters' in the Morning Chronicle. WW and Dorothy Wordsworth are reunited in Keswick. Execution of Robespierre. Treason Trials in London, in which radical intellectuals, including Thomas Hardy and John Thelwall, are tried for sedition, and acquitted.

1795 STC delivers political and religious lectures in Bristol, where he meets WW briefly for the first time. STC marries Sara Fricker on 4 October. WW is in London, moving in radical circles, but moves with Dorothy to Racedown, in Dorset.

1796 STC publishes Poems on Various Subjects and ten issues of The Watchman, a political journal. Hartley Coleridge born 19 September. The Coleridges move to Nether Stowey in Somerset in December.

1797 STC visits Racedown in June. The Wordsworths move to Alfoxden in July. WW writes 'The Ruined Cottage', completes The Borderers, and tries, unsuccessfully, to get his play accepted at Covent Garden. STC completes Osorio and tries, unsuccessfully, to get it accepted at Drury Lane. Walking tour in November and the composition of 'The Rime of the Ancyent Marinere'.

1798 STC writes 'Fears in Solitude', published with 'Frost at Midnight' and 'France: An Ode'. Birth of Berkeley Coleridge, 14 May. WW engaged in major period of composition for Lyrical Ballads. The Wordsworths go on a walking tour of the Wye in July, delivering 'Lines written a few miles above Tintern Abbey' to Joseph Cottle in Bristol as they return. Lyrical Ballads published. STC and the Wordsworths travel to Germany in September. The rising of the United Irishmen is suppressed. Napoleon invades Egypt, but is defeated by Nelson at the Battle of the Nile in August.

1799 STC and the Wordsworths in Germany. Berkeley Coleridge dies 10 February. In Goslar, WW writes several of the shorter poems that will be part of the expanded *Lyrical Ballads* and begins work on *The Prelude*. The Wordsworths return to England in April and stay with the Hutchinson family in Sockburn on Tees, in Yorkshire. STC returns to England in July to be reunited with Sara and Hartley, and then moves between London and Bristol, working for the *Morning Post*. STC and the Wordsworths meet again and tour the Lakes, with WW's brother, John. At Sockburn, STC falls in love with Sara Hutchinson. WW and Dorothy Wordsworth settle in Dove Cottage, Grasmere, in December.

1800 WW composes most of the poems that form the second volume of *Lyrical Ballads*, and also works on 'Home at Grasmere'. John Wordsworth stays at Dove Cottage between January and September. STC moves to the Lakes in July, revises 'The Ancient Mariner', and generally helps with preparing the second edition of *Lyrical Ballads*. Derwent Coleridge born 14 September. Preface to *Lyrical Ballads* written in September–October. Act of Union between Britain and Ireland passed.

1801 Second edition of *Lyrical Ballads* published in January. WW writes to Charles James Fox, sending a copy. STC writes several letters promoting the enlarged edition.

1802 WW expands the Preface to *Lyrical Ballads* and makes minor revisions to the poems for the third edition, published in April. Letter from the Glasgow student John Wilson received in May, and long reply composed and despatched in early June. Spring spent composing many shorter lyrics, and also the first four stanzas of the 'Ode: There was a Time' and 'Resolution and Independence', later published in *Poems, in Two Volumes*, 1807. The Peace of Amiens, signed in March, allows WW and Dorothy to cross the Channel and meet Annette and Caroline Vallon in August, prior to WW's marriage to Mary Hutchinson. Napoleon proclaimed life consul. France invades Switzerland in October. WW begins composing a sequence of political sonnets, published in 1807. STC, suffering from serious health problems and passionate and hopeless love for Sara Hutchinson, writes the verse letter 'To Asra', published in revised form as 'Dejection: An Ode' on his seventh wedding anniversary, 4 October, which is also the day of WW's marriage to Mary Hutchinson. Sara Coleridge born 23 December. *Edinburgh Review* launched in October with hostile review of Southey's *Thalaba* and attack on the 'Lake School of Poetry'.

1803 Renewal of the war with France, which provokes fears of an invasion. Robert Emmet leads a further uprising in Ireland, but is defeated and executed. WW and Mary Wordsworth's first son, John, is born. WW and Dorothy Wordsworth and STC travel through Scotland in July–September, parting company during the trip. First meeting with

Walter Scott. The tour is described in Dorothy's *Recollections of a Tour Made in Scotland, A.D. 1803.*

1804 WW's 'Ode: There was a Time' completed and much of *The Prelude.* Coleridge leaves for Malta in May. Napoleon becomes emperor of France on 18 May. Spain declares war on Britain in December.

1805 Publication of the fourth edition of *Lyrical Ballads.* Death of WW and Dorothy's brother, John, who drowns off Weymouth when his ship, *The Earl of Abergavenny,* is wrecked in February. WW completes the thirteen-book *Prelude.* Nelson is killed at the Battle of Trafalgar. Napoleon defeats the Russians and Austrians at Austerlitz.

1806 WW spends the winter at Coleorton, Leicestershire home of Sir George Beaumont. STC returns from Malta. Thomas Wordsworth born.

1807 STC writes 'To William Wordsworth' after hearing *The Prelude* in January. WW's *Poems, in Two Volumes* published and received very unsympathetically by reviewers. Act for the Abolition of the Slave Trade passed. The Peninsular War begins.

1808 STC lectures on poetry in London. Catherine Wordsworth born. The Wordsworth household leaves Dove Cottage and moves to a larger house, Allan Bank, on the west side of Grasmere village. France invades Spain.

1809 WW publishes *The Convention of Cintra.* STC goes to stay with the Wordsworths in Allan Bank, and begins *The Friend,* helped by Sara Hutchinson and WW, who contributes the *Essays Upon Epitaphs,* published early the following year.

1810 WW and STC fall out and STC moves to London, staying with John Morgan. William Wordsworth born 12 May. WW publishes a *Guide to the Lakes* as the preface to Joseph Wilkinson's *Select Views in Cumberland, Westmoreland and Lancashire.*

1811 Beginning of the Regency, after George III is declared insane. STC delivers lectures on Shakespeare and Milton in London from November to January 1812. Spenser Percival, the prime minister of Britain, is assassinated.

1812 WW's daughter, Catherine, dies in June and his son, Thomas, in December during a bout of measles. STC and WW reconciled after two-year breach. Napoleon's forced retreat from Moscow. America declares war on Britain.

1813 STC's tragedy, *Osorio,* now revised as *Remorse,* meets with success at the Drury Lane Theatre. The Wordsworths move into Rydal Mount and WW accepts a post as distributor of stamps. Napoleon defeated at Leipzig.

1814 WW publishes *The Excursion* and receives some very hostile reviews. Coleridge gives lectures in Bristol. Napoleon defeated at Toulouse and sent into exile in Elba. War between Britain and America ends in December.

1815 Napoleon escapes from Elba, but is then defeated at the Battle of Waterloo on 18 June, which finally brings an end to the long war with France. WW publishes his collected volume of *Poems*, which includes most of *Lyrical Ballads*, now rearranged by theme and grouped with other poems. WW also publishes *The White Doe of Rylstone* (written in 1806–7).

1816 STC moves into the home of Dr Gillman in Highgate. He is persuaded by Byron to publish 'Christabel' (written in 1798) which appears in a small volume, with 'The Pains of Sleep' and 'Kubla Khan' from the house of John Murray. STC also publishes *The Statesman's Manual*. WW publishes *A Letter to a Friend of Robert Burns*. Riots at Spa Fields in London.

1817 STC publishes *Biographia Literaria*, *A Lay Sermon*, and his collected poems, *Sibylline Leaves*, which includes 'The Ancient Mariner', complete with new marginal glosses. Death of Princess Charlotte. Trial and acquittal of William Hone, the radical publisher.

1818 STC lectures on Milton and Shakespeare.

1819 WW publishes *Peter Bell* (written in 1798). STC lectures on literature and philosophy. Peterloo Massacre in Manchester in August. Trial and conviction of Richard Carlile, radical publisher.

1820 WW publishes *The River Duddon* to critical acclaim and an enlarged collected edition of his *Poems*. Death of George III ends the Regency. Cato Street Conspiracy fails in its attempt to destroy the government. Queen Caroline on trial for infidelity and acquitted.

1821 George IV is crowned. Napoleon dies at St Helena.

1822 WW publishes *Memorials of a Tour on the Continent* and *Ecclesiastical Sketches*. Castlereagh commits suicide.

1823 Hazlitt publishes 'My first Acquaintance with Poets' in *The Liberal*, in April.

1825 STC publishes *Aids to Reflection*. Hazlitt publishes *The Spirit of the Age*, with pen portraits of WW and STC.

1827 WW publishes another collected edition of his *Poems*.

1828 WW and his daughter, Dora, tour Germany with STC. STC publishes his *Poetical Works*.

1829 STC publishes *On the Constitution of the Church and State* and second edition of *Poetical Works*. Catholic Emancipation Act passed.

1830 George IV dies childless and so his brother becomes King William IV. Earl Grey becomes prime minister after many years of the Tory administration.

1831   WW tours Scotland and visits Walter Scott.

1832   The First Reform Act passed. Death of Walter Scott.

1833   Emancipation Act which abolishes slavery throughout the British colonies is passed.

1834   STC dies on 25 July. Third edition of STC's *Poetical Works* published. Poor Law Reform Act passed. Houses of Parliament burn down.

1835   WW publishes *Yarrow Revisited*, including a brief essay on the new Poor Law.

1837   William IV dies childless and so his niece becomes Queen Victoria. WW tours France and Italy.

1838   Chartists present their Charter to Parliament, but it is rejected, sparking riots in Birmingham. The Opium War with China begins.

1839   De Quincey publishes the first of his 'Lake Reminiscences' in *Tait's Edinburgh Magazine*.

1842   WW publishes *Poems, Chiefly of Early and Later Years*, which includes *The Borderers* and 'Salisbury Plain', now entitled 'Guilt and Sorrow'.

1843   WW comments on his poems in a long sequence of notes dictated to his friend, Isabella Fenwick. He becomes Poet Laureate after the death of Southey.

1847   Death of WW's daughter, Dora.

1849   Death of Hartley Coleridge.

1850   WW dies on 23 April. *The Prelude* published in July.

1855   Dorothy Wordsworth dies on 25 January.

1859   Mary Wordsworth, wife of WW, dies.

LYRICAL BALLADS,

WITH

A FEW OTHER POEMS

1798

ADVERTISEMENT

It is the honourable characteristic of Poetry that its materials are to be found in every subject which can interest the human mind. The evidence of this fact is to be sought, not in the writings of Critics, but in those of Poets themselves.

The majority of the following poems are to be considered as experiments. They were written chiefly with a view to ascertain how far the language of conversation in the middle and lower classes of society is adapted to the purposes of poetic pleasure. Readers accustomed to the gaudiness and inane phraseology of many modern writers, if they persist in reading this book to its conclusion, will perhaps frequently have to struggle with feelings of strangeness and aukwardness: they will look round for poetry, and will be induced to enquire by what species of courtesy these attempts can be permitted to assume that title. It is desirable that such readers, for their own sakes, should not suffer the solitary word Poetry, a word of very disputed meaning, to stand in the way of their gratification; but that, while they are perusing this book, they should ask themselves if it contains a natural delineation of human passions, human characters, and human incidents; and if the answer be favorable to the author's wishes, that they should consent to be pleased in spite of that most dreadful enemy to our pleasures, our own pre-established codes of decision.

Readers of superior judgment may disapprove of the style in which many of these pieces are executed it must be expected that many lines and phrases will not exactly suit their taste. It will perhaps appear to them, that wishing to avoid the prevalent fault of the day, the author has sometimes descended too low, and that many of his expressions are too familiar, and not of sufficient dignity. It is apprehended, that the more conversant the reader is with our elder writers, and with those in modern times who have been the most successful in painting manners and passions, the fewer complaints of this kind will he have to make.

An accurate taste in poetry, and in all the other arts, Sir Joshua Reynolds° has observed, is an acquired talent, which can only be produced by severe thought, and a long continued intercourse with the best models of composition. This is mentioned not with so ridiculous a purpose as to prevent the most inexperienced reader from judging for himself; but merely to temper the rashness of decision, and to suggest that if poetry be a subject on which much time has not been bestowed, the judgment may be erroneous, and that in many cases it necessarily will be so.

The tale of Goody Blake and Harry Gill is founded on a well-authenticated fact which happened in Warwickshire. Of the other poems in the collection, it may be proper to say that they are either absolute inventions of the author, or facts which took place within his personal observation or that of his friends. The poem of the Thorn, as the reader will soon discover, is not supposed to be spoken in the author's own person: the character of the loquacious narrator will sufficiently shew itself in the course of the story. The Rime of the Ancyent Marinere was professedly written in imitation of the *style*, as well as of the spirit of the elder poets;° but with a few exceptions, the Author believes that the language adopted in it has been equally intelligible for these three last centuries. The lines entitled Expostulation and Reply, and those which follow, arose out of conversation with a friend° who was somewhat unreasonably attached to modern books of moral philosophy.

THE RIME OF THE ANCYENT MARINERE,
IN SEVEN PARTS

ARGUMENT

How a Ship having passed the Line° was driven by Storms to the cold Country towards the South Pole; and how from thence she made her course to the tropical Latitude of the Great Pacific Ocean; and of the strange things that befell; and in what manner the Ancyent Marinere came back to his own Country.

I

It is an ancyent Marinere,
    And he stoppeth one of three:
'By thy long grey beard and thy glittering eye
    Now wherefore stoppest me?

The Bridegroom's doors are open'd wide   5
    And I am next of kin;
The Guests are met, the Feast is set,—
    May'st hear the merry din.'

But still he holds the wedding-guest—
    There was a Ship, quoth he—   10
'Nay, if thou'st got a laughsome tale,
    Marinere! come with me.'

He holds him with his skinny hand,
    Quoth he, there was a Ship—
'Now get thee hence, thou grey-beard Loon!°   15
    Or my Staff shall make thee skip.'

He holds him with his glittering eye—
    The wedding guest stood still
And listens like a three year's child;
    The Marinere hath his will.   20

The wedding-guest sate on a stone,
    He cannot chuse but hear:
And thus spake on that ancyent man,
    The bright-eyed Marinere.

The Ship was cheer'd, the Harbour clear'd—   25
  Merrily did we drop
Below the Kirk, below the Hill,°
  Below the Light-house top.

The Sun came up upon the left,
  Out of the Sea came he: 30
And he shone bright, and on the right
  Went down into the Sea.

Higher and higher every day,
  Till over the mast at noon—
The wedding-guest here beat his breast,   35
  For he heard the loud bassoon.

The Bride hath pac'd into the Hall,
  Red as a rose is she;
Nodding their heads before her goes
  The merry Minstralsy.   40

The wedding-guest he beat his breast,
  Yet he cannot chuse but hear:
And thus spake on that ancyent Man,
  The bright-eyed Marinere.

Listen, Stranger! Storm and Wind,   45
  A Wind and Tempest strong!
For days and weeks it play'd us freaks—°
  Like Chaff we drove along.

Listen, Stranger! Mist and Snow,
  And it grew wond'rous cauld:°   50
And Ice mast-high came floating by
  As green as Emerauld.

And thro' the drifts the snowy clifts
  Did send a dismal sheen;
Ne shapes of men ne beasts we ken—°   55
  The Ice was all between.

The Ice was here, the Ice was there,
  The Ice was all around:

It crack'd and growl'd, and roar'd and howl'd—
   Like noises of a swound.°   60

At length did cross an Albatross,°
   Thorough the Fog it came;
And an it were a Christian Soul,°
   We hail'd it in God's name.

The Marineres gave it biscuit-worms,   65
   And round and round it flew:
The Ice did split with a Thunder-fit;
   The Helmsman steer'd us thro'.

And a good south wind sprung up behind,
   The Albatross did follow;   70
And every day for food or play
   Came to the Marinere's hollo!

In mist or cloud on mast or shroud
   It perch'd for vespers nine,°
Whiles all the night thro' fog-smoke white   75
   Glimmer'd the white moon-shine.

'God save thee, ancyent Marinere!
   From the fiends that plague thee thus—
Why look'st thou so?'—with my cross bow
   I shot the Albatross.   80

II

The Sun came up upon the right,
   Out of the Sea came he;
And broad as a weft upon the left°
   Went down into the Sea.

And the good south wind still blew behind,   85
   But no sweet Bird did follow
Ne any day for food or play
   Came to the Marinere's hollo!

And I had done an hellish thing
   And it would work 'em woe: 90

For all averr'd, I had kill'd the Bird
    That made the Breeze to blow.

Ne dim ne red, like God's own head,
    The glorious Sun uprist:
Then all averr'd, I had kill'd the Bird   95
    That brought the fog and mist.
'Twas right, said they, such birds to slay
    That bring the fog and mist.

The breezes blew, the white foam flew,
    The furrow follow'd free: 100
We were the first that ever burst
    Into that silent Sea.

Down dropt the breeze, the Sails dropt down,
    'Twas sad as sad could be
And we did speak only to break   105
    The silence of the Sea.

All in a hot and copper sky
    The bloody sun at noon,
Right up above the mast did stand,
    No bigger than the moon.   110

Day after day, day after day,
    We stuck, ne breath ne motion,
As idle as a painted Ship
    Upon a painted Ocean.

Water, water, every where   115
    And all the boards did shrink;
Water, water, every where,
    Ne any drop to drink.

The very deeps did rot: O Christ!
    That ever this should be!   120
Yea, slimy things did crawl with legs
    Upon the slimy Sea.

About, about, in reel and rout
    The Death-fires danc'd at night;

The water, like a witch's oils,   125
    Burnt green and blue and white.

And some in dreams assured were
    Of the Spirit that plagued us so:
Nine fathom deep he had follow'd us°
    From the Land of Mist and Snow.   130

And every tongue thro' utter drouth°
    Was wither'd at the root;
We could not speak no more than if
    We had been choked with soot.

Ah wel-a-day! what evil looks°   135
    Had I from old and young;
Instead of the Cross the Albatross
    About my neck was hung.

III

I saw a something in the Sky
    No bigger than my fist;   140
At first it seem'd a little speck
    And then it seem'd a mist:
It mov'd and mov'd, and took at last
    A certain shape, I wist.°

A speck, a mist, a shape, I wist!   145
    And still it ner'd and ner'd;
And, an it dodg'd a water-sprite,°
    It plung'd and tack'd and veer'd.

With throat unslack'd, with black lips bak'd°
    Ne could we laugh, ne wail: 150
Then while thro' drouth all dumb they stood
I bit my arm and suck'd the blood
    And cry'd, A sail! a sail!

With throat unslack'd, with black lips bak'd°
    Agape they hear'd me call: 155
Gramercy! they for joy did grin°
And all at once their breath drew in
    As they were drinking all.

She doth not tack from side to side—
    Hither to work us weal°   160
Withouten wind, withouten tide
    She steddies with upright keel.

The western wave was all a flame,
    The day was well nigh done!
Almost upon the western wave   165
    Rested the broad bright Sun;
When that strange shape drove suddenly
    Betwixt us and the Sun.

And strait the Sun was fleck'd with bars
    (Heaven's mother send us grace)   170
As if thro' a dungeon grate he peer'd
    With broad and burning face.

Alas! (thought I, and my heart beat loud)
    How fast she neres and neres!
Are those *her* Sails that glance in the Sun   175
    Like restless gossameres?°

Are these *her* naked ribs, which fleck'd
    The sun that did behind them peer?
And are these two all, all the crew,
    That woman and her fleshless Pheere?°   180

His bones were black with many a crack,
    All black and bare, I ween;°
Jet-black and bare, save where with rust
Of mouldy damps and charnel crust
    They're patch'd with purple and green.   185

Her lips are red, *her* looks are free,
    Her locks are yellow as gold:
Her skin is white as leprosy,
And she is far liker Death than he;
    Her flesh makes the still air cold.   190

The naked Hulk alongside came
    And the Twain were playing dice;

'The Game is done! I've won, I've won!'
    Quoth she, and whistled thrice.

A gust of wind sterte up behind°   195
    And whistled thro' his bones;
Thro' the holes of his eyes and the hole of his mouth
    Half-whistles and half-groans.

With never a whisper in the Sea
    Oft darts the Spectre-ship;   200
While clombe above the Eastern bar
The horned Moon, with one bright Star°
    Almost atween the tips.

One after one by the horned Moon°
    (Listen, O Stranger! to me)   205
Each turn'd his face with a ghastly pang°
    And curs'd me with his ee.°

Four times fifty living men,
    With never a sigh or groan,
With heavy thump, a lifeless lump   210
    They dropp'd down one by one.

Their souls did from their bodies fly,—
    They fled to bliss or woe;
And every soul it pass'd me by,
    Like the whiz of my Cross-bow.   215

IV

'I fear thee, ancyent Marinere!
    I fear thy skinny hand;
And thou art long and lank and brown
    As is the ribb'd Sea-sand.

I fear thee and thy glittering eye   220
    And thy skinny hand so brown'—
Fear not, fear not, thou wedding guest!
    This body dropt not down.

Alone, alone, all all alone
    Alone on the wide wide Sea;   225

And Christ would take no pity on
        My soul in agony.

The many men so beautiful,
        And they all dead did lie!
And a million million slimy things   230
        Liv'd on—and so did I.

I look'd upon the rotting Sea,
        And drew my eyes away;
I look'd upon the eldritch deck,°
        And there the dead men lay.   235

I look'd to Heaven, and try'd to pray;
        But or ever a prayer had gusht,
A wicked whisper came and made
        My heart as dry as dust.

I clos'd my lids and kept them close,   240
        Till the balls like pulses beat;
For the sky and the sea, and the sea and the sky
Lay like a load on my weary eye,
        And the dead were at my feet.

The cold sweat melted from their limbs,   245
        Ne rot, ne reek did they;
The look with which they look'd on me,
        Had never pass'd away.

An orphan's curse would drag to Hell
        A spirit from on high: 250
But O! more horrible than that
        Is the curse in a dead man's eye!
Seven days, seven nights I saw that curse,
        And yet I could not die.

The moving Moon went up the sky   255
        And no where did abide:
Softly she was going up
        And a star or two beside—

Her beams bemock'd the sultry main
   Like morning frosts yspread;   260
But where the ship's huge shadow lay,
The charmed water burnt alway
   A still and awful red.

Beyond the shadow of the ship
   I watch'd the water-snakes: 265
They mov'd in tracks of shining white;
And when they rear'd, the elfish light
   Fell off in hoary flakes.

Within the shadow of the ship
   I watch'd their rich attire: 270
Blue, glossy green, and velvet black
They coil'd and swam; and every track
   Was a flash of golden fire.

O happy living things! no tongue
   Their beauty might declare: 275
A spring of love gusht from my heart,
   And I bless'd them unaware!
Sure my kind saint took pity on me,
   And I bless'd them unaware.

The self-same moment I could pray;   280
   And from my neck so free
The Albatross fell off, and sank
   Like lead into the sea.

V

O sleep, it is a gentle thing
   Belov'd from pole to pole!   285
To Mary-queen the praise be yeven°
She sent the gentle sleep from heaven
   That slid into my soul.

The silly buckets on the deck°
   That had so long remain'd,   290
I dreamt that they were fill'd with dew
   And when I awoke it rain'd.

My lips were wet, my throat was cold,
   My garments all were dank;
Sure I had drunken in my dreams   295
   And still my body drank.

I mov'd and could not feel my limbs,
   I was so light, almost
I thought that I had died in sleep,
   And was a blessed Ghost.   300

The roaring wind! it roar'd far off,
   It did not come anear;°
But with its sound it shook the sails
   That were so thin and sere.

The upper air bursts into life,   305
   And a hundred fire-flags sheen
To and fro they are hurried about;
And to and fro, and in and out
   The stars dance on between.

The coming wind doth roar more loud;   310
   The sails do sigh, like sedge:
The rain pours down from one black cloud
   And the Moon is at its edge.

Hark! hark! the thick black cloud is cleft,
   And the Moon is at its side: 315
Like waters shot from some high crag,
The lightning falls with never a jag
   A river steep and wide.

The strong wind reach'd the ship: it roar'd
   And dropp'd down, like a stone!   320
Beneath the lightning and the moon
   The dead men gave a groan.

They groan'd, they stirr'd, they all uprose,
   Ne spake, ne mov'd their eyes:
It had been strange, even in a dream   325
   To have seen those dead men rise.

The helmsman steerd, the ship mov'd on;
   Yet never a breeze up-blew;
The Marineres all 'gan work the ropes,
   Where they were wont to do: 330
They rais'd their limbs like lifeless tools—
   We were a ghastly crew.

The body of my brother's son
   Stood by me knee to knee:
The body and I pull'd at one rope,   335
   But he said nought to me—
And I quak'd to think of my own voice
   How frightful it would be!

The day-light dawn'd—they dropp'd their arms,
   And cluster'd round the mast: 340
Sweet sounds rose slowly thro' their mouths
   And from their bodies pass'd.

Around, around, flew each sweet sound,
   Then darted to the sun:
Slowly the sounds came back again   345
   Now mix'd, now one by one.

Sometimes a dropping from the sky
   I heard the Lavrock sing;°
Sometimes all little birds that are
How they seem'd to fill the sea and air   350
   With their sweet jargoning,°

And now 'twas like all instruments,
   Now like a lonely flute;
And now it is an angel's song
   That makes the heavens be mute.   355

It ceas'd: yet still the sails made on
   A pleasant noise till noon,
A noise like of a hidden brook
   In the leafy month of June,
That to the sleeping woods all night   360
   Singeth a quiet tune.

Listen, O listen, thou Wedding-guest!
   'Marinere! thou hast thy will:
For that, which comes out of thine eye, doth make
   My body and soul to be still.'   365

Never sadder tale was told
   To a man of woman born:°
Sadder and wiser thou wedding-guest!
   Thou'lt rise to morrow morn.

Never sadder tale was heard   370
   By a man of woman born:°
The Marineres all return'd to work
   As silent as beforne.

The Marineres all 'gan pull the ropes,
   But look at me they n'old:°   375
Thought I, I am as thin as air—
   They cannot me behold.°

Till noon we silently sail'd on
   Yet never a breeze did breathe:
Slowly and smoothly went the ship   380
   Mov'd onward from beneath.

Under the keel nine fathom deep
   From the land of mist and snow
The spirit slid: and it was He
   That made the Ship to go.   385
The sails at noon left off their tune
   And the Ship stood still also.

The sun right up above the mast
   Had fix'd her to the ocean:
But in a minute she 'gan stir   390
   With a short uneasy motion—
Backwards and forwards half her length
   With a short uneasy motion.

Then, like a pawing horse let go,
   She made a sudden bound: 395

It flung the blood into my head,
  And I fell into a swound.

How long in that same fit I lay,
  I have not to declare;
But ere my living life return'd,   400
I heard and in my soul discern'd
  Two voices in the air,

'Is it he?' quoth one, 'Is this the man?
  By him who died on cross,
With his cruel bow he lay'd full low   405
  The harmless Albatross.

The spirit who 'bideth by himself
  In the land of mist and snow,
He lov'd the bird that lov'd the man
  Who shot him with his bow.'   410

The other was a softer voice,
  As soft as honey-dew:°
Quoth he 'the man hath penance done,
  And penance more will do.'

VI

FIRST VOICE

'But tell me, tell me! speak again,   415
  Thy soft response renewing—
What makes that ship drive on so fast?
  What is the Ocean doing?'

SECOND VOICE

'Still as a Slave before his Lord,°
  The Ocean hath no blast: 420
His great bright eye most silently
  Up to the moon is cast—

If he may know which way to go,
  For she guides him smooth or grim.

See, brother, see! how graciously   425
    She looketh down on him.'

FIRST VOICE
'But why drives on that ship so fast
    Withouten wave or wind?'

SECOND VOICE
'The air is cut away before,
    And closes from behind.   430

Fly, brother, fly! more high, more high,
    Or we shall be belated:°
For slow and slow that ship will go,
    When the Marinere's trance is abated.'

I woke, and we were sailing on   435
    As in a gentle weather:
'Twas night, calm night, the moon was high;
    The dead men stood together.

All stood together on the deck,
    For a charnel-dungeon fitter: 440
All fix'd on me their stony eyes
    That in the moon did glitter.

The pang, the curse, with which they died,
    Had never pass'd away:
I could not draw my een from theirs°   445
    Ne turn them up to pray.

And in its time the spell was snapt,
    And I could move my een:
I look'd far-forth, but little saw
    Of what might else be seen.   450

Like one, that on a lonely road
    Doth walk in fear and dread,
And having once turn'd round, walks on
    And turns no more his head:
Because he knows, a frightful fiend   455
    Doth close behind him tread.

But soon there breath'd a wind on me,
   Ne sound ne motion made:
Its path was not upon the sea
   In ripple or in shade.   460

It rais'd my hair, it fann'd my cheek,
   Like a meadow-gale of spring—
It mingled strangely with my fears,
   Yet it felt like a welcoming.

Swiftly, swiftly flew the ship,   465
   Yet she sail'd softly too:
Sweetly, sweetly blew the breeze—
   On me alone it blew.

O dream of joy! is this indeed
   The light-house top I see?   470
Is this the Hill? Is this the Kirk?
   Is this mine own countrée?

We drifted o'er the Harbour-bar,
   And I with sobs did pray—
'O let me be awake, my God!   475
   Or let me sleep alway!'

The harbour-bay was clear as glass,
   So smoothly it was strewn!
And on the bay the moon light lay,
   And the shadow of the moon.   480

The moonlight bay was white all o'er,
   Till rising from the same,
Full many shapes, that shadows were,
   Like as of torches came.

A little distance from the prow   485
   Those dark-red shadows were;
But soon I saw that my own flesh
   Was red as in a glare.

I turn'd my head in fear and dread,
   And by the holy rood,°   490

The bodies had advanc'd, and now
    Before the mast they stood.

They lifted up their stiff right arms,
    They held them strait and tight;
And each right-arm burnt like a torch,   495
    A torch that's borne upright.
Their stony eye-balls glitter'd on
    In the red and smoky light.

I pray'd and turn'd my head away
    Forth looking as before.   500
There was no breeze upon the bay,
    No wave against the shore.

The rock shone bright, the kirk no less
    That stands above the rock:
The moonlight steep'd in silentness   505
    The steady weathercock.

And the bay was white with silent light,
    Till rising from the same
Full many shapes, that shadows were,
    In crimson colours came.   510

A little distance from the prow
    Those crimson shadows were:
I turn'd my eyes upon the deck—
    O Christ! what saw I there?

Each corse lay flat, lifeless and flat;   515
    And by the Holy rood
A man all light, a seraph-man,
    On every corse there stood.

This seraph-band, each wav'd his hand:
    It was a heavenly sight: 520
They stood as signals to the land,
    Each one a lovely light:

This seraph-band, each wav'd his hand,
    No voice did they impart—

No voice; but O! the silence sank,   525
    Like music on my heart.

Eftsones I heard the dash of oars,°
    I heard the pilot's cheer:°
My head was turn'd perforce away
    And I saw a boat appear.   530

Then vanish'd all the lovely lights;
    The bodies rose anew:
With silent pace, each to his place,
    Came back the ghastly crew.
The wind, that shade nor motion made,   535
    On me alone it blew.

The pilot, and the pilot's boy
    I heard them coming fast:
Dear Lord in Heaven! it was a joy,
    The dead men could not blast.   540

I saw a third—I heard his voice:
    It is the Hermit good!°
He singeth loud his godly hymns
    That he makes in the wood.
He'll shrieve my soul, he'll wash away°   545
    The Albatross's blood.

VII

This Hermit good lives in that wood
    Which slopes down to the Sea.
How loudly his sweet voice he rears!
He loves to talk with Marineres   550
    That come from a far countrée.

He kneels at morn and noon and eve—
    He hath a cushion plump:
It is the moss, that wholly hides
    The rotted old Oak-stump.   555

The Skiff-boat ne'rd: I heard them talk,°
    'Why, this is strange, I trow!°

Where are those lights so many and fair
    That signal made but now?'

'Strange, by my faith!' the Hermit said—   560
    'And they answer'd not our cheer.
The planks look warp'd, and see those sails
    How thin they are and sere!
I never saw aught like to them
    Unless perchance it were   565

The skeletons of leaves that lag
    My forest brook along:
When the Ivy-tod is heavy with snow,°
And the Owlet whoops to the wolf below
    That eats the she-wolf's young.'   570

'Dear Lord! it has a fiendish look'—
    (The Pilot made reply)
'I am a-fear'd.'—'Push on, push on!'
    Said the Hermit cheerily.

The Boat came closer to the Ship,   575
    But I ne spake ne stirr'd!
The Boat came close beneath the Ship,
    And strait a sound was heard!

Under the water it rumbled on,
    Still louder and more dread: 580
It reach'd the Ship, it split the bay;
    The Ship went down like lead.

Stunn'd by that loud and dreadful sound,
    Which sky and ocean smote:
Like one that hath been seven days drown'd   585
    My body lay afloat:
But, swift as dreams, myself I found
    Within the Pilot's boat.

Upon the whirl, where sank the Ship,
    The boat spun round and round: 590

And all was still, save that the hill
  Was telling of the sound.

I mov'd my lips: the Pilot shriek'd
  And fell down in a fit.
The Holy Hermit rais'd his eyes   595
  And pray'd where he did sit.

I took the oars: the Pilot's boy,
  Who now doth crazy go,
Laugh'd loud and long, and all the while
  His eyes went to and fro,   600
'Ha! ha!' quoth he—'full plain I see,
  The devil knows how to row.'

And now all in mine own countrée
  I stood on the firm land!
The Hermit stepp'd forth from the boat,   605
  And scarcely he could stand.

'O shrieve me, shrieve me, holy Man!'
  The Hermit cross'd his brow—
'Say quick,' quoth he, 'I bid thee say
  What manner man art thou?'°   610

Forthwith this frame of mine was wrench'd
  With a woeful agony,
Which forc'd me to begin my tale
  And then it left me free.

Since then at an uncertain hour,   615
  Now oftimes and now fewer,
That anguish comes and makes me tell
  My ghastly aventure.

I pass, like night, from land to land;
  I have strange power of speech;°   620
The moment that his face I see
I know the man that must hear me;
  To him my tale I teach.

What loud uproar bursts from that door!
　　The Wedding-guests are there;   625
But in the Garden-bower the Bride
　　And Bride-maids singing are:
And hark the little Vesper-bell
　　Which biddeth me to prayer.

O Wedding-guest! this soul hath been   630
　　Alone on a wide wide sea:
So lonely 'twas, that God himself
　　Scarce seemed there to be.

O sweeter than the Marriage-feast,
　　'Tis sweeter far to me   635
To walk together to the Kirk
　　With a goodly company.

To walk together to the Kirk
　　And all together pray,
While each to his great father bends,   640
Old men, and babes, and loving friends,
　　And Youths, and Maidens gay.

Farewell, farewell! but this I tell
　　To thee, thou wedding-guest!
He prayeth well who loveth well   645
　　Both man and bird and beast.

He prayeth best who loveth best,
　　All things both great and small:
For the dear God, who loveth us,
　　He made and loveth all.   650

The Marinere, whose eye is bright,
　　Whose beard with age is hoar,
Is gone; and now the wedding-guest
　　Turn'd from the bridegroom's door.

He went, like one that hath been stunn'd   655
　　And is of sense forlorn:°
A sadder and a wiser man
　　He rose the morrow morn.

THE FOSTER-MOTHER'S TALE,

A DRAMATIC FRAGMENT

FOSTER-MOTHER. I never saw the man whom you describe.

MARIA. 'Tis strange! he spake of you familiarly
As mine and Albert's common Foster-mother.

FOSTER-MOTHER. Now blessings on the man, whoe'er he be,
That joined your names with mine! O my sweet lady,   5
As often as I think of those dear times
When you two little ones would stand at eve
On each side of my chair, and make me learn
All you had learnt in the day; and how to talk
In gentle phrase, then bid me sing to you—   10
'Tis more like heaven to come than what *has* been.

MARIA. O my dear Mother! this strange man has left me
Troubled with wilder fancies, than the moon
Breeds in the love-sick maid who gazes at it,
Till lost in inward vision, with wet eye   15
She gazes idly!—But that entrance, Mother!

FOSTER-MOTHER. Can no one hear? It is a perilous tale!

MARIA. No one.

FOSTER-MOTHER. My husband's father told it me,
Poor old Leoni!—Angels rest his soul!
He was a woodman, and could fell and saw   20
With lusty arm. You know that huge round beam
Which props the hanging wall of the old chapel?
Beneath that tree, while yet it was a tree
He found a baby wrapt in mosses, lined
With thistle-beards, and such small locks of wool   25
As hang on brambles. Well, he brought him home,
And reared him at the then Lord Velez' cost.
And so the babe grew up a pretty boy,
A pretty boy, but most unteachable—
And never learnt a prayer, nor told a bead,   30
But knew the names of birds, and mocked their notes,
And whistled, as he were a bird himself:
And all the autumn 'twas his only play

To get the seeds of wild flowers, and to plant them
With earth and water, on the stumps of trees.   35
A Friar, who gathered simples in the wood,°
A grey-haired man—he loved this little boy,
The boy loved him—and, when the Friar taught him,
He soon could write with the pen: and from that time,
Lived chiefly at the Convent or the Castle.   40
So he became a very learned youth.
But Oh! poor wretch!—he read, and read, and read,
'Till his brain turned—and ere his twentieth year,
He had unlawful thoughts of many things:
And though he prayed, he never loved to pray   45
With holy men, nor in a holy place—
But yet his speech, it was so soft and sweet,
The late Lord Velez ne'er was wearied with him.
And once, as by the north side of the Chapel
They stood together, chained in deep discourse,   50
The earth heaved under them with such a groan,
That the wall tottered, and had well-nigh fallen
Right on their heads. My Lord was sorely frightened;
A fever seized him, and he made confession
Of all the heretical and lawless talk   55
Which brought this judgment: so the youth was seized
And cast into that hole. My husband's father
Sobbed like a child—it almost broke his heart:
And once as he was working in the cellar,
He heard a voice distinctly; 'twas the youth's,   60
Who sung a doleful song about green fields,
How sweet it were on lake or wild savannah,°
To hunt for food, and be a naked man,
And wander up and down at liberty.
He always doted on the youth, and now   65
His love grew desperate; and defying death,
He made that cunning entrance I described:
And the young man escaped.

MARIA.   'Tis a sweet tale:
Such as would lull a listening child to sleep,
His rosy face besoiled with unwiped tears.—   70
And what became of him?

FOSTER-MOTHER.   He went on ship-board
With those bold voyagers, who made discovery

Of golden lands. Leoni's younger brother
Went likewise, and when he returned to Spain,
He told Leoni, that the poor mad youth,   75
Soon after they arrived in that new world,
In spite of his dissuasion, seized a boat,
And all alone, set sail by silent moonlight
Up a great river, great as any sea,
And ne'er was heard of more: but 'tis supposed,   80
He lived and died among the savage men.

LINES

Left upon a seat in a yew-tree which stands near the lake of Esthwaite,
on a desolate part of the shore, yet commanding a beautiful prospect

—Nay, Traveller! rest. This lonely yew-tree stands°
Far from all human dwelling: what if here
No sparkling rivulet spread the verdant herb;
What if these barren boughs the bee not loves;
Yet, if the wind breathe soft, the curling waves,   5
That break against the shore, shall lull thy mind
By one soft impulse saved from vacancy.
                              Who he was
That piled these stones, and with the mossy sod
First covered o'er, and taught this aged tree,   10
Now wild, to bend its arms in circling shade,
I well remember.—He was one who own'd
No common soul. In youth, by genius nurs'd,
And big with lofty views, he to the world
Went forth, pure in his heart, against the taint   15
Of dissolute tongues, 'gainst jealousy, and hate,
And scorn, against all enemies prepared,
All but neglect: and so, his spirit damped
At once, with rash disdain he turned away,
And with the food of pride sustained his soul   20
In solitude.—Stranger! these gloomy boughs
Had charms for him; and here he loved to sit,
His only visitants a straggling sheep,
The stone-chat, or the glancing sand-piper;°
And on these barren rocks, with juniper,   25

And heath, and thistle, thinly sprinkled o'er,
Fixing his downward eye, he many an hour
A morbid pleasure nourished, tracing here
An emblem of his own unfruitful life:
And lifting up his head, he then would gaze   30
On the more distant scene; how lovely 'tis
Thou seest, and he would gaze till it became
Far lovelier, and his heart could not sustain
The beauty still more beauteous. Nor, that time,
Would he forget those beings, to whose minds,   35
Warm from the labours of benevolence,
The world, and man himself, appeared a scene
Of kindred loveliness: then he would sigh
With mournful joy, to think that others felt
What he must never feel: and so, lost man!   40
On visionary views would fancy feed,
Till his eye streamed with tears. In this deep vale
He died, this seat his only monument.
If thou be one whose heart the holy forms
Of young imagination have kept pure,   45
Stranger! henceforth be warned; and know, that pride,
Howe'er disguised in its own majesty,
Is littleness; that he, who feels contempt
For any living thing, hath faculties
Which he has never used; that thought with him   50
Is in its infancy. The man, whose eye
Is ever on himself, doth look on one,
The least of nature's works, one who might move
The wise man to that scorn which wisdom holds
Unlawful, ever. O, be wiser thou!   55
Instructed that true knowledge leads to love,
True dignity abides with him alone
Who, in the silent hour of inward thought,
Can still suspect, and still revere himself,
In lowliness of heart.   60

THE NIGHTINGALE;

A CONVERSATIONAL POEM, WRITTEN IN APRIL, 1798

No cloud, no relique of the sunken day
Distinguishes the West, no long thin slip
Of sullen Light, no obscure trembling hues.
Come, we will rest on this old mossy Bridge!
You see the glimmer of the stream beneath,   5
But hear no murmuring: it flows silently
O'er its soft bed of verdure. All is still,
A balmy night! and tho' the stars be dim,
Yet let us think upon the vernal showers
That gladden the green earth, and we shall find   10
A pleasure in the dimness of the stars.
And hark! the Nightingale begins its song,
'Most musical, most melancholy'* Bird!°
A melancholy Bird? O idle thought!
In nature there is nothing melancholy.   15
—But some night-wandering Man, whose heart was pierc'd
With the remembrance of a grievous wrong,
Or slow distemper or neglected love,°
(And so, poor Wretch! fill'd all things with himself
And made all gentle sounds tell back the tale   20
Of his own sorrows) he and such as he
First nam'd these notes a melancholy strain;
And many a poet echoes the conceit,°
Poet, who hath been building up the rhyme
When he had better far have stretch'd his limbs   25
Beside a brook in mossy forest-dell
By sun or moonlight, to the influxes
Of shapes and sounds and shifting elements
Surrendering his whole spirit, of his song
And of his fame forgetful! so his fame   30
Should share in nature's immortality,

---

* *'Most musical, most melancholy'*. This passage in Milton possesses an excellence far
superior to that of mere description: it is spoken in the character of the melancholy Man,
and has therefore a *dramatic* propriety. The Author makes this remark in order to rescue
himself from the charge of having alluded with levity to a line in Milton: a charge than
which nothing could be more painful to him, except that perhaps of having ridiculed his
Bible.

A venerable thing! and so his song
Should make all nature lovelier, and itself
Be lov'd, like nature !—But 'twill not be so;
And youths and maidens most poetical   35
Who lose the deep'ning twilights of the spring
In ball-rooms and hot theatres, they still
Full of meek sympathy must heave their sighs
O'er Philomela's pity-pleading strains.°
My Friend, and my Friend's Sister! we have learnt°   40
A different lore: we may not thus profane°
Nature's sweet voices always full of love
And joyance! 'Tis the merry Nightingale
That crowds, and hurries, and precipitates
With fast thick warble his delicious notes,   45
As he were fearful, that an April night
Would be too short for him to utter forth
His love-chant, and disburthen his full soul
Of all its music ! And I know a grove
Of large extent, hard by a castle huge   50
Which the great lord inhabits not: and so
This grove is wild with tangling underwood,
And the trim walks are broken up, and grass,
Thin grass and king-cups grow within the paths.
But never elsewhere in one place I knew   55
So many Nightingales: and far and near
In wood and thicket over the wide grove
They answer and provoke each other's songs—
With skirmish and capricious passagings,
And murmurs musical and swift jug jug°   60
And one low piping sound more sweet than all—
Stirring the air with such an harmony,
That should you close your eyes, you might almost
Forget it was not day! On moonlight bushes,
Whose dewy leafits are but half disclos'd,   65
You may perchance behold them on the twigs,
Their bright, bright eyes, their eyes both bright and full,
Glistning, while many a glow-worm in the shade°
Lights up her love-torch.°
                              A most gentle maid
Who dwelleth in her hospitable home   70
Hard by the Castle, and at latest eve,

(Even like a Lady vow'd and dedicate
To something more than nature in the grove)
Glides thro' the pathways; she knows all their notes,
That gentle Maid! and oft, a moment's space,   75
What time the moon was lost behind a cloud,
Hath heard a pause of silence: till the Moon
Emerging, hath awaken'd earth and sky
With one sensation, and those wakeful Birds
Have all burst forth in choral minstrelsy,   80
As if one quick and sudden Gale had swept
An hundred airy harps! And she hath watch'd°
Many a Nightingale perch giddily
On blosmy twig still swinging from the breeze,°
And to that motion tune his wanton song,   85
Like tipsy Joy that reels with tossing head.

Farewell, O Warbler! till to-morrow eve,
And you, my friends! farewell, a short farewell!
We have been loitering long and pleasantly,
And now for our dear homes.—That strain again!°   90
Full fain would it delay me!—My dear Babe,°
Who, capable of no articulate sound,
Mars all things with his imitative lisp,
How he would place his hand beside his ear,
His little hand, the small forefinger up,   95
And bid us listen! And I deem it wise
To make him Nature's playmate. He knows well
The evening star: and once when he awoke
In most distressful mood (some inward pain
Had made up that strange thing, an infant's dream)   100
I hurried with him to our orchard plot,
And he beholds the moon, and hush'd at once
Suspends his sobs, and laughs most silently,
While his fair eyes that swam with undropt tears°
Did glitter in the yellow moon-beam! Well—   105
It is a father's tale. But if that Heaven
Should give me life, his childhood shall grow up
Familiar with these songs, that with the night
He may associate Joy! Once more farewell,°
Sweet Nightingale! once more, my friends! farewell.   110

THE FEMALE VAGRANT

By Derwent's side my Father's cottage stood,°
(The Woman thus her artless story told)
One field, a flock, and what the neighbouring flood
Supplied, to him were more than mines of gold.
Light was my sleep; my days in transport roll'd: 5
With thoughtless joy I stretch'd along the shore
My father's nets, or watched, when from the fold
High o'er the cliffs I led my fleecy store,
A dizzy depth below! his boat and twinkling oar.

My father was a good and pious man,   10
An honest man by honest parents bred,
And I believe that, soon as I began
To lisp, he made me kneel beside my bed,
And in his hearing there my prayers I said:
And afterwards, by my good father taught,   15
I read, and loved the books in which I read;
For books in every neighbouring house I sought,
And nothing to my mind a sweeter pleasure brought.

Can I forget what charms did once adorn
My garden, stored with pease, and mint, and thyme,   20
And rose and lilly for the sabbath morn?
The sabbath bells, and their delightful chime;
The gambols and wild freaks at shearing time;°
My hen's rich nest through long grass scarce espied;
The cowslip-gathering at May's dewy prime;   25
The swans, that, when I sought the water-side,
From far to meet me came, spreading their snowy pride.

The staff I yet remember which upbore
The bending body of my active sire;
His seat beneath the honeyed sycamore   30
When the bees hummed, and chair by winter fire;
When market-morning came, the neat attire
With which, though bent on haste, myself I deck'd;
My watchful dog, whose starts of furious ire,
When stranger passed, so often I have check'd;   35
The red-breast known for years, which at my casement peck'd.

The suns of twenty summers danced along,—
Ah! little marked, how fast they rolled away:
Then rose a mansion proud our woods among,
And cottage after cottage owned its sway,   40
No joy to see a neighbouring house, or stray
Through pastures not his own, the master took;
My Father dared his greedy wish gainsay;
He loved his old hereditary nook,°
And ill could I the thought of such sad parting brook.   45

But, when he had refused the proffered gold,
To cruel injuries he became a prey,
Sore traversed in whate'er he bought and sold:
His troubles grew upon him day by day,
Till all his substance fell into decay.   50
His little range of water was denied;*
All but the bed where his old body lay,
All, all was seized, and weeping, side by side,
We sought a home where we uninjured might abide.

Can I forget that miserable hour,   55
When from the last hill-top, my sire surveyed,
Peering above the trees, the steeple tower,
That on his marriage-day sweet music made?
Till then he hoped his bones might there be laid,
Close by my mother in their native bowers: 60
Bidding me trust in God, he stood and prayed,—
I could not pray:—through tears that fell in showers,
Glimmer'd our dear-loved home, alas! no longer ours!

There was a youth whom I had loved so long,
That when I loved him not I cannot say.   65
'Mid the green mountains many and many a song
We two had sung, like little birds in May.
When we began to tire of childish play
We seemed still more and more to prize each other:
We talked of marriage and our marriage day;   70
And I in truth did love him like a brother,
For never could I hope to meet with such another.

* Several of the Lakes in the north of England are let out to different Fishermen, in parcels marked out by imaginary lines drawn from rock to rock.

His father said, that to a distant town
He must repair, to ply the artist's trade.°
What tears of bitter grief till then unknown!   75
What tender vows our last sad kiss delayed!
To him we turned:—we had no other aid.
Like one revived, upon his neck I wept,
And her whom he had loved in joy, he said
He well could love in grief: his faith he kept;   80
And in a quiet house once more my father slept.

Four years each day with daily bread was blest,
By constant toil and constant prayer supplied.
Three lovely infants lay upon my breast;
And often, viewing their sweet smiles, I sighed,   85
And knew not why. My happy father died
When sad distress reduced the children's meal:
Thrice happy! that from him the grave did hide
The empty loom, cold hearth, and silent wheel,°
And tears that flowed for ills which patience could not heal.   90

'Twas a hard change, an evil time was come;
We had no hope, and no relief could gain.°
But soon, with proud parade, the noisy drum
Beat round, to sweep the streets of want and pain.
My husband's arms now only served to strain   95
Me and his children hungering in his view:
In such dismay my prayers and tears were vain:
To join those miserable men he flew;
And now to the sea-coast, with numbers more, we drew.

There foul neglect for months and months we bore,   100
Nor yet the crowded fleet its anchor stirred.
Green fields before us and our native shore,
By fever, from polluted air incurred,
Ravage was made, for which no knell was heard.
Fondly we wished, and wished away, nor knew,   105
'Mid that long sickness, and those hopes deferr'd,
That happier days we never more must view:
The parting signal streamed, at last the land withdrew,°

But from delay the summer calms were past.
On as we drove, the equinoctial deep°   110

Ran mountains-high before the howling blast.
We gazed with terror on the gloomy sleep
Of them that perished in the whirlwind's sweep,
Untaught that soon such anguish must ensue,
Our hopes such harvest of affliction reap,   115
That we the mercy of the waves should rue.
We reached the western world, a poor, devoted crew.

Oh! dreadful price of being to resign
All that is dear *in* being! better far
In Want's most lonely cave till death to pine,   120
Unseen, unheard, unwatched by any star;
Or in the streets and walks where proud men are,
Better our dying bodies to obtrude,
Than dog-like, wading at the heels of war,°
Protract a curst existence, with the brood   125
That lap (their very nourishment!) their brother's blood.

The pains and plagues that on our heads came down,
Disease and famine, agony and fear,
In wood or wilderness, in camp or town,
It would thy brain unsettle even to hear.   130
All perished—all, in one remorseless year,
Husband and children! one by one, by sword
And ravenous plague, all perished: every tear
Dried up, despairing, desolate, on board
A British ship I waked, as from a trance restored.   135

Peaceful as some immeasurable plain
By the first beams of dawning light impress'd,
In the calm sunshine slept the glittering main.
The very ocean has its hour of rest,
That comes not to the human mourner's breast.   140
Remote from man, and storms of mortal care,
A heavenly silence did the waves invest;
I looked and looked along the silent air,
Until it seemed to bring a joy to my despair.

Ah! how unlike those late terrific sleeps!   145
And groans, that rage of racking famine spoke,
Where looks inhuman dwelt on festering heaps!
The breathing pestilence that rose like smoke!

The shriek that from the distant battle broke!
The mine's dire earthquake, and the pallid host   150
Driven by the bomb's incessant thunder-stroke
To loathsome vaults, where heart-sick anguish toss'd,
Hope died, and fear itself in agony was lost!

Yet does that burst of woe congeal my frame,
When the dark streets appeared to heave and gape,   155
While like a sea the storming army came,
And Fire from Hell reared his gigantic shape,
And Murder, by the ghastly gleam, and Rape
Seized their joint prey, the mother and the child!
But from these crazing thoughts my brain, escape!   160
—For weeks the balmy air breathed soft and mild,
And on the gliding vessel Heaven and Ocean smiled.

Some mighty gulph of separation past,
I seemed transported to another world:—
A thought resigned with pain, when from the mast   165
The impatient mariner the sail unfurl'd,
And whistling, called the wind that hardly curled
The silent sea. From the sweet thoughts of home,
And from all hope I was forever hurled.
For me—farthest from earthly port to roam   170
Was best, could I but shun the spot where man might come.

And oft, robb'd of my perfect mind, I thought
At last my feet a resting-place had found:
Here will I weep in peace, (so fancy wrought,)
Roaming the illimitable waters round;   175
Here watch, of every human friend disowned,
All day, my ready tomb the ocean-flood—
To break my dream the vessel reached its bound:
And homeless near a thousand homes I stood,
And near a thousand tables pined, and wanted food.   180

By grief enfeebled was I turned adrift,
Helpless as sailor cast on desart rock;
Nor morsel to my mouth that day did lift,
Nor dared my hand at any door to knock.

I lay, where with his drowsy mates, the cock   185
From the cross timber of an out-house hung;
How dismal tolled, that night, the city clock!
At morn my sick heart hunger scarcely stung,
Nor to the beggar's language could I frame my tongue.

So passed another day, and so the third: 190
Then did I try, in vain, the crowd's resort,
In deep despair by frightful wishes stirr'd,
Near the sea-side I reached a ruined fort:
There, pains which nature could no more support,
With blindness linked, did on my vitals fall;   195
Dizzy my brain, with interruption short
Of hideous sense; I sunk, nor step could crawl,
And thence was borne away to neighbouring hospital.

Recovery came with food: but still, my brain
Was weak, nor of the past had memory.   200
I heard my neighbours, in their beds, complain
Of many things which never troubled me;
Of feet still bustling round with busy glee,
Of looks where common kindness had no part,
Of service done with careless cruelty,   205
Fretting the fever round the languid heart,
And groans, which, as they said, would make a dead man start.

These things just served to stir the torpid sense,
Nor pain nor pity in my bosom raised.
Memory, though slow, returned with strength; and thence   210
Dismissed, again on open day I gazed,
At houses, men, and common light, amazed.
The lanes I sought, and as the sun retired,
Came, where beneath the trees a faggot blazed;
The wild brood saw me weep, my fate enquired,°   215
And gave me food, and rest, more welcome, more desired.

My heart is touched to think that men like these,
The rude earth's tenants, were my first relief:
How kindly did they paint their vagrant ease!
And their long holiday that feared not grief,   220

For all belonged to all, and each was chief.
No plough their sinews strained; on grating road
No wain they drove, and yet, the yellow sheaf
In every vale for their delight was stowed:
For them, in nature's meads, the milky udder flowed.   225

Semblance, with straw and panniered ass, they made°
Of potters wandering on from door to door:
But life of happier sort to me pourtrayed,
And other joys my fancy to allure;
The bag-pipe dinning on the midnight moor°   230
In barn uplighted, and companions boon
Well met from far with revelry secure,
In depth of forest glade, when jocund June
Rolled fast along the sky his warm and genial moon.

But ill it suited me, in journey dark   235
O'er moor and mountain, midnight theft to hatch;
To charm the surly house-dog's faithful bark,
Or hang on tiptoe at the lifted latch;
The gloomy lantern, and the dim blue match,
The black disguise, the warning whistle shrill,   240
And ear still busy on its nightly watch,
Were not for me, brought up in nothing ill;
Besides, on griefs so fresh my thoughts were brooding still.

What could I do, unaided and unblest?
Poor Father! gone was every friend of thine: 245
And kindred of dead husband are at best
Small help, and, after marriage such as mine,
With little kindness would to me incline.
Ill was I then for toil or service fit:
With tears whose course no effort could confine,   250
By high-way side forgetful would I sit
Whole hours, my idle arms in moping sorrow knit.

I lived upon the mercy of the fields,
And oft of cruelty the sky accused;
On hazard, or what general bounty yields,   255
Now coldly given, now utterly refused.

The fields I for my bed have often used:
But, what afflicts my peace with keenest ruth°
Is, that I have my inner self abused,
Foregone the home delight of constant truth,   260
And clear and open soul, so prized in fearless youth.

Three years a wanderer, often have I view'd,
In tears, the sun towards that country tend
Where my poor heart lost all its fortitude:
And now across this moor my steps I bend—   265
Oh! tell me whither—for no earthly friend
Have I.—She ceased, and weeping turned away,
As if because her tale was at an end
She wept;—because she had no more to say
Of that perpetual weight which on her spirit lay.   270

GOODY BLAKE, AND HARRY GILL,
A TRUE STORY

Oh! what's the matter? what's the matter?
What is't that ails young Harry Gill?
That evermore his teeth they chatter,
Chatter, chatter, chatter still.
Of waistcoats Harry has no lack,   5
Good duffle grey, and flannel fine;
He has a blanket on his back,
And coats enough to smother nine.

In March, December, and in July,
'Tis all the same with Harry Gill;   10
The neighbours tell, and tell you truly,
His teeth they chatter, chatter still.
At night, at morning, and at noon,
'Tis all the same with Harry Gill;
Beneath the sun, beneath the moon,   15
His teeth they chatter, chatter still.

Young Harry was a lusty drover,°
And who so stout of limb as he?
His cheeks were red as ruddy clover,
His voice was like the voice of three.   20

Auld Goody Blake was old and poor,
Ill fed she was, and thinly clad;
And any man who pass'd her door,
Might see how poor a hut she had.

All day she spun in her poor dwelling,°   25
And then her three hours' work at night!
Alas! 'twas hardly worth the telling,
It would not pay for candle-light.
—This woman dwelt in Dorsetshire,
Her hut was on a cold hill-side,   30
And in that country coals are dear,°
For they come far by wind and tide.

By the same fire to boil their pottage,°
Two poor old dames, as I have known,
Will often live in one small cottage,   35
But she, poor woman, dwelt alone.
'Twas well enough when summer came,
The long, warm, lightsome summer-day,
Then at her door the *canty* dame°
Would sit, as any linnet gay.   40

But when the ice our streams did fetter,
Oh! then how her old bones would shake!
You would have said, if you had met her,
'Twas a hard time for Goody Blake.
Her evenings then were dull and dead;   45
Sad case it was, as you may think,
For very cold to go to bed,
And then for cold not sleep a wink.

Oh joy for her! when e'er in winter
The winds at night had made a rout,   50
And scatter'd many a lusty splinter,
And many a rotten bough about.
Yet never had she, well or sick,
As every man who knew her says,
A pile before-hand, wood or stick,   55
Enough to warm her for three days.

Now, when the frost was past enduring,
And made her poor old bones to ache,
Could any thing be more alluring,
Than an old hedge to Goody Blake?°   60
And now and then, it must be said,
When her old bones were cold and chill,
She left her fire, or left her bed,
To seek the hedge of Harry Gill.

Now Harry he had long suspected   65
This trespass of old Goody Blake,°
And vow'd that she should be detected,
And he on her would vengeance take.
And oft from his warm fire he'd go,
And to the fields his road would take,   70
And there, at night, in frost and snow,
He watch'd to seize old Goody Blake.

And once, behind a rick of barley,
Thus looking out did Harry stand;
The moon was full and shining clearly,   75
And crisp with frost the stubble-land.°
—He hears a noise—he's all awake—
Again?—on tip-toe down the hill
He softly creeps—'Tis Goody Blake,
She's at the hedge of Harry Gill.   80

Right glad was he when he beheld her:
Stick after stick did Goody pull,
He stood behind a bush of elder,
Till she had filled her apron full.
When with her load she turned about,   85
The bye-road back again to take,
He started forward with a shout,
And sprang upon poor Goody Blake.

And fiercely by the arm he took her,
And by the arm he held her fast,   90
And fiercely by the arm he shook her,
And cried, 'I've caught you then at last!'

Then Goody, who had nothing said,
Her bundle from her lap let fall;
And kneeling on the sticks, she pray'd   95
To God that is the judge of all.

She pray'd, her wither'd hand uprearing,
While Harry held her by the arm—
'God! who art never out of hearing,
O may he never more be warm!'   100
The cold, cold moon above her head,
Thus on her knees did Goody pray,
Young Harry heard what she had said,
And icy-cold he turned away.

He went complaining all the morrow   105
That he was cold and very chill:
His face was gloom, his heart was sorrow,
Alas! that day for Harry Gill!
That day he wore a riding-coat,
But not a whit the warmer he: 110
Another was on Thursday brought,
And ere the Sabbath he had three.

'Twas all in vain, a useless matter,
And blankets were about him pinn'd;
Yet still his jaws and teeth they clatter,   115
Like a loose casement in the wind.
And Harry's flesh it fell away;
And all who see him say 'tis plain,
That, live as long as live he may,
He never will be warm again.   120

No word to any man he utters,
A-bed or up, to young or old;
But ever to himself he mutters,
'Poor Harry Gill is very cold.'
A-bed or up, by night or day;   125
His teeth they chatter, chatter still.
Now think, ye farmers all, I pray,
Of Goody Blake and Harry Gill.

LINES

Written at a small distance from my House, and sent by my little boy to the person to whom they are addressed

It is the first mild day of March:
Each minute sweeter than before,
The red-breast sings from the tall larch°
That stands beside our door.

There is a blessing in the air,   5
Which seems a sense of joy to yield
To the bare trees, and mountains bare,
And grass in the green field.

My Sister! ('tis a wish of mine)
Now that our morning meal is done,   10
Make haste, your morning task resign;
Come forth and feel the sun.

Edward will come with you, and pray,
Put on with speed your woodland dress,
And bring no book, for this one day   15
We'll give to idleness.

No joyless forms shall regulate
Our living Calendar:
We from to-day, my friend, will date
The opening of the year.   20

Love, now an universal birth,
From heart to heart is stealing,
From earth to man, from man to earth,
—It is the hour of feeling.

One moment now may give us more   25
Than fifty years of reason;
Our minds shall drink at every pore
The spirit of the season.

Some silent laws our hearts may make,
Which they shall long obey;   30

We for the year to come may take
Our temper from to-day.

And from the blessed power that rolls
About, below, above;
We'll frame the measure of our souls,   35
They shall be tuned to love.

Then come, my sister! come, I pray,
With speed put on your woodland dress,
And bring no book; for this one day
We'll give to idleness.   40

SIMON LEE,

THE OLD HUNTSMAN,

With an incident in which he was concerned

In the sweet shire of Cardigan,°
Not far from pleasant Ivor-hall,°
An old man dwells, a little man,
I've heard he once was tall.
Of years he has upon his back,   5
No doubt, a burthen weighty;
He says he is three score and ten,
But others say he's eighty.

A long blue livery-coat has he,
That's fair behind, and fair before;   10
Yet, meet him where you will, you see
At once that he is poor.
Full five and twenty years he lived
A running huntsman merry;°
And, though he has but one eye left,   15
His cheek is like a cherry.°

No man like him the horn could sound,
And no man was so full of glee;
To say the least, four counties round
Had heard of Simon Lee;   20

His master's dead, and no one now
Dwells in the hall of Ivor;
Men, dogs, and horses, all are dead;
He is the sole survivor.

His hunting feats have him bereft   25
Of his right eye, as you may see:
And then, what limbs those feats have left
To poor old Simon Lee!
He has no son, he has no child,
His wife, an aged woman,   30
Lives with him, near the waterfall,
Upon the village common.

And he is lean and he is sick,
His little body's half awry
His ancles they are swoln and thick;°   35
His legs are thin and dry.
When he was young he little knew
Of husbandry or tillage;°
And now he's forced to work, though weak,
—The weakest in the village.   40

He all the country could outrun,
Could leave both man and horse behind;
And often, ere the race was done,
He reeled and was stone-blind.°
And still there's something in the world   45
At which his heart rejoices;
For when the chiming hounds are out,
He dearly loves their voices!

Old Ruth works out of doors with him,
And does what Simon cannot do;   50
For she, not over stout of limb,
Is stouter of the two.
And though you with your utmost skill
From labour could not wean them,
Alas! 'tis very little, all   55
Which they can do between them.

Beside their moss-grown hut of clay,
Not twenty paces from the door,
A scrap of land they have, but they
Are poorest of the poor.   60
This scrap of land he from the heath
Enclosed when he was stronger;°
But what avails the land to them,
Which they can till no longer?

Few months of life has he in store,   65
As he to you will tell,
For still, the more he works, the more
His poor old ancles swell.
My gentle reader, I perceive°
How patiently you've waited,   70
And I'm afraid that you expect
Some tale will be related.

O reader! had you in your mind
Such stores as silent thought can bring,
O gentle reader! you would find   75
A tale in every thing.
What more I have to say is short,
I hope you'll kindly take it;
It is no tale; but should you think,
Perhaps a tale you'll make it.   80

One summer-day I chanced to see
This old man doing all he could
About the root of an old tree,
A stump of rotten wood.
The mattock totter'd in his hand;°   85
So vain was his endeavour
That at the root of the old tree
He might have worked for ever.

'You're overtasked, good Simon Lee,
Give me your tool' to him I said;   90
And at the word right gladly he
Received my proffer'd aid.

I struck, and with a single blow
The tangled root I sever'd,
At which the poor old man so long   95
And vainly had endeavour'd.

The tears into his eyes were brought,
And thanks and praises seemed to run
So fast out of his heart, I thought
They never would have done.   100
—I've heard of hearts unkind, kind deeds
With coldness still returning.
Alas! the gratitude of men
Has oftner left me mourning.

ANECDOTE FOR FATHERS,

Shewing how the art of lying may be taught

I have a boy of five years old,
His face is fair and fresh to see;
His limbs are cast in beauty's mould,°
And dearly he loves me.

One morn we stroll'd on our dry walk,   5
Our quiet house all full in view,
And held such intermitted talk
As we are wont to do.

My thoughts on former pleasures ran;
I thought of Kilve's delightful shore,°   10
My pleasant home, when spring began,
A long, long year before.

A day it was when I could bear
To think, and think, and think again;
With so much happiness to spare,   15
I could not feel a pain.

My boy was by my side, so slim
And graceful in his rustic dress!

And oftentimes I talked to him,
In very idleness.   20

The young lambs ran a pretty race;
The morning sun shone bright and warm;
'Kilve,' said I, 'was a pleasant place,
And so is Liswyn farm.°

My little boy, which like you more,'   25
I said and took him by the arm—
'Our home by Kilve's delightful shore,
Or here at Liswyn farm?'

'And tell me, had you rather be,'
I said and held him by the arm,   30
'At Kilve's smooth shore by the green sea,
Or here at Liswyn farm?'

In careless mood he looked at me,
While still I held him by the arm,
And said, 'At Kilve I'd rather be   35
Than here at Liswyn farm.'

'Now, little Edward, say why so;
My little Edward, tell me why;'
'I cannot tell, I do not know.'
'Why this is strange,' said I.   40

'For, here are woods and green-hills warm;
There surely must some reason be
Why you would change sweet Liswyn farm
For Kilve by the green sea.'

At this, my boy, so fair and slim,   45
Hung down his head, nor made reply;
And five times did I say to him,
'Why? Edward, tell me why?'

His head he raised—there was in sight,
It caught his eye, he saw it plain—   50
Upon the house-top, glittering bright,
A broad and gilded vane.

Then did the boy his tongue unlock,
And thus to me he made reply;
'At Kilve there was no weather-cock,   55
And that's the reason why.'

Oh dearest, dearest boy! my heart
For better lore would seldom yearn,
Could I but teach the hundredth part
Of what from thee I learn.   60

WE ARE SEVEN

A simple child, dear brother Jim,
That lightly draws its breath,
And feels its life in every limb,
What should it know of death?

I met a little cottage girl,   5
She was eight years old, she said;
Her hair was thick with many a curl
That cluster'd round her head.

She had a rustic, woodland air,
And she was wildly clad;   10
Her eyes were fair, and very fair,
—Her beauty made me glad.

'Sisters and brothers, little maid,
How many may you be?'
'How many? seven in all,' she said,   15
And wondering looked at me.

'And where are they, I pray you tell?'
She answered, 'Seven are we,
And two of us at Conway dwell,°
And two are gone to sea.   20

Two of us in the church-yard lie,
My sister and my brother,
And in the church-yard cottage, I
Dwell near them with my mother.'

'You say that two at Conway dwell,   25
And two are gone to sea,
Yet you are seven; I pray you tell
Sweet Maid, how this may be?'

Then did the little Maid reply,
'Seven boys and girls are we;   30
Two of us in the church-yard lie,
Beneath the church-yard tree.'

'You run about, my little maid,
Your limbs they are alive;
If two are in the church-yard laid,   35
Then ye are only five.'

'Their graves are green, they may be seen,'
The little Maid replied,
'Twelve steps or more from my mother's door,
And they are side by side.   40

My stockings there I often knit,
My 'kerchief there I hem;
And there upon the ground I sit—
I sit and sing to them.

And often after sunset, Sir,   45
When it is light and fair,
I take my little porringer,°
And eat my supper there.

The first that died was little Jane;
In bed she moaning lay,   50
Till God released her of her pain,
And then she went away.

So in the church-yard she was laid,
And all the summer dry,
Together round her grave we played,   55
My brother John and I.

And when the ground was white with snow,
And I could run and slide,

My brother John was forced to go,
And he lies by her side.' 60

'How many are you then,' said I,
'If they two are in Heaven?'
The little Maiden did reply,
'O Master! we are seven.'

'But they are dead; those two are dead! 65
Their spirits are in heaven!'
'Twas throwing words away; for still
The little Maid would have her will,
And said, 'Nay, we are seven!'

LINES
Written in early spring

I heard a thousand blended notes,
While in a grove I sate reclined,
In that sweet mood when pleasant thoughts
Bring sad thoughts to the mind.

To her fair works did nature link 5
The human soul that through me ran;
And much it griev'd my heart to think
What man has made of man.°

Through primrose-tufts, in that sweet bower,
The periwinkle trail'd its wreathes; 10
And 'tis my faith that every flower
Enjoys the air it breathes.

The birds around me hopp'd and play'd:
Their thoughts I cannot measure,
But the least motion which they made, 15
It seem'd a thrill of pleasure.

The budding twigs spread out their fan,
To catch the breezy air;

And I must think, do all I can,
That there was pleasure there.   20

If I these thoughts may not prevent,
If such be of my creed the plan,
Have I not reason to lament
What man has made of man?

THE THORN

I

There is a thorn; it looks so old,
In truth you'd find it hard to say,
How it could ever have been young,
It looks so old and grey.
Not higher than a two-years' child,   5
It stands erect this aged thorn;
No leaves it has, no thorny points;
It is a mass of knotted joints,
A wretched thing forlorn.
It stands erect, and like a stone   10
With lichens it is overgrown.

II

Like rock or stone, it is o'ergrown
With lichens to the very top,
And hung with heavy tufts of moss,
A melancholy crop: 15
Up from the earth these mosses creep,
And this poor thorn they clasp it round
So close, you'd say that they were bent
With plain and manifest intent,
To drag it to the ground;   20
And all had joined in one endeavour
To bury this poor thorn for ever.

III

High on a mountain's highest ridge,
Where oft the stormy winter gale
Cuts like a scythe, while through the clouds   25

It sweeps from vale to vale;
Not five yards from the mountain-path,
This thorn you on your left espy;
And to the left, three yards beyond,
You see a little muddy pond   30
Of water, never dry;
I've measured it from side to side:
'Tis three feet long, and two feet wide.

IV

And close beside this aged thorn,
There is a fresh and lovely sight,   35
A beauteous heap, a hill of moss,
Just half a foot in height.
All lovely colours there you see,
All colours that were ever seen,
And mossy network too is there,   40
As if by hand of lady fair
The work had woven been,
And cups, the darlings of the eye,
So deep is their vermilion dye.

V

Ah me! what lovely tints are there!   45
Of olive-green and scarlet bright,
In spikes, in branches, and in stars,
Green, red, and pearly white.
This heap of earth o'ergrown with moss,
Which close beside the thorn you see,   50
So fresh in all its beauteous dyes,
Is like an infant's grave in size
As like as like can be:
But never, never any where,
An infant's grave was half so fair.   55

VI

Now would you see this aged thorn,
This pond and beauteous hill of moss,
You must take care and chuse your time
The mountain when to cross.
For oft there sits, between the heap   60

That's like an infant's grave in size,
And that same pond of which I spoke,
A woman in a scarlet cloak,°
And to herself she cries,
'Oh misery! oh misery!°   65
Oh woe is me! oh misery!'

VII

At all times of the day and night
This wretched woman thither goes,
And she is known to every star,
And every wind that blows;   70
And there beside the thorn she sits
When the blue day-light's in the skies,
And when the whirlwind's on the hill,
Or frosty air is keen and still,
And to herself she cries,   75
'Oh misery! oh misery!
Oh woe is me! oh misery!'

VIII

'Now wherefore thus, by day and night,
In rain, in tempest, and in snow,
Thus to the dreary mountain-top   80
Does this poor woman go?
And why sits she beside the thorn
When the blue day-light's in the sky,
Or when the whirlwind's on the hill,
Or frosty air is keen and still,   85
And wherefore does she cry?—
Oh wherefore? wherefore? tell me why
Does she repeat that doleful cry?'

IX

I cannot tell; I wish I could;
For the true reason no one knows,   90
But if you'd gladly view the spot,
The spot to which she goes;
The heap that's like an infant's grave,
The pond—and thorn, so old and grey;
Pass by her door—'tis seldom shut—   95

And if you see her in her hut,
Then to the spot away!—
I never heard of such as dare
Approach the spot when she is there.

X

'But wherefore to the mountain-top   100
Can this unhappy woman go,
Whatever star is in the skies,
Whatever wind may blow?'
Nay rack your brain—'tis all in vain,
I'll tell you every thing I know;   105
But to the thorn, and to the pond
Which is a little step beyond,
I wish that you would go:
Perhaps when you are at the place
You something of her tale may trace.   110

XI

I'll give you the best help I can:
Before you up the mountain go,
Up to the dreary mountain-top,
I'll tell you all I know.
'Tis now some two and twenty years,   115
Since she (her name is Martha Ray)°
Gave with a maiden's true good will
Her company to Stephen Hill;
And she was blithe and gay,°
And she was happy, happy still°   120
Whene'er she thought of Stephen Hill.

XII

And they had fix'd the wedding-day,
The morning that must wed them both;
But Stephen to another maid
Had sworn another oath;   125
And with this other maid to church
Unthinking Stephen went—
Poor Martha! on that woful day
A cruel, cruel fire, they say,
Into her bones was sent: 130

It dried her body like a cinder,
And almost turn'd her brain to tinder.

XIII

They say, full six months after this,
While yet the summer leaves were green,
She to the mountain-top would go,   135
And there was often seen.
'Tis said, a child was in her womb,
As now to any eye was plain;
She was with child, and she was mad,
Yet often she was sober sad   140
From her exceeding pain.
Oh me! ten thousand times I'd rather
That he had died, that cruel father!

XIV

Sad case for such a brain to hold
Communion with a stirring child!   145
Sad case, as you may think, for one
Who had a brain so wild!
Last Christmas when we talked of this,
Old Farmer Simpson did maintain,
That in her womb the infant wrought   150
About its mother's heart, and brought
Her senses back again:
And when at last her time drew near,
Her looks were calm, her senses clear.

XV

No more I know, I wish I did,   155
And I would tell it all to you;
For what became of this poor child
There's none that ever knew:
And if a child was born or no,
There's no one that could ever tell;   160
And if 'twas born alive or dead,
There's no one knows, as I have said,
But some remember well,
That Martha Ray about this time
Would up the mountain often climb.   165

XVI

And all that winter, when at night
The wind blew from the mountain-peak,
'Twas worth your while, though in the dark,
The church-yard path to seek:
For many a time and oft were heard   170
Cries coming from the mountain-head,
Some plainly living voices were,
And others, I've heard many swear,
Were voices of the dead:
I cannot think, whate'er they say,   175
They had to do with Martha Ray.

XVII

But that she goes to this old thorn,
The thorn which I've described to you,
And there sits in a scarlet cloak,
I will be sworn is true.   180
For one day with my telescope,°
To view the ocean wide and bright,
When to this country first I came,
Ere I had heard of Martha's name,
I climbed the mountain's height: 185
A storm came on, and I could see
No object higher than my knee.

XVIII

'Twas mist and rain, and storm and rain,
No screen, no fence could I discover,
And then the wind! in faith, it was   190
A wind full ten times over.
I looked around, I thought I saw
A jutting crag, and off I ran,
Head-foremost, through the driving rain,
The shelter of the crag to gain,   195
And, as I am a man,
Instead of jutting crag, I found
A woman seated on the ground.

XIX

I did not speak—I saw her face,
Her face it was enough for me;   200
I turned about and heard her cry,
'Oh misery! oh misery!'
And there she sits, until the moon
Through half the clear blue sky will go,
And when the little breezes make   205
The waters of the pond to shake,°
As all the country know,
She shudders and you hear her cry,
'Oh misery! oh misery!'

XX

'But what's the thorn? and what's the pond?   210
And what's the hill of moss to her?
And what's the creeping breeze that comes
The little pond to stir?'
I cannot tell; but some will say
She hanged her baby on the tree,   215
Some say she drowned it in the pond,
Which is a little step beyond,
But all and each agree,
The little babe was buried there,
Beneath that hill of moss so fair.   220

XXI

I've heard the scarlet moss is red
With drops of that poor infant's blood;
But kill a new-born infant thus!
I do not think she could.
Some say, if to the pond you go,   225
And fix on it a steady view,
The shadow of a babe you trace,
A baby and a baby's face,
And that it looks at you;
Whene'er you look on it, 'tis plain   230
The baby looks at you again.

XXII

And some had sworn an oath that she
Should be to public justice brought;
And for the little infant's bones
With spades they would have sought.   235
But then the beauteous hill of moss
Before their eyes began to stir;
And for full fifty yards around,
The grass it shook upon the ground;
But all do still aver   240
The little babe is buried there,
Beneath that hill of moss so fair.

XXIII

I cannot tell how this may be,
But plain it is, the thorn is bound
With heavy tufts of moss, that strive   245
To drag it to the ground.
And this I know, full many a time,
When she was on the mountain high,
By day, and in the silent night,
When all the stars shone clear and bright,   250
That I have heard her cry,
'Oh misery! oh misery!
O woe is me! oh misery!'

THE LAST OF THE FLOCK

In distant countries I have been,
And yet I have not often seen
A healthy man, a man full grown,
Weep in the public roads alone.°
But such a one, on English ground,   5
And in the broad high-way, I met;
Along the broad high-way he came,
His cheeks with tears were wet.
Sturdy he seemed, though he was sad;
And in his arms a lamb he had.   10

He saw me, and he turned aside,
As if he wished himself to hide:
Then with his coat he made essay
To wipe those briny tears away.
I follow'd him, and said, 'My friend   15
What ails you? wherefore weep you so?'
—'Shame on me, Sir! this lusty lamb,
He makes my tears to flow.
To-day I fetched him from the rock;
He is the last of all my flock.   20

When I was young, a single man,
And after youthful follies ran,
Though little given to care and thought,
Yet, so it was, a ewe I bought;
And other sheep from her I raised,   25
As healthy sheep as you might see,
And then I married, and was rich
As I could wish to be;
Of sheep I number'd a full score,
And every year encreas'd my store.   30

Year after year my stock it grew,
And from this one, this single ewe,
Full fifty comely sheep I raised,
As sweet a flock as ever grazed!
Upon the mountain did they feed;   35
They throve, and we at home did thrive.
—This lusty lamb of all my store
Is all that is alive:
And now I care not if we die,
And perish all of poverty.   40

Ten children, Sir! had I to feed,°
Hard labour in a time of need!
My pride was tamed, and in our grief,
I of the parish ask'd relief.°
They said I was a wealthy man;   45
My sheep upon the mountain fed,
And it was fit that thence I took
Whereof to buy us bread:

"Do this; how can we give to you,"
They cried, "what to the poor is due?"   50

I sold a sheep as they had said,
And bought my little children bread,
And they were healthy with their food;
For me it never did me good.
A woeful time it was for me,   55
To see the end of all my gains,
The pretty flock which I had reared
With all my care and pains,
To see it melt like snow away!
For me it was woeful day.   60

Another still! and still another!
A little lamb, and then its mother!
It was a vein that never stopp'd,
Like blood-drops from my heart they dropp'd.
Till thirty were not left alive   65
They dwindled, dwindled, one by one,
And I may say that many a time
I wished they all were gone:
They dwindled one by one away;
For me it was a woeful day.   70

To wicked deeds I was inclined,
And wicked fancies cross'd my mind,
And every man I chanc'd to see,
I thought he knew some ill of me.
No peace, no comfort could I find,   75
No ease, within doors or without,
And crazily, and wearily,
I went my work about.
Oft-times I thought to run away;
For me it was a woeful day.   80

Sir! 'twas a precious flock to me,
As dear as my own children be;
For daily with my growing store
I loved my children more and more.
Alas! it was an evil time;   85

God cursed me in my sore distress,
I prayed, yet every day I thought
I loved my children less;
And every week, and every day,
My flock, it seemed to melt away.   90

They dwindled, Sir, sad sight to see!
From ten to five, from five to three,
A lamb, a weather, and a ewe;
And then at last, from three to two;
And of my fifty, yesterday   95
I had but only one,
And here it lies upon my arm,
Alas! and I have none;
To-day I fetched it from the rock;
It is the last of all my flock.'   100

THE DUNGEON

And this place our forefathers made for man!
This is the process of our love and wisdom,
To each poor brother who offends against us—
Most innocent, perhaps—and what if guilty?
Is this the only cure? Merciful God!   5
Each pore and natural outlet shrivell'd up
By ignorance and parching poverty,
His energies roll back upon his heart,
And stagnate and corrupt; till changed to poison,
They break out on him, like a loathsome plague-spot; 10
Then we call in our pamper'd mountebanks—°
And this is their best cure! uncomforted
And friendless solitude, groaning and tears,
And savage faces, at the clanking hour,
Seen through the steams and vapour of his dungeon,   15
By the lamp's dismal twilight! So he lies
Circled with evil, till his very soul
Unmoulds its essence, hopelessly deformed
By sights of ever more deformity!

With other ministrations thou, O nature!°   20
Healest thy wandering and distempered child:°
Thou pourest on him thy soft influences,
Thy sunny hues, fair forms, and breathing sweets,
Thy melodies of woods, and winds, and waters,
Till he relent, and can no more endure   25
To be a jarring and a dissonant thing,
Amid this general dance and minstrelsy;
But, bursting into tears, wins back his way,
His angry spirit healed and harmonized
By the benignant touch of love and beauty.   30

THE MAD MOTHER

Her eyes are wild, her head is bare,
The sun has burnt her coal-black hair,
Her eye-brows have a rusty stain,
And she came far from over the main.°
She has a baby on her arm,   5
Or else she were alone;
And underneath the hay-stack warm,
And on the green-wood stone,
She talked and sung the woods among;
And it was in the English tongue.   10

'Sweet babe! they say that I am mad,
But nay, my heart is far too glad;
And I am happy when I sing
Full many a sad and doleful thing:
Then, lovely baby, do not fear!   15
I pray thee have no fear of me,
But, safe as in a cradle, here
My lovely baby! thou shalt be,
To thee I know too much I owe;
I cannot work thee any woe.   20

A fire was once within my brain;
And in my head a dull, dull pain;
And fiendish faces one, two, three,
Hung at my breasts, and pulled at me.

But then there came a sight of joy;   25
It came at once to do me good;
I waked, and saw my little boy,
My little boy of flesh and blood;
Oh joy for me that sight to see!
For he was here, and only he.   30

Suck, little babe, oh suck again!
It cools my blood; it cools my brain;
Thy lips I feel them, baby! they
Draw from my heart the pain away.
Oh! press me with thy little hand;   35
It loosens something at my chest;
About that tight and deadly band
I feel thy little fingers press'd.
The breeze I see is in the tree;
It comes to cool my babe and me.   40

Oh! love me, love me, little boy!
Thou art thy mother's only joy;
And do not dread the waves below,
When o'er the sea-rock's edge we go;
The high crag cannot work me harm,   45
Nor leaping torrents when they howl;
The babe I carry on my arm,
He saves for me my precious soul;
Then happy lie, for blest am I;
Without me my sweet babe would die.   50

Then do not fear, my boy! for thee
Bold as a lion I will be;
And I will always be thy guide,
Through hollow snows and rivers wide.
I'll build an Indian bower; I know   55
The leaves that make the softest bed:
And if from me thou wilt not go,
But still be true 'till I am dead,
My pretty thing! then thou shalt sing,
As merry as the birds in spring.   60

Thy father cares not for my breast,
'Tis thine, sweet baby, there to rest:

'Tis all thine own! and if its hue
Be changed, that was so fair to view,
'Tis fair enough for thee, my dove!   65
My beauty, little child, is flown;
But thou wilt live with me in love,
And what if my poor cheek be brown?
'Tis well for me; thou canst not see
How pale and wan it else would be.   70

Dread not their taunts, my little life!
I am thy father's wedded wife;
And underneath the spreading tree
We two will live in honesty.
If his sweet boy he could forsake,   75
With me he never would have stay'd:
From him no harm my babe can take,
But he, poor man! is wretched made,
And every day we two will pray
For him that's gone and far away.   80

I'll teach my boy the sweetest things;
I'll teach him how the owlet sings.
My little babe! thy lips are still,
And thou hast almost suck'd thy fill.
—Where art thou gone my own dear child?   85
What wicked looks are those I see?
Alas! alas! that look so wild,
It never, never came from me:
If thou art mad, my pretty lad,
Then I must be for ever sad.   90

Oh! smile on me, my little lamb!
For I thy own dear mother am.
My love for thee has well been tried:
I've sought thy father far and wide.
I know the poisons of the shade,   95
I know the earth-nuts fit for food;°
Then, pretty dear, be not afraid;
We'll find thy father in the wood.
Now laugh and be gay, to the woods away!
And there, my babe; we'll live for aye.'   100

THE IDIOT BOY

'Tis eight o'clock,—a clear March night,
The moon is up—the sky is blue,
The owlet in the moonlight air,
He shouts from nobody knows where;
He lengthens out his lonely shout,   5
Halloo! halloo! a long halloo!°

—Why bustle thus about your door,
What means this bustle, Betty Foy?
Why are you in this mighty fret?
And why on horseback have you set   10
Him whom you love, your idiot boy?

Beneath the moon that shines so bright,
Till she is tired, let Betty Foy
With girt and stirrup fiddle-faddle;
But wherefore set upon a saddle   15
Him whom she loves, her idiot boy?

There's scarce a soul that's out of bed;
Good Betty! put him down again;
His lips with joy they burr at you,
But, Betty! what has he to do   20
With stirrup, saddle, or with rein?

The world will say 'tis very idle,
Bethink you of the time of night;
There's not a mother, no not one,
But when she hears what you have done,   25
Oh! Betty she'll be in a fright.

But Betty's bent on her intent,
For her good neighbour, Susan Gale,
Old Susan, she who dwells alone,
Is sick, and makes a piteous moan,   30
As if her very life would fail.

There's not a house within a mile,
No hand to help them in distress:

Old Susan lies a bed in pain,
And sorely puzzled are the twain,   35
For what she ails they cannot guess.

And Betty's husband's at the wood,
Where by the week he doth abide,
A woodman in the distant vale;
There's none to help poor Susan Gale,   40
What must be done? what will betide?

And Betty from the lane has fetched
Her pony, that is mild and good,
Whether he be in joy or pain,
Feeding at will along the lane,   45
Or bringing faggots from the wood.

And he is all in travelling trim,
And by the moonlight, Betty Foy
Has up upon the saddle set,
The like was never heard of yet,   50
Him whom she loves, her idiot boy.

And he must post without delay
Across the bridge that's in the dale,
And by the church, and o'er the down,
To bring a doctor from the town,   55
Or she will die, old Susan Gale.

There is no need of boot or spur,
There is no need of whip or wand,
For Johnny has his holly-bough,
And with a hurly-burly now°   60
He shakes the green bough in his hand.

And Betty o'er and o'er has told
The boy who is her best delight,
Both what to follow, what to shun,
What do, and what to leave undone,   65
How turn to left, and how to right.

And Betty's most especial charge,
Was, 'Johnny! Johnny! mind that you

Come home again, nor stop at all,
Come home again, whate'er befal,   70
My Johnny do, I pray you do.'

To this did Johnny answer make,
Both with his head, and with his hand,
And proudly shook the bridle too,
And then! his words were not a few,   75
Which Betty well could understand.

And now that Johnny is just going,
Though Betty's in a mighty flurry,
She gently pats the pony's side,
On which her idiot boy must ride,   80
And seems no longer in a hurry.

But when the pony moved his legs,
Oh! then for the poor idiot boy!
For joy he cannot hold the bridle,
For joy his head and heels are idle,   85
He's idle all for very joy.

And while the pony moves his legs,
In Johnny's left-hand you may see,
The green bough's motionless and dead;
The moon that shines above his head   90
Is not more still and mute than he.

His heart it was so full of glee,
That till full fifty yards were gone,
He quite forgot his holly whip,
And all his skill in horsemanship,   95
Oh! happy, happy, happy John.

And Betty's standing at the door,
And Betty's face with joy o'erflows,
Proud of herself, and proud of him,
She sees him in his travelling trim;   100
How quietly her Johnny goes.

The silence of her idiot boy,
What hopes it sends to Betty's heart!

He's at the guide-post—he turns right,
She watches till he's out of sight,   105
And Betty will not then depart.

Burr, burr—now Johnny's lips they burr,
As loud as any mill, or near it,
Meek as a lamb the pony moves,
And Johnny makes the noise he loves,   110
And Betty listens, glad to hear it.

Away she hies to Susan Gale:
And Johnny's in a merry tune,
The owlets hoot, the owlets curr,
And Johnny's lips they burr, burr, burr,   115
And on he goes beneath the moon.°

His steed and he right well agree,
For of this pony there's a rumour,
That should he lose his eyes and ears,
And should he live a thousand years,   120
He never will be out of humour.

But then he is a horse that thinks!
And when he thinks his pace is slack;
Now, though he knows poor Johnny well,
Yet for his life he cannot tell   125
What he has got upon his back.°

So through the moonlight lanes they go,
And far into the moonlight dale,
And by the church, and o'er the down,
To bring a doctor from the town,   130
To comfort poor old Susan Gale.

And Betty, now at Susan's side,
Is in the middle of her story,
What comfort Johnny soon will bring,
With many a most diverting thing,   135
Of Johnny's wit and Johnny's glory.

And Betty's still at Susan's side:
By this time she's not quite so flurried;

Demure with porringer and plate°
She sits, as if in Susan's fate   140
Her life and soul were buried.

But Betty, poor good woman! she,
You plainly in her face may read it,
Could lend out of that moment's store
Five years of happiness or more,   145
To any that might need it.

But yet I guess that now and then
With Betty all was not so well,
And to the road she turns her ears,
And thence full many a sound she hears,   150
Which she to Susan will not tell.

Poor Susan moans, poor Susan groans,
'As sure as there's a moon in heaven,'
Cries Betty, 'he'll be back again;
They'll both be here, 'tis almost ten,   155
They'll both be here before eleven.'

Poor Susan moans, poor Susan groans,
The clock gives warning for eleven;
'Tis on the stroke—'If Johnny's near,'
Quoth Betty 'he will soon be here,   160
As sure as there's a moon in heaven.'

The clock is on the stroke of twelve,
And Johnny is not yet in sight,
The moon's in heaven, as Betty sees,
But Betty is not quite at ease;   165
And Susan has a dreadful night.

And Betty, half an hour ago,
On Johnny vile reflections cast;
'A little idle sauntering thing!'
With other names, an endless string,   170
But now that time is gone and past.

And Betty's drooping at the heart,
That happy time all past and gone,

'How can it be he is so late?
The doctor he has made him wait,   175
Susan! they'll both be here anon.'

And Susan's growing worse and worse,
And Betty's in a sad quandary;
And then there's nobody to say
If she must go or she must stay: 180
—She's in a sad quandary.

The clock is on the stroke of one;
But neither Doctor nor his guide
Appear along the moonlight road,
There's neither horse nor man abroad,   185
And Betty's still at Susan's side.

And Susan she begins to fear
Of sad mischances not a few,
That Johnny may perhaps be drown'd,
Or lost perhaps, and never found;   190
Which they must both for ever rue.

She prefaced half a hint of this
With, 'God forbid it should be true!'
At the first word that Susan said
Cried Betty, rising from the bed,   195
'Susan, I'd gladly stay with you.

I must be gone, I must away,
Consider, Johnny's but half-wise;
Susan, we must take care of him,
If he is hurt in life or limb'—   200
'Oh God forbid!' poor Susan cries.

'What can I do?' says Betty, going,
'What can I do to ease your pain?
Good Susan tell me, and I'll stay;
I fear you're in a dreadful way,   205
But I shall soon be back again.'

'Good Betty go, good Betty go,
There's nothing that can ease my pain.'

Then off she hies, but with a prayer
That God poor Susan's life would spare,   210
Till she comes back again.

So, through the moonlight lane she goes,
And far into the moonlight dale;
And how she ran, and how she walked,
And all that to herself she talked,   215
Would surely be a tedious tale.

In high and low, above, below,
In great and small, in round and square,
In tree and tower was Johnny seen,
In bush and brake, in black and green,°   220
'Twas Johnny, Johnny, every where.

She's past the bridge that's in the dale,
And now the thought torments her sore,
Johnny perhaps his horse forsook,
To hunt the moon that's in the brook,°   225
And never will be heard of more.

And now she's high upon the down,
Alone amid a prospect wide;
There's neither Johnny nor his horse,
Among the fern or in the gorse;   230
There's neither doctor nor his guide.

'Oh saints! what is become of him?
Perhaps he's climbed into an oak,
Where he will stay till he is dead;
Or sadly he has been misled,   235
And joined the wandering gypsey-folk.

Or him that wicked pony's carried
To the dark cave, the goblins' hall,
Or in the castle he's pursuing,
Among the ghosts, his own undoing;   240
Or playing with the waterfall.'

At poor old Susan then she railed,
While to the town she posts away;

'If Susan had not been so ill,
Alas! I should have had him still,   245
My Johnny, till my dying day.'

Poor Betty! in this sad distemper,°
The doctor's self would hardly spare,
Unworthy things she talked and wild,
Even he, of cattle the most mild,   250
The pony had his share.

And now she's got into the town,
And to the doctor's door she hies;
'Tis silence all on every side;
The town so long, the town so wide,   255
Is silent as the skies.

And now she's at the doctor's door,
She lifts the knocker, rap, rap, rap,
The doctor at the casement shews,
His glimmering eyes that peep and doze;   260
And one hand rubs his old night-cap.

'Oh Doctor! Doctor! where's my Johnny?'
'I'm here, what is't you want with me?'
'Oh Sir! you know I'm Betty Foy,
And I have lost my poor dear boy,   265
You know him—him you often see;

He's not so wise as some folks be,'
'The devil take his wisdom!' said
The Doctor, looking somewhat grim,
'What, woman! should I know of him?'   270
And, grumbling, he went back to bed.

'O woe is me! O woe is me!
Here will I die; here will I die;
I thought to find my Johnny here,
But he is neither far nor near,   275
Oh! what a wretched mother I!'

She stops, she stands, she looks about,
Which way to turn she cannot tell.

Poor Betty! it would ease her pain
If she had heart to knock again;   280
—The clock strikes three—a dismal knell!

Then up along the town she hies,
No wonder if her senses fail,
This piteous news so much it shock'd her,
She quite forgot to send the Doctor,   285
To comfort poor old Susan Gale.

And now she's high upon the down,
And she can see a mile of road,
'Oh cruel! I'm almost three-score;
Such night as this was ne'er before,   290
There's not a single soul abroad.'

She listens, but she cannot hear
The foot of horse, the voice of man;
The streams with softest sound are flowing,
The grass you almost hear it growing,   295
You hear it now if e'er you can.

The owlets through the long blue night
Are shouting to each other still:
Fond lovers, yet not quite hob nob,
They lengthen out the tremulous sob,   300
That echoes far from hill to hill.

Poor Betty now has lost all hope,
Her thoughts are bent on deadly sin;°
A green-grown pond she just has pass'd,
And from the brink she hurries fast,   305
Lest she should drown herself therein.

And now she sits her down and weeps;
Such tears she never shed before;
'Oh dear, dear pony! my sweet joy!
Oh carry back my idiot boy!   310
And we will ne'er o'erload thee more.'

A thought is come into her head;
'The pony he is mild and good,

And we have always used him well;
Perhaps he's gone along the dell,   315
And carried Johnny to the wood.'

Then up she springs as if on wings;
She thinks no more of deadly sin;°
If Betty fifty ponds should see,
The last of all her thoughts would be,   320
To drown herself therein.

Oh reader! now that I might tell
What Johnny and his horse are doing!
What they've been doing all this time,
Oh could I put it into rhyme,   325
A most delightful tale pursuing!

Perhaps, and no unlikely thought!
He with his pony now doth roam
The cliffs and peaks so high that are,
To lay his hands upon a star,   330
And in his pocket bring it home.

Perhaps he's turned himself about,
His face unto his horse's tail,
And still and mute, in wonder lost,
All like a silent horseman-ghost,°   335
He travels on along the vale.

And now, perhaps, he's hunting sheep,
A fierce and dreadful hunter he!
Yon valley, that's so trim and green,
In five months' time, should he be seen,   340
A desart wilderness will be.

Perhaps, with head and heels on fire,
And like the very soul of evil,
He's galloping away, away,
And so he'll gallop on for aye,   345
The bane of all that dread the devil.

I to the muses have been bound,
These fourteen years, by strong indentures;

Oh gentle muses! let me tell
But half of what to him befel,   350
For sure he met with strange adventures.

Oh gentle muses! is this kind?
Why will ye thus my suit repel?
Why of your further aid bereave me?
And can ye thus unfriended leave me?   355
Ye muses! whom I love so well.

Who's yon, that, near the waterfall,
Which thunders down with headlong force,
Beneath the moon, yet shining fair,
As careless as if nothing were,   360
Sits upright on a feeding horse?

Unto his horse, that's feeding free,
He seems, I think, the rein to give;
Of moon or stars he takes no heed;
Of such we in romances read,   365
—'Tis Johnny! Johnny! as I live.

And that's the very pony too.
Where is she, where is Betty Foy?
She hardly can sustain her fears;
The roaring water-fall she hears,   370
And cannot find her idiot boy.

Your pony's worth his weight in gold,
Then calm your terrors, Betty Foy!
She's coming from among the trees,
And now, all full in view, she sees   375
Him whom she loves, her idiot boy.

And Betty sees the pony too:
Why stand you thus Good Betty Foy?
It is no goblin, 'tis no ghost,
'Tis he whom you so long have lost,   380
He whom you love, your idiot boy.

She looks again—her arms are up—
She screams—she cannot move for joy;

She darts as with a torrent's force,
She almost has o'erturned the horse,   385
And fast she holds her idiot boy.

And Johnny burrs and laughs aloud,
Whether in cunning or in joy,
I cannot tell; but while he laughs,
Betty a drunken pleasure quaffs,   390
To hear again her idiot boy.

And now she's at the pony's tail,
And now she's at the pony's head,
On that side now, and now on this,
And almost stifled with her bliss,   395
A few sad tears does Betty shed.

She kisses o'er and o'er again,
Him whom she loves, her idiot boy,
She's happy here, she's happy there,
She is uneasy every where;   400
Her limbs are all alive with joy.

She pats the pony, where or when
She knows not, happy Betty Foy!
The little pony glad may be,
But he is milder far than she,   405
You hardly can perceive his joy.

'Oh! Johnny, never mind the Doctor;
You've done your best, and that is all.'
She took the reins, when this was said,
And gently turned the pony's head   410
From the loud water-fall.

By this the stars were almost gone,
The moon was setting on the hill,
So pale you scarcely looked at her:
The little birds began to stir,   415
Though yet their tongues were still.

The pony, Betty, and her boy,
Wind slowly through the woody dale:

And who is she, be-times abroad,
That hobbles up the steep rough road?   420
Who is it, but old Susan Gale?

Long Susan lay deep lost in thought,
And many dreadful fears beset her,
Both for her messenger and nurse;
And as her mind grew worse and worse,   425
Her body it grew better.

She turned, she toss'd herself in bed,
On all sides doubts and terrors met her;
Point after point did she discuss;
And while her mind was fighting thus,   430
Her body still grew better.

'Alas! what is become of them?
These fears can never be endured,
I'll to the wood.'—The word scarce said,
Did Susan rise up from her bed,   435
As if by magic cured.

Away she posts up hill and down,
And to the wood at length is come,
She spies her friends, she shouts a greeting;
Oh me! it is a merry meeting,   440
As ever was in Christendom.

The owls have hardly sung their last,
While our four travellers homeward wend;
The owls have hooted all night long,
And with the owls began my song,   445
And with the owls must end.

For while they all were travelling home,
Cried Betty, 'Tell us Johnny, do,
Where all this long night you have been,
What you have heard, what you have seen,   450
And Johnny, mind you tell us true.'

Now Johnny all night long had heard
The owls in tuneful concert strive;

No doubt too he the moon had seen;
For in the moonlight he had been   455
From eight o'clock till five.

And thus to Betty's question, he
Made answer, like a traveller bold,
(His very words I give to you,)
'The cocks did crow to-whoo, to-whoo,   460
And the sun did shine so cold.'
—Thus answered Johnny in his glory,°
And that was all his travel's story.

LINES

Written near Richmond, upon the Thames, at Evening

How rich the wave, in front, imprest
With evening-twilight's summer hues,
While, facing thus the crimson west,
The boat her silent path pursues!
And see how dark the backward stream!   5
A little moment past, so smiling!
And still, perhaps, with faithless gleam,
Some other loiterer beguiling.

Such views the youthful bard allure,
But, heedless of the following gloom,   10
He deems their colours shall endure
'Till peace go with him to the tomb.
—And let him nurse his fond deceit,
And what if he must die in sorrow!
Who would not cherish dreams so sweet,   15
Though grief and pain may come to-morrow?

Glide gently, thus for ever glide,
O Thames! that other bards may see,
As lovely visions by thy side
As now, fair river! come to me.   20
Oh glide, fair stream! for ever so;
Thy quiet soul on all bestowing,

'Till all our minds for ever flow,
As thy deep waters now are flowing.

Vain thought! yet be as now thou art,   25
That in thy waters may be seen
The image of a poet's heart,
How bright, how solemn, how serene!
Such heart did once the poet bless,
Who, pouring here a* *later* ditty,°   30
Could find no refuge from distress,
But in the milder grief of pity.

Remembrance! as we glide along,
For him suspend the dashing oar,°
And pray that never child of Song   35
May know his freezing sorrows more.
How calm! how still! the only sound,
The dripping of the oar suspended!
—The evening darkness gathers round
By virtue's holiest powers attended.   40

EXPOSTULATION AND REPLY

'Why William, on that old grey stone,
Thus for the length of half a day,
Why William, sit you thus alone,
And dream your time away?

Where are your books? that light bequeath'd   5
To beings else forlorn and blind!
Up! Up! and drink the spirit breath'd
From dead men to their kind.

You look round on your mother earth,
As if she for no purpose bore you;   10
As if you were her first-born birth,
And none had lived before you!'

---

* Collins's Ode on the death of Thomson, the last written, I believe, of the poems
which were published during his life-time. This Ode is also alluded to in the next stanza.

One morning thus, by Esthwaite lake,°
When life was sweet I knew not why,
To me my good friend Matthew spake,°   15
And thus I made reply.

'The eye it cannot chuse but see,
We cannot bid the ear be still;
Our bodies feel, where'er they be,
Against, or with our will.   20

Nor less I deem that there are powers,
Which of themselves our minds impress,
That we can feed this mind of ours,
In a wise passiveness.

Think you, mid all this mighty sum   25
Of things for ever speaking,
That nothing of itself will come,
But we must still be seeking?

—Then ask not wherefore, here, alone,
Conversing as I may,   30
I sit upon this old grey stone,
And dream my time away.'

THE TABLES TURNED;

AN EVENING SCENE, ON THE SAME SUBJECT

Up! up! my friend, and clear your looks,
Why all this toil and trouble?
Up! up! my friend, and quit your books,
Or surely you'll grow double.

The sun above the mountain's head,   5
A freshening lustre mellow,
Through all the long green fields has spread,
His first sweet evening yellow.

Books! 'tis a dull and endless strife,
Come, hear the woodland linnet,   10

How sweet his music; on my life
There's more of wisdom in it.

And hark! how blithe the throstle sings!
And he is no mean preacher;
Come forth into the light of things,   15
Let Nature be your teacher.

She has a world of ready wealth,
Our minds and hearts to bless—
Spontaneous wisdom breathed by health,
Truth breathed by chearfulness.   20

One impulse from a vernal wood
May teach you more of man;
Of moral evil and of good,
Than all the sages can.

Sweet is the lore which nature brings;°   25
Our meddling intellect
Mishapes the beauteous forms of things;
—We murder to dissect.°

Enough of science and of art;
Close up these barren leaves;°   30
Come forth, and bring with you a heart
That watches and receives.

OLD MAN TRAVELLING;
ANIMAL TRANQUILLITY AND DECAY, A SKETCH

            The little hedge-row birds,
That peck along the road, regard him not.
He travels on, and in his face, his step,
His gait, is one expression; every limb,
His look and bending figure, all bespeak   5
A man who does not move with pain, but moves
With thought—He is insensibly subdued
To settled quiet: he is one by whom

All effort seems forgotten, one to whom
Long patience has such mild composure given,   10
That patience now doth seem a thing, of which
He hath no need. He is by nature led
To peace so perfect, that the young behold
With envy, what the old man hardly feels.
—I asked him whither he was bound, and what   15
The object of his journey; he replied
'Sir! I am going many miles to take
A last leave of my son, a mariner,
Who from a sea-fight has been brought to Falmouth,°
And there is dying in an hospital.'   20

THE COMPLAINT OF A FORSAKEN
INDIAN WOMAN

*When a Northern Indian, from sickness, is unable to continue his
journey with his companions; he is left behind, covered over with
Deer-skins, and is supplied with water, food, and fuel if the situation
of the place will afford it. He is informed of the track which his com-
panions intend to pursue, and if he is unable to follow, or overtake
them, he perishes alone in the Desart; unless he should have the good
fortune to fall in with some other Tribes of Indians. It is unnecessary
to add that the females are equally, or still more, exposed to the same
fate. See that very interesting work,* Hearne's Journey *from*
Hudson's Bay *to the* Northern Ocean. *When the Northern Lights,
as the same writer informs us, vary their position in the air, they make
a rustling and a crackling noise. This circumstance is alluded to in the
first stanza of the following poem.*

> Before I see another day,
> Oh let my body die away!
> In sleep I heard the northern gleams;°
> The stars they were among my dreams;
> In sleep did I behold the skies,   5
> I saw the crackling flashes drive;
> And yet they are upon my eyes,
> And yet I am alive.
> Before I see another day,
> Oh let my body die away!   10

My fire is dead: it knew no pain;
Yet it is dead, and I remain.
All stiff with ice the ashes lie;
And they are dead, and I will die.
When I was well, I wished to live,   15
For clothes, for warmth, for food, and fire;
But they to me no joy can give,
No pleasure now, and no desire.
Then here contented will I lie;
Alone I cannot fear to die.   20

Alas! you might have dragged me on
Another day, a single one!
Too soon despair o'er me prevailed;
Too soon my heartless spirit failed;°
When you were gone my limbs were stronger,   25
And Oh how grievously I rue,
That, afterwards, a little longer,
My friends, I did not follow you!
For strong and without pain I lay,
My friends, when you were gone away.   30

My child! they gave thee to another,
A woman who was not thy mother.
When from my arms my babe they took,
On me how strangely did he look!
Through his whole body something ran,   35
A most strange something did I see;
—As if he strove to be a man,
That he might pull the sledge for me.
And then he stretched his arms, how wild!
Oh mercy! like a little child.   40

My little joy! my little pride!
In two days more I must have died.
Then do not weep and grieve for me;
I feel I must have died with thee.
Oh wind that o'er my head art flying,   45
The way my friends their course did bend,
I should not feel the pain of dying,
Could I with thee a message send.

Too soon, my friends, you went away;
For I had many things to say.   50

I'll follow you across the snow,
You travel heavily and slow:
In spite of all my weary pain,
I'll look upon your tents again.
My fire is dead, and snowy white   55
The water which beside it stood;
The wolf has come to me to-night,
And he has stolen away my food.
For ever left alone am I,
Then wherefore should I fear to die?   60

My journey will be shortly run,
I shall not see another sun,
I cannot lift my limbs to know
If they have any life or no.
My poor forsaken child! if I°   65
For once could have thee close to me,
With happy heart I then would die,
And my last thoughts would happy be.
I feel my body die away,
I shall not see another day.   70

THE CONVICT

The glory of evening was spread through the west;
  —On the slope of a mountain I stood,
While the joy that precedes the calm season of rest
  Rang loud through the meadow and wood.

'And must we then part from a dwelling so fair?'   5
  In the pain of my spirit I said,
And with a deep sadness I turned, to repair
  To the cell where the convict is laid.

The thick-ribbed walls that o'ershadow the gate
  Resound; and the dungeons unfold: 10
I pause; and at length, through the glimmering grate,
  That outcast of pity behold.

His black matted head on his shoulder is bent,
    And deep is the sigh of his breath,
And with stedfast dejection his eyes are intent   15
    On the fetters that link him to death.

'Tis sorrow enough on that visage to gaze,
    That body dismiss'd from his care;
Yet my fancy has pierced to his heart, and pourtrays
    More terrible images there.   20

His bones are consumed, and his life-blood is dried,
    With wishes the past to undo;
And his crime, through the pains that o'erwhelm him, descried,
    Still blackens and grows on his view.

When from the dark synod, or blood-reeking field,°   25
    To his chamber the monarch is led,
All soothers of sense their soft virtue shall yield,
    And quietness pillow his head.

But if grief, self-consumed, in oblivion would doze,
    And conscience her tortures appease,   30
'Mid tumult and uproar this man must repose;
    In the comfortless vault of disease.

When his fetters at night have so press'd on his limbs,
    That the weight can no longer be borne,
If, while a half-slumber his memory bedims,   35
    The wretch on his pallet should turn,

While the jail-mastiff howls at the dull clanking chain,°
    From the roots of his hair there shall start
A thousand sharp punctures of cold-sweating pain,
    And terror shall leap at his heart.   40

But now he half-raises his deep-sunken eye,
    And the motion unsettles a tear;
The silence of sorrow it seems to supply,
    And asks of me why I am here.

'Poor victim! no idle intruder has stood   45
    With o'erweening complacence our state to compare,°

But one, whose first wish is the wish to be good,
  Is come as a brother thy sorrows to share.

At thy name though compassion her nature resign,
  Though in virtue's proud mouth thy report be a stain,   50
My care, if the arm of the mighty were mine,
  Would plant thee where yet thou might'st blossom again.'

LINES

*Written a few miles above Tintern Abbey, on revisiting the Banks
of the Wye during a tour, July 13, 1798.*

Five years have passed; five summers, with the length°
Of five long winters! and again I hear
These waters, rolling from their mountain-springs
With a sweet inland murmur.*—Once again°
Do I behold these steep and lofty cliffs,°   5
Which on a wild secluded scene impress
Thoughts of more deep seclusion; and connect
The landscape with the quiet of the sky.
The day is come when I again repose
Here, under this dark sycamore, and view°   10
These plots of cottage-ground, these orchard-tufts,
Which, at this season, with their unripe fruits,
Among the woods and copses lose themselves,
Nor, with their green and simple hue, disturb
The wild green landscape. Once again I see   15
These hedge-rows, hardly hedge-rows, little lines
Of sportive wood run wild; these pastoral farms°
Green to the very door; and wreathes of smoke°
Sent up, in silence, from among the trees,°
With some uncertain notice, as might seem,   20
Of vagrant dwellers in the houseless woods,
Or of some hermit's cave, where by his fire
The hermit sits alone.°

                          Though absent long,
These forms of beauty have not been to me,
As is a landscape to a blind man's eye:°   25

* The river is not affected by the tides a few miles above Tintern.

But oft, in lonely rooms, and mid the din
Of towns and cities, I have owed to them,
In hours of weariness, sensations sweet,
Felt in the blood, and felt along the heart,
And passing even into my purer mind   30
With tranquil restoration:—feelings too
Of unremembered pleasure; such, perhaps,
As may have had no trivial influence
On that best portion of a good man's life;°
His little, nameless, unremembered acts   35
Of kindness and of love. Nor less, I trust,
To them I may have owed another gift,
Of aspect more sublime; that blessed mood,
In which the burthen of the mystery,
In which the heavy and the weary weight   40
Of all this unintelligible world
Is lighten'd:—that serene and blessed mood,
In which the affections gently lead us on,
Until, the breath of this corporeal frame,
And even the motion of our human blood   45
Almost suspended, we are laid asleep
In body, and become a living soul:°
While with an eye made quiet by the power
Of harmony, and the deep power of joy,
We see into the life of things.°   50

                              If this
Be but a vain belief, yet, oh! how oft,
In darkness, and amid the many shapes
Of joyless day-light; when the fretful stir
Unprofitable, and the fever of the world,
Have hung upon the beatings of my heart,   55
How oft, in spirit, have I turned to thee°
O sylvan Wye! Thou wanderer through the woods,°
How often has my spirit turned to thee!°

And now, with gleams of half-extinguish'd thought,
With many recognitions dim and faint,   60
And somewhat of a sad perplexity,
The picture of the mind revives again:
While here I stand, not only with the sense
Of present pleasure, but with pleasing thoughts

That in this moment there is life and food   65
For future years. And so I dare to hope
Though changed, no doubt, from what I was, when first
I came among these hills; when like a roe°
I bounded o'er the mountains, by the sides
Of the deep rivers, and the lonely streams,   70
Wherever nature led; more like a man
Flying from something that he dreads, than one
Who sought the thing he loved. For nature then
(The coarser pleasures of my boyish days,°
And their glad animal movements all gone by,)   75
To me was all in all.—I cannot paint°
What then I was. The sounding cataract
Haunted me like a passion: the tall rock,
The mountain, and the deep and gloomy wood,
Their colours and their forms, were then to me   80
An appetite: a feeling and a love,
That had no need of a remoter charm,
By thought supplied, or any interest
Unborrowed from the eye.—That time is past,
And all its aching joys are now no more,   85
And all its dizzy raptures. Not for this
Faint I, nor mourn nor murmur: other gifts
Have followed, for such loss, I would believe,
Abundant recompence. For I have learned°
To look on nature, not as in the hour   90
Of thoughtless youth, but hearing oftentimes
The still, sad music of humanity,
Not harsh nor grating, though of ample power
To chasten and subdue. And I have felt
A presence that disturbs me with the joy   95
Of elevated thoughts; a sense sublime
Of something far more deeply interfused,
Whose dwelling is the light of setting suns,
And the round ocean, and the living air,
And the blue sky, and in the mind of man,   100
A motion and a spirit, that impels
All thinking things, all objects of all thought,
And rolls through all things. Therefore am I still
A lover of the meadows and the woods,
And mountains; and of all that we behold   105

From this green earth; of all the mighty world
Of eye and ear, both what they half-create,*
And what perceive; well pleased to recognize°
In nature and the language of the sense,
The anchor of my purest thoughts, the nurse,   110
The guide, the guardian of my heart, and soul
Of all my moral being.

                              Nor, perchance,
If I were not thus taught, should I the more
Suffer my genial spirits to decay:°
For thou art with me, here, upon the banks°   115
Of this fair river; thou, my dearest Friend,
My dear, dear Friend, and in thy voice I catch
The language of my former heart, and read
My former pleasures in the shooting lights
Of thy wild eyes. Oh! yet a little while   120
May I behold in thee what I was once,
My dear, dear Sister! And this prayer I make,
Knowing that Nature never did betray°
The heart that loved her; 'tis her privilege,
Through all the years of this our life, to lead   125
From joy to joy: for she can so inform
The mind that is within us, so impress
With quietness and beauty, and so feed
With lofty thoughts, that neither evil tongues,°
Rash judgments, nor the sneers of selfish men,   130
Nor greetings where no kindness is, nor all
The dreary intercourse of daily life,
Shall e'er prevail against us, or disturb
Our chearful faith that all which we behold
Is full of blessings. Therefore let the moon°   135
Shine on thee in thy solitary walk;
And let the misty mountain winds be free
To blow against thee: and in after years,
When these wild ecstasies shall be matured
Into a sober pleasure, when thy mind   140
Shall be a mansion for all lovely forms,

* This line has a close resemblance to an admirable line of Young, the exact expression of which I cannot recollect.

Thy memory be as a dwelling-place
For all sweet sounds and harmonies; Oh! then,
If solitude, or fear, or pain, or grief,
Should be thy portion, with what healing thoughts   145
Of tender joy wilt thou remember me,
And these my exhortations! Nor, perchance,
If I should be, where I no more can hear
Thy voice, nor catch from thy wild eyes these gleams
Of past existence, wilt thou then forget   150
That on the banks of this delightful stream
We stood together; and that I, so long
A worshipper of Nature, hither came,
Unwearied in that service: rather say
With warmer love, oh! with far deeper zeal   155
Of holier love. Nor wilt thou then forget,
That after many wanderings, many years
Of absence, these steep woods and lofty cliffs,
And this green pastoral landscape, were to me
More dear, both for themselves, and for thy sake.   160

LYRICAL BALLADS,

WITH

PASTORAL

AND OTHER

POEMS

IN TWO VOLUMES

BY W. WORDSWORTH.

Quam nihil ad genium, Papiniane, tuum!

Pectus enim id est quod disertos facit, & vis mentis;
ideoque imperitis quoquo, si modo sint aliquo
affectu concitati, verba non desunt.

VOL. I

1802

PREFACE

The first Volume of these Poems has already been submitted to general perusal. It was published, as an experiment, which, I hoped, might be of some use to ascertain, how far, by fitting to metrical arrangement a selection of the real language of men in a state of vivid sensation, that sort of pleasure and that quantity of pleasure may be imparted, which a Poet may rationally endeavour to impart.

I had formed no very inaccurate estimate of the probable effect of those Poems: I flattered myself that they who should be pleased with them would read them with more than common pleasure: and, on the other hand, I was well aware, that by those who should dislike them they would be read with more than common dislike. The result has differed from my expectation in this only, that I have pleased a greater number, than I ventured to hope I should please.

For the sake of variety, and from a consciousness of my own weakness, I was induced to request the assistance of a Friend, who furnished me with the Poems of the ANCIENT MARINER, the FOSTER-MOTHER'S TALE, the NIGHTINGALE, and the Poem entitled LOVE. I should not, however, have requested this assistance, had I not believed that the Poems of my Friend would in a great measure have the same tendency as my own, and that, though there would be found a difference, there would be found no discordance in the colours of our style; as our opinions on the subject of poetry do almost entirely coincide.°

Several of my Friends are anxious for the success of these Poems from a belief, that, if the views with which they were composed were indeed realized, a class of Poetry would be produced, well adapted to interest mankind permanently, and not unimportant in the multiplicity, and in the quality of its moral relations: and on this account they have advised me to prefix a systematic defence of the theory, upon which the poems were written. But I was unwilling to undertake the task, because I knew that on this occasion the Reader would look coldly upon my arguments, since I might be suspected of having been principally influenced by the selfish and foolish hope of *reasoning* him into an approbation of these particular Poems: and I was still more unwilling to undertake the task, because, adequately to display my opinions, and fully to enforce my arguments, would require a space wholly disproportionate to the nature of a preface. For to treat the subject with the clearness and coherence, of which I believe it susceptible, it would be

necessary to give a full account of the present state of the public taste
in this country, and to determine how far this taste is healthy or
depraved; which, again, could not be determined, without pointing
out, in what manner language and the human mind act and re-act on
each other, and without retracing the revolutions, not of literature
alone, but likewise of society itself. I have therefore altogether declined
to enter regularly upon this defence; yet I am sensible, that there would
be some impropriety in abruptly obtruding upon the Public, without
a few words of introduction, Poems so materially different from those,
upon which general approbation is at present bestowed.

It is supposed, that by the act of writing in verse an Author makes
a formal engagement that he will gratify certain known habits of asso-
ciation; that he not only thus apprizes the Reader that certain classes of
ideas and expressions will be found in his book, but that others will
be carefully excluded. This exponent or symbol held forth by metri-
cal language must in different æras of literature have excited very dif-
ferent expectations: for example, in the age of Catullus, Terence, and
Lucretius and that of Statius or Claudian; and in our own country, in
the age of Shakespeare and Beaumont and Fletcher, and that of Donne
and Cowley, or Dryden, or Pope.° I will not take upon me to determine
the exact import of the promise which by the act of writing in verse an
Author, in the present day, makes to his Reader; but I am certain, it will
appear to many persons that I have not fulfilled the terms of an engage-
ment thus voluntarily contracted. They who have been accustomed
to the gaudiness and inane phraseology of many modern writers, if
they persist in reading this book to its conclusion, will, no doubt, fre-
quently have to struggle with feelings of strangeness and aukwardness:
they will look round for poetry, and will be induced to inquire by what
species of courtesy these attempts can be permitted to assume that
title.° I hope therefore the Reader will not censure me, if I attempt to
state what I have proposed to myself to perform; and also, (as far as the
limits of a preface will permit) to explain some of the chief reasons
which have determined me in the choice of my purpose: that at least he
may be spared any unpleasant feeling of disappointment, and that
I myself may be protected from the most dishonorable accusation
which can be brought against an Author, namely, that of an indolence
which prevents him from endeavouring to ascertain what is his duty,
or, when his duty is ascertained, prevents him from performing it.

The principal object, then, which I proposed to myself in these
Poems was to chuse incidents and situations from common life, and
to relate or describe them, throughout, as far as was possible, in a

selection of language really used by men; and, at the same time, to throw over them a certain colouring of imagination, whereby ordinary things should be presented to the mind in an unusual way; and, further, and above all, to make these incidents and situations interesting° by tracing in them, truly though not ostentatiously, the primary laws of our nature: chiefly, as far as regards the manner in which we associate ideas in a state of excitement. Low and rustic life was generally chosen, because in that condition,° the essential passions of the heart find a better soil in which they can attain their maturity, are less under restraint, and speak a plainer and more emphatic language; because in that condition of life our elementary feelings co-exist in a state of greater simplicity, and, consequently, may be more accurately contemplated, and more forcibly communicated; because the manners of rural life germinate from those elementary feelings; and, from the necessary character of rural occupations, are more easily comprehended; and are more durable; and lastly, because in that condition the passions of men are incorporated with the beautiful and permanent forms of nature. The language, too, of these men is adopted (purified indeed from what appear to be its real defects, from all lasting and rational causes of dislike or disgust) because such men hourly communicate with the best objects from which the best part of language is originally derived; and because, from their rank in society and the sameness and narrow circle of their intercourse, being less under the influence of social vanity they convey their feelings and notions in simple and unelaborated expressions. Accordingly, such a language, arising out of repeated experience and regular feelings, is a more permanent, and a far more philosophical language, than that which is frequently substituted for it by Poets, who think that they are conferring honour upon themselves and their art, in proportion as they separate themselves from the sympathies of men, and indulge in arbitrary and capricious habits of expression, in order to furnish food for fickle tastes, and fickle appetites, of their own creation.*

I cannot, however, be insensible of the present outcry against the triviality and meanness both of thought and language, which some of my contemporaries have occasionally introduced into their metrical compositions; and I acknowledge, that this defect, where it exists, is more dishonorable to the Writer's own character than false refinement or arbitrary innovation, though I should contend at the same time that it is far less pernicious in the sum of its consequences. From such

---

* It is worth while here to observe that the affecting parts of Chaucer are almost always expressed in language pure and universally intelligible even to this day.

verses the Poems in these volumes will be found distinguished at least by one mark of difference, that each of them has a worthy *purpose*. Not that I mean to say, that I always began to write with a distinct purpose formally conceived; but I believe that my habits of meditation have so formed my feelings, as that my descriptions of such objects as strongly excite those feelings, will be found to carry along with them a *purpose*. If in this opinion I am mistaken, I can have little right to the name of a Poet. For all good poetry is the spontaneous overflow of powerful feelings: but though this be true, Poems to which any value can be attached, were never produced on any variety of subjects but by a man, who being possessed of more than usual organic sensibility, had also thought long and deeply. For our continued influxes of feeling are modified and directed by our thoughts, which are indeed the representatives of all our past feelings; and, as by contemplating the relation of these general representatives to each other we discover what is really important to men, so, by the repetition and continuance of this act, our feelings will be connected with important subjects, till at length, if we be originally possessed of much sensibility, such habits of mind will be produced, that, by obeying blindly and mechanically the impulses of those habits, we shall describe objects, and utter sentiments, of such a nature and in such connection with each other, that the understanding of the being to whom we address ourselves, if he be in a healthful state of association, must necessarily be in some degree enlightened, and his affections ameliorated.

I have said that each of these poems has a purpose. I have also informed my Reader what this purpose will be found principally to be: namely to illustrate the manner in which our feelings and ideas are associated in a state of excitement. But, speaking in language somewhat more appropriate, it is to follow the fluxes and refluxes of the mind when agitated by the great and simple affections of our nature. This object I have endeavoured in these short essays to attain by various means; by tracing the maternal passion through many of its more subtle windings, as in the poems of the IDIOT BOY and the MAD MOTHER; by accompanying the last struggles of a human being, at the approach of death, cleaving in solitude to life and society, as in the Poem of the FORSAKEN INDIAN; by shewing, as in the Stanzas entitled WE ARE SEVEN, the perplexity and obscurity which in childhood attend our notion of death, or rather our utter inability to admit that notion; or by displaying the strength of fraternal, or to speak more philosophically, of moral attachment when early associated with the great and beautiful objects of nature, as in THE BROTHERS; or, as in the Incident of

SIMON LEE, by placing my Reader in the way of receiving from ordinary moral sensations another and more salutary impression than we are accustomed to receive from them. It has also been part of my general purpose to attempt to sketch characters under the influence of less impassioned feelings, as in the TWO APRIL MORNINGS, THE FOUNTAIN, THE OLD MAN TRAVELLING, THE TWO THIEVES, &c. characters of which the elements are simple, belonging rather to nature than to manners, such as exist now, and will probably always exist, and which from their constitution may be distinctly and profitably contemplated. I will not abuse the indulgence of my Reader by dwelling longer upon this subject; but it is proper that I should mention one other circumstance which distinguishes these Poems from the popular Poetry of the day; it is this, that the feeling therein developed gives importance to the action and situation, and not the action and situation to the feeling. My meaning will be rendered perfectly intelligible by referring my Reader to the Poems entitled POOR SUSAN and the CHILDLESS FATHER, particularly to the last Stanza of the latter Poem.

I will not suffer a sense of false modesty to prevent me from asserting, that I point my Reader's attention to this mark of distinction, far less for the sake of these particular Poems than from the general importance of the subject. The subject is indeed important! For the human mind is capable of being excited without the application of gross and violent stimulants; and he must have a very faint perception of its beauty and dignity who does not know this, and who does not further know, that one being is elevated above another, in proportion as he possesses this capability. It has therefore appeared to me, that to endeavour to produce or enlarge this capability is one of the best services in which, at any period, a Writer can be engaged; but this service, excellent at all times, is especially so at the present day. For a multitude of causes, unknown to former times, are now acting with a combined force to blunt the discriminating powers of the mind, and unfitting it for all voluntary exertion to reduce it to a state of almost savage torpor. The most effective of these causes are the great national events which are daily taking place, and the encreasing accumulation of men in cities, where the uniformity of their occupations produces a craving for extraordinary incident, which the rapid communication of intelligence hourly gratifies.° To this tendency of life and manners the literature and theatrical exhibitions of the country have conformed themselves. The invaluable works of our elder writers, I had almost said the works of Shakespear and Milton, are driven into neglect by frantic novels,

sickly and stupid German Tragedies, and deluges of idle and extrava-
gant stories in verse.°—When I think upon this degrading thirst after
outrageous stimulation, I am almost ashamed to have spoken of the
feeble effort with which I have endeavoured to counteract it; and,
reflecting upon the magnitude of the general evil, I should be oppressed
with no dishonorable melancholy, had I not a deep impression of
certain inherent and indestructible qualities of the human mind, and
likewise of certain powers in the great and permanent objects that act
upon it which are equally inherent and indestructible; and did I not
further add to this impression a belief, that the time is approaching
when the evil will be systematically opposed, by men of greater powers,
and with far more distinguished success.

Having dwelt thus long on the subjects and aim of these Poems,
I shall request the Reader's permission to apprize him of a few circum-
stances relating to their *style*, in order, among other reasons, that I may
not be censured for not having performed what I never attempted.°
The Reader will find that personifications of abstract ideas rarely occur
in these volumes; and, I hope, are utterly rejected as an ordinary device
to elevate the style, and raise it above prose. I have proposed to myself
to imitate, and, as far as is possible, to adopt the very language of men;
and assuredly such personifications do not make any natural or regular
part of that language. They are, indeed, a figure of speech occasionally
prompted by passion, and I have made use of them as such; but I have
endeavoured utterly to reject them as a mechanical device of style, or as
a family language which Writers in metre seem to lay claim to by pre-
scription. I have wished to keep my Reader in the company of flesh and
blood, persuaded that by so doing I shall interest him. I am, however,
well aware that others who pursue a different track may interest him
likewise; I do not interfere with their claim, I only wish to prefer a dif-
ferent claim of my own. There will also be found in these volumes little
of what is usually called poetic diction; I have taken as much pains to
avoid it as others ordinarily take to produce it; this I have done for the
reason already alleged, to bring my language near to the language of
men, and further, because the pleasure which I have proposed to
myself to impart is of a kind very different from that which is supposed
by many persons to be the proper object of poetry. I do not know how
without being culpably particular I can give my Reader a more exact
notion of the style in which I wished these poems to be written than by
informing him that I have at all times endeavoured to look steadily at
my subject, consequently, I hope that there is in these Poems little
falsehood of description, and that my ideas are expressed in language

fitted to their respective importance. Something I must have gained by this practice, as it is friendly to one property of all good poetry, namely, good sense; but it has necessarily cut me off from a large portion of phrases and figures of speech which from father to son have long been regarded as the common inheritance of Poets. I have also thought it expedient to restrict myself still further, having abstained from the use of many expressions, in themselves proper and beautiful, but which have been foolishly repeated by bad Poets, till such feelings of disgust are connected with them as it is scarcely possible by any art of association to overpower.

If in a Poem there should be found a series of lines, or even a single line, in which the language, though naturally arranged and according to the strict laws of metre, does not differ from that of prose, there is a numerous class of critics, who, when they stumble upon these prosaisms as they call them, imagine that they have made a notable discovery, and exult over the Poet as over a man ignorant of his own profession. Now these men would establish a canon of criticism which the Reader will conclude he must utterly reject, if he wishes to be pleased with these volumes. And it would be a most easy task to prove to him, that not only the language of a large portion of every good poem, even of the most elevated character, must necessarily, except with reference to the metre, in no respect differ from that of good prose, but likewise that some of the most interesting parts of the best poems will be found to be strictly the language of prose, when prose is well written. The truth of this assertion might be demonstrated by innumerable passages from almost all the poetical writings, even of Milton himself. I have not space for much quotation; but, to illustrate the subject in a general manner, I will here adduce a short composition of Gray, who was at the head of those who by their reasonings have attempted to widen the space of separation betwixt Prose and Metrical composition, and was more than any other man curiously elaborate in the structure of his own poetic diction.

> In vain to me the smiling mornings shine,
> And reddening Phœbus lifts his golden fire:
> The birds in vain their amorous descant join,
> Or chearful fields resume their green attire:
> These ears alas! for other notes repine;
> *A different object do these eyes require;*
> *My lonely anguish melts no heart but mine;*
> *And in my breast the imperfect joys expire;*

> Yet Morning smiles the busy race to cheer,
> And new-born pleasure brings to happier men;
> The fields to all their wonted tribute bear;
> To warm their little loves the birds complain.
> *I fruitless mourn to him that cannot hear*
> *And weep the more because I weep in vain.*°

It will easily be perceived that the only part of this Sonnet which is of any value is the lines printed in Italics: it is equally obvious, that, except in the rhyme, and in the use of the single word 'fruitless' for fruitlessly, which is so far a defect, the language of these lines does in no respect differ from that of prose.

By the foregoing quotation I have shewn that the language of Prose may yet be well adapted to Poetry; and I have previously asserted that a large portion of the language of every good poem can in no respect differ from that of good Prose. I will go further. I do not doubt that it may be safely affirmed, that there neither is, nor can be, any essential difference between the language of prose and metrical composition. We are fond of tracing the resemblance between Poetry and Painting, and, accordingly, we call them Sisters:° but where shall we find bonds of connection sufficiently strict to typify the affinity betwixt metrical and prose composition? They both speak by and to the same organs; the bodies in which both of them are clothed may be said to be of the same substance, their affections are kindred and almost identical, not necessarily differing even in degree; Poetry* sheds no tears 'such as Angels weep,' but natural and human tears; she can boast of no celestial Ichor that distinguishes her vital juices from those of prose; the same human blood circulates through the veins of them both.°

If it be affirmed that rhyme and metrical arrangement of themselves constitute a distinction which overturns what I have been saying on the strict affinity of metrical language with that of prose, and paves the way for other artificial distinctions which the mind voluntarily admits, I answer that the language of such Poetry as I am recommending is, as far as is possible, a selection of the language really spoken by men; that this selection, wherever it is made with true taste and feeling, will of

---

* I here use the word 'Poetry' (though against my own judgment) as opposed to the word Prose, and synonomous with metrical composition. But much confusion has been introduced into criticism by this contradistinction of Poetry and Prose, instead of the more philosophical one of Poetry and Matter of fact, or Science. The only strict antithesis to Prose is Metre; nor is this in truth a *strict* antithesis; because lines and passages of metre so naturally occur in writing Prose, that it would be scarcely possible to avoid them, even were it desirable.

itself form a distinction far greater than would at first be imagined, and will entirely separate the composition from the vulgarity and meanness of ordinary life; and, if metre be superadded thereto, I believe that a dissimilitude will be produced altogether sufficient for the gratification of a rational mind. What other distinction would we have? Whence is it to come? And where is it to exist? Not, surely, where the Poet speaks through the mouths of his characters: it cannot be necessary here, either for elevation of style, or any of its supposed ornaments: for, if the Poet's subject be judiciously chosen, it will naturally, and upon fit occasion, lead him to passions the language of which, if selected truly and judiciously, must necessarily be dignified and variegated, and alive with metaphors and figures. I forbear to speak of an incongruity which would shock the intelligent Reader, should the Poet interweave any foreign splendour of his own with that which the passion naturally suggests: it is sufficient to say that such addition is unnecessary. And, surely, it is more probable that those passages, which with propriety abound with metaphors and figures, will have their due effect, if, upon other occasions where the passions are of a milder character, the style also be subdued and temperate.

But, as the pleasure which I hope to give by the Poems I now present to the Reader must depend entirely on just notions upon this subject, and, as it is in itself of the highest importance to our taste and moral feelings, I cannot content myself with these detached remarks. And if, in what I am about to say, it shall appear to some that my labour is unnecessary, and that I am like a man fighting a battle without enemies, I would remind such persons, that, whatever may be the language outwardly holden by men, a practical faith in the opinions which I am wishing to establish is almost unknown. If my conclusions are admitted, and carried as far as they must be carried if admitted at all, our judgments concerning the works of the greatest Poets both ancient and modern will be far different from what they are at present, both when we praise, and when we censure: and our moral feelings influencing, and influenced by these judgments will, I believe, be corrected and purified.

Taking up the subject, then, upon general grounds, I ask what is meant by the word Poet? What is a Poet? To whom does he address himself? And what language is to be expected from him? He is a man speaking to men: a man, it is true, endued with more lively sensibility, more enthusiasm and tenderness, who has a greater knowledge of human nature, and a more comprehensive soul, than are supposed to be common among mankind; a man pleased with his own passions and volitions, and who rejoices more than other men in the spirit of life that is in him; delighting to contemplate similar volitions and passions as manifested in the goings-on of the Universe, and habitually impelled to create them where he does not find them. To these qualities he has added a disposition to be affected more than other men by absent things as if they were present; an ability of conjuring up in himself passions, which are indeed far from being the same as those produced by real events, yet (especially in those parts of the general sympathy which are pleasing and delightful) do more nearly resemble the passions produced by real events, than any thing which, from the motions of their own minds merely, other men are accustomed to feel in themselves; whence, and from practice, he has acquired a greater readiness and power in expressing what he thinks and feels, and especially those thoughts and feelings which, by his own choice, or from the structure of his own mind, arise in him without immediate external excitement.

But, whatever portion of this faculty we may suppose even the greatest Poet to possess, there cannot be a doubt but that the language which it will suggest to him, must, in liveliness and truth, fall far short of that which is uttered by men in real life, under the actual pressure of those passions, certain shadows of which the Poet thus produces, or feels to be produced, in himself. However exalted a notion we would wish to cherish of the character of a Poet, it is obvious, that, while he describes and imitates passions, his situation is altogether slavish and mechanical, compared with the freedom and power of real and substantial action and suffering. So that it will be the wish of the Poet to bring his feelings near to those of the persons whose feelings he describes, nay, for short spaces of time perhaps, to let himself slip into an entire delusion, and even confound and identify his own feelings with theirs; modifying only the language which is thus suggested to him, by a consideration that he describes for a particular purpose, that of giving pleasure. Here, then, he will apply the principle on which I have so much insisted, namely, that of selection; on this he will depend for removing what would otherwise be painful or disgusting in the passion; he will feel that there is no necessity to trick out or to elevate nature: and, the more industriously he applies this principle, the deeper will be his faith that no words, which his fancy or imagination can suggest, will be to be compared with those which are the emanations of reality and truth.

But it may be said by those who do not object to the general spirit of these remarks, that, as it is impossible for the Poet to produce upon all occasions language as exquisitely fitted for the passion as that which the real passion itself suggests, it is proper that he should consider himself as in the situation of a translator, who deems himself justified when he substitutes excellences of another kind for those which are unattainable by him; and endeavours occasionally to surpass his original, in order to make some amends for the general inferiority to which he feels that he must submit. But this would be to encourage idleness and unmanly despair. Further, it is the language of men who speak of what they do not understand; who talk of Poetry as of a matter of amusement and idle pleasure; who will converse with us as gravely about a *taste* for Poetry, as they express it, as if it were a thing as indifferent as a taste for Rope-dancing, or Frontiniac or Sherry.° Aristotle, I have been told, hath said, that Poetry is the most philosophic of all writing:° it is so: its object is truth, not individual and local, but general, and operative; not standing upon external testimony, but carried alive into the heart by passion; truth which is its own testimony, which gives strength and divinity to the tribunal to which it appeals, and receives them from the same tribunal. Poetry is the image of man and nature. The obstacles which stand in the way of the fidelity of the Biographer and Historian, and of their consequent utility, are incalculably greater than those which are to be encountered by the Poet who has an adequate notion of the dignity of his art. The Poet writes under one restriction only, namely, that of the necessity of giving immediate pleasure to a human Being possessed of that information which may be expected from him, not as a lawyer, a physician, a mariner, an astronomer or a natural philosopher, but as a Man. Except this one restriction, there is no object standing between the Poet and the image of things; between this, and the Biographer and Historian there are a thousand.

Nor let this necessity of producing immediate pleasure be considered as a degradation of the Poet's art. It is far otherwise. It is an acknowledgment of the beauty of the universe, an acknowledgment the more sincere because it is not formal, but indirect; it is a task light and easy to him who looks at the world in the spirit of love: further, it is a homage paid to the native and naked dignity of man, to the grand elementary principle of pleasure, by which he knows, and feels, and lives, and moves. We have no sympathy but what is propagated by pleasure: I would not be misunderstood; but wherever we sympathize with pain it will be found that the sympathy is produced and carried on by subtle combinations with pleasure. We have no knowledge, that is, no general principles drawn from the contemplation of particular facts, but what has been built up by pleasure, and exists in us by pleasure alone. The Man of Science, the Chemist and Mathematician, whatever difficulties and disgusts they may have had to struggle with, know and feel this. However painful may be the objects with which the Anatomist's knowledge is connected, he feels that his knowledge is pleasure; and where he has no pleasure he has no knowledge. What then does the Poet? He considers man and the objects that surround him as acting and re-acting upon each other, so as to produce an infinite complexity of pain and pleasure; he considers man in his own nature and in his ordinary life as contemplating this with a certain quantity of immediate knowledge, with certain convictions, intuitions, and deductions which by habit become of the nature of intuitions; he considers him as looking upon this complex scene of ideas and sensations, and finding every where objects that immediately excite in him sympathies which, from the necessities of his nature, are accompanied by an overbalance of enjoyment.

To this knowledge which all men carry about with them, and to these sympathies in which without any other discipline than that of our daily life we are fitted to take delight, the Poet principally directs his attention. He considers man and nature as essentially adapted to each other, and the mind of man as naturally the mirror of the fairest and most interesting qualities of nature. And thus the Poet, prompted by this feeling of pleasure which accompanies him through the whole course of his studies, converses with general nature with affections akin to those, which, through labour and length of time, the Man of Science has raised up in himself, by conversing with those particular parts of nature which are the objects of his studies. The knowledge both of the Poet and the Man of Science is pleasure; but the knowledge of the one cleaves to us as a necessary part of our existence, our natural and unalienable inheritance; the other is a personal and individual acquisition, slow to come to us, and by no habitual and direct sympathy connecting us with our fellow-beings. The Man of Science seeks truth as a remote and unknown benefactor; he cherishes and loves it in his solitude: the Poet, singing a song in which all human beings join with him, rejoices in the presence of truth as our visible friend and hourly companion. Poetry is the breath and finer spirit of all knowledge; it is the impassioned expression which is in the countenance of all Science. Emphatically may it be said of the Poet, as Shakespeare hath said of man, 'that he looks before and after.'° He is the rock of defence of human nature; an upholder and preserver, carrying every where with him relationship and love. In spite of difference of soil and climate, of language and manners, of laws and customs, in spite of things silently gone out of mind and things violently destroyed, the Poet binds together by passion and knowledge the vast empire of human society, as it is spread over the whole earth, and over all time. The objects of the Poet's thoughts are every where; though the eyes and senses of man are, it is true, his favorite guides, yet he will follow wheresoever he can find an atmosphere of sensation in which to move his wings. Poetry is the first and last of all knowledge—it is as immortal as the heart of man. If the labours of men of Science should ever create any material revolution, direct or indirect, in our condition, and in the impressions which we habitually receive, the Poet will sleep then no more than at present, but he will be ready to follow the steps of the man of Science, not only in those general indirect effects, but he will be at his side, carrying sensation into the midst of the objects of the Science itself. The remotest discoveries of the Chemist, the Botanist, or Mineralogist, will be as proper objects of the Poet's art as any upon which it can be employed, if the time should ever come when these things shall be familiar to us, and the relations under which they are contemplated by the followers of these respective Sciences shall be manifestly and palpably material to us as enjoying and suffering beings. If the time should ever come when what is now called Science, thus familiarized to men, shall be ready to put on, as it were, a form of flesh and blood, the Poet will lend his divine spirit to aid the transfiguration, and will welcome the Being thus produced, as a dear and genuine inmate of the household of man.—It is not, then, to be supposed that any one, who holds that sublime notion of Poetry which I have attempted to convey, will break in upon the sanctity and truth of his pictures by transitory and accidental ornaments, and endeavour to excite admiration of himself by arts, the necessity of which must manifestly depend upon the assumed meanness of his subject.

What I have thus far said applies to Poetry in general; but especially to those parts of composition where the Poet speaks through the mouths of his characters; and upon this point it appears to have such weight that I will conclude, there are few persons, of good sense, who would not allow that the dramatic parts of composition are defective, in proportion as they deviate from the real language of nature, and are coloured by a diction of the Poet's own, either peculiar to him as an individual Poet, or belonging simply to Poets in general, to a body of men who, from the circumstance of their compositions being in metre, it is expected will employ a particular language.

It is not, then, in the dramatic parts of composition that we look for this distinction of language; but still it may be proper and necessary where the Poet speaks to us in his own person and character. To this

I answer by referring my Reader to the description which I have before given of a Poet. Among the qualities which I have enumerated as principally conducing to form a Poet, is implied nothing differing in kind from other men, but only in degree. The sum of what I have there said is, that the Poet is chiefly distinguished from other men by a greater promptness to think and feel without immediate external excitement, and a greater power in expressing such thoughts and feelings as are produced in him in that manner. But these passions and thoughts and feelings are the general passions and thoughts and feelings of men. And with what are they connected? Undoubtedly with our moral sentiments and animal sensations, and with the causes which excite these; with the operations of the elements and the appearances of the visible universe; with storm and sun-shine, with the revolutions of the seasons, with cold and heat, with loss of friends and kindred, with injuries and resentments, gratitude and hope, with fear and sorrow. These, and the like, are the sensations and objects which the Poet describes, as they are the sensations of other men, and the objects which interest them. The Poet thinks and feels in the spirit of the passions of men. How, then, can his language differ in any material degree from that of all other men who feel vividly and see clearly? It might be *proved* that it is impossible. But supposing that this were not the case, the Poet might then be allowed to use a peculiar language, when expressing his feelings for his own gratification, or that of men like himself. But Poets do not write for Poets alone, but for men. Unless therefore we are advocates for that admiration which depends upon ignorance, and that pleasure which arises from hearing what we do not understand, the Poet must descend from this supposed height, and, in order to excite rational sympathy, he must express himself as other men express themselves. To this it may be added, that while he is only selecting from the real language of men, or, which amounts to the same thing, composing accurately in the spirit of such selection, he is treading upon safe ground, and we know what we are to expect from him. Our feelings are the same with respect to metre; for, as it may be proper to remind the Reader, the distinction of metre° is regular and uniform, and not like that which is produced by what is usually called poetic diction, arbitrary, and subject to infinite caprices upon which no calculation whatever can be made. In the one case, the Reader is utterly at the mercy of the Poet respecting what imagery or diction he may choose to connect with the passion, whereas, in the other, the metre obeys certain laws, to which the Poet and Reader both willingly submit because they are certain, and because no interference is made by them with the passion but such as the concurring testimony of ages has shewn to heighten and improve the pleasure which co-exists with it.

It will now be proper to answer an obvious question, namely, why, professing these opinions, have I written in verse? To this, in addition to such answer as is included in what I have already said, I reply in the first place, because, however I may have restricted myself, there is still left open to me what confessedly constitutes the most valuable object of all writing whether in prose or verse, the great and universal passions of men, the most general and interesting of their occupations, and the entire world of nature, from which I am at liberty to supply myself with endless combinations of forms and imagery. Now, supposing for a moment that whatever is interesting in these objects may be as vividly described in prose, why am I to be condemned, if to such description I have endeavoured to superadd the charm which, by the consent of all nations, is acknowledged to exist in metrical language? To this, by such as are unconvinced by what I have already said, it may be answered, that a very small part of the pleasure given by Poetry depends upon the metre, and that it is injudicious to write in metre, unless it be accompanied with the other artificial distinctions of style with which metre is usually accompanied, and that by such deviation more will be lost from the shock which will be thereby given to the Reader's associations, than will be counterbalanced by any pleasure which he can derive from the general power of numbers. In answer to those who still contend for the necessity of accompanying metre with certain appropriate colours of style in order to the accomplishment of its appropriate end, and who also, in my opinion, greatly under-rate the power of metre in itself, it might perhaps, as far as relates to these Poems, have been almost sufficient to observe, that poems are extant, written upon more humble subjects, and in a more naked and simple style than I have aimed at, which poems have continued to give pleasure from generation to generation. Now, if nakedness and simplicity be a defect, the fact here mentioned affords a strong presumption that poems somewhat less naked and simple are capable of affording pleasure at the present day; and, what I wished *chiefly* to attempt, at present, was to justify myself for having written under the impression of this belief.

But I might point out various causes why, when the style is manly, and the subject of some importance, words metrically arranged will long continue to impart such a pleasure to mankind as he who is sensible of the extent of that pleasure will be desirous to impart. The end of Poetry is to produce excitement in co-existence with an over-balance of pleasure. Now, by the supposition, excitement is an unusual and

irregular state of the mind; ideas and feelings do not in that state suc-
ceed each other in accustomed order. But, if the words by which this
excitement is produced are in themselves powerful, or the images and
feelings have an undue proportion of pain connected with them, there
is some danger that the excitement may be carried beyond its proper
bounds. Now the co-presence of something regular, something to
which the mind has been accustomed in various moods and in a less
excited state, cannot but have great efficacy in tempering and restrain-
ing the passion by an intertexture of ordinary feeling, and of feeling not
strictly and necessarily connected with the passion. This is unques-
tionably true, and hence, though the opinion will at first appear para-
doxical, from the tendency of metre to divest language in a certain
degree of its reality, and thus to throw a sort of half consciousness of
unsubstantial existence over the whole composition, there can be little
doubt but that more pathetic situations and sentiments, that is, those
which have a greater proportion of pain connected with them, may be
endured in metrical composition, especially in rhyme, than in prose.
The metre of the old Ballads is very artless; yet they contain many
passages which would illustrate this opinion, and, I hope, if the follow-
ing Poems be attentively perused, similar instances will be found in
them. This opinion may be further illustrated by appealing to the
Reader's own experience of the reluctance with which he comes to the
re-perusal of the distressful parts of Clarissa Harlowe, or the Gamester.°
While Shakespeare's writings, in the most pathetic scenes, never act
upon us as pathetic beyond the bounds of pleasure—an effect which,
in a much greater degree than might at first be imagined, is to be
ascribed to small, but continual and regular impulses of pleasurable
surprise from the metrical arrangement.—On the other hand (what it
must be allowed will much more frequently happen) if the Poet's words
should be incommensurate with the passion, and inadequate to raise
the Reader to a height of desirable excitement, then, (unless the Poet's
choice of his metre has been grossly injudicious) in the feelings of
pleasure which the Reader has been accustomed to connect with metre
in general, and in the feeling, whether chearful or melancholy, which
he has been accustomed to connect with that particular movement of
metre, there will be found something which will greatly contribute to
impart passion to the words, and to effect the complex end which the
Poet proposes to himself.

If I had undertaken a systematic defence of the theory upon which
these poems are written, it would have been my duty to develope
the various causes upon which the pleasure received from metrical

language depends. Among the chief of these causes is to be reckoned a principle which must be well known to those who have made any of the Arts the object of accurate reflection; I mean the pleasure which the mind derives from the perception of similitude in dissimilitude. This principle is the great spring of the activity of our minds, and their chief feeder. From this principle the direction of the sexual appetite, and all the passions connected with it take their origin: It is the life of our ordinary conversation; and upon the accuracy with which similitude in dissimilitude, and dissimilitude in similitude are perceived, depend our taste and our moral feelings. It would not have been a useless employment to have applied this principle to the consideration of metre, and to have shewn that metre is hence enabled to afford much pleasure, and to have pointed out in what manner that pleasure is produced. But my limits will not permit me to enter upon this subject, and I must content myself with a general summary.

I have said that Poetry is the spontaneous overflow of powerful feelings: it takes its origin from emotion recollected in tranquillity: the emotion is contemplated till by a species of reaction the tranquillity gradually disappears, and an emotion, kindred to that which was before the subject of contemplation, is gradually produced, and does itself actually exist in the mind. In this mood successful composition generally begins, and in a mood similar to this it is carried on; but the emotion, of whatever kind and in whatever degree, from various causes is qualified by various pleasures, so that in describing any passions whatsoever, which are voluntarily described, the mind will upon the whole be in a state of enjoyment. Now, if Nature be thus cautious in preserving in a state of enjoyment a being thus employed, the Poet ought to profit by the lesson thus held forth to him, and ought especially to take care, that whatever passions he communicates to his Reader, those passions, if his Reader's mind be sound and vigorous, should always be accompanied with an overbalance of pleasure. Now the music of harmonious metrical language, the sense of difficulty overcome, and the blind association of pleasure which has been previously received from works of rhyme or metre of the same or similar construction,° an indistinct perception perpetually renewed of language closely resembling that of real life, and yet, in the circumstance of metre, differing from it so widely, all these imperceptibly make up a complex feeling of delight, which is of the most important use in tempering the painful feeling which will always be found intermingled with powerful descriptions of the deeper passions. This effect is always produced in pathetic and impassioned poetry; while, in lighter compositions, the ease and gracefulness with which the Poet manages his numbers are themselves confessedly a principal source of the gratification of the Reader. I might perhaps include all which it is *necessary* to say upon this subject by affirming, what few persons will deny, that, of two descriptions, either of passions, manners, or characters, each of them equally well executed, the one in prose and the other in verse, the verse will be read a hundred times where the prose is read once. We see that Pope by the power of verse alone, has contrived to render the plainest common sense interesting, and even frequently to invest it with the appearance of passion.° In consequence of these convictions I related in metre the Tale of GOODY BLAKE and HARRY GILL, which is one of the rudest of this collection. I wished to draw attention to the truth that the power of the human imagination is sufficient to produce such changes even in our physical nature as might almost appear miraculous. The truth is an important one; the fact (for it is a *fact*) is a valuable illustration of it. And I have the satisfaction of knowing that it has been communicated to many hundreds of people who would never have heard of it, had it not been narrated as a Ballad, and in a more impressive metre than is usual in Ballads.

Having thus explained a few of the reasons why I have written in verse, and why I have chosen subjects from common life, and endeavoured to bring my language near to the real language of men, if I have been too minute in pleading my own cause, I have at the same time been treating a subject of general interest; and it is for this reason that I request the Reader's permission to add a few words with reference solely to these particular poems, and to some defects which will probably be found in them. I am sensible that my associations must have sometimes been particular instead of general, and that, consequently, giving to things a false importance, sometimes from diseased impulses I may have written upon unworthy subjects; but I am less apprehensive on this account, than that my language may frequently have suffered from those arbitrary connections of feelings and ideas with particular words and phrases, from which no man can altogether protect himself. Hence I have no doubt, that, in some instances, feelings even of the ludicrous may be given to my Readers by expressions which appeared to me tender and pathetic. Such faulty expressions, were I convinced they were faulty at present, and that they must necessarily continue to be so, I would willingly take all reasonable pains to correct. But it is dangerous to make these alterations on the simple authority of a few individuals, or even of certain classes of men; for where the understanding of an Author is not convinced, or his feelings altered, this cannot be done without great injury to himself: for his own feelings are his stay and support, and, if he sets them aside in one instance, he may be induced to repeat this act till his mind loses all confidence in itself, and becomes utterly debilitated. To this it may be added, that the Reader ought never to forget that he is himself exposed to the same errors as the Poet, and perhaps in a much greater degree: for there can be no presumption in saying, that it is not probable he will be so well acquainted with the various stages of meaning through which words have passed, or with the fickleness or stability of the relations of particular ideas to each other; and above all, since he is so much less interested in the subject, he may decide lightly and carelessly.

Long as I have detained my Reader, I hope he will permit me to caution him against a mode of false criticism which has been applied to Poetry in which the language closely resembles that of life and nature. Such verses have been triumphed over in parodies of which Dr. Johnson's Stanza is a fair specimen.

> 'I put my hat upon my head,
> And walk'd into the Strand,
> And there I met another man
> Whose hat was in his hand.'°

Immediately under these lines I will place one of the most justly admired stanzas of the 'Babes in the Wood.'

> "These pretty Babes with hand in hand
> Went wandering up and down;
> But never more they saw the Man
> Approaching from the Town."°

In both of these stanzas the words, and the order of the words, in no respect differ from the most unimpassioned conversation. There are words in both, for example, 'the Strand,' and 'the Town,' connected with none but the most familiar ideas; yet the one stanza we admit as admirable, and the other as a fair example of the superlatively contemptible. Whence arises this difference? Not from the metre, not from the language, not from the order of the words; but the *matter* expressed in Dr. Johnson's stanza is contemptible. The proper method of treating trivial and simple verses to which Dr. Johnson's stanza would be a fair parallelism is not to say, this is a bad kind of poetry, or this is not poetry; but this wants sense; it is neither interesting in itself, nor can *lead* to any thing interesting; the images neither originate in that sane state of feeling which arises out of thought, nor can excite thought or feeling in the Reader. This is the only sensible manner of dealing with such verses: Why trouble yourself about the species till you have previously decided upon the genus? Why take pains to prove that an Ape is not a Newton when it is self-evident that he is not a man?

I have one request to make of my Reader, which is, that in judging these Poems he would decide by his own feelings genuinely, and not by reflection upon what will probably be the judgment of others. How common is it to hear a person say, 'I myself do not object to this style of composition or this or that expression, but to such and such classes of people it will appear mean or ludicrous.' This mode of criticism, so destructive of all sound unadulterated judgment, is almost universal: I have therefore to request, that the Reader would abide independently by his own feelings, and that if he finds himself affected he would not suffer such conjectures to interfere with his pleasure.

If an Author by any single composition has impressed us with respect for his talents, it is useful to consider this as affording a presumption, that, on other occasions where we have been displeased, he nevertheless may not have written ill or absurdly; and, further, to give him so much credit for this one composition as may induce us to review what has displeased us with more care than we should otherwise have bestowed upon it. This is not only an act of justice, but in our decisions upon poetry especially, may conduce in a high degree to the improvement of our own taste: for an *accurate* taste in poetry, and in all the other arts, as Sir Joshua Reynolds° has observed, is an *acquired* talent, which can only be produced by thought and a long continued intercourse with the best models of composition. This is mentioned, not with so ridiculous a purpose as to prevent the most inexperienced Reader from judging for himself, (I have already said that I wish him to judge for himself;) but merely to temper the rashness of decision, and to suggest, that, if Poetry be a subject on which much time has not been bestowed, the judgment may be erroneous; and that in many cases it necessarily will be so.

I know that nothing would have so effectually contributed to further the end which I have in view as to have shewn of what kind the pleasure is, and how the pleasure is produced, which is confessedly produced by metrical composition essentially different from that which I have here endeavoured to recommend: for the Reader will say that he has been pleased by such composition; and what can I do more for him? The power of any art is limited; and he will suspect, that, if I propose to furnish him with new friends, it is only upon condition of his abandoning his old friends. Besides, as I have said, the Reader is himself

conscious of the pleasure which he has received from such compos-
ition, composition to which he has peculiarly attached the endearing
name of Poetry; and all men feel an habitual gratitude, and something
of an honorable bigotry for the objects which have long continued to
please them: we not only wish to be pleased, but to be pleased in that
particular way in which we have been accustomed to be pleased. There
is a host of arguments in these feelings; and I should be the less able to
combat them successfully, as I am willing to allow, that, in order
entirely to enjoy the Poetry which I am recommending, it would be
necessary to give up much of what is ordinarily enjoyed. But, would
my limits have permitted me to point out how this pleasure is pro-
duced, I might have removed many obstacles, and assisted my Reader
in perceiving that the powers of language are not so limited as he may
suppose; and that it is possible that poetry may give other enjoyments,
of a purer, more lasting, and more exquisite nature. This part of my
subject I have not altogether neglected; but it has been less my present
aim to prove, that the interest excited by some other kinds of poetry is
less vivid, and less worthy of the nobler powers of the mind, than to
offer reasons for presuming, that, if the object which I have proposed
to myself were adequately attained, a species of poetry would be pro-
duced, which is genuine poetry; in its nature well adapted to interest
mankind permanently, and likewise important in the multiplicity and
quality of its moral relations.

From what has been said, and from a perusal of the Poems, the
Reader will be able clearly to perceive the object which I have proposed
to myself: he will determine how far I have attained this object; and,
what is a much more important question, whether it be worth attain-
ing; and upon the decision of these two questions will rest my claim to
the approbation of the public.

EXPOSTULATION AND REPLY

'Why, William, on that old grey stone,
Thus for the length of half a day,
Why, William, sit you thus alone,
And dream your time away?

Where are your books?—that light bequeath'd   5
To beings else forlorn and blind!
Up! Up! and drink the spirit breath'd
From dead men to their kind.

You look round on your mother earth,
As if she for no purpose bore you;   10
As if you were her first-born birth,
And none had lived before you!'

One morning thus, by Esthwaite lake,
When life was sweet, I knew not why,
To me my good friend Matthew spake,   15
And thus I made reply.

'The eye it cannot chuse but see;
We cannot bid the ear be still;
Our bodies feel, where'er they be,
Against, or with our will.   20

Nor less I deem that there are powers
Which of themselves our minds impress;
That we can feed this mind of ours
In a wise passiveness.

Think you, mid all this mighty sum   25
Of things for ever speaking,
That nothing of itself will come,
But we must still be seeking?

—Then ask not wherefore, here, alone,
Conversing as I may,   30
I sit upon this old grey stone,
And dream my time away.'

THE TABLES TURNED;

An EVENING SCENE, *on the same subject*

Up! up! my Friend, and clear your looks;
Why all this toil and trouble?
Up! up! my Friend, and quit your books,
Or surely you'll grow double.

The sun, above the mountain's head,   5
A freshening lustre mellow
Through all the long green fields has spread,
His first sweet evening yellow.

Books! 'tis a dull and endless strife:
Come, hear the woodland Linnet,   10
How sweet his music; on my life
There's more of wisdom in it.

And hark! how blithe the Throstle sings!
And he is no mean preacher:
Come forth into the light of things,   15
Let Nature be your teacher.

She has a world of ready wealth,
Our minds and hearts to bless—
Spontaneous wisdom breathed by health,
Truth breathed by chearfulness.   20

One impulse from a vernal wood
May teach you more of man;
Of moral evil and of good,
Than all the sages can.

Sweet is the lore which nature brings;   25
Our meddling intellect
Mishapes the beauteous forms of things;
—We murder to dissect.

Enough of science and of art;
Close up these barren leaves;   30

Come forth, and bring with you a heart
That watches and receives.

ANIMAL TRANQUILLITY AND DECAY,

A SKETCH

      The little hedge-row birds
That peck along the road, regard him not.
He travels on, and in his face, his step,
His gait, is one expression; every limb,
His look and bending figure, all bespeak   5
A man who does not move with pain, but moves
With thought.—He is insensibly subdued
To settled quiet: he is one by whom
All effort seems forgotten, one to whom
Long patience has such mild composure given,   10
That patience now doth seem a thing, of which
He hath no need. He is by nature led
To peace so perfect, that the young behold
With envy, what the Old Man hardly feels.
—I asked him whither he was bound, and what   15
The object of his journey; he replied
That he was going many miles to take
A last leave of his Son, a Mariner,
Who from a sea-fight had been brought to Falmouth,
And there was dying in an hospital.   20

GOODY BLAKE AND HARRY GILL,

A TRUE STORY

Oh! what's the matter? what's the matter?
What is't that ails young Harry Gill?
That evermore his teeth they chatter,
Chatter, chatter, chatter still.
Of waistcoats Harry has no lack,   5
Good duffle grey, and flannel fine;
He has a blanket on his back,
And coats enough to smother nine.

In March, December, and in July,
'Tis all the same with Harry Gill;   10
The neighbours tell, and tell you truly,
His teeth they chatter, chatter still.
At night, at morning, and at noon,
'Tis all the same with Harry Gill;
Beneath the sun, beneath the moon,   15
His teeth they chatter, chatter still.

Young Harry was a lusty drover,
And who so stout of limb as he?
His cheeks were red as ruddy clover;
His voice was like the voice of three.   20
Old Goody Blake was old and poor;
Ill fed she was, and thinly clad;
And any man who pass'd her door,
Might see how poor a hut she had.

All day she spun in her poor dwelling: 25
And then her three hours' work at night!
Alas! 'twas hardly worth the telling,
It would not pay for candle light.
—This woman dwelt in Dorsetshire,
Her hut was on a cold hill side,   30
And in that country coals are dear,
For they come far by wind and tide.

By the same fire to boil their pottage,
Two poor old Dames, as I have known,
Will often live in one small cottage;   35
But she, poor Woman! dwelt alone.
'Twas well enough when summer came,
The long, warm, lightsome summer-day,
Then at her door the *canty* Dame
Would sit, as any linnet gay.   40

But when the ice our streams did fetter,
Oh! then how her old bones would shake!
You would have said, if you had met her,
'Twas a hard time for Goody Blake.

Her evenings then were dull and dead;   45
Sad case it was, as you may think,
For very cold to go to bed;
And then for cold not sleep a wink.

Oh joy for her! whene'er in winter
The winds at night had made a rout;   50
And scatter'd many a lusty splinter,
And many a rotten bough about.
Yet never had she, well or sick,
As every man who knew her says,
A pile before hand, wood or stick,   55
Enough to warm her for three days.

Now, when the frost was past enduring,
And made her poor old bones to ache,
Could any thing be more alluring,
Than an old hedge to Goody Blake;   60
And, now and then, it must be said,
When her old bones were cold and chill,
She left her fire, or left her bed,
To seek the hedge of Harry Gill.

Now Harry he had long suspected   65
This trespass of old Goody Blake;
And vow'd that she should be detected,
And he on her would vengeance take.
And oft from his warm fire he'd go,
And to the fields his road would take;   70
And there, at night, in frost and snow,
He watch'd to seize old Goody Blake.

And once, behind a rick of barley,
Thus looking out did Harry stand:
The moon was full and shining clearly,   75
And crisp with frost the stubble land.
—He hears a noise—he's all awake—
Again?—on tip-toe down the hill
He softly creeps—'Tis Goody Blake,
She's at the hedge of Harry Gill.   80

Right glad was he when he beheld her:
Stick after stick did Goody pull:
He stood behind a bush of elder,
Till she had filled her apron full.
When with her load she turned about,   85
The bye-road back again to take,
He started forward with a shout,
And sprang upon poor Goody Blake.

And fiercely by the arm he took her,
And by the arm he held her fast,   90
And fiercely by the arm he shook her,
And cried, 'I've caught you then at last!'
Then Goody, who had nothing said,
Her bundle from her lap let fall;
And, kneeling on the sticks, she pray'd   95
To God that is the judge of all.

She pray'd, her wither'd hand uprearing,
While Harry held her by the arm—
'God! who art never out of hearing,
O may he never more be warm!'   100
The cold, cold moon above her head,
Thus on her knees did Goody pray,
Young Harry heard what she had said:
And icy cold he turned away.

He went complaining all the morrow   105
That he was cold and very chill:
His face was gloom, his heart was sorrow,
Alas! that day for Harry Gill!
That day he wore a riding coat,
But not a whit the warmer he: 110
Another was on Thursday brought,
And ere the Sabbath he had three.

'Twas all in vain, a useless matter,
And blankets were about him pinn'd;
Yet still his jaws and teeth they clatter,   115
Like a loose casement in the wind.

And Harry's flesh it fell away;
And all who see him say, 'tis plain,
That live as long as live he may,
He never will be warm again.   120

No word to any man he utters,
A-bed or up, to young or old;
But ever to himself he mutters,
'Poor Harry Gill is very cold.'
A-bed or up, by night or day;   125
His teeth they chatter, chatter still.
Now think, ye farmers all, I pray,
Of Goody Blake and Harry Gill.

THE LAST OF THE FLOCK

In distant countries I have been;
And yet I have not often seen
A healthy Man, a Man full grown,
Weep in the public roads alone.
But such a one, on English ground,   5
And in the broad high-way, I met;
Along the broad high-way he came,
His cheeks with tears were wet.
Sturdy he seemed, though he was sad;
And in his arms a Lamb he had.   10

He saw me, and he turned aside,
As if he wished himself to hide:
Then with his coat he made essay
To wipe those briny tears away.
I followed him, and said, 'My Friend   15
What ails you? wherefore weep you so?'
—'Shame on me, Sir! this lusty Lamb,
He makes my tears to flow.
To-day I fetched him from the rock;
He is the last of all my flock.   20

When I was young, a single Man,
And after youthful follies ran,

Though little given to care and thought,
Yet, so it was, a Ewe I bought;
And other sheep from her I raised,   25
As healthy sheep as you might see;
And then I married, and was rich
As I could wish to be;
Of sheep I numbered a full score,
And every year increas'd my store.   30

Year after year my stock it grew,
And from this one, this single Ewe,
Full fifty comely sheep I raised,
As sweet a flock as ever grazed!
Upon the mountain did they feed,   35
They throve, and we at home did thrive.
—This lusty Lamb of all my store
Is all that is alive;
And now I care not if we die,
And perish all of poverty.   40

Six Children, Sir! had I to feed,
Hard labour in a time of need!
My pride was tamed, and in our grief,
I of the Parish ask'd relief.
They said I was a wealthy man;   45
My sheep upon the mountain fed,
And it was fit that thence I took
Whereof to buy us bread:
"Do this; how can we give to you,"
They cried, "what to the poor is due?"   50

I sold a sheep, as they had said,
And bought my little children bread,
And they were healthy with their food;
For me it never did me good.
A woeful time it was for me,   55
To see the end of all my gains,
The pretty flock which I had reared
With all my care and pains,
To see it melt like snow away!
For me it was woeful day.   60

Another still! and still another!
A little lamb, and then its mother!
It was a vein that never stopp'd—
Like blood-drops from my heart they dropp'd.
Till thirty were not left alive   65
They dwindled, dwindled, one by one,
And I may say, that many a time
I wished they all were gone:
They dwindled one by one away;
For me it was a woeful day.   70

To wicked deeds I was inclined,
And wicked fancies cross'd my mind;
And every man I chanc'd to see,
I thought he knew some ill of me.
No peace no comfort could I find,   75
No ease, within doors or without,
And crazily, and wearily,
I went my work about.
Oft-times I thought to run away;
For me it was a woeful day.   80

Sir! 'twas a precious flock to me,
As dear as my own Children be;
For daily with my growing store
I loved my Children more and more.
Alas! it was an evil time;   85
God cursed me in my sore distress;
I prayed, yet every day I thought
I loved my children less;
And every week, and every day,
My flock, it seemed to melt away.   90

They dwindled, Sir, sad sight to see!
From ten to five, from five to three,
A lamb, a weather, and a ewe;—
And then at last, from three to two;
And of my fifty, yesterday   95
I had but only one:
And here it lies upon my arm,
Alas! and I have none;—

To-day I fetched it from the rock;
It is the last of all my flock.'   100

LINES

*Left upon a seat in a YEW-TREE, which stands near the Lake
of ESTHWAITE, on a desolate part of the shore, yet commanding
a beautiful prospect*

—Nay, Traveller! rest. This lonely Yew-tree stands
Far from all human dwelling: what if here
No sparkling rivulet spread the verdant herb;
What if these barren boughs the bee not loves;
Yet, if the wind breathe soft, the curling waves,   5
That break against the shore, shall lull thy mind
By one soft impulse saved from vacancy.

————————Who he was
That piled these stones, and with the mossy sod
First covered o'er, and taught this aged Tree   10
With its dark arms to form a circling bower,
I well remember.—He was one who owned
No common soul. In youth by science nursed,
And led by nature into a wild scene
Of lofty hopes, he to the world went forth,   15
A favored being, knowing no desire
Which genius did not hallow, 'gainst the taint
Of dissolute tongues, and jealousy, and hate,
And scorn, against all enemies prepared,
All but neglect. The world, for so it thought,   20
Owed him no service: wherefore he at once
With indignation turn'd himself away
And with the food of pride sustained his soul
In solitude.—Stranger! these gloomy boughs
Had charms for him; and here he loved to sit,   25
His only visitants a straggling sheep,
The stone-chat, or the glancing sand-piper;
And on these barren rocks, with juniper,
And heath, and thistle, thinly sprinkled o'er,
Fixing his down-cast eye, he many an hour   30

A morbid pleasure nourished, tracing here
An emblem of his own unfruitful life:
And lifting up his head, he then would gaze
On the more distant scene; how lovely 'tis
Thou seest, and he would gaze till it became   35
Far lovelier, and his heart could not sustain
The beauty still more beauteous. Nor, that time,
When Nature had subdued him to herself,
Would he forget those beings, to whose minds,
Warm from the labours of benevolence,   40
The world, and man himself, appeared a scene
Of kindred loveliness: then he would sigh
With mournful joy, to think that others felt
What he must never feel: and so, lost Man!
On visionary views would fancy feed,   45
Till his eye streamed with tears. In this deep vale
He died, this seat his only monument.

If Thou be one whose heart the holy forms
Of young imagination have kept pure,
Stranger! henceforth be warned; and know, that pride, 50
Howe'er disguised in its own majesty,
Is littleness; that he, who feels contempt
For any living thing, hath faculties
Which he has never used; that thought with him
Is in its infancy. The man, whose eye   55
Is ever on himself, doth look on one,
The least of Nature's works, one who might move
The wise man to that scorn which wisdom holds
Unlawful, ever. O, be wiser Thou!
Instructed that true knowledge leads to love,   60
True dignity abides with him alone
Who, in the silent hour of inward thought,
Can still suspect, and still revere himself,
In lowliness of heart.

THE FOSTER-MOTHER'S TALE
A Narration in Dramatic Blank Verse

                              But that entrance, Mother!

FOSTER-MOTHER. Can no one hear ? It is a perilous tale!

MARIA. No one.

FOSTER-MOTHER. My husband's father told it me,
Poor old Leoni!—Angels rest his soul!
He was a woodman, and could fell and saw   5
With lusty arm. You know that huge round beam
Which props the hanging wall of the old chapel;
Beneath that tree, while yet it was a tree
He found a baby wrapt in mosses, lined
With thistle beards, and such small locks of wool   10
As hang on brambles. Well, he brought him home,
And reared him at the then Lord Velez' cost.
And so the babe grew up a pretty boy,
A pretty boy, but most unteachable—
And never learnt a prayer, nor told a bead,   15
But knew the names of birds, and mocked their notes,
And whistled, as he were a bird himself:
And all the autumn 'twas his only play
To gather seeds of wild flowers, and to plant them
With earth and water, on the stumps of trees.   20
A Friar, who sought for simples in the wood,
A grey-haired man—he loved this little boy,
The boy loved him—and, when the Friar taught him,
He soon could write with the pen: and from that time,
Lived chiefly at the Convent or the Castle.   25
So he became a very learned youth.
But Oh! poor wretch—he read, and read, and read,
'Till his brain turned—and ere his twentieth year,
He had unlawful thoughts of many things:
And though he prayed, he never loved to pray   30
With holy men, nor in a holy place—
But yet his speech, it was so soft and sweet,
The late Lord Velez ne'er was wearied with him.
And once, as by the north side of the Chapel

They stood together, chained in deep discourse,   35
The earth heaved under them with such a groan,
That the wall tottered, and had well-nigh fallen
Right on their heads. My Lord was sorely frightened;
A fever seized him, and he made confession
Of all the heretical and lawless talk   40
Which brought this judgment: so the youth was seized
And cast into that cell. My husband's father
Sobbed like a child—it almost broke his heart:
And once as he was working near the cell
He heard a voice distinctly; 'twas the youth's   45
Who sang a doleful song about green fields,
How sweet it were on lake or wild savannah, .
To hunt for food, and be a naked man,
And wander up and down at liberty.

Leoni doted on the youth, and now   50
His love grew desperate; and defying death,
He made that cunning entrance I described:
And the young man escaped.

MARIA.   'Tis a sweet tale.
And what became of him?

FOSTER-MOTHER.   He went on ship-board
With those bold voyagers, who made discovery   55
Of golden lands. Leoni's younger brother
Went likewise, and when he returned to Spain,
He told Leoni, that the poor mad youth,
Soon after they arrived in that new world,
In spite of his dissuasion, seized a boat,   60
And all alone, set sail by silent moonlight
Up a great river, great as any sea,
And ne'er was heard of more: but 'tis supposed,
He lived and died among the savage men.

THE THORN

I

There is a Thorn—it looks so old,
In truth, you'd find it hard to say

How it could ever have been young—
It looks so old and grey.
Not higher than a two years' child   5
It stands erect, this aged Thorn;
No leaves it has, no thorny points;
It is a mass of knotted joints,
A wretched thing forlorn.
It stands erect, and like a stone   10
With lichens it is overgrown.

II

Like rock or stone, it is o'ergrown
With lichens to the very top,
And hung with heavy tufts of moss,
A melancholy crop: 15
Up from the earth these mosses creep,
And this poor Thorn they clasp it round
So close, you'd say that they were bent
With plain and manifest intent,
To drag it to the ground;   20
And all had join'd in one endeavour
To bury this poor Thorn for ever.

III

High on a mountain's highest ridge,
Where oft the stormy winter gale
Cuts like a scythe, while through the clouds 25
It sweeps from vale to vale;
Not five yards from the mountain-path,
This Thorn you on your left espy;
And to the left, three yards beyond,
You see a little muddy Pond   30
Of water never dry;
I've measured it from side to side:
'Tis three feet long, and two feet wide.

IV

And, close beside this aged Thorn,
There is a fresh and lovely sight,   35
A beauteous heap, a Hill of moss,
Just half a foot in height.

All lovely colours there you see,
All colours that were ever seen;
And mossy network too is there,   40
As if by hand of lady fair
The work had woven been;
And cups, the darlings of the eye,
So deep is their vermilion dye.

V

Ah me! what lovely tints are there!   45
Of olive green and scarlet bright,
In spikes, in branches, and in stars,
Green, red, and pearly white.
This heap of earth o'ergrown with moss,
Which close beside the Thorn you see,   50
So fresh in all its beauteous dyes,
Is like an infant's grave in size,
As like as like can be:
But never, never any where,
An infant's grave was half so fair.   55

VI

Now would you see this aged Thorn,
This Pond, and beauteous Hill of moss,
You must take care and chuse your time
The mountain when to cross.
For oft there sits, between the Heap   60
That's like an infant's grave in size,
And that same Pond of which I spoke,
A Woman in a scarlet cloak,
And to herself she cries,
'Oh misery! oh misery!   65
Oh woe is me! oh misery!'

VII

At all times of the day and night
This wretched Woman thither goes;
And she is known to every star,
And every wind that blows;   70
And there beside the Thorn she sits
When the blue day-light's in the skies,

And when the whirlwind's on the hill,
Or frosty air is keen and still,
And to herself she cries,   75
'Oh misery! oh misery!
Oh woe is me! oh misery!'

VIII

'Now wherefore, thus, by day and night,
In rain, in tempest, and in snow,
Thus to the dreary mountain-top   80
Does this poor Woman go?
And why sits she beside the Thorn
When the blue day-light's in the sky,
Or when the whirlwind's on the hill,
Or frosty air is keen and still,   85
And wherefore does she cry?—
Oh wherefore? wherefore? tell me why
Does she repeat that doleful cry?'

IX

I cannot tell; I wish I could;
For the true reason no one knows: 90
But if you'd gladly view the spot,
The spot to which she goes;
The Heap that's like an infant's grave,
The Pond—and Thorn, so old and grey,
Pass by her door—'tis seldom shut—   95
And, if you see her in her hut,
Then to the spot away!—
I never heard of such as dare
Approach the spot when she is there.

X

'But wherefore to the mountain-top,   100
Can this unhappy Woman go,
Whatever star is in the skies,
Whatever wind may blow?'
Nay rack your brain—'tis all in vain,
I'll tell you every thing I know;   105
But to the Thorn, and to the Pond

Which is a little step beyond,
I wish that you would go:
Perhaps, when you are at the place,
You something of her tale may trace.   110

XI

I'll give you the best help I can:
Before you up the mountain go,
Up to the dreary mountain-top,
I'll tell you all I know.
'Tis now some two and twenty years,   115
Since she (her name is Martha Ray)
Gave with a maiden's true good will
Her company to Stephen Hill;
And she was blithe and gay,
And she was happy, happy still   120
Whene'er she thought of Stephen Hill.

XII

And they had fix'd the wedding-day,
The morning that must wed them both;
But Stephen to another Maid
Had sworn another oath;   125
And with this other Maid to church
Unthinking Stephen went—
Poor Martha! on that woful day
A cruel, cruel fire, they say,
Into her bones was sent: 130
It dried her body like a cinder,
And almost turned her brain to tinder.

XIII

They say, full six months after this,
While yet the summer leaves were green,
She to the mountain-top would go,   135
And there was often seen.
'Tis said, a child was in her womb,
As now to any eye was plain;
She was with child, and she was mad;
Yet often she was sober sad   140
From her exceeding pain.

Oh me! ten thousand times I'd rather,
That he had died, that cruel father!

XIV

Sad case for such a brain to hold
Communion with a stirring child! 145
Sad case, as you may think, for one
Who had a brain so wild!
Last Christmas when we talked of this,
Old Farmer Simpson did maintain,
That in her womb the infant wrought 150
About its mother's heart, and brought
Her senses back again:
And when at last her time drew near,
Her looks were calm, her senses clear.

XV

No more I know, I wish I did, 155
And I would tell it all to you;
For what became of this poor child
There's none that ever knew:
And if a child was born or no,
There's no one that could ever tell; 160
And if 'twas born alive or dead,
There's no one knows, as I have said;
But some remember well,
That Martha Ray about this time
Would up the mountain often climb. 165

XVI

And all that winter, when at night
The wind blew from the mountain-peak,
'Twas worth your while, though in the dark,
The church-yard path to seek:
For many a time and oft were heard 170
Cries coming from the mountain-head:
Some plainly living voices were;
And others, I've heard many swear,
Were voices of the dead:
I cannot think, whate'er they say, 175
They had to do with Martha Ray.

XVII

But that she goes to this old Thorn,
The Thorn which I've described to you,
And there sits in a scarlet cloak,
I will be sworn is true.   180
For one day with my telescope,
To view the ocean wide and bright,
When to this country first I came,
Ere I had heard of Martha's name,
I climbed the mountain's height: 185
A storm came on, and I could see
No object higher than my knee.

XVIII

'Twas mist and rain, and storm and rain,
No screen, no fence could I discover,
And then the wind! in faith, it was   190
A wind full ten times over.
I looked around, I thought I saw
A jutting crag, and off I ran,
Head-foremost, through the driving rain,
The shelter of the crag to gain,   195
And, as I am a man,
Instead of jutting crag, I found
A Woman seated on the ground.

XIX

I did not speak—I saw her face,
In truth it was enough for me;   200
I turned about and heard her cry,
'O misery! O misery!'
And there she sits, until the moon
Through half the clear blue sky will go;
And, when the little breezes make   205
The waters of the Pond to shake,
As all the country know,
She shudders, and you hear her cry,
'Oh misery! oh misery!'

XX

'But what's the Thorn? and what's the Pond?   210
And what's the Hill of moss to her?
And what's the creeping breeze that comes
The little Pond to stir?'
I cannot tell; but some will say
She hanged her baby on the tree;   215
Some say, she drowned it in the pond,
Which is a little step beyond;
But all and each agree,
The little babe was buried there,
Beneath that Hill of moss so fair.   220

XXI

I've heard, the moss is spotted red
With drops of that poor infant's blood:
But kill a new-born infant thus!
I do not think she could.
Some say, if to the Pond you go,   225
And fix on it a steady view,
The shadow of a babe you trace,
A baby and a baby's face,
And that it looks at you;
Whene'er you look on it, 'tis plain   230
The baby looks at you again.

XXII

And some had sworn an oath that she
Should be to public justice brought:
And for the little infant's bones
With spades they would have sought.   235
But then the beauteous Hill of moss
Before their eyes began to stir;
And for full fifty yards around,
The grass it shook upon the ground;
But all do still aver   240
The little babe is buried there,
Beneath that Hill of moss so fair.

XXIII

I cannot tell how this may be,
But plain it is, the Thorn is bound
With heavy tufts of moss, that strive   245
To drag it to the ground.
And this I know, full many a time,
When she was on the mountain high,
By day, and in the silent night,
When all the stars shone clear and bright,   250
That I have heard her cry,
'Oh misery! oh misery!
O woe is me! oh misery!'

WE ARE SEVEN

A simple child, dear brother Jim,
That lightly draws its breath,
And feels its life in every limb,
What should it know of death?

I met a little cottage Girl: 5
She was eight years old, she said;
Her hair was thick with many a curl
That cluster'd round her head.

She had a rustic, woodland air,
And she was wildly clad;   10
Her eyes were fair, and very fair;
—Her beauty made me glad.

'Sisters and brothers, little Maid,
How many may you be?'
'How many? seven in all,' she said,   15
And wondering looked at me.

'And where are they, I pray you tell?'
She answered, 'Seven are we;
And two of us at Conway dwell,
And two are gone to sea.   20

Two of us in the church-yard lie,
My sister and my brother,
And in the church-yard cottage, I
Dwell near them with my mother.'

'You say that two at Conway dwell,   25
And two are gone to sea,
Yet you are seven; I pray you tell,
Sweet Maid, how this may be?'

Then did the little Maid reply,
'Seven boys and girls are we;   30
Two of us in the church-yard lie,
Beneath the church-yard tree.'

'You run about, my little Maid,
Your limbs they are alive;
If two are in the church-yard laid,   35
Then ye are only five.'

'Their graves are green, they may be seen,'
The little Maid replied,
'Twelve steps or more from my mother's door,
And they are side by side.   40

My stockings there I often knit,
My 'kerchief there I hem;
And there upon the ground I sit—
I sit and sing to them.

And often after sun-set, Sir,   45
When it is light and fair,
I take my little porringer,
And eat my supper there.

The first that died was little Jane;
In bed she moaning lay,
Till God released her of her pain;   50
And then she went away.

So in the church-yard she was laid;
And all the summer dry,

Together round her grave we played,
My brother John and I.   55

And, when the ground was white with snow,
And I could run and slide,
My brother John was forced to go,
And he lies by her side.'

'How many are you then,' said I,   60
If they two are in Heaven?'
The little Maiden did reply,
'O Master! we are seven.'

'But they are dead: those two are dead!
Their spirits are in Heaven!'   65
'Twas throwing words away: for still
The little Maid would have her will,
And said, 'Nay, we are seven!'

ANECDOTE FOR FATHERS,

Shewing how the practice of Lying may be taught

I have a Boy of five years old;
His face is fair and fresh to see;
His limbs are cast in beauty's mould,
And dearly he loves me.

One morn we stroll'd on our dry walk,   5
Our quiet home all full in view,
And held such intermitted talk
As we are wont to do.

My thoughts on former pleasures ran:
I thought of Kilve's delightful shore,   10
Our pleasant home, when Spring began,
A long, long year before.

A day it was when I could bear
To think, and think, and think again;

With so much happiness to spare,
I could not feel a pain.

My Boy was by my side, so slim
And graceful in his rustic dress!
And oftentimes I talked to him.
In very idleness.   20

The young lambs ran a pretty race;
The morning sun shone bright and warm;
'Kilve,' said I, 'was a pleasant place;
And so is Liswyn farm.

My little Boy, which like you more,'   25
I said, and took him by the arm—
'Our home by Kilve's delightful shore,
Or here at Liswyn farm?

And tell me, had you rather be,'
I said, and held him by the arm,   30
'At Kilve's smooth shore by the green sea,
Or here at Liswyn farm?'

In careless mood he looked at me,
While still I held him by the arm,
And said, 'At Kilve I'd rather be   35
Than here at Liswyn farm.'

'Now, little Edward, say why so;
My little Edward, tell me why;'—
'I cannot tell, I do not know.'
'Why this is strange,' said I.   40

'For, here are woods, and green-hills warm:
There surely must some reason be
Why you would change sweet Liswyn farm
For Kilve by the green sea.'

At this, my Boy hung down his head,   45
He blush'd with shame, nor made reply;
And five times to the Child I said,
'Why, Edward, tell me why?'

His head he raised—there was in sight,
It caught his eye, he saw it plain—   50
Upon the house-top, glittering bright,
A broad and gilded vane.

Then did the Boy his tongue unlock;
And thus to me he made reply;
'At Kilve there was no weather-cock,   55
And that's the reason why.'

Oh dearest, dearest Boy! my heart
For better lore would seldom yearn,
Could I but teach the hundredth part
Of what from thee I learn.   60

LINES

*Written at a small distance from my House, and sent by my
little boy to the person to whom they are addressed*

It is the first mild day of March:
Each minute sweeter than before,
The Red-breast sings from the tall Larch
That stands beside our door.

There is a blessing in the air,   5
Which seems a sense of joy to yield
To the bare trees, and mountains bare,
And grass in the green field.

My Sister! ('tis a wish of mine)
Now that our morning meal is done,   10
Make haste, your morning task resign;
Come forth and feel the sun.

Edward will come with you; and pray,
Put on with speed your woodland dress;
And bring no book: for this one day   15
We'll give to idleness.

No joyless forms shall regulate
Our living Calendar:
We from to-day, my Friend, will date
The opening of the year.   20

Love, now an universal birth,
From heart to heart is stealing,
From earth to man, from man to earth:
—It is the hour of feeling.

One moment now may give us more   25
Than fifty years of reason:
Our minds shall drink at every pore
The spirit of the season.

Some silent laws our hearts may make,
Which they shall long obey: 30
We for the year to come may take
Our temper from to-day.

And from the blessed power that rolls
About, below, above,
We'll frame the measure of our souls: 35
They shall be tuned to love.

Then come, my sister! come, I pray,
With speed put on your woodland dress;
—And bring no book: for this one day
We'll give to idleness.   40

THE FEMALE VAGRANT

'My Father was a good and pious man,
An honest man by honest parents bred;
And I believe, that, soon as I began
To lisp, he made me kneel beside my bed,
And in his hearing there my prayers I said: 5
And, afterwards, by my good Father taught,
I read, and loved the books in which I read;
For books in every neighbouring house I sought,
And nothing to my mind a sweeter pleasure brought.

The suns of twenty summers danced along,—   10
Ah! little marked how fast they rolled away:
Then rose a stately Hall our woods among,
And cottage after cottage owned its sway.
No joy to see a neighbouring House, or stray
Through pastures not his own, the master took;   15
My Father dared his greedy wish gainsay;
He loved his old hereditary nook,
And ill could I the thought of such sad parting brook.

But, when he had refused the proffered gold,
To cruel injuries he became a prey,   20
Sore traversed in whate'er he bought and sold:
His troubles grew upon him day by day,
And all his substance fell into decay.
They dealt most hardly with him, and he tried
To move their hearts—but it was vain—for they   25
Seized all he had; and, weeping side by side,
We sought a home where we uninjured might abide.

It was in truth a lamentable hour
When, from the last hill-top, my Sire surveyed,
Peering above the trees, the steeple tower   30
That on his marriage-day sweet music made.
Till then he hoped his bones might there be laid,
Close by my Mother, in their native bowers;
Bidding me trust in God, he stood and prayed,—
I could not pray:—through tears that fell in showers,   35
I saw our own dear home, that was no longer ours.

There was a Youth, whom I had loved so long,
That when I loved him not I cannot say.
'Mid the green mountains many and many a song
We two had sung, like gladsome birds in May.   40
When we began to tire of childish play
We seemed still more and more to prize each other;
We talked of marriage and our marriage day;
And I in truth did love him like a brother;
For never could I hope to meet with such another.   45

Two years were pass'd, since to a distant Town
He had repair'd to ply the artist's trade.

What tears of bitter grief till then unknown!
What tender vows our last sad kiss delayed!
To him we turned:—we had no other aid.   50
Like one revived, upon his neck I wept:
And her whom he had loved in joy, he said
He well could love in grief: his faith he kept;
And in a quiet home once more my Father slept.

We lived in peace and comfort; and were blest   55
With daily bread, by constant toil supplied.
Three lovely Infants lay upon my breast;
And often, viewing their sweet smiles, I sighed,
And knew not why. My happy Father died
When sad distress reduced the Children's meal: 60
Thrice happy! that from him the grave did hide
The empty loom, cold hearth, and silent wheel,
And tears that flowed for ills which patience could not heal.

'Twas a hard change, an evil time was come;
We had no hope, and no relief could gain.   65
But soon, day after day, the noisy drum
Beat round, to sweep the streets of want and pain.
My husband's arms now only served to strain
Me and his children hungering in his view:
In such dismay my prayers and tears were vain: 70
To join those miserable men he flew:
And now to the sea-coast, with numbers more, we drew.

There, long were we neglected, and we bore
Much sorrow ere the fleet its anchor weigh'd;
Green fields before us and our native shore,   75
We breath'd a pestilential air that made
Ravage for which no knell was heard. We pray'd
For our departure; wish'd and wish'd—nor knew
'Mid that long sickness, and those hopes delay'd,
That happier days we never more must view: 80
The parting signal streamed, at last the land withdrew.

But the calm summer season now was past.
On as we drove, the equinoctial Deep

Ran mountains-high before the howling blast;
And many perish'd in the whirlwind's sweep.   85
We gazed with terror on their gloomy sleep,
Untaught that soon such anguish must ensue,
Our hopes such harvest of affliction reap,
That we the mercy of the waves should rue.
We reach'd the Western World, a poor, devoted crew.   90

The pains and plagues that on our heads came down,
Disease and famine, agony and fear,
In wood or wilderness, in camp or town,
It would thy brain unsettle, even to hear.
All perished—all, in one remorseless year,   95
Husband and Children! one by one, by sword
And ravenous plague, all perished: every tear
Dried up, despairing, desolate, on board
A British ship I waked, as from a trance restored.

Peaceful as some immeasurable plain   100
By the first beams of dawning light imprcss'd,
In the calm sun-shine slept the glittering main.
The very ocean has its hour of rest.
I too was calm, though hcavily distress'd!
Oh me, how quiet sky and ocean were!   105
My heart was healed within me, I was bless'd,
And looked, and looked along the silent air,
Until it seemed to bring a joy to my despair.

Ah! how unlike those late terrific sleeps!
And groans, that rage of racking famine spoke: 110
The unburied dead that lay in festering heaps!
The breathing pestilence that rose like smoke!
The shriek that from the distant battle broke!
The mine's dire earthquake, and the pallid host
Driven by the bomb's incessant thunder-stroke   115
To loathsome vaults, where heart-sick anguish toss'd,
Hope died, and fear itself in agony was lost!

At midnight once the storming Army came,
Yet do I see the miserable sight,

The Bayonet, the Soldier, and the Flame   120
That followed us and faced us in our flight:
When Rape and Murder by the ghastly light
Seized their joint prey, the Mother and the Child!
But I must leave these thoughts.—From night to night,
From day to day, the air breathed soft and mild;   125
And on the gliding vessel Heaven and Ocean smiled.

Some mighty gulph of separation past,
I seemed transported to another world:—
A thought resigned with pain, when from the mast
The impatient mariner the sail unfurl'd,   130
And whistling, called the wind that hardly curled
The silent sea. From the sweet thoughts of home,
And from all hope I was forever hurled.
For me—farthest from earthly port to roam
Was best, could I but shun the spot where man might come.   135

And oft I thought (my fancy was so strong)
That I at last a resting-place had found;
Here will I dwell, said I, my whole life-long,
Roaming the illimitable waters round:
Here will I live:—of every friend disown'd,   140
Here will I roam about the ocean-flood.—
To break my dream the vessel reached its bound:
And homeless near a thousand homes I stood,
And near a thousand tables pin'd, and wanted food.

By grief enfeebled was I turned adrift,   145
Helpless as sailor cast on desart rock;
Nor morsel to my mouth that day did lift,
Nor dared my hand at any door to knock.
I lay, where with his drowsy Mates, the Cock
From the cross timber of an out-house hung;   150
Dismally tolled, that night, the city clock!
At morn my sick heart hunger scarcely stung,
Nor to the beggar's language could I frame my tongue.

So pass'd another day, and so the third;
Then did I try in vain the crowd's resort.   155

—In deep despair by frightful wishes stirr'd,
Near the sea-side I reached a ruined Fort:
There, pains which nature could no more support,
With blindness link'd, did on my vitals fall,
And I had many interruptions short   160
Of hideous sense; I sank, nor step could crawl,
And thence was carried to a neighbouring Hospital.

Recovery came with food: but still, my brain
Was weak, nor of the past had memory.
I heard my neighbours, in their beds, complain   165
Of many things which never troubled me;
Of feet still bustling round with busy glee;
Of looks where common kindness had no part;
Of service done with careless cruelty,
Fretting the fever round the languid heart;   170
And groans, which, as they said, would make a dead man start.

These things just served to stir the torpid sense,
Nor pain nor pity in my bosom raised.
My memory and my strength returned; and thence
Dismissed, again on open day I gazed,   175
At houses, men, and common light, amazed.
The lanes I sought, and as the sun retired,
Came, where beneath the trees a faggot blazed;
The Travellers saw me weep, my fate enquired,
And gave me food, and rest, more welcome, more desired.   180

My heart is touched to think that men like these,
Wild houseless Wanderers, were my first relief:
How kindly did they paint their vagrant ease!
And their long holiday that feared not grief!
For all belonged to all, and each was chief.   185
No plough their sinews strained; on grating road
No wain they drove; and yet the yellow sheaf
In every vale for their delight was stow'd;
In every field, with milk their dairy overflow'd.

They with their pannier'd Asses semblance made   190
Of Potters wandering on from door to door:

But life of happier sort to me pourtray'd,
And other joys my fancy to allure;
The bag-pipe dinning on the midnight moor
In barn uplighted, and Companions boon   195
Well met from far with revelry secure,
Among the forest glades, when jocund June
Rolled fast along the sky his warm and genial moon.

But ill they suited me; those journies dark
O'er moor and mountain, midnight theft to hatch!   200
To charm the surly House-dog's faithful bark,
Or hang on tip-toe at the lifted latch;
The gloomy lantern, and the dim blue match,
The black disguise, the warning whistle shrill,
And ear still busy on its nightly watch,   205
Were not for me, brought up in nothing ill:
Besides, on griefs so fresh my thoughts were brooding still.

What could I do, unaided and unblest?
My Father! gone was every friend of thine:
And kindred of dead husband are at best   210
Small help; and, after marriage such as mine,
With little kindness would to me incline.
Ill was I then for toil or service fit:
With tears whose course no effort could confine,
By the road-side forgetful would I sit   215
Whole hours, my idle arms in moping sorrow knit.

I led a wandering life among the fields;
Contentedly, yet sometimes self-accused,
I liv'd upon what casual bounty yields,
Now coldly given, now utterly refused.   220
The ground I for my bed have often used:
But, what afflicts my peace with keenest ruth
Is, that I have my inner self abused,
Forgone the home delight of constant truth,
And clear and open soul, so prized in fearless youth.   225

Three years thus wandering, often have I view'd,
In tears, the sun towards that country tend

Where my poor heart lost all its fortitude:
And now across this moor my steps I bend—
Oh! tell me whither——for no earthly friend   230
Have I.'——She ceased, and weeping turned away,
As if because her tale was at an end
She wept;—because she had no more to say
Of that perpetual weight which on her spirit lay.

LINES

Written in early spring

I heard a thousand blended notes,
While in a grove I sate reclined,
In that sweet mood when pleasant thoughts
Bring sad thoughts to the mind.

To her fair works did Nature link   5
The human soul that through me ran;
And much it griev'd my heart to think
What man has made of man.

Through primrose tufts, in that sweet bower,
The periwinkle trail'd its wreathes;   10
And 'tis my faith that every flower
Enjoys the air it breathes.

The birds around me hopp'd and play'd:
Their thoughts I cannot measure:—
But the least motion which they made,   15
It seem'd a thrill of pleasure.

The budding twigs spread out their fan,
To catch the breezy air;
And I must think, do all I can,
That there was pleasure there.   20

If I these thoughts may not prevent,
If such be of my creed the plan,
Have I not reason to lament
What man has made of man?

SIMON LEE,

THE OLD HUNTSMAN,

With an incident in which he was concerned

In the sweet shire of Cardigan,
Not far from pleasant Ivor-hall,
An Old Man dwells, a little man,
I've heard he once was tall.
Of years he has upon his back,   5
No doubt, a burthen weighty;
He says he is three score and ten,
But others say he's eighty.

A long blue livery-coat has he,
That's fair behind, and fair before;   10
Yet, meet him where you will, you see
At once that he is poor.
Full five and twenty years he lived
A running Huntsman merry;
And, though he has but one eye left,   15
His cheek is like a cherry.

No man like him the horn could sound,
And no man was so full of glee;
To say the least, four counties round
Had heard of Simon Lee;   20
His Master's dead, and no one now
Dwells in the hall of Ivor;
Men, Dogs, and Horses, all are dead;
He is the sole survivor.

And he is lean and he is sick,   25
His dwindled body's half awry;
His ancles they are swoln and thick;
His legs are thin and dry.
When he was young he little knew
Of husbandry or tillage;   30
And now he's forced to work, though weak,
—The weakest in the village.

He all the country could outrun,
Could leave both man and horse behind;
And often, ere the race was done,   35
He reeled and was stone-blind.
And still there's something in the world
At which his heart rejoices;
For when the chiming hounds are out,
He dearly loves their voices!   40

His hunting feats have him bereft
Of his right eye, as you may see:
And then, what limbs those feats have left
To poor old Simon Lee!
He has no son, he has no child,   45
His Wife, an aged woman,
Lives with him, near the waterfall,
Upon the village Common.

Old Ruth works out of doors with him,
And does what Simon cannot do;   50
For she, not over stout of limb,
Is stouter of the two.
And, though you with your utmost skill
From labour could not wean them,
Alas! 'tis very little, all   55
Which they can do between them.

Beside their moss-grown hut of clay,
Not twenty paces from the door,
A scrap of land they have, but they
Are poorest of the poor.   60
This scrap of land he from the heath
Enclosed when he was stronger;
But what avails the land to them,
Which they can till no longer?

Few months of life has he in store,   65
As he to you will tell,
For still, the more he works, the more
His poor old ancles swell.

My gentle Reader, I perceive
How patiently you've waited,   70
And I'm afraid that you expect
Some tale will be related.

O Reader! had you in your mind
Such stores as silent thought can bring,
O gentle Reader! you would find   75
A tale in every thing.
What more I have to say is short,
I hope you'll kindly take it:
It is no tale; but should you think,
Perhaps a tale you'll make it.   80

One summer-day I chanced to see
This Old Man doing all he could
About the root of an old tree,
A stump of rotten wood.
The mattock totter'd in his hand;   85
So vain was his endeavour
That at the root of the old tree
He might have worked for ever.

'You're overtasked, good Simon Lee,
Give me your tool' to him I said;   90
And at the word right gladly he
Received my proffer'd aid.
I struck, and with a single blow
The tangled root I sever'd,
At which the poor Old Man so long   95
And vainly had endeavoured.

The tears into his eyes were brought,
And thanks and praises seemed to run
So fast out of his heart, I thought
They never would have done.   100
—I've heard of hearts unkind, kind deeds
With coldness still returning.
Alas! the gratitude of men
Has oftner left me mourning.

THE NIGHTINGALE,

Written in April, 1798

No cloud, no relique of the sunken day
Distinguishes the West, no long thin slip
Of sullen Light, no obscure trembling hues.
Come, we will rest on this old mossy Bridge!
You see the glimmer of the stream beneath,   5
But hear no murmuring: it flows silently
O'er its soft bed of verdure. All is still,
A balmy night! and tho' the stars be dim,
Yet let us think upon the vernal showers
That gladden the green earth, and we shall find   10
A pleasure in the dimness of the stars.
And hark! the Nightingale begins its song,
'Most musical, most melancholy'* Bird!
A melancholy Bird? O idle thought!
In nature there is nothing melancholy.   15
—But some night-wandering Man, whose heart was pierc'd
With the remembrance of a grievous wrong,
Or slow distemper, or neglected love,
(And so, poor wretch! fill'd all things with himself,
And made all gentle sounds tell back the tale   20
Of his own sorrows) he and such as he
First named these notes a melancholy strain:
And many a poet echoes the conceit;
Poet, who hath been building up the rhyme
When he had better far have stretched his limbs   25
Beside a brook in mossy forest-dell
By sun or moon-light, to the influxes
Of shapes and sounds and shifting elements
Surrendering his whole spirit, of his song
And of his fame forgetful! so his fame   30
Should share in nature's immortality,

---

* '*Most musical, most melancholy.*' This passage in Milton possesses an excellence
far superior to that of mere description: it is spoken in the character of the melancholy
Man, and has therefore a *dramatic* propriety. The Author makes this remark, to rescue
himself from the charge of having alluded with levity to a line in Milton: a charge than
which none could be more painful to him, except perhaps that of having ridiculed his
Bible.

A venerable thing! and so his song
Should make all nature lovelier, and itself
Be lov'd, like nature!—But 'twill not be so;
And youths and maidens most poetical   35
Who lose the deep'ning twilights of the spring
In ball-rooms and hot theatres, they still
Full of meek sympathy must heave their sighs
O'er Philomela's pity-pleading strains.
My Friend, and my Friend's Sister! we have learnt   40
A different lore: we may not thus profane
Nature's sweet voices always full of love
And joyance! 'Tis the merry Nightingale
That crowds, and hurries, and precipitates
With fast thick warble his delicious notes,   45
As he were fearful, that an April night
Would be too short for him to utter forth
His love-chant, and disburthen his full soul
Of all its music! And I know a grove
Of large extent, hard by a castle huge   50
Which the great lord inhabits not: and so
This grove is wild with tangling underwood,
And the trim walks are broken up, and grass,
Thin grass and king-cups grow within the paths.
But never elsewhere in one place I knew   55
So many Nightingales: and far and near
In wood and thicket over the wide grove
They answer and provoke each other's songs—
With skirmish and capricious passagings,
And murmurs musical and swift jug jug   60
And one low piping sound more sweet than all—
Stirring the air with such an harmony,
That should you close your eyes, you might almost
Forget it was not day.

                A most gentle Maid
Who dwelleth in her hospitable home   65
Hard by the Castle, and at latest eve,
(Even like a Lady vow'd and dedicate
To something more than nature in the grove)
Glides thro' the pathways; she knows all their notes,
That gentle Maid! and oft, a moment's space,   70

What time the moon was lost behind a cloud,
Hath heard a pause of silence: till the Moon
Emerging, hath awaken'd earth and sky
With one sensation, and those wakeful Birds
Have all burst forth in choral minstrelsy,   75
As if one quick and sudden Gale had swept
An hundred airy harps! And she hath watch'd
Many a Nightingale perch giddily
On blosmy twig still swinging from the breeze,
And to that motion tune his wanton song,   80
Like tipsy Joy that reels with tossing head.

Farewell, O Warbler! till to-morrow eve,
And you, my friends! farewell, a short farewell!
We have been loitering long and pleasantly
And now for our dear homes.—That strain again!   85
Full fain would it delay me! My dear Babe,
Who, capable of no articulate sound,
Mars all things with his imitative lisp,
How he would place his hand beside his ear,
His little hand, the small forefinger up,   90
And bid us listen! And I deem it wise
To make him Nature's playmate. He knows well
The evening star: and once when he awoke
In most distressful mood (some inward pain
Had made up that strange thing, an infant's dream)   95
I hurried with him to our orchard plot,
And he beholds the moon, and hush'd at once
Suspends his sobs, and laughs most silently,
While his fair eyes that swam with undropt tears
Did glitter in the yellow moon-beam! Well—   100
It is a father's tale. But if that Heaven
Should give me life, his childhood shall grow up
Familiar with these songs, that with the night
He may associate Joy! Once more farewell,
Sweet Nightingale! once more, my friends! farewell.   105

THE IDIOT BOY

'Tis eight o'clock,—a clear March night,
The Moon is up—the Sky is blue,
The Owlet in the moonlight air,
He shouts from nobody knows where;
He lengthens out his lonely shout,　　　　5
Halloo! halloo! a long halloo!

—Why bustle thus about your door,
What means this bustle, Betty Foy?
Why are you in this mighty fret?
And why on horseback have you set　　　10
Him whom you love, your Idiot Boy?

Beneath the Moon that shines so bright,
Till she is tired, let Betty Foy
With girt and stirrup fiddle-faddle;
But wherefore set upon a saddle　　　　15
Him whom she loves, her Idiot Boy?

There's scarce a soul that's out of bed;
Good Betty put him down again;
His lips with joy they burr at you;
But, Betty! what has he to do　　　　20
With stirrup, saddle, or with rein?

The world will say 'tis very idle,
Bethink you of the time of night;
There's not a mother, no not one,
But when she hears what you have done,　　25
Oh! Betty she'll be in a fright.

But Betty's bent on her intent,
For her good neighbour, Susan Gale,
Old Susan, she who dwells alone,
Is sick, and makes a piteous moan,　　　30
As if her very life would fail.

There's not a house within a mile,
No hand to help them in distress:
Old Susan lies a-bed in pain,
And sorely puzzled are the twain,   35
For what she ails they cannot guess.

And Betty's Husband's at the wood,
Where by the week he doth abide,
A Woodman in the distant vale;
There's none to help poor Susan Gale,   40
What must be done? what will betide?

And Betty from the lane has fetched
Her Pony, that is mild and good,
Whether he be in joy or pain,
Feeding at will along the lane,   45
Or bringing faggots from the wood.

And he is all in travelling trim,
And by the moonlight, Betty Foy
Has up upon the saddle set,
The like was never heard of yet,   50
Him whom she loves, her Idiot Boy.

And he must post without delay
Across the bridge that's in the dale,
And by the church, and o'er the down,
To bring a Doctor from the town,   55
Or she will die, old Susan Gale.

There is no need of boot or spur,
There is no need of whip or wand,
For Johnny has his holly-bough,
And with a hurly-burly now   60
He shakes the green bough in his hand.

And Betty o'er and o'er has told
The Boy who is her best delight,
Both what to follow, what to shun,
What do, and what to leave undone,   65
How turn to left, and how to right.

And Betty's most especial charge,
Was, 'Johnny! Johnny! mind that you
Come home again, nor stop at all,
Come home again, whate'er befal,   70
My Johnny do, I pray you do.'

To this did Johnny answer make,
Both with his head, and with his hand,
And proudly shook the bridle too,
And then! his words were not a few,   75
Which Betty well could understand.

And now that Johnny is just going,
Though Betty's in a mighty flurry,
She gently pats the Pony's side,
On which her Idiot Boy must ride,   80
And seems no longer in a hurry.

But when the Pony moved his legs,
Oh! then for the poor Idiot Boy!
For joy he cannot hold the bridle,
For joy his head and heels are idle,   85
He's idle all for very joy.

And while the Pony moves his legs,
In Johnny's left hand you may see,
The green bough's motionless and dead:
The Moon that shines above his head   90
Is not more still and mute than he.

His heart it was so full of glee,
That till full fifty yards were gone,
He quite forgot his holly whip,
And all his skill in horsemanship,   95
Oh! happy, happy, happy John.

And Betty's standing at the door,
And Betty's face with joy o'erflows,
Proud of herself, and proud of him,
She sees him in his travelling trim;   100
How quietly her Johnny goes.

The silence of her Idiot Boy,
What hopes it sends to Betty's heart!
He's at the Guide-post—he turns right,
She watches till he's out of sight,   105
And Betty will not then depart.

Burr, burr—now Johnny's lips they burr,
As loud as any mill, or near it,
Meek as a lamb the Pony moves,
And Johnny makes the noise he loves,   110
And Betty listens, glad to hear it.

Away she hies to Susan Gale:
And Johnny's in a merry tune,
The Owlets hoot, the Owlets curr,
And Johnny's lips they burr, burr, burr,   115
And on he goes beneath the Moon.

His Steed and He right well agree,
For of this Pony there's a rumour,
That should he lose his eyes and ears,
And should he live a thousand years,   120
He never will be out of humour.

But then he is a Horse that thinks!
And when he thinks his pace is slack;
Now, though he knows poor Johnny well,
Yet for his life he cannot tell   125
What he has got upon his back.

So through the moonlight lanes they go,
And far into the moonlight dale,
And by the church, and o'er the down,
To bring a Doctor from the town,   130
To comfort poor old Susan Gale.

And Betty, now at Susan's side,
Is in the middle of her story,
What comfort Johnny soon will bring,
With many a most diverting thing,   135
Of Johnny's wit and Johnny's glory.

And Betty's still at Susan's side:
By this time she's not quite so flurried;
Demure with porringer and plate
She sits, as if in Susan's fate   140
Her life and soul were buried.

But Betty, poor good woman! she,
You plainly in her face may read it,
Could lend out of that moment's store
Five years of happiness or more,   145
To any that might need it.

But yet I guess that now and then
With Betty all was not so well,
And to the road she turns her ears,
And thence full many a sound she hears,   150
Which she to Susan will not tell.

Poor Susan moans, poor Susan groans;
'As sure as there's a moon in heaven,'
Cries Betty, 'he'll be back again;
They'll both be here—'tis almost ten—   155
They'll both be here before eleven.'

Poor Susan moans, poor Susan groans;
The clock gives warning for eleven;
'Tis on the stroke—'If Johnny's near,'
Quoth Betty 'he will soon be here,   160
As sure as there's a moon in heaven.'

The clock is on the stroke of twelve,
And Johnny is not yet in sight,
—The Moon's in heaven, as Betty sees,
But Betty is not quite at ease;   165
And Susan has a dreadful night.

And Betty, half an hour ago,
On Johnny vile reflections cast:
'A little idle sauntering Thing!'
With other names, an endless string,   170
But now that time is gone and past.

And Betty's drooping at the heart,
That happy time all past and gone,
'How can it be he is so late?
The Doctor he has made him wait,   175
Susan! they'll both be here anon.'

And Susan's growing worse and worse,
And Betty's in a sad quandary;
And then there's nobody to say
If she must go or she must stay!   180
—She's in a sad quandary.

The clock is on the stroke of one;
But neither Doctor nor his Guide
Appear along the moonlight road;
There's neither horse nor man abroad,   185
And Betty's still at Susan's side.

And Susan she begins to fear
Of sad mischances not a few,
That Johnny may perhaps be drown'd,
Or lost perhaps, and never found;   190
Which they must both for ever rue.

She prefaced half a hint of this
With, 'God forbid it should be true!'
At the first word that Susan said
Cried Betty, rising from the bed,   195
'Susan, I'd gladly stay with you.

I must be gone, I must away,
Consider, Johnny's but half-wise;
Susan, we must take care of him,
If he is hurt in life or limb'—   200
'Oh God forbid!' poor Susan cries.

'What can I do?' says Betty, going,
'What can I do to ease your pain?
Good Susan tell me, and I'll stay;
I fear you're in a dreadful way,   205
But I shall soon be back again.'

'Nay, Betty, go! good Betty, go!
There's nothing that can ease my pain.'
Then off she hies, but with a prayer
That God poor Susan's life would spare,   210
Till she comes back again.

So, through the moonlight lane she goes,
And far into the moonlight dale;
And how she ran, and how she walked,
And all that to herself she talked,   215
Would surely be a tedious tale.

In high and low, above, below,
In great and small, in round and square,
In tree and tower was Johnny seen,
In bush and brake, in black and green,   220
'Twas Johnny, Johnny, every where.

She's past the bridge that's in the dale,
And now the thought torments her sore,
Johnny perhaps his horse forsook,
To hunt the moon that's in the brook,   225
And never will be heard of more.

And now she's high upon the down,
Alone amid a prospect wide;
There's neither Johnny nor his Horse,
Among the fern or in the gorse;   230
There's neither Doctor nor his Guide.

'Oh saints! what is become of him?
Perhaps he's climbed into an oak,
Where he will stay till he is dead;
Or, sadly he has been misled,   235
And joined the wandering gypsey-folk.

Or him that wicked Pony's carried
To the dark cave, the goblin's hall;
Or in the castle he's pursuing,
Among the ghosts, his own undoing;   240
Or playing with the waterfall.'

At poor old Susan then she railed,
While to the town she posts away;
'If Susan had not been so ill,
Alas! I should have had him still,   245
My Johnny, till my dying day.'

Poor Betty! in this sad distemper,
The Doctor's self would hardly spare,
Unworthy things she talked and wild,
Even he, of cattle the most mild,   250
The Pony had his share.

And now she's got into the town,
And to the Doctor's door she hies;
'Tis silence all on every side;
The town so long, the town so wide,   255
Is silent as the skies.

And now she's at the Doctor's door,
She lifts the knocker, rap, rap, rap;
The Doctor at the casement shews
His glimmering eyes that peep and dose;   260
And one hand rubs his old night-cap.

'Oh Doctor! Doctor! where's my Johnny?'
'I'm here, what is't you want with me?'
'Oh Sir! you know I'm Betty Foy,
And I have lost my poor dear Boy,   265
You know him—him you often see;

He's not so wise as some folks be,'
'The devil take his wisdom!' said
The Doctor, looking somewhat grim,
'What, Woman! should I know of him?'   270
And, grumbling, he went back to bed.

'O woe is me! O woe is me!
Here will I die; here will I die;
I thought to find my Johnny here,
But he is neither far nor near,   275
Oh! what a wretched Mother I!'

She stops, she stands, she looks about,
Which way to turn she cannot tell.
Poor Betty! it would ease her pain
If she had heart to knock again;   280
—The clock strikes three—a dismal knell!

Then up along the town she hies,
No wonder if her senses fail,
This piteous news so much it shock'd her,
She quite forgot to send the Doctor,   285
To comfort poor old Susan Gale.

And now she's high upon the down,
And she can see a mile of road;
'Oh cruel! I'm almost threescore;
Such night as this was ne'er before,   290
There's not a single soul abroad.'

She listens, but she cannot hear
The foot of horse, the voice of man;
The streams with softest sound are flowing,
The grass you almost hear it growing,   295
You hear it now if e'er you can.

The Owlets through the long blue night
Are shouting to each other still:
Fond lovers! yet not quite hob nob,
They lengthen out the tremulous sob,   300
That echoes far from hill to hill.

Poor Betty now has lost all hope,
Her thoughts are bent on deadly sin:
A green-grown pond she just has pass'd,
And from the brink she hurries fast,   305
Lest she should drown herself therein.

And now she sits her down and weeps;
Such tears she never shed before;
'Oh dear, dear Pony! my sweet joy!
Oh carry back my Idiot Boy!   310
And we will ne'er o'erload thee more.'

A thought is come into her head:
'The Pony he is mild and good,
And we have always used him well;
Perhaps he's gone along the dell,   315
And carried Johnny to the wood.'

Then up she springs as if on wings;
She thinks no more of deadly sin;
If Betty fifty ponds should see,
The last of all her thoughts would be,   320
To drown herself therein.

Oh Reader! now that I might tell
What Johnny and his Horse are doing!
What they've been doing all this time,
Oh could I put it into rhyme,   325
A most delightful tale pursuing!

Perhaps, and no unlikely thought!
He with his Pony now doth roam
The cliffs and peaks so high that are,
To lay his hands upon a star,   330
And in his pocket bring it home.

Perhaps he's turned himself about,
His face unto his horse's tail,
And still and mute, in wonder lost,
All like a silent Horseman-Ghost,   335
He travels on along the vale.

And now, perhaps, he's hunting sheep,
A fierce and dreadful hunter he;
Yon valley, that's so trim and green,
In five months' time, should he be seen,   340
A desart wilderness will be.

Perhaps, with head and heels on fire,
And like the very soul of evil,
He's galloping away, away,
And so he'll gallop on for aye,   345
The bane of all that dread the devil.

I to the Muses have been bound
These fourteen years, by strong indentures:
Oh gentle Muses! let me tell
But half of what to him befel,   350
He surely met with strange adventures.

Oh gentle Muses! is this kind?
Why will ye thus my suit repel?
Why of your further aid bereave me?
And can ye thus unfriended leave me;   355
Ye Muses! whom I love so well.

Who's yon, that, near the waterfall,
Which thunders down with headlong force,
Beneath the Moon, yet shining fair,
As careless as if nothing were,   360
Sits upright on a feeding Horse;

Unto his Horse, that's feeding free,
He seems, I think, the rein to give;
Of Moon or Stars he takes no heed;
Of such we in romances read,   365
—'Tis Johnny! Johnny! as I live.

And that's the very Pony too.
Where is she, where is Betty Foy?
She hardly can sustain her fears;
The roaring water-fall she hears,   370
And cannot find her Idiot Boy.

Your Pony's worth his weight in gold,
Then calm your terrors, Betty Foy!
She's coming from among the trees,
And now all full in view she sees   375
Him whom she loves, her Idiot Boy.

And Betty sees the Pony too:
Why stand you thus, good Betty Foy?
It is no goblin, 'tis no ghost,
'Tis he whom you so long have lost,   380
He whom you love, your Idiot Boy.

She looks again—her arms are up—
She screams—she cannot move for joy;
She darts as with a torrent's force,
She almost has o'erturned the Horse,   385
And fast she holds her Idiot Boy.

And Johnny burrs, and laughs aloud,
Whether in cunning or in joy,
I cannot tell; but while he laughs,
Betty a drunken pleasure quaffs,   390
To hear again her Idiot Boy.

And now she's at the Pony's tail,
And now she's at the Pony's head,
On that side now, and now on this,
And almost stifled with her bliss,   395
A few sad tears does Betty shed.

She kisses o'er and o'er again,
Him whom she loves, her Idiot Boy,
She's happy here, she's happy there,
She is uneasy every where;   400
Her limbs are all alive with joy.

She pats the Pony, where or when
She knows not, happy Betty Foy!
The little Pony glad may be,
But he is milder far than she,   405
You hardly can perceive his joy.

'Oh! Johnny, never mind the Doctor;
You've done your best, and that is all.'
She took the reins, when this was said,
And gently turned the Pony's head   410
From the loud water-fall.

By this the stars were almost gone,
The moon was setting on the hill,
So pale you scarcely looked at her:
The little birds began to stir,   415
Though yet their tongues were still.

The Pony, Betty, and her Boy,
Wind slowly through the woody dale;
And who is she, be-times abroad,
That hobbles up the steep rough road?   420
Who is it, but old Susan Gale?

Long Susan lay deep lost in thought,
And many dreadful fears beset her,
Both for her Messenger and Nurse;
And as her mind grew worse and worse,   425
Her body it grew better.

She turned, she toss'd herself in bed,
On all sides doubts and terrors met her;
Point after point did she discuss;
And while her mind was fighting thus,   430
Her body still grew better.

'Alas! what is become of them?
These fears can never be endured,
I'll to the wood.'—The word scarce said,
Did Susan rise up from her bed,   435
As if by magic cured.

Away she posts up hill and down,
And to the wood at length is come,
She spies her Friends, she shouts a greeting;
Oh me! it is a merry meeting,   440
As ever was in Christendom.

The Owls have hardly sung their last,
While our four Travellers homeward wend;
The Owls have hooted all night long,
And with the Owls began my song,   445
And with the Owls must end.

For, while they all were travelling home,
Cried Betty, 'Tell us Johnny, do,
Where all this long night you have been,
What you have heard, what you have seen,   450
And Johnny, mind you tell us true.'

Now Johnny all night long had heard
The Owls in tuneful concert strive;
No doubt too he the Moon had seen;
For in the moonlight he had been   455
From eight o'clock till five.

And thus to Betty's question, he,
Made answer, like a Traveller bold,
(His very words I give to you,)
'The Cocks did crow to-whoo, to-whoo,   460
And the Sun did shine so cold.'
—Thus answered Johnny in his glory,
And that was all his travel's story.

LOVE

All Thoughts, all Passions, all Delights,
Whatever stirs this mortal Frame,
All are but Ministers of Love,
    And feed his sacred flame.

Oft in my waking dreams do I°   5
Live o'er again that happy hour,
When midway on the Mount I lay
    Beside the Ruin'd Tower.

The Moonshine stealing o'er the scene
Had blended with the Lights of Eve;°   10
And she was there, my Hope, my Joy,
    My own dear Genevieve!

She lean'd against the Armed Man
The Statue of the Armed Knight:
She stood and listen'd to my Harp   15
    Amid the ling'ring Light.

Few Sorrows hath she of her own,
My Hope, my Joy, my Genevieve!
She loves me best, whene'er I sing
    The Songs, that make her grieve.   20

I play'd a soft and doleful Air,
I sang an old and moving Story—
An old rude Song that fitted well
    The Ruin wild and hoary.

She listen'd with a flitting Blush,   25
With downcast Eyes and modest Grace;
For well she knew, I could not choose
    But gaze upon her Face.

I told her of the Knight, that wore
Upon his Shield a burning Brand;   30
And that for ten long Years he woo'd
    The Lady of the Land.

I told her, how he pin'd: and, ah!
The low, the deep, the pleading tone,
With which I sang another's Love,   35
    Interpreted my own.

She listen'd with a flitting Blush,
With downcast Eyes and modest Grace;
And she forgave me, that I gaz'd
    Too fondly on her Face!   40

But when I told the cruel scorn
Which craz'd this bold and lovely Knight,
And that he cross'd the mountain woods
    Nor rested day nor night;

That sometimes from the savage Den,   45
And sometimes from the darksome Shade,
And sometimes starting up at once
    In green and sunny Glade,

There came, and look'd him in the face,
An Angel beautiful and bright;   50
And that he knew, it was a Fiend,
    This miserable Knight!

And how, unknowing what he did,
He leapt amid a murd'rous Band,

And sav'd from Outrage worse than Death   55
   The Lady of the Land;

And how she wept and clasp'd his knees,
And how she tended him in vain—
And ever strove to expiate
   The Scorn, that craz'd his Brain: 60

And that she nurs'd him in a Cave;
And how his Madness went away
When on the yellow forest leaves
   A dying Man he lay;

His dying words—but when I reach'd   65
That tenderest strain of all the Ditty,
My falt'ring Voice and pausing Harp
   Disturb'd her Soul with Pity!

All Impulses of Soul and Sense
Had thrill'd my guileless Genevieve,   70
The Music, and the doleful Tale,
   The rich and balmy Eve;

And Hopes, and Fears that kindle Hope,
An undistinguishable Throng!
And gentle Wishes long subdued,   75
   Subdued and cherish'd long!

She wept with pity and delight,
She blush'd with love and maiden shame;
And, like the murmur of a dream,
   I heard her breathe my name.   80

Her bosom heav'd—she stepp'd aside;
As conscious of my Look, she stepp'd—
Then suddenly with timorous eye
   She fled to me and wept.

She half inclosed me with her arms,   85
She press'd me with a meek embrace;
And bending back her head look'd up,
   And gaz'd upon my face.

'Twas partly Love, and partly Fear,
And partly 'twas a bashful Art   90
That I might rather feel than see
    The Swelling of her Heart.

I calm'd her fears; and she was calm,
And told her love with virgin Pride.
And so I won my Genevieve,   95
    My bright and beauteous Bride!

THE MAD MOTHER

Her eyes are wild, her head is bare,
The sun has burnt her coal-black hair,
Her eye-brows have a rusty stain,
And she came far from over the main.
She has a baby on her arm,   5
Or else she were alone;
And underneath the hay-stack warm,
And on the green-wood stone,
She talked and sung the woods among;
And it was in the English tongue.   10

'Sweet Babe! they say that I am mad,
But nay, my heart is far too glad;
And I am happy when I sing
Full many a sad and doleful thing:
Then, lovely Baby, do not fear!   15
I pray thee have no fear of me,
But, safe as in a cradle, here
My lovely Baby! thou shalt be,
To thee I know too much I owe;
I cannot work thee any woe.   20

A fire was once within my brain;
And in my head a dull, dull pain;
And fiendish faces one, two, three,
Hung at my breasts, and pulled at me.
But then there came a sight of joy;   25
It came at once to do me good;

I waked, and saw my little Boy,
My little Boy of flesh and blood;
Oh joy for me that sight to see!
For he was here, and only he.   30

Suck, little Babe, oh suck again!
It cools my blood; it cools my brain;
Thy lips I feel them, Baby! they
Draw from my heart the pain away.
Oh! press me with thy little hand;   35
It loosens something at my chest;
About that tight and deadly band
I feel thy little fingers press'd.
The breeze I see is in the tree;
It comes to cool my Babe and me.   40

Oh! love me, love me, little Boy!
Thou art thy Mother's only joy;
And do not dread the waves below,
When o'er the sea-rock's edge we go;
The high crag cannot work me harm,   45
Nor leaping torrents when they howl;
The Babe I carry on my arm,
He saves for me my precious soul;
Then happy lie, for blest am I;
Without me my sweet Babe would die.   50

Then do not fear, my Boy! for thee
Bold as a lion I will be;
And I will always be thy guide,
Through hollow snows and rivers wide.
I'll build an Indian bower; I know   55
The leaves that make the softest bed:
And, if from me thou wilt not go,
But still be true 'till I am dead,
My pretty thing! then thou shalt sing
As merry as the birds in spring.   60

Thy Father cares not for my breast,
'Tis thine, sweet Baby, there to rest:

'Tis all thine own! and, if its hue
Be changed, that was so fair to view,
'Tis fair enough for thee, my dove!   65
My beauty, little Child, is flown;
But thou wilt live with me in love,
And what if my poor cheek be brown?
'Tis well for me, thou canst not see
How pale and wan it else would be.   70

Dread not their taunts, my little life!
I am thy Father's wedded Wife;
And underneath the spreading tree
We two will live in honesty.
If his sweet Boy he could forsake,   75
With me he never would have stay'd:
From him no harm my Babe can take,
But he, poor Man! is wretched made,
And every day we two will pray
For him that's gone and far away.   80

I'll teach my Boy the sweetest things;
I'll teach him how the owlet sings.
My little Babe! thy lips are still,
And thou hast almost suck'd thy fill.
—Where art thou gone my own dear Child?   85
What wicked looks are those I see?
Alas! alas! that look so wild,
It never, never came from me:
If thou art mad, my pretty lad,
Then I must be for ever sad.   90

Oh! smile on me, my little lamb!
For I thy own dear Mother am.
My love for thee has well been tried:
I've sought thy Father far and wide.
I know the poisons of the shade,   95
I know the earth-nuts fit for food;
Then, pretty dear, be not afraid;
We'll find thy Father in the wood.
Now laugh and be gay, to the woods away!
And there, my babe; we'll live for aye.'   100

THE ANCIENT MARINER,

A POET'S REVERIE

I

It is an ancient Mariner,
    And he stoppeth one of three:
'By thy long grey beard and thy glittering eye
    Now wherefore stoppest me?

The Bridegroom's doors are open'd wide   5
    And I am next of kin;
The Guests are met, the Feast is set,—
    May'st hear the merry din.'

But still he holds the wedding guest—
    There was a Ship, quoth he—   10
'Nay, if thou'st got a laughsome tale,
    Mariner! come with me.'

He holds him with his skinny hand,
    Quoth he, there was a Ship—
'Now get thee hence, thou grey-beard Loon!   15
    Or my Staff shall make thee skip.'

He holds him with his glittering eye—
    The wedding guest stood still
And listens like a three year's child;
    The Mariner hath his will.   20

The wedding-guest sate on a stone,
    He cannot chuse but hear:
And thus spake on that ancient man,
    The bright-eyed Mariner.

The Ship was cheer'd, the Harbour clear'd—   25
    Merrily did we drop
Below the Kirk, below the Hill,
    Below the Light-house top.

The Sun came up upon the left,
  Out of the Sea came he: 30
And he shone bright, and on the right
  Went down into the sea.

Higher and higher every day,
  Till over the mast at noon—
The wedding-guest here beat his breast,   35
  For he heard the loud bassoon.

The Bride hath pac'd into the Hall,
  Red as a rose is she;
Nodding their heads before her goes
  The merry Minstralsy.   40

The wedding-guest he beat his breast,
  Yet he cannot chuse but hear:
And thus spake on that ancient Man,
  The bright-eyed Mariner.

But now the Northwind came more fierce,   45
  There came a Tempest strong!
And Southward still for days and weeks
  Like Chaff we drove along.

And now there came both Mist and Snow,
  And it grew wond'rous cold;   50
And Ice mast-high came floating by
  As green as Emerald.

And thro' the drifts the snowy clifts
  Did send a dismal sheen;
Nor shapes of men nor beasts we ken—   55
  The Ice was all between.

The Ice was here, the Ice was there,
  The Ice was all around:
It crack'd and growl'd, and roar'd and howl'd—
  A wild and ceaseless sound.   60

At length did cross an Albatross,
  Thorough the Fog it came;

As if it had been a Christian Soul,
    We hail'd it in God's name.

The Mariners gave it biscuit-worms,   65
    And round and round it flew:
The Ice did split with a Thunder-fit;
    The Helmsman steer'd us thro'.

And a good south wind sprung up behind,
    The Albatross did follow;   70
And every day for food or play
    Came to the Mariner's hollo!

In mist or cloud on mast or shroud
    It perch'd for vespers nine,
Whiles all the night thro' fog-smoke white   75
    Glimmer'd the white moon-shine.

'God save thee, ancient Mariner!
    From the fiends that plague thee thus—
Why look'st thou so?'—with my cross bow
    I shot the Albatross.   80

II

The Sun now rose upon the right,
    Out of the Sea came he;
Still hid in mist; and on the left
    Went down into the Sea.

And the good south wind still blew behind,   85
    But no sweet Bird did follow
Nor any day for food or play
    Came to the Mariner's hollo!

And I had done an hellish thing
    And it would work 'em woe: 90
For all averr'd, I had kill'd the Bird
    That made the Breeze to blow.

Nor dim nor red, like an Angel's head,
    The glorious Sun uprist:

Then all averr'd, I had kill'd the Bird   95
    That brought the fog and mist.
'Twas right, said they, such birds to slay
    That bring the fog and mist.

The breezes blew, the white foam flew,
    The furrow follow'd free: 100
We were the first that ever burst
    Into that silent sea.

Down dropt the breeze, the Sails dropt down,
    'Twas sad as sad could be,
And we did speak only to break   105
    The silence of the Sea.

All in a hot and copper sky
    The bloody sun at noon,
Right up above the mast did stand,
    No bigger than the moon.   110

Day after day, day after day,
    We stuck, nor breath nor motion,
As idle as a painted Ship
    Upon a painted Ocean.

Water, water, every where,   115
    And all the boards did shrink;
Water, water, every where,
    Nor any drop to drink.

The very deeps did rot: O Christ!
    That ever this should be!   120
Yea, slimy things did crawl with legs
    Upon the slimy Sea.

About, about, in reel and rout
    The Death-fires danc'd at night;
The water, like a witch's oils,   125
    Burnt green and blue and white.

And some in dreams assured were
    Of the Spirit that plagued us so:

Nine fathom deep he had follow'd us
  From the Land of Mist and Snow.   130

And every tongue thro' utter drouth
  Was wither'd at the root;
We could not speak no more than if
  We had been choked with soot.

Ah well-a-day! what evil looks   135
  Had I from old and young;
Instead of the Cross the Albatross
  About my neck was hung.

III

So past a weary time; each throat
  Was parch'd, and glaz'd each eye,   140
When, looking westward, I beheld
  A something in the sky.

At first it seem'd a little speck
  And then it seem'd a mist:
It mov'd and mov'd, and took at last   145
  A certain shape, I wist.

A speck, a mist, a shape, I wist!
  And still it ner'd and ner'd;
And, as if it dodg'd a water-sprite,
  It plung'd and tack'd and veer'd.   150

With throat unslack'd, with black lips bak'd
  We could nor laugh nor wail;
Thro' utter drouth all dumb we stood
Till I bit my arm and suck'd the blood,
  And cry'd, A sail! a sail!   155

With throat unslack'd, with black lips bak'd
  Agape they heard me call:
Gramercy! they for joy did grin
And all at once their breath drew in
  As they were drinking all.   160

See! See! (I cry'd) she tacks no more!
　Hither to work us weal
Without a breeze, without a tide
　She steddies with upright keel!

The western wave was all a flame.   165
　The day was well nigh done!
Almost upon the western wave
Rested the broad bright Sun;
When that strange shape drove suddenly
　Betwixt us and the Sun.   170

And strait the Sun was fleck'd with bars
　(Heaven's Mother send us grace)
As if thro' a dungeon grate he peer'd
　With broad and burning face.

Alas! (thought I, and my heart beat loud)   175
　How fast she neres and neres!
Are those *her* Sails that glance in the Sun
　Like restless gossameres?

Are those *her* Ribs, thro' which the Sun
　Did peer, as thro' a grate?   180
And are those two all, all her crew,
　That Woman, and her Mate?

His bones were black with many a crack,
　All black and bare, I ween;
Jet-black and bare, save where with rust   185
Of mouldy damps and charnel crust
　They were patch'd with purple and green.

Her lips were red, *her* looks were free,
　Her locks were yellow as gold:
Her skin was white as leprosy,   190
And she was far liker Death than he;
　Her flesh made the still air cold.

The naked Hulk alongside came
　And the Twain were playing dice;

'The Game is done! I've won, I've won!'   195
   Quoth she, and whistled thrice.

A gust of wind sterte up behind
   And whistled thro' his bones;
Thro' the hole of his eyes and the hole of his mouth
   Half whistles and half-groans.   200

With never a whisper in the Sea
   Off darts the Spectre-ship;
While clombe above the Eastern bar
The horned Moon, with one bright Star
   Almost between the tips.   205

One after one by the horned Moon
   (Listen, O Stranger! to me)
Each turn'd his face with a ghastly pang
   And curs'd me with his ee.

Four times fifty living men,   210
   With never a sigh or groan,
With heavy thump, a lifeless lump
   They dropp'd down one by one.

Their souls did from their bodies fly,—
   They fled to bliss or woe;   215
And every soul it pass'd me by,
   Like the whiz of my Cross-bow.

IV

'I fear thee, ancient Mariner!
   I fear thy skinny hand;
And thou art long and lank and brown   220
   As is the ribb'd Sea-sand.

I fear thee and thy glittering eye
   And thy skinny hand so brown'—
Fear not, fear not, thou wedding guest!
   This body dropt not down.   225

Alone, alone, all all alone,
   Alone on the wide wide Sea;

And Christ would take no pity on
   My soul in agony.

The many men so beautiful,   230
   And they all dead did lie!
And a million million slimy things
   Liv'd on—and so did I.

I look'd upon the rotting Sea,
   And drew my eyes away;   235
I look'd upon the ghastly deck,
   And there the dead men lay.

I look'd to Heaven, and try'd to pray;
   But or ever a prayer had gusht,
A wicked whisper came and made   240
   My heart as dry as dust.

I clos'd my lids and kept them close,
   Till the balls like pulses beat;
For the sky and the sea, and the sea and the sky
Lay like a load on my weary eye,   245
   And the dead were at my feet.

The cold sweat melted from their limbs,
   Nor rot, nor reek did they;
The look with which they look'd on me,
   Had never pass'd away.   250

An orphan's curse would drag to Hell
   A spirit from on high:
But O! more horrible than that
   Is the curse in a dead man's eye!
Seven days, seven nights I saw that curse,   255
   And yet I could not die.

The moving Moon went up the sky
   And no where did abide:
Softly she was going up
   And a star or two beside—   260

Her beams bemock'd the sultry main
    Like April hoar-frost spread;
But where the Ship's huge shadow lay,
The charmed water burnt alway
    A still and awful red.   265

Beyond the shadow of the ship
    I watch'd the water-snakes:
They mov'd in tracks of shining white;
And when they rear'd, the elfish light
    Fell off in hoary flakes.   270

Within the shadow of the ship
    I watch'd their rich attire:
Blue, glossy green, and velvet black
They coil'd and swam; and every track
    Was a flash of golden fire.   275

O happy living things! no tongue
    Their beauty might declare:
A spring of love gusht from my heart,
    And I bless'd them unaware!
Sure my kind saint took pity on me,   280
    And I bless'd them unaware.

The self-same moment I could pray;
    And from my neck so free
The Albatross fell off, and sank
    Like lead into the sea.   285

V

O sleep, it is a gentle thing
    Belov'd from pole to pole!
To Mary-queen the praise be given
She sent the gentle sleep from heaven
    That slid into my soul.   290

The silly buckets on the deck
    That had so long remain'd,
I dreamt that they were fill'd with dew
    And when I awoke it rain'd.

My lips were wet, my throat was cold,   295
   My garments all were dank;
Sure I had drunken in my dreams
   And still my body drank.

I mov'd and could not feel my limbs,
   I was so light, almost   300
I thought that I had died in sleep,
   And was a blessed Ghost.

And soon I heard a roaring wind,
   It did not come anear;
But with its sound it shook the sails   305
   That were so thin and sere.

The upper air burst into life
   And a hundred fire-flags sheen
To and fro they were hurried about;
And to and fro, and in and out   310
   The wan stars danc'd between.

And the coming wind did roar more loud;
   And the sails did sigh like sedge:
And the rain pour'd down from one black cloud
   The moon was at its edge.   315

The thick black cloud was cleft, and still
   The Moon was at its side:
Like waters shot from some high crag,
The lightning fell with never a jag
   A river steep and wide.   320

The loud wind never reach'd the Ship,
   Yet now the Ship mov'd on!
Beneath the lightning and the moon
   The dead men gave a groan.

They groan'd, they stirr'd, they all uprose,   325
   Nor spake, nor mov'd their eyes:
It had been strange, even in a dream
   To have seen those dead men rise.

The helmsman steer'd, the ship mov'd on;
   Yet never a breeze up-blew;   330
The Mariners all 'gan work the ropes,
   Where they were wont to do:
They rais'd their limbs like lifeless tools—
   We were a ghastly crew.

The body of my brother's son   335
   Stood by me knee to knee:
The body and I pull'd at one rope,
   But he said nought to me.

'I fear thee, ancient Mariner!'
   Be calm, thou wedding guest!   340
'Twas not those souls, that fled in pain,
Which to their corses came again,
   But a troop of Spirits blest:

For when it dawn'd—they dropp'd their arms,
   And cluster'd round the mast: 345
Sweet sounds rose slowly thro' their mouths
   And from their bodies pass'd.

Around, around, flew each sweet sound,
   Then darted to the sun:
Slowly the sounds came back again   350
   Now mix'd, now one by one.

Sometimes a dropping from the sky
   I heard the Sky-lark sing;
Sometimes all little birds that are
How they seem'd to fill the sea and air   355
   With their sweet jargoning.

And now 'twas like all instruments,
   Now like a lonely flute;
And now it is an angel's song
   That makes the heavens be mute.   360

It ceas'd: yet still the sails made on
   A pleasant noise till noon,

A noise like of a hidden brook
  In the leafy month of June,
That to the sleeping woods all night   365
  Singeth a quiet tune.

Till noon we silently sail'd on
  Yet never a breeze did breathe:
Slowly and smoothly went the Ship
  Mov'd onward from beneath.   370

Under the keel nine fathom deep
  From the land of mist and snow
The spirit slid: and it was He
  That made the Ship to go.
The sails at noon left off their tune   375
  And the Ship stood still also.

The sun right up above the mast
  Had fix'd her to the ocean:
But in a minute she 'gan stir
  With a short uneasy motion—   380
Backwards and forwards half her length
  With a short uneasy motion.

Then, like a pawing horse let go,
  She made a sudden bound:
It flung the blood into my head,   385
  And I fell into a swound.

How long in that same fit I lay,
  I have not to declare;
But ere my living life return'd,
  I heard and in my soul discern'd   390
  Two voices in the air.

'Is it he?' quoth one, 'Is this the man?
  By him who died on cross,
With his cruel bow he lay'd full low
  The harmless Albatross.   395

The spirit who 'bideth by himself
  In the land of mist and snow,

He lov'd the bird that lov'd the man
  Who shot him with his bow.'

The other was a softer voice,   400
  As soft as honey-dew:
Quoth he 'the man hath penance done,
  And penance more will do.'

VI

FIRST VOICE

'But tell me, tell me! speak again,
  Thy soft response renewing—   405
What makes that ship drive on so fast?
  What is the Ocean doing?'

SECOND VOICE

'Still as a Slave before his Lord,
  The Ocean hath no blast:
His great bright eye most silently   410
  Up to the moon is cast—

If he may know which way to go,
  For she guides him smooth or grim.
See, brother, see! how graciously
  She looketh down on him.'   415

FIRST VOICE

'But why drives on that ship so fast
  Without or wave or wind?'

SECOND VOICE

'The air is cut away before,
  And closes from behind.

Fly, brother, fly! more high, more high,   420
  Or we shall be belated:
For slow and slow that ship will go,
  When the Mariner's trance is abated.'

I woke, and we were sailing on
  As in a gentle weather: 425

'Twas night, calm night, the moon was high;
   The dead men stood together.

All stood together on the deck,
   For a charnel-dungeon fitter:
All fix'd on me their stony eyes   430
   That in the moon did glitter.

The pang, the curse, with which they died,
   Had never pass'd away;
I could not draw my eyes from theirs
   Nor turn them up to pray.   435

And now this spell was snapt: once more
   I view'd the ocean green,
And look'd far forth, yet little saw
   Of what had else been seen.

Like one, that on a lonesome road   440
   Doth walk in fear and dread,
And having once turn'd round, walks on
   And turns no more his head:
Because he knows, a frightful fiend
   Doth close behind him tread.   445

But soon there breath'd a wind on me,
   Nor sound nor motion made:
Its path was not upon the sea
   In ripple or in shade.

It rais'd my hair, it fann'd my cheek,   450
   Like a meadow-gale of spring—
It mingled strangely with my fears,
   Yet it felt like a welcoming.

Swiftly, swiftly flew the ship
   Yet she sail'd softly too: 455
Sweetly, sweetly blew the breeze—
   On me alone it blew.

O dream of joy! is this indeed
   The light-house top I see?
Is this the Hill? Is this the Kirk?   460
   Is this mine own countrée?

We drifted o'er the Harbour-bar,
   And I with sobs did pray—
'O let me be awake, my God!
   Or let me sleep alway!'   465

The harbour-bay was clear as glass,
   So smoothly it was strewn!
And on the bay the moonlight lay,
   And the shadow of the moon.

The rock shone bright, the kirk no less   470
   That stands above the rock:
The moonlight steep'd in silentness
   The steady weathercock.

And the bay was white with silent light,
   Till rising from the same   475
Full many shapes, that shadows were,
   In crimson colours came.

A little distance from the prow
   Those crimson shadows were:
I turn'd my eyes upon the deck—   480
   O Christ! what saw I there?

Each corse lay flat, lifeless and flat;
   And by the Holy rood
A man all light, a seraph-man,
   On every corse there stood.   485

This seraph-band, each wav'd his hand:
   It was a heavenly sight:
They stood as signals to the land,
   Each one a lovely light:

This seraph-band, each wav'd his hand,   490
   No voice did they impart—

No voice; but O! the silence sank,
  Like music on my heart.

But soon I heard the dash of oars,
  I heard the pilot's cheer: 495
My head was turn'd perforce away
  And I saw a boat appear.

The pilot, and the pilot's boy
  I heard them coming fast:
Dear Lord in Heaven! it was a joy,   500
  The dead men could not blast.

I saw a third—I heard his voice:
  It is the Hermit good!
He singeth loud his godly hymns
  That he makes in the wood.   505
He'll shrieve my soul, he'll wash away
  The Albatross's blood.

VII

This Hermit good lives in that wood
  Which slopes down to the Sea.
How loudly his sweet voice he rears!   510
He loves to talk with Mariners
  That come from a far countrée.

He kneels at morn and noon and eve—
  He hath a cushion plump:
It is the moss that wholly hides   515
  The rotted old Oak-stump.

The Skiff-boat ner'd: I heard them talk,
  'Why, this is strange, I trow!
Where are those lights so many and fair
  That signal made but now?'   520

'Strange, by my faith!' the Hermit said—
  'And they answer'd not our cheer.
The planks look warp'd, and see those sails
  How thin they are and sere!

I never saw aught like to them   525
   Unless perchance it were

The skeletons of leaves that lag
   My forest brook along:
When the Ivy-tod is heavy with snow,
And the Owlet whoops to the wolf below   530
   That eats the she-wolf's young.'

'Dear Lord! it has a fiendish look'—
   (The Pilot made reply)
'I am a-fear'd.'—'Push on, push on!'
   Said the Hermit cheerily.   535

The Boat came closer to the Ship,
   But I nor spake nor stirr'd!
The Boat came close beneath the Ship,
   And strait a sound was heard!

Under the water it rumbled on,   540
   Still louder and more dread:
It reach'd the Ship, it split the bay;
   The Ship went down like lead.

Stunn'd by that loud and dreadful sound,
   Which sky and ocean smote: 545
Like one that hath been seven days drown'd
   My body lay afloat:
But, swift as dreams, myself I found
   Within the Pilot's boat.

Upon the whirl, where sank the Ship,   550
   The boat spun round and round,
And all was still, save that the hill
   Was telling of the sound.

I mov'd my lips: the Pilot shriek'd
   And fell down in a fit.   555
The Holy Hermit rais'd his eyes
   And pray'd where he did sit.

I took the oars: the Pilot's boy,
    Who now doth crazy go,
Laugh'd loud and long, and all the while   560
    His eyes went to and fro,
'Ha! ha!' quoth he—'full plain I see,
    The devil knows how to row.'

And now all in mine own countrée
    I stood on the firm land!   565
The Hermit stepp'd forth from the boat,
    And scarcely he could stand.

'O shrieve me, shrieve me, holy Man!'
    The Hermit cross'd his brow—
'Say quick,' quoth he, 'I bid thee say   570
    What manner man art thou?'

Forthwith this frame of mind was wrench'd
    With a woeful agony,
Which forc'd me to begin my tale
    And then it left me free.   575

Since then at an uncertain hour,
    That agony returns;
And till my ghastly tale is told
    This heart within me burns.

I pass, like night, from land to land;   580
    I have strange power of speech;
The moment that his face I see
I know the man that must hear me;
    To him my tale I teach.

What loud uproar bursts from that door!   585
    The Wedding-guests are there;
But in the Garden-bower the Bride
    And Bride-maids singing are;
And hark the little Vesper-bell
    Which biddeth me to prayer.   590

O Wedding-guest! this soul hath been
    Alone on a wide wide sea:

So lonely 'twas, that God himself
    Scarce seemed there to be.

O sweeter than the Marriage-feast,   595
    'Tis sweeter far to me
To walk together to the Kirk
    With a goodly company.

To walk together to the Kirk
    And all together pray,   600
While each to his great father bends,
Old men, and babes, and loving friends,
    And Youths, and Maidens gay.

Farewell, farewell! but this I tell
    To thee, thou wedding-guest!   605
He prayeth well who loveth well
    Both man and bird and beast.

He prayeth best who loveth best
    All things both great and small:
For the dear God, who loveth us,   610
    He made and loveth all.

The Mariner, whose eye is bright,
    Whose beard with age is hoar,
Is gone; and now the wedding-guest
    Turn'd from the bridegroom's door.   615

He went, like one that hath been stunn'd
    And is of sense forlorn:
A sadder and a wiser man
    He rose the morrow morn.

LINES

*Written a few miles above TINTERN ABBEY, on revisiting
the banks of the WYE during a Tour. July 13, 1798.*

Five years have passed; five summers, with the length
Of five long winters! and again I hear

These waters, rolling from their mountain-springs
With a sweet inland murmur.*——Once again
Do I behold these steep and lofty cliffs,   5
Which on a wild secluded scene impress
Thoughts of more deep seclusion; and connect
The landscape with the quiet of the sky.
The day is come when I again repose
Here, under this dark sycamore, and view   10
These plots of cottage ground, these orchard-tufts,
Which, at this season, with their unripe fruits,
Are clad in one green hue, and lose themselves
Among the woods and copses, nor disturb
The wild green landscape. Once again I see   15
These hedge-rows, hardly hedge-rows, little lines
Of sportive wood run wild; these pastoral farms
Green to the very door; and wreathes of smoke
Sent up, in silence, from among the trees,
With some uncertain notice, as might seem,   20
Of vagrant Dwellers in the houseless woods,
Or of some Hermit's cave, where by his fire
The Hermit sits alone.

                              Though absent long,
These forms of beauty have not been to me,
As is a landscape to a blind man's eye: 25
But oft, in lonely rooms, and mid the din
Of towns and cities, I have owed to them,
In hours of weariness, sensations sweet,
Felt in the blood, and felt along the heart,
And passing even into my purer mind,   30
With tranquil restoration:——feelings too
Of unremembered pleasure: such, perhaps,
As may have had no trivial influence
On that best portion of a good man's life;
His little, nameless, unremembered acts   35
Of kindness and of love. Nor less, I trust,
To them I may have owed another gift,
Of aspect more sublime; that blessed mood,
In which the burthen of the mystery,

* The river is not affected by the tides a few miles above Tintern.

In which the heavy and the weary weight   40
Of all this unintelligible world
Is lighten'd:—that serene and blessed mood,
In which the affections gently lead us on,
Until, the breath of this corporeal frame,
And even the motion of our human blood   45
Almost suspended, we are laid asleep
In body, and become a living soul:
While with an eye made quiet by the power
Of harmony, and the deep power of joy,
We see into the life of things.   50

            If this
Be but a vain belief, yet, oh! how oft,
In darkness, and amid the many shapes
Of joyless day-light; when the fretful stir
Unprofitable, and the fever of the world,
Have hung upon the beatings of my heart,   55
How oft, in spirit, have I turned to thee
O sylvan Wye! Thou wanderer through the woods,
How often has my spirit turned to thee!

And now, with gleams of half-extinguish'd thought,
With many recognitions dim and faint,   60
And somewhat of a sad perplexity,
The picture of the mind revives again:
While here I stand, not only with the sense
Of present pleasure, but with pleasing thoughts
That in this moment there is life and food   65
For future years. And so I dare to hope
Though changed, no doubt, from what I was, when first
I came among these hills; when like a roe
I bounded o'er the mountains, by the sides
Of the deep rivers, and the lonely streams,   70
Wherever nature led: more like a man
Flying from something that he dreads, than one
Who sought the thing he loved. For nature then
(The coarser pleasures of my boyish days,
And their glad animal movements all gone by,)   75
To me was all in all.—I cannot paint
What then I was. The sounding cataract

Haunted me like a passion: the tall rock,
The mountain, and the deep and gloomy wood,
Their colours and their forms, were then to me   80
An appetite: a feeling and a love,
That had no need of a remoter charm,
By thought supplied, or any interest
Unborrowed from the eye.—That time is past,
And all its aching joys are now no more,   85
And all its dizzy raptures. Not for this
Faint I, nor mourn nor murmur; other gifts
Have followed, for such loss, I would believe,
Abundant recompence. For I have learned
To look on nature, not as in the hour   90
Of thoughtless youth, but hearing oftentimes
The still, sad music of humanity,
Nor harsh nor grating, though of ample power
To chasten and subdue. And I have felt
A presence that disturbs me with the joy   95
Of elevated thoughts; a sense sublime
Of something far more deeply interfused,
Whose dwelling is the light of setting suns,
And the round ocean, and the living air,
And the blue sky, and in the mind of man,   100
A motion and a spirit, that impels
All thinking things, all objects of all thought,
And rolls through all things. Therefore am I still
A lover of the meadows and the woods,
And mountains; and of all that we behold   105
From this green earth; of all the mighty world
Of eye and ear, both what they half create,*
And what perceive; well pleased to recognize
In nature and the language of the sense,
The anchor of my purest thoughts, the nurse,   110
The guide, the guardian of my heart, and soul
Of all my moral being.

                              Nor, perchance,
If I were not thus taught, should I the more

* This line has a close resemblance to an admirable line of Young, the exact expression of which I cannot recollect.

Suffer my genial spirits to decay:
For thou art with me, here, upon the banks   115
Of this fair river; thou, my dearest Friend,
My dear, dear Friend, and in thy voice I catch
The language of my former heart, and read
My former pleasures in the shooting lights
Of thy wild eyes. Oh! yet a little while   120
May I behold in thee what I was once,
My dear, dear Sister! And this prayer I make,
Knowing that Nature never did betray
The heart that loved her; 'tis her privilege,
Through all the years of this our life, to lead   125
From joy to joy: for she can so inform
The mind that is within us, so impress
With quietness and beauty, and so feed
With lofty thoughts, that neither evil tongues,
Rash judgments, nor the sneers of selfish men,   130
Nor greetings where no kindness is, nor all
The dreary intercourse of daily life,
Shall e'er prevail against us, or disturb
Our chearful faith that all which we behold
Is full of blessings. Therefore let the moon   135
Shine on thee in thy solitary walk;
And let the misty mountain winds be free
To blow against thee: and, in after years,
When these wild ecstasies shall be matured
Into a sober pleasure, when thy mind   140
Shall be a mansion for all lovely forms,
Thy memory be as a dwelling-place
For all sweet sounds and harmonies; Oh! then,
If solitude, or fear, or pain, or grief,
Should be thy portion, with what healing thoughts   145
Of tender joy wilt thou remember me,
And these my exhortations! Nor, perchance,
If I should be, where I no more can hear
Thy voice, nor catch from thy wild eyes these gleams
Of past existence, wilt thou then forget   150
That on the banks of this delightful stream
We stood together; and that I, so long
A worshipper of Nature, hither came,
Unwearied in that service: rather say

With warmer love, oh! with far deeper zeal   155
Of holier love. Nor wilt thou then forget,
That after many wanderings, many years
Of absence, these steep woods and lofty cliffs,
And this green pastoral landscape, were to me
More dear, both for themselves, and for thy sake.   160

WORDSWORTH'S ENDNOTES

Note to The Thorn.—This Poem ought to have been preceded by an introductory Poem, which I have been prevented from writing by never having felt myself in a mood when it was probable that I should write it well.—The character which I have here introduced speaking is sufficiently common. The Reader will perhaps have a general notion of it, if he has ever known a man, a Captain of a small trading vessel, for example, who, being past the middle age of life, had retired upon an annuity or small independent income to some village or country town of which he was not a native, or in which he had not been accustomed to live. Such men having little to do become credulous and talkative from indolence; and from the same cause, and other predisposing causes by which it is probable that such men may have been affected, they are prone to superstition. On which account it appeared to me proper to select a character like this to exhibit some of the general laws by which superstition acts upon the mind.° Superstitious men are almost always men of slow faculties and deep feelings; their minds are not loose but adhesive; they have a reasonable share of imagination, by which word I mean the faculty which produces impressive effects out of simple elements; but they are utterly destitute of fancy,° the power by which pleasure and surprize are excited by sudden varieties of situation and by accumulated imagery.

It was my wish in this poem to shew the manner in which such men cleave to the same ideas; and to follow the turns of passion, always different, yet not palpably different, by which their conversation is swayed. I had two objects to attain; first, to represent a picture which should not be unimpressive yet consistent with the character that should describe it, secondly, while I adhered to the style in which such persons describe, to take care that words, which in their minds are impregnated with passion, should likewise convey passion to Readers who are not accustomed to sympathize with men feeling in that manner or using such language. It seemed to me that this might be done by calling in the assistance of Lyrical and rapid Metre. It was necessary that the Poem, to be natural, should in reality move slowly; yet I hoped, that, by the aid of the metre, to those who should at all enter into the spirit of the Poem, it would appear to move quickly. The Reader will have the kindness to excuse this note as I am sensible that an introductory Poem is necessary to give this Poem its full effect.

Upon this occasion I will request permission to add a few words closely connected with THE THORN and many other Poems in these Volumes. There is a numerous class of readers who imagine that the same words cannot be repeated without tautology: this is a great error: virtual tautology is much oftener produced by using different words when the meaning is exactly the same. Words, a Poet's words more particularly, ought to be weighed in the balance of feeling, and not measured by the space which they occupy upon paper. For the Reader cannot be too often reminded that Poetry is passion: it is the history or science of feelings: now every man must know that an attempt is rarely made to communicate impassioned feelings without something of an accompanying consciousness of the inadequateness of our own powers, or the deficiencies of language. During such efforts there will be a craving in the mind, and as long as it is unsatisfied the Speaker will cling to the same words, or words of the same character. There are also various other reasons why repetition and apparent tautology are frequently beauties of the highest kind. Among the chief of these reasons is the interest which the mind attaches to words, not only as symbols of the passion, but as *things*, active and efficient, which are of themselves part of the passion. And further, from a spirit of fondness, exultation, and gratitude, the mind luxuriates in the repetition of words which appear successfully to communicate its feelings. The truth of these remarks might be shewn by innumerable passages from the Bible° and from the impassioned poetry of every nation.

'Awake, awake Deborah: awake, awake, utter a song:
   Arise Barak, and lead thy captivity captive, thou Son of Abinoam.
   At her feet he bowed, he fell, he lay down: at her feet he bowed, he fell; where he bowed there he fell down dead.
   Why is his Chariot so long in coming? Why tarry the Wheels of his Chariot?'—Judges, Chap 5th. Verses 12th, 27th, and part of 28th.—See also the whole of that tumultuous and wonderful Poem.

Note to the Poem On Revisiting the Wye.—I have not ventured to call this Poem an Ode; but it was written with a hope that in the transitions, and the impassioned music of the versification, would be found the principal requisites of that species of composition.

LYRICAL BALLADS,

WITH

PASTORAL

AND

OTHER POEMS

VOL. II

HART-LEAP WELL

Hart-Leap Well is a small spring of water, about five miles from Richmond in Yorkshire, and near the side of the road which leads from Richmond to Askrigg. Its name is derived from a remarkable Chace, the memory of which is preserved by the monuments spoken of in the second Part of the following Poem, which monuments do now exist as I have there described them.

The Knight had ridden down from Wensley moor°
With the slow motion of a summer's cloud;
He turn'd aside towards a Vassal's door,
And, 'Bring another Horse!' he cried aloud.

'Another Horse!'—That shout the Vassal heard,   5
And saddled his best steed, a comely Grey;
Sir Walter mounted him; he was the third
Which he had mounted on that glorious day.

Joy sparkled in the prancing Courser's eyes;
The Horse and Horseman are a happy pair;   10
But, though Sir Walter like a falcon flies,
There is a doleful silence in the air.

A rout this morning left Sir Walter's Hall,
That as they gallop'd made the echoes roar;
But Horse and Man are vanish'd, one and all;   15
Such race, I think, was never seen before.

Sir Walter, restless as a veering wind,
Calls to the few tired Dogs that yet remain:
Brach, Swift and Music, noblest of their kind,
Follow, and up the weary mountain strain.   20

The Knight halloo'd, he chid and cheer'd them on
With suppliant gestures and upbraidings stern;
But breath and eye-sight fail, and, one by one,
The Dogs are stretch'd among the mountain fern.

Where is the throng, the tumult of the race?   25
The bugles that so joyfully were blown?

—This Chase it looks not like an earthly Chase;
Sir Walter and the Hart are left alone.°

The poor Hart toils along the mountain side;
I will not stop to tell how far he fled,   30
Nor will I mention by what death he died;
But now the Knight beholds him lying dead.

Dismounting then, he lean'd against a thorn;
He had no follower, Dog, nor Man, nor Boy:
He neither smak'd his whip, nor blew his horn,   35
But gaz'd upon the spoil with silent joy.

Close to the thorn on which Sir Walter lean'd,
Stood his dumb partner in this glorious act;
Weak as a lamb the hour that it is yean'd,
And foaming like a mountain cataract.   40

Upon his side the Hart was lying stretch'd:
His nose half-touch'd a spring beneath a hill,
And with the last deep groan his breath had fetch'd
The waters of the spring were trembling still.

And now, too happy for repose or rest,   45
(Was never man in such a joyful case!)
Sir Walter walk'd all round, north, south, and west,
And gaz'd, and gaz'd upon that darling place.

And climbing up the hill—(it was at least
Nine roods of sheer ascent) Sir Walter found°   50
Three several hoof-marks which the hunted Beast
Had left imprinted on the verdant ground.

Sir Walter wiped his face, and cried, 'Till now
Such sight was never seen by living eyes:
Three leaps have borne him from this lofty brow,   55
Down to the very fountain where he lies.°

I'll build a Pleasure-house upon this spot,
And a small Arbour, made for rural joy;
'Twill be the Traveller's shed, the Pilgrim's cot,
A place of love for Damsels that are coy.   60

A cunning Artist will I have to frame
A bason for that Fountain in the dell;
And they, who do make mention of the same,
From this day forth, shall call it HART-LEAP WELL.

And, gallant brute! to make thy praises known,   65
Another monument shall here be rais'd;
Three several Pillars, each a rough hewn Stone,
And planted where thy hoofs the turf have graz'd.

And in the summer-time when days are long,
I will come hither with my Paramour;   70
And with the Dancers, and the Minstrel's song,
We will make merry in that pleasant Bower.

Till the foundations of the mountains fail
My Mansion with its Arbour shall endure;
—The joy of them who till the fields of Swale,   75
And them who dwell among the woods of Ure!"°

Then home he went, and left the Hart, stone-dead,
With breathless nostrils stretch'd above the spring.
And soon the Knight perform'd what he had said,
The fame whereof through many a land did ring.   80

Ere thrice the moon into her port had steer'd,
A Cup of Stone receiv'd the living Well;
Three Pillars of rude stone Sir Walter rear'd,
And built a House of Pleasure in the dell.

And near the fountain, flowers of stature tall   85
With trailing plants and trees were intertwin'd,
Which soon composed a little sylvan Hall,
A leafy shelter from the sun and wind.

And thither, when the summer days were long,
Sir Walter journey'd with his Paramour;   90
And with the Dancers and the Minstrel's song
Made merriment within that pleasant Bower.

The Knight, Sir Walter, died in course of time,
And his bones lie in his paternal vale.—

But there is matter for a second rhyme,   95
And I to this would add another tale.

PART SECOND

The moving accident is not my trade:°
To freeze the blood I have no ready arts:°
'Tis my delight, alone in summer shade,
To pipe a simple song to thinking hearts.   100

As I from Hawes to Richmond did repair,°
It chanc'd that I saw standing in a Dell
Three Aspins at three corners of a square,°
And one, not four yards distant, near a Well.

What this imported I could ill divine: 105
And, pulling now the rein my horse to stop,
I saw three Pillars standing in a line,
The last Stone Pillar on a dark hill-top.

The Trees were grey, with neither arms nor head;
Half-wasted the square Mound of tawny green;   110
So that you just might say, as then I said,
'Here in old time the hand of man has been.'

I look'd upon the hills both far and near,
More doleful place did never eye survey;
·It seem'd as if the spring-time came not here,   115
And Nature here were willing to decay.

I stood in various thoughts and fancies lost,
When one, who was in Shepherd's garb attir'd,
Came up the Hollow. Him did I accost,
And what this place might be I then inquir'd.   120

The Shepherd stopp'd, and that same story told
Which in my former rhyme I have rehears'd.
'A jolly place,' said he, 'in times of old!
But something ails it now; the spot is curs'd.

You see these lifeless Stumps of aspin wood,   125
Some say that they are beeches, others elms—

These were the Bower; and here a Mansion stood,
The finest palace of a hundred realms!

The Arbour does its own condition tell;
You see the Stones, the Fountain, and the Stream,   130
But as to the great Lodge! you might as well
Hunt half a day for a forgotten dream.

There's neither dog nor heifer, horse nor sheep,
Will wet his lips within that Cup of Stone;
And, oftentimes, when all are fast asleep,   135
This water doth send forth a dolorous groan.

Some say that here a murder has been done,
And blood cries out for blood: but, for my part,
I've guess'd, when I've been sitting in the sun,
That it was all for that unhappy Hart.   140

What thoughts must through the creature's brain have pass'd!
From the stone upon the summit of the steep
Are but three bounds—and look, Sir, at this last—
—O Master! it has been a cruel leap.

For thirteen hours he ran a desperate race;   145
And in my simple mind we cannot tell
What cause the Hart might have to love this place,
And come and make his death-bed near the Well.

Here on the grass perhaps asleep he sank,
Lull'd by this Fountain in the summer-tide;   150
This water was perhaps the first he drank
When he had wander'd from his mother's side.

In April here beneath the scented thorn
He heard the birds their morning carols sing;
And he, perhaps, for aught we know, was born   155
Not half a furlong from that self-same spring.

But now here's neither grass nor pleasant shade;
The sun on drearier Hollow never shone:

So will it be, as I have often said,
Till Trees, and Stones, and Fountain all are gone.'   160

'Grey-headed Shepherd, thou hast spoken well;
Small difference lies between thy creed and mine:
This Beast not unobserv'd by Nature fell;
His death was mourn'd by sympathy divine.

The Being, that is in the clouds and air,   165
That is in the green leaves among the groves,
Maintains a deep and reverential care
For them the quiet creatures whom he loves.

The Pleasure-house is dust:—behind, before,
This is no common waste, no common gloom;   170
But Nature, in due course of time, once more
Shall here put on her beauty and her bloom.

She leaves these objects to a slow decay,
That what we are, and have been, may be known;
But, at the coming of the milder day,   175
These monuments shall all be overgrown.

One lesson, Shepherd, let us two divide,
Taught both by what she shews, and what conceals,
Never to blend our pleasure or our pride
With sorrow of the meanest thing that feels.'   180

'There was a Boy'

There was a Boy, ye knew him well, ye Cliffs
And Islands of Winander! many a time,°
At evening, when the stars had just begun
To move along the edges of the hills,
Rising or setting, would he stand alone,   5
Beneath the trees, or by the glimmering lake;
And there, with fingers interwoven, both hands
Press'd closely palm to palm and to his mouth
Uplifted, he, as through an instrument,
Blew mimic hootings to the silent owls°   10
That they might answer him.—And they would shout

Across the wat'ry vale and shout again
Responsive to his call, with quivering peals,
And long halloos, and screams, and echoes loud
Redoubled and redoubled; a wild scene   15
Of mirth and jocund din! And, when it chanced
That pauses of deep silence mock'd his skill,
Then, sometimes, in that silence, while he hung
Listening, a gentle shock of mild surprise
Has carried far into his heart the voice   20
Of mountain torrents; or the visible scene
Would enter unawares into his mind
With all its solemn imagery, its rocks,
Its woods, and that uncertain heaven, receiv'd
Into the bosom of the steady lake.   25

Fair are the woods, and beauteous is the spot,
The vale where he was born: the Church-yard hangs
Upon a slope above the village School,
And there, along that bank, when I have pass'd
At evening, I believe, that near his grave   30
A full half-hour together I have stood
Mute——for he died when he was ten years old.

THE BROTHERS,

A PASTORAL POEM*

'These Tourists, Heaven preserve us! needs must live°
A profitable life: some glance along,
Rapid and gay, as if the earth were air,
And they were butterflies to wheel about
Long as their summer lasted: some, as wise,   5
Upon the forehead of a jutting crag,
Sit perch'd with book and pencil on their knee,
And look and scribble, scribble on and look,
Until a man might travel twelve stout miles,
Or reap an acre of his neighbour's corn.   10
But, for that moping Son of Idleness,

* This Poem was intended to be the concluding poem of a series of pastorals, the scene of which was laid among the mountains of Cumberland and Westmoreland. I mention this to apologise for the abruptness with which the poem begins.

Why can he tarry *yonder?*—In our church-yard
Is neither epitaph nor monument,°
Tomb-stone nor name—only the turf we tread,
And a few natural graves.' To Jane, his Wife,   15
Thus spake the homely Priest of Ennerdale.°
It was a July evening; and he sate
Upon the long stone-seat beneath the eaves
Of his old cottage, as it chanced, that day,
Employ'd in winter's work. Upon the stone   20
His wife sate near him, teasing matted wool,
While, from the twin cards tooth'd with glittering wire,
He fed the spindle of his youngest Child,°
Who turn'd her large round wheel in the open air
With back and forward steps. Towards the field   25
In which the Parish Chapel stood alone,
Girt round with a bare ring of mossy wall,
While half an hour went by, the Priest had sent
Many a long look of wonder, and at last,
Risen from his seat, beside the snow-white ridge   30
Of carded wool which the old man had piled
He laid his implements with gentle care,
Each in the other lock'd; and, down the path
Which from his cottage to the church-yard led,
He took his way, impatient to accost   35
The Stranger, whom he saw still lingering there.

        'Twas one well known to him in former days,
A Shepherd-lad: who ere his thirteenth year
Had chang'd his calling, with the mariners°
A fellow-mariner, and so had fared   40
Through twenty seasons; but he had been rear'd
Among the mountains, and he in his heart
Was half a Shepherd on the stormy seas.
Oft in the piping shrouds had Leonard heard
The tones of waterfalls, and inland sounds   45
Of caves and trees:—and, when the regular wind
Between the tropics fill'd the steady sail,
And blew with the same breath through days and weeks,
Lengthening invisibly its weary line
Along the cloudless Main, he, in those hours   50
Of tiresome indolence, would often hang

Over the vessel's side, and gaze and gaze,
And, while the broad green wave and sparkling foam,
Flash'd round him images and hues, that wrought
In union with the employment of his heart,   55
He, thus by feverish passion overcome,
Even with the organs of his bodily eye,
Below him, in the bosom of the deep,
Saw mountains, saw the forms of sheep that graz'd
On verdant hills, with dwellings among trees,   60
And Shepherds clad in the same country grey
Which he himself had worn.*
                          And now at length
From perils manifold, with some small wealth
Acquir'd by traffic in the Indian Isles,
To his paternal home he is return'd,   65
With a determin'd purpose to resume
The life which he liv'd there; both for the sake
Of many darling pleasures, and the love
Which to an only brother he has borne
In all his hardships, since that happy time   70
When, whether it blew foul or fair, they two
Were brother Shepherds on their native hills.
—They were the last of all their race: and now°
When Leonard had approach'd his home, his heart
Fail'd in him; and, not venturing to inquire   75
Tidings of one whom he so dearly lov'd,
Towards the church-yard he had turn'd aside,
That, as he knew in what particular spot
His family were laid, he thence might learn
If still his Brother liv'd, or to the file   80
Another grave was added.—He had found
Another grave, near which a full half hour
He had remain'd; but, as he gaz'd, there grew
Such a confusion in his memory,
That he began to doubt, and he had hopes   85
That he had seen this heap of turf before,
That it was not another grave, but one,
He had forgotten. He had lost his path,

* This description of the Calenture° is sketched from an imperfect recollection of an admirable one in prose, by Mr. Gilbert, Author of the Hurricane.

As up the vale he came that afternoon,
Through fields which once had been well known to him.   90
And Oh! what joy the recollection now
Sent to his heart! he lifted up his eyes,
And looking round he thought that he perceiv'd
Strange alteration wrought on every side
Among the woods and fields, and that the rocks,   95
And the eternal hills, themselves were chang'd.

By this the Priest who down the field had come
Unseen by Leonard, at the church-yard gate
Stopp'd short, and thence, at leisure, limb by limb
He scann'd him with a gay complacency.°   100
Aye, thought the Vicar, smiling to himself,
'Tis one of those who needs must leave the path
Of the world's business to go wild alone:
His arms have a perpetual holiday;
The happy Man will creep about the fields   105
Following his fancies by the hour, to bring
Tears down his cheeks, or solitary smiles
Into his face, until the setting sun
Write Fool upon his forehead. Planted thus
Beneath a shed that overarch'd the gate   110
Of this rude church-yard, till the stars appear'd
The good man might have commun'd with himself
But that the stranger, who had left the grave,
Approach'd; he recogniz'd the Priest at once,
And, after greetings interchang'd, and given   115
By Leonard to the Vicar as to one
Unknown to him, this dialogue ensued.

LEONARD. You live, Sir, in these dales, a quiet life:
    Your years make up one peaceful family;
    And who would grieve and fret, if, welcome come   120
    And welcome gone, they are so like each other,
    They cannot be remember'd. Scarce a funeral
    Comes to this church-yard once in eighteen months;
    And yet, some changes must take place among you:
    And you, who dwell here, even among these rocks   125
    Can trace the finger of mortality,
    And see, that with our threescore years and ten

We are not all that perish.——I remember,
For many years ago I pass'd this road,
There was a foot-way all along the fields   130
By the brook-side——'tis gone——and that dark cleft!
To me it does not seem to wear the face
Which then it had.

PRIEST.   Why, Sir, for aught I know,
That chasm is much the same——

LEONARD.   But, surely, yonder——

PRIEST.   Aye, there indeed, your memory is a friend   135
That does not play you false.——On that tall pike,
(It is the loneliest place of all these hills)
There were two Springs which bubbled side by side,
As if they had been made that they might be
Companions for each other: ten years back,   140
Close to those brother fountains, the huge crag
Was rent with lightning——one is dead and gone,
The other, left behind, is flowing still.——°
For accidents and changes such as these,
Why we have store of them! a water-spout   145
Will bring down half a mountain; what a feast
For folks that wander up and down like you
To see an acre's breadth of that wide cliff
One roaring cataract!——a sharp May storm
Will come with loads of January snow,   150
And in one night send twenty score of sheep
To feed the ravens; or a Shepherd dies
By some untoward death among the rocks:
The ice breaks up and sweeps away a bridge——
A wood is fell'd:——and then for our own homes!   155
A Child is born or christen'd, a Field plough'd,
A Daughter sent to service, a Web spun,
The old House-clock is deck'd with a new face;
And hence, so far from wanting facts or dates
To chronicle the time, we all have here   160
A pair of diaries, one serving, Sir,
For the whole dale, and one for each fire-side——
Your's was a stranger's judgment: for Historians
Commend me to these vallies.

LEONARD.   Yet your Church-yard
 Seems, if such freedom may be used with you,   165
 To say that you are heedless of the past.
 An orphan could not find his mother's grave:
 Here's neither head nor foot-stone, plate of brass,
 Cross-bones or skull, type of our earthly state
 Or emblem of our hopes: the dead man's home   170
 Is but a fellow to that pasture-field.

PRIEST. Why there, Sir, is a thought that's new to me.
 The Stone-cutters, 'tis true, might beg their bread°
 If every English Church-yard were like ours:
 Yet your conclusion wanders from the truth.   175
 We have no need of names and epitaphs;
 We talk about the dead by our fire-sides,
 And then, for our immortal part! *we* want
 No symbols, Sir, to tell us that plain tale:
 The thought of death sits easy on the man   180
 Who has been born and dies among the mountains.°

LEONARD. Your Dalesmen, then, do in each other's thoughts
 Possess a kind of second life: no doubt
 You, Sir, could help me to the history
 Of half these Graves?

PRIEST.   For eight-score winters past,   185
 With what I've witness'd, and with what I've heard,
 Perhaps I might; and, on a winter's evening,
 If you were seated at my chimney's nook,°
 By turning o'er these hillocks one by one
 We two could travel, Sir, through a strange round,   190
 Yet all in the broad high-way of the world.
 Now there's a grave—your foot is half upon it,
 It looks just like the rest; and yet that Man
 Died broken-hearted.

LEONARD.   'Tis a common case,
 We'll take another: who is he that lies   195
 Beneath yon ridge, the last of those three graves;—
 It touches on that piece of native rock
 Left in the church-yard wall.

PRIEST.   That's Walter Ewbank.
    He had as white a head and fresh a cheek
    As ever were produc'd by youth and age   200
    Engendering in the blood of hale fourscore.
    For five long generations had the heart
    Of Walter's forefathers o'erflow'd the bounds
    Of their inheritance, that single cottage,
    —You see it yonder! and those few green fields.   205
    They toil'd and wrought, and still, from Sire to Son,
    Each struggled, and each yielded as before
    A little—yet a little—and old Walter,
    They left to him the family heart, and land
    With other burthens than the crop it bore.   210
    Year after year the old man still kept up°
    A chearful mind, and buffetted with bond,
    Interest and mortgages; at last he sank,
    And went into his grave before his time.
    Poor Walter! whether it was care that spurr'd him   215
    God only knows, but to the very last
    He had the lightest foot in Ennerdale:
    His pace was never that of an old man:
    I almost see him tripping down the path
    With his two Grandsons after him—but You,   220
    Unless our Landlord be your host to night,
    Have far to travel, and in these rough paths
    Even in the longest day of midsummer—

LEONARD. But these two Orphans!

PRIEST.   Orphans! such they were—
    Yet not while Walter liv'd—for, though their Parents   225
    Lay buried side by side as now they lie,
    The old Man was a father to the boys,
    Two fathers in one father: and if tears,
    Shed when he talk'd of them where they were not,
    And hauntings from the infirmity of love,   230
    Are aught of what makes up a mother's heart,
    This old Man in the day of his old age
    Was half a mother to them.—If you weep, Sir,
    To hear a Stranger talking about Strangers,
    Heaven bless you when you are among your kindred!   235

Aye. You may turn that way—it is a grave
Which will bear looking at.

LEONARD.   These Boys—I hope
They lov'd this good old Man—

PRIEST.   They did—and truly:
But that was what we almost overlook'd,
They were such darlings of each other. For   240
Though from their cradles they had liv'd with Walter,
The only Kinsman near them in the house,
Yet he being old, they had much love to spare,
And it all went into each other's hearts.
Leonard, the elder by just eighteen months,   245
Was two years taller: 'twas a joy to see,
To hear, to meet them! from their house the School
Was distant three short miles—and in the time
Of storm and thaw, when every water-course
And unbridg'd stream, such as you may have notic'd   250
Crossing our roads at every hundred steps,
Was swoln into a noisy rivulet,
Would Leonard then, when elder boys perhaps
Remain'd at home, go staggering through the fords
Bearing his Brother on his back.—I've seen him,   255
On windy days, in one of those stray brooks,
Aye, more than once I've seen him mid-leg deep,
Their two books lying both on a dry stone
Upon the hither side: and once I said,
As I remember, looking round these rocks   260
And hills on which we all of us were born,
That God who made the great book of the world°
Would bless such piety—

LEONARD.   It may be then—

PRIEST. Never did worthier lads break English bread!
The finest Sunday that the Autumn saw,   265
With all its mealy clusters of ripe nuts,
Could never keep these boys away from church,
Or tempt them to an hour of sabbath breach.
Leonard and James! I warrant, every corner

Among these rocks and every hollow place   270
Where foot could come, to one or both of them
Was known as well as to the flowers that grow there.
Like Roe-bucks they went bounding o'er the hills:°
They play'd like two young Ravens on the crags:
Then they could write, aye and speak too, as well   275
As many of their betters—and for Leonard!
The very night before he went away,
In my own house I put into his hand
A Bible, and I'd wager twenty pounds,
That, if he is alive, he has it yet.   280

LEONARD. It seems, these Brothers have not liv'd to be
A comfort to each other.—

PRIEST.   That they might
Live to that end, is what both old and young
In this our valley all of us have wish'd,
And what, for my part, I have often pray'd: 285
But Leonard—

LEONARD.   Then James still is left among you!

PRIEST. 'Tis of the elder Brother I am speaking:
They had an Uncle, he was at that time
A thriving man, and traffick'd on the seas:
And, but for this same Uncle, to this hour   290
Leonard had never handled rope or shroud.
For the Boy lov'd the life which we lead here;
And, though a very Stripling, twelve years old,
His soul was knit to this his native soil.
But, as I said, old Walter was too weak   295
To strive with such a torrent; when he died,
The Estate and House were sold, and all their Sheep,
A pretty flock, and which for aught I know,
Had clothed the Ewbanks for a thousand years.
Well—all was gone, and they were destitute.   300
And Leonard, chiefly for his Brother's sake,
Resolv'd to try his fortune on the seas.
'Tis now twelve years since we had tidings from him.
If there was one among us who had heard

That Leonard Ewbank was come home again,   305
From the great Gavel,* down by Leeza's Banks,
And down the Enna, far as Egremont,°
The day would be a very festival,
And those two bells of ours, which there you see
Hanging in the open air—but, O good Sir!   310
This is sad talk—they'll never sound for him
Living or dead—When last we heard of him
He was in slavery among the Moors
Upon the Barbary Coast—'Twas not a little°
That would bring down his spirit, and, no doubt,   315
Before it ended in his death, the Lad
Was sadly cross'd—Poor Leonard! when we parted,
He took me by the hand and said to me,
If ever the day came when he was rich,
He would return, and on his Father's Land   320
He would grow old among us.

LEONARD.   If that day
Should come, 'twould needs be a glad day for him;
He would himself, no doubt, be happy then
As any that should meet him—

PRIEST.   Happy! Sir—

LEONARD. You said his kindred all were in their graves,   325
And that he had one Brother—

PRIEST.   That is but
A fellow tale of sorrow. From his youth
James, though not sickly, yet was delicate,
And Leonard being always by his side
Had done so many offices about him,   330
That, though he was not of a timid nature,
Yet still the spirit of a Mountain Boy
In him was somewhat check'd; and, when his Brother

* The Great Gavel, so called, I imagine, from its resemblance to the Gable end of a
house, is one of the highest of the Cumberland mountains. It stands at the head of the
several vales of Ennerdale, Wastdale, and Borrowdale. The Leeza is a river which flows
into the Lake of Ennerdale: on issuing from the Lake, it changes its name, and is called
the End, Eyne, or Enna. It falls into the sea a little below Egremont.

Was gone to sea and he was left alone,
The little colour that he had was soon   335
Stolen from his cheek, he droop'd, and pin'd and pin'd—

LEONARD. But these are all the graves of full-grown men!

PRIEST. Aye, Sir, that pass'd away: we took him to us.
      He was the Child of all the dale—he liv'd
      Three months with one, and six months with another;   340
      And wanted neither food, nor clothes, nor love:
      And many, many happy days were his.
      But, whether blithe or sad, 'tis my belief
      His absent Brother still was at his heart.
      And, when he liv'd beneath our roof, we found   345
      (A practice till this time unknown to him)
      That often, rising from his bed at night,
      He in his sleep would walk about, and sleeping
      He sought his Brother Leonard—You are mov'd!
      Forgive me, Sir: before I spoke to you,   350
      I judg'd you most unkindly.

LEONARD.   But this Youth,
      How did he die at last?

PRIEST.   One sweet May morning,
      It will be twelve years since, when Spring returns,
      He had gone forth among the new-dropp'd lambs,
      With two or three Companions whom it chanc'd   355
      Some further business summon'd to a house
      Which stands at the Dale-head. James, tir'd perhaps,
      Or from some other cause, remain'd behind.
      You see yon Precipice—it almost looks
      Like some vast building made of many crags;   360
      And in the midst is one particular rock
      That rises like a column from the vale,
      Whence by our Shepherds it is call'd, the Pillar.°
      James, pointed to its summit, over which
      They all had purpos'd to return together,   365
      And told them that he there would wait for them:
      They parted, and his Comrades pass'd that way
      Some two hours after, but they did not find him

Upon the Pillar—at the appointed place.
Of this they took no heed: but one of them,   370
Going by chance, at night, into the house
Which at that time was James's home, there learn'd
That nobody had seen him all that day:
The morning came, and still, he was unheard of:
The neighbours were alarm'd, and to the Brook   375
Some went, and some towards the Lake; ere noon
They found him at the foot of that same Rock—
Dead, and with mangled limbs. The third day after
I buried him, poor Lad, and there he lies.

LEONARD. And that then *is* his grave!—Before his death   380
You said that he saw many happy years?

PRIEST. Aye, that he did—

LEONARD.   And all went well with him—

PRIEST. If he had one, the Lad had twenty homes.

LEONARD. And you believe then, that his mind was easy—

PRIEST. Yes, long before he died, he found that time   385
Is a true friend to sorrow; and unless
His thoughts were turn'd on Leonard's luckless fortune,
He talk'd about him with a chearful love.

LEONARD. He could not come to an unhallow'd end!

PRIEST. Nay, God forbid! You recollect I mention'd   390
A habit which disquietude and grief
Had brought upon him; and we all conjectur'd
That, as the day was warm, he had lain down
Upon the grass, and, waiting for his comrades
He there had fallen asleep; that in his sleep   395
He to the margin of the precipice
Had walk'd, and from the summit had fallen head-long,
And so no doubt he perish'd: at the time,
We guess, that in his hands he must have had
His Shepherd's staff; for midway in the cliff,   400

It had been caught; and there for many years
It hung—and moulder'd there.

                The Priest here ended—
The Stranger would have thank'd him, but he felt
Tears rushing in; both left the spot in silence,
And Leonard, when they reach'd the church-yard gate,   405
As the Priest lifted up the latch, turn'd round,
And, looking at the grave, he said, 'My Brother.'
The Vicar did not hear the words: and now,
Pointing towards the Cottage, he entreated
That Leonard would partake his homely fare: 410
The other thank'd him with a fervent voice,
But added, that, the evening being calm,
He would pursue his journey. So they parted.

It was not long ere Leonard reach'd a grove
That overhung the road: he there stopp'd short,   415
And, sitting down beneath the trees, review'd
All that the Priest had said: his early years
Were with him in his heart: his cherish'd hopes,
And thoughts which had been his an hour before,
All press'd on him with such a weight, that now,   420
This vale, where he had been so happy, seem'd
A place in which he could not bear to live:
So he relinquish'd all his purposes.
He travell'd on to Egremont: and thence,
That night, he wrote a letter to the Priest   425
Reminding him of what had pass'd between them;
And adding, with a hope to be forgiven,
That it was from the weakness of his heart,
He had not dared to tell him who he was.

This done, he went on shipboard, and is now   430
A Seaman, a grey headed Mariner.

ELLEN IRWIN,
Or The Braes of Kirtle. *

Fair Ellen Irwin, when she sate
Upon the Braes of Kirtle,°
Was lovely as a Grecian Maid
Adorn'd with wreaths of myrtle.
Young Adam Bruce beside her lay;   5
And there did they beguile the day
With love and gentle speeches,
Beneath the budding beeches.

From many Knights and many Squires
The Bruce had been selected;   10
And Gordon, fairest of them all,
By Ellen was rejected.
Sad tidings to that noble Youth!
For it may be proclaim'd with truth,
If Bruce hath lov'd sincerely,   15
The Gordon loves as dearly.

But what is Gordon's beauteous face?
And what are Gordon's crosses
To them who sit by Kirtle's Braes
Upon the verdant mosses?   20
Alas that ever he was born!
The Gordon, couch'd behind a thorn,
Sees them and their caressing,
Beholds them bless'd and blessing.

Proud Gordon cannot bear the thoughts   25
That through his brain are travelling,
And, starting up, to Bruce's heart
He launch'd a deadly jav'lin!
Fair Ellen saw it when it came,
And, stepping forth to meet the same,   30
Did with her body cover
The Youth her chosen lover.

* The Kirtle is a River in the Southern part of Scotland, on whose banks the events
here related took place.

And, falling into Bruce's arms,
Thus died the beauteous Ellen,
Thus from the heart of her true-love   35
The mortal spear repelling.
And Bruce, as soon as he had slain
The Gordon, sail'd away to Spain;
And fought with rage incessant
Against the Moorish Crescent.°   40

But many days, and many months,
And many years ensuing,
This wretched Knight did vainly seek
The death that he was wooing:
And coming back across the wave,   45
Without a groan on Ellen's grave
His body he extended,
And there his sorrow ended.

Now ye, who willingly have heard
The tale I have been telling,   50
May in Kirkonnel church-yard view°
The grave of lovely Ellen:
By Ellen's side the Bruce is laid;
And, for the stone upon his head,
May no rude hand deface it,   55
And its forlorn HIC JACET.°

'Strange fits of passion I have known'

Strange fits of passion I have known:
And I will dare to tell,
But in the Lover's ear alone,
What once to me befel.

When she I lov'd, was strong and gay   5
And like a rose in June,
I to her cottage bent my way,
Beneath the evening Moon.

Upon the Moon I fix'd my eye,
All over the wide lea: 10
My Horse trudg'd on—and we drew nigh
Those paths so dear to me.

And now we reach'd the orchard plot;
And, as we climb'd the hill,
Towards the roof of Lucy's cot   15
The Moon descended still.

In one of those sweet dreams I slept,
Kind Nature's gentlest boon!
And, all the while, my eyes I kept
On the descending Moon.   20

My Horse mov'd on; hoof after hoof
He rais'd, and never stopp'd:
When down behind the cottage roof
At once the Planet dropp'd.

What fond and wayward thoughts will slide   25
Into a Lover's head—
'O mercy!' to myself I cried,
'If Lucy should be dead!'

'She dwelt among th' untrodden ways'

She dwelt among th' untrodden ways
    Beside the springs of Dove,°
A Maid whom there were none to praise,
    A very few to love.

A Violet by a mossy stone   5
    Half-hidden from the Eye!
—Fair as a star, when only one
    Is shining in the sky.

She liv'd unknown, and few could know°
    When Lucy ceas'd to be;   10
But she is in her Grave, and Oh!
    The difference to me.

'A slumber did my spirit seal'

A slumber did my spirit seal;
  I had no human fears:
She seem'd a thing that could not feel
  The touch of earthly years.

No motion has she now, no force;   5
  She neither hears nor sees,
Roll'd round in earth's diurnal course
  With rocks and stones and trees!

THE WATERFALL AND THE EGLANTINE

'Begone, thou fond presumptuous Elf,'
Exclaim'd a thundering Voice,
'Nor dare to thrust thy foolish self
Between me and my choice!'
A falling Water swoln with snows   5
Thus spake to a poor Briar-rose,
That, all bespatter'd with his foam,
And dancing high, and dancing low,
Was living, as a child might know,
In an unhappy home.   10

'Dost thou presume my course to block?
Off, off! or, puny Thing!
I'll hurl thee headlong with the rock
To which thy fibres cling.'
The Flood was tyrannous and strong;   15
The patient Briar suffer'd long,
Nor did he utter groan or sigh,
Hoping the danger would be pass'd:
But seeing no relief, at last
He ventur'd to reply.   20

'Ah!' said the Briar, 'Blame me not!
Why should we dwell in strife?
We who in this, our natal spot,
Once liv'd a happy life!

You stirr'd me on my rocky bed—   25
What pleasure thro' my veins you spread!
The Summer long from day to day
My leaves you freshen'd and bedew'd;
Nor was it common gratitude
That did your cares repay.   30

When Spring came on with bud and bell,
Among these rocks did I
Before you hang my wreath to tell
That gentle days were nigh!
And in the sultry summer hours   35
I shelter'd you with leaves and flowers;
And in my leaves, now shed and gone,
The Linnet lodg'd, and for us two
Chaunted his pretty songs, when You
Had little voice or none.   40

But now proud thoughts are in your breast—
What grief is mine you see.
Ah! would you think, ev'n yet how blest
Together we might be!
Though of both leaf and flower bereft,   45
Some ornaments to me are left—
Rich store of scarlet hips is mine,
With which I in my humble way
Would deck you many a winter's day,
A happy Eglantine!'   50

What more he said, I cannot tell.
The stream came thundering down the dell,
And gallop'd loud and fast;
I listen'd, nor aught else could hear,
The Briar quak'd—and much I fear,   55
Those accents were his last.

THE OAK AND THE BROOM,

A PASTORAL

His simple truths did Andrew glean
Beside the babbling rills;
A careful student he had been
Among the woods and hills.
One winter's night, when through the Trees   5
The wind was thundering, on his knees
His youngest born did Andrew hold:
And while the rest, a ruddy quire,
Were seated round their blazing fire,
This Tale the Shepherd told.   10

I saw a crag, a lofty stone
As ever tempest beat!
Out of its head an Oak had grown,
A Broom out of its feet.
The time was March, a chearful noon—   15
The thaw-wind with the breath of June
Breath'd gently from the warm South-west;
When, in a voice sedate with age,
This Oak, half giant and half sage,
His neighbour thus address'd.   20

'Eight weary weeks, through rock and clay,
Along this mountain's edge
The Frost hath wrought both night and day,
Wedge driving after wedge.
Look up! and think, above your head   25
What trouble surely will be bred;
Last night I heard a crash—'tis true,
The splinters took another road—
I see them yonder—what a load
For such a Thing as you!   30

You are preparing as before
To deck your slender shape;
And yet, just three years back—no more—
You had a strange escape.

Down from yon Cliff a fragment broke,   35
It came, you know, with fire and smoke
And hitherward it bent its way.
This pond'rous Block was caught by me,
And o'er your head, as you may see,
'Tis hanging to this day!   40

The Thing had better been asleep,
Whatever thing it were,
Or Breeze, or Bird, or Dog, or Sheep,
That first did plant you there.
For you and your green twigs decoy   45
The little witless Shepherd-boy
To come and slumber in your bower;
And, trust me, on some sultry noon,
Both you and he, Heaven knows how soon!
Will perish in one hour.   50

From me this friendly warning take'—
—The Broom began to doze,
And thus to keep herself awake
Did gently interpose.
'My thanks for your discourse are due;   55
That it is true, and more than true,
I know and I have known it long;
Frail is the bond, by which we hold
Our being, be we young or old,
Wise, foolish, weak or strong.   60

Disasters, do the best we can,
Will reach both great and small;
And he is oft the wisest man,
Who is not wise at all.
For me, why should I wish to roam?   65
This spot is my paternal home,
It is my pleasant Heritage;
My Father many a happy year
Here spread his careless blossoms, here
Attain'd a good old age.   70

Even such as his may be my lot.
What cause have I to haunt

My heart with terrors? Am I not
In truth a favor'd plant!
The Spring for me a garland weaves   75
Of yellow flowers and verdant leaves;
And, when the Frost is in the sky,
My branches are so fresh and gay
That You might look at me and say,
This Plant can never die.   80

The Butterfly, all green and gold,
To me hath often flown,
Here in my Blossoms to behold
Wings lovely as his own.
When grass is chill with rain or dew,   85
Beneath my shade the mother Ewe
Lies with her infant Lamb; I see
The love they to each other make,
And the sweet joy, which they partake,
It is a joy to me.'   90

Her voice was blithe, her heart was light;
The Broom might have pursued
Her speech, until the stars of night
Their journey had renew'd.
But in the branches of the Oak   95
Two Ravens now began to croak
Their nuptial song, a gladsome air;
And to her own green bower the breeze
That instant brought two stripling Bees
To feed and murmur there.   100

One night the Wind came from the North
And blew a furious blast;
At break of day I ventur'd forth
And near the Cliff I pass'd.
The storm had fall'n upon the Oak   105
And struck him with a mighty stroke,
And whirl'd and whirl'd him far away;
And in one hospitable Cleft
The little careless Broom was left
To live for many a day.   110

THE COMPLAINT OF A FORSAKEN INDIAN WOMAN

When a Northern Indian, from sickness, is unable to continue his journey with his companions; he is left behind, covered over with Deer-skins; and is supplied with water, food, and fuel, if the situation of the place will afford it. He is informed of the track which his companions intend to pursue, and if he is unable to follow, or overtake them, he perishes alone in the Desart; unless he should have the good fortune to fall in with some other Tribes of Indians. The females are equally, or still more, exposed to the same fate. See that very interesting work, Hearne's Journey from Hudson's Bay to the Northern Ocean. In the high Northern Latitudes, as the same writer informs us, when the Northern Lights vary their position in the air, they make a rustling and a crackling noise. This circumstance is alluded to in the first stanza of the following poem.

Before I see another day,
Oh let my body die away!
In sleep I heard the northern gleams;
The stars they were among my dreams;
In sleep did I behold the skies,   5
I saw the crackling flashes drive;
And yet they are upon my eyes,
And yet I am alive.
Before I see another day,
Oh let my body die away!   10

My fire is dead: it knew no pain;
Yet it is dead, and I remain.
All stiff with ice the ashes lie;
And they are dead, and I will die.
When I was well, I wished to live,   15
For clothes, for warmth, for food, and fire;
But they to me no joy can give,
No pleasure now, and no desire.
Then here contented will I lie!
Alone I cannot fear to die.   20

Alas! you might have dragged me on
Another day, a single one!
Too soon despair o'er me prevail'd;

Too soon my heartless spirit fail'd;
When you were gone my limbs were stronger;   25
And Oh how grievously I rue,
That, afterwards, a little longer,
My Friends, I did not follow you!
For strong and without pain I lay,
My Friends, when you were gone away.   30

My Child! they gave thee to another,
A woman who was not thy mother.
When from my arms my Babe they took,
On me how strangely did he look!
Through his whole body something ran,   35
A most strange something did I see;
—As if he strove to be a man,
That he might pull the sledge for me.
And then he stretched his arms, how wild!
Oh mercy! like a little child.   40

My little joy! my little pride!
In two days more I must have died.
Then do not weep and grieve for me;
I feel I must have died with thee.
Oh wind, that o'er my head art flying   45
The way my Friends their course did bend,
I should not feel the pain of dying,
Could I with thee a message send!
Too soon, my Friends, you went away;
For I had many things to say.   50

I'll follow you across the snow;
You travel heavily and slow:
In spite of all my weary pain,
I'll look upon your tents again.
—My fire is dead, and snowy white   55
The water which beside it stood;
The wolf has come to me to-night,
And he has stolen away my food.
For ever left alone am I,
Then wherefore should I fear to die?   60

My journey will be shortly run,
I shall not see another sun;
I cannot lift my limbs to know
If they have any life or no.
My poor forsaken child! if I   65
For once could have thee close to me,
With happy heart I then should die,
And my last thoughts would happy be.
I feel my body die away,
I shall not see another day.   70

LUCY GRAY

Oft I had heard of Lucy Gray:
And, when I cross'd the Wild,°
I chanc'd to see at break of day
The solitary Child.

No Mate, no comrade Lucy knew;   5
She dwelt on a wide Moor,
—The sweetest thing that ever grew
Beside a human door!

You yet may spy the Fawn at play,
The Hare upon the Green;   10
But the sweet face of Lucy Gray
Will never more be seen.

'To-night will be a stormy night—
You to the Town must go;
And take a lantern, Child, to light   15
Your Mother thro' the snow.'

'That, Father! will I gladly do;
'Tis scarcely afternoon—
The Minster-clock has just struck two,
And yonder is the Moon.'   20

At this the Father rais'd his hook
And snap'd a faggot-band;

He plied his work, and Lucy took
The lantern in her hand.

Not blither is the mountain roe: 25
With many a wanton stroke
Her feet disperse the powd'ry snow,°
That rises up like smoke.

The storm came on before its time:
She wander'd up and down;°   30
And many a hill did Lucy climb,
But never reach'd the Town.

The wretched Parents all that night
Went shouting far and wide;
But there was neither sound nor sight   35
To serve them for a guide.

At day-break on a hill they stood
That overlook'd the Moor;
And thence they saw the Bridge of wood,
A furlong from their door.°   40

And now they homeward turn'd, and cry'd
'In Heaven we all shall meet!'
—When in the snow the Mother spied
The print of Lucy's feet.

Then downward from the steep hill's edge   45
They track'd the footmarks small;
And through the broken hawthorn-edge,
And by the long stone-wall;

And then an open field they cross'd:
The marks were still the same;   50
They track'd them on, nor ever lost;
And to the Bridge they came.

They follow'd from the snowy bank,
The footmarks, one by one,
Into the middle of the plank;   55
And further there was none.

—Yet some maintain that to this day
She is a living Child;
That you may see sweet Lucy Gray
Upon the lonesome Wild.   60

O'er rough and smooth she trips along,
And never looks behind;
And sings a solitary song
That whistles in the wind.

''Tis said that some have died for Love'

'Tis said, that some have died for love:
And here and there a church-yard grave is found
In the cold North's unhallow'd ground,
Because the wretched Man himself had slain,
His love was such a grievous pain.   5
And there is one whom I five years have known;
He dwells alone
Upon Helvellyn's side:°
He loved——the pretty Barbara died,°
And thus he makes his moan: 10
Three years had Barbara in her grave been laid
When thus his moan he made.

'Oh move thou Cottage from behind that oak!
Or let the aged tree uprooted lie,
That in some other way yon smoke   15
May mount into the sky!
The clouds pass on; they from the Heavens depart:
I look—the sky is empty space;
I know not what I trace;
But, when I cease to look, my hand is on my heart.   20

O! what a weight is in these shades! Ye leaves,
When will that dying murmur be suppress'd?
Your sound my heart of peace bereaves,
It robs my heart of rest.
Thou Thrush, that singest loud and loud and free,   25
Into yon row of willows flit,

Upon that alder sit;
Or sing another song, or chuse another tree.

Roll back, sweet Rill! back to thy mountain bounds,
And there for ever be thy waters chain'd!   30
For thou dost haunt the air with sounds
That cannot be sustain'd;
If still beneath that pine-tree's ragged bough
Headlong yon waterfall must come,
Oh let it then be dumb!—   35
Be any thing, sweet Rill, but that which thou art now.

Thou Eglantine whose arch so proudly towers
(Even like the rainbow spanning half the vale)
Thou one fair shrub, oh! shed thy flowers,
And stir not in the gale.   40
For thus to see thee nodding in the air,
To see thy arch thus stretch and bend,
Thus rise and thus descend,
Disturbs me, till the sight is more than I can bear.'

The Man who makes this feverish complaint   45
Is one of giant stature, who could dance
Equipp'd from head to foot in iron mail.
Ah gentle Love! if ever thought was thine
To store up kindred hours for me, thy face
Turn from me, gentle Love! nor let me walk   50
Within the sound of Emma's voice, or know
Such happiness as I have known to-day.

THE IDLE SHEPHERD-BOYS,

OR, DUNGEON-GILL FORCE,*A PASTORAL

I

The valley rings with mirth and joy;
Among the hills the Echoes play

---

* *Gill* in the dialect of Cumberland and Westmoreland is a short, and for the most part, a steep narrow valley, with a stream running through it. *Force* is the word universally employed in these dialects for Waterfall.

A never, never ending song
To welcome in the May.
The Magpie chatters with delight;   5
The mountain Raven's youngling Brood
Have left the Mother and the Nest;
And they go rambling east and west
In search of their own food;
Or thro' the glittering Vapors dart   10
In very wantonness of heart.

II

Beneath a rock, upon the grass,
Two Boys are sitting in the sun;
It seems they have no work to do,
Or that their work is done.   15
On pipes of sycamore they play
The fragments of a Christmas Hymn;
Or with that plant, which in our dale
We call Stag-horn, or Fox's Tail,°
Their rusty Hats they trim:°   20
And thus, as happy as the Day,
Those Shepherds wear the time away.

III

Along the river's stony marge
The Sand-lark chaunts a joyous song;
The Thrush is busy in the wood,   25
And carols loud and strong.
A thousand Lambs are on the rocks,
All newly born! both earth and sky
Keep jubilee; and more than all,
Those Boys with their green Coronal;   30
They never hear the cry,
That plaintive cry! which up the hill
Comes from the depth of Dungeon-Gill.

IV

Said Walter, leaping from the ground,
'Down to the stump of yon old yew   35
We'll for this Whistle run a race.'
—Away the Shepherds flew.

They leapt—they ran—and when they came
Right opposite to Dungeon-Gill,   40
Seeing that he should lose the prize,
'Stop!' to his comrade Walter cries—
James stopp'd with no good will:
Said Walter then, 'Your task is here,
'Twill keep you working half a year.'

V

'Now cross where I shall cross—come on   45
And follow me where I shall lead'—°
James proudly took him at his word,
But did not like the deed.°
It was a spot, which you may see
If ever you to Langdale go:°   50
Into a chasm a mighty Block
Hath fallen, and made a Bridge of rock:
The gulph is deep below;
And in a bason black and small
Receives a lofty Waterfall.   55

VI

With staff in hand across the cleft
The Challenger began his march;
And now, all eyes and feet, hath gain'd
The middle of the arch.
When list! he hears a piteous moan—   60
Again!—his heart within him dies—
His pulse is stopp'd, his breath is lost,
He totters, pale as any ghost,
And, looking down, he spies
A Lamb, that in the pool is pent   65
Within that black and frightful Rent.

VII

The Lamb had slipp'd into the stream,
And safe without a bruise or wound
The Cataract had borne him down
Into the gulph profound.°   70
His Dam had seen him when he fell,
She saw him down the torrent borne;

And, while with all a mother's love
She from the lofty rocks above
Sent forth a cry forlorn,   75
The Lamb, still swimming round and round,
Made answer to that plaintive sound.

VIII

When he had learnt, what thing it was,
That sent this rueful cry; I ween,°
The Boy recover'd heart, and told   80
The sight which he had seen.
Both gladly now deferr'd their task;
Nor was there wanting other aid—
A Poet, one who loves the brooks,
Far better than the sages' books,   85
By chance had thither stray'd;
And there the helpless Lamb he found
By those huge rocks encompass'd round.

IX

He drew it gently from the pool,
And brought it forth into the light: 90
The Shepherds met him with his Charge,
An unexpected sight!
Into their arms the Lamb they took,
Said they, 'He's neither maim'd nor scarr'd'—
Then up the steep ascent they hied   95
And placed him at his Mother's side;
And gently did the Bard
Those idle Shepherd-boys upbraid,
And bade them better mind their trade.

POOR SUSAN

At the corner of Wood-Street, when day-light appears,°
There's a Thrush that sings loud, it has sung for three years:
Poor Susan has pass'd by the spot, and has heard
In the silence of morning the song of the Bird.

'Tis a note of enchantment; what ails her? She sees   5
A mountain ascending, a vision of trees;

Bright volumes of vapour through Lothbury glide,
And a river flows on through the vale of Cheapside.°

Green pastures she views in the midst of the dale,
Down which she so often has tripp'd with her pail;   10
And a single small cottage, a nest like a dove's,
The one only Dwelling on earth that she loves.

She looks, and her Heart is in Heaven:—but they fade,
The mist and the river, the hill and the shade;
The stream will not flow, and the hill will not rise,   15
And the colours have all pass'd away from her eyes.

INSCRIPTION
for the spot where the Hermitage stood on St. Herbert's Island, Derwent-Water

If Thou in the dear love of some one Friend
Hast been so happy, that thou know'st what thoughts
Will, sometimes, in the happiness of love
Make the heart sick, then wilt thou reverence
This quiet spot.—St. Herbert hither came,   5
And here, for many seasons, from the world
Remov'd, and the affections of the world,
He dwelt in solitude.—But he had left
A Fellow-labourer, whom the good Man lov'd   10
As his own soul. And, when within his cave
Alone he knelt before the crucifix
While o'er the Lake the cataract of Lodore°
Peal'd to his orisons, and when he pac'd
Along the beach of this small isle and thought   15
Of his Companion, he would pray that both
Might die in the same moment. Nor in vain
So pray'd he:—as our Chronicles report,
Though here the Hermit number'd his last days,
Far from St. Cuthbert his beloved Friend,   20
Those holy Men both died in the same hour.

LINES

*Written with a pencil upon a stone in the wall of the House
(an Out-house) on the Island at Grasmere*

Rude is this Edifice, and Thou hast seen°
Buildings, albeit rude, that have maintain'd
Proportions more harmonious, and approach'd
To somewhat of a closer fellowship
With the ideal grace. Yet as it is   5
Do take it in good part; for he, the poor
Vitruvius of our village, had no help°
From the great City; never on the leaves
Of red Morocco folio saw display'd
The skeletons and pre-existing ghosts   10
Of Beauties yet unborn, the rustic Box,
Snug Cot, with Coach-house, Shed and Hermitage.°
It is a homely Pile, yet to these walls
The heifer comes in the snow-storm, and here
The new-dropp'd lamb finds shelter from the wind.   15
And hither does one Poet sometimes row
His Pinnace, a small vagrant Barge, up-piled
With plenteous store of heath and wither'd fern,
(A lading which he with his sickle cuts
Among the mountains,) and beneath this roof°   20
He makes his summer couch, and here at noon
Spreads out his limbs, while, yet unshorn, the Sheep°
Panting beneath the burthen of their wool
Lie round him, even as if they were a part
Of his own Household: nor, while from his bed   25
He through that door-place looks toward the lake
And to the stirring breezes, does he want
Creations lovely as the work of sleep,
Fair sights, and visions of romantic joy.

TO A SEXTON

Let thy wheel-barrow alone.
Wherefore, Sexton, piling still
In thy Bone-house bone on bone?

'Tis already like a hill
In a field of battle made,   5
Where three thousand skulls are laid.
——These died in peace each with the other,
Father, Sister, Friend, and Brother.

Mark the spot to which I point!
From this platform eight feet square   10
Take not even a finger-joint:
Andrew's whole fire-side is there.
Here, alone, before thine eyes,
Simon's sickly Daughter lies,
From weakness, now, and pain defended,   15
Whom he twenty winters tended.

Look but at the gardener's pride—
How he glories, when he sees
Roses, Lilies, side by side,
Violets in families!   20
By the heart of Man, his tears,
By his hopes and by his fears,
Thou, old Grey-beard! art the Warden
Of a far superior garden.

Thus then, each to other dear,   25
Let them all in quiet lie,
Andrew there and Susan here,
Neighbours in mortality.
And, should I live through sun and rain
Seven widow'd years without my Jane,   30
O Sexton, do not then remove her,
Let one grave hold the Lov'd and Lover!

ANDREW JONES

'I hate that Andrew Jones: he'll breed
His children up to waste and pillage.
I wish the press-gang or the drum°
With its tantara sound, would come
And sweep him from the village!'   5

I said not this, because he loves
Through the long day to swear and tipple;
But for the poor dear sake of one
To whom a foul deed he had done,
A friendless Man, a travelling Cripple.   10

For this poor crawling helpless wretch
Some Horseman who was passing by
A penny on the ground had thrown;
But the poor Cripple was alone
And could not stoop—no help was nigh.   15

Inch-thick the dust lay on the ground,
For it had long been droughty weather:
So with his staff the Cripple wrought
Among the dust till he had brought
The halfpennies together.   20

It chanc'd that Andrew pass'd that way
Just at that time; and there he found
The Cripple in the mid-day heat
Standing alone, and at his feet
He saw the penny on the ground.   25

He stoop'd and took the penny up:
And when the Cripple nearer drew,
Quoth Andrew, 'Under half-a-crown,
What a man finds is all his own,
And so, my friend, good day to you.'   30

And *hence* I said, that Andrew's boys
Will all be train'd to waste and pillage;
And wish'd the press-gang, or the drum
With its tantara sound, would come
And sweep him from the village!   35

RUTH

When Ruth was left half desolate
Her Father took another Mate;
And Ruth, not seven years old,

A slighted Child, at her own will
Went wandering over dale and hill,   5
In thoughtless freedom bold.

And she had made a Pipe of straw,
And from that oaten Pipe could draw°
All sounds of winds and floods;
Had built a Bower upon the green,   10
As if she from her birth had been
An Infant of the woods.

Beneath her Father's roof, alone
She seem'd to live; her thoughts her own;
Herself her own delight: 15
Pleas'd with herself, nor sad nor gay,
She pass'd her time; and in this way
Grew up to Woman's height.°

There came a Youth from Georgia's shore—°
A military Casque he wore°   20
With splendid feathers drest;
He brought them from the Cherokees;°
The feathers nodded in the breeze
And made a gallant crest.

From Indian blood you deem him sprung: 25
Ah no! he spake the English tongue,
And bare a Soldier's name;
And, when America was free°
From battle and from jeopardy,
He cross the ocean came.   30

With hues of genius on his cheek°
In finest tones the Youth could speak.
—While he was yet a Boy
The moon, the glory of the sun,
And streams that murmur as they run   35
Had been his dearest joy.

He was a lovely Youth! I guess
The panther in the wilderness

Was not so fair as he;
And when he chose to sport and play,   40
No dolphin ever was so gay
Upon the tropic sea.

Among the Indians he had fought;
And with him many tales he brought°
Of pleasure and of fear;   45
Such tales as told to any Maid
By such a Youth in the green shade
Were perilous to hear.

He told of Girls, a happy rout!
Who quit their fold with dance and shout   50
Their pleasant Indian Town
To gather strawberries all day long,°
Returning with a choral song
When day-light is gone down.

He spake of plants divine and strange   55
That every day their blossoms change,
Ten thousand lovely hues!°
With budding, fading, faded flowers
They stand the wonder of the bowers
From morn to evening dews.   60

Of march and ambush, siege and fight,
Then did he tell; and with delight
The heart of Ruth would ache;
Wild histories they were, and dear:
But 'twas a thing of heaven to hear   65
When of himself he spake!

Sometimes most earnestly he said;
'O Ruth! I have been worse than dead:
False thoughts, thoughts bold and vain
Encompass'd me on every side   70
When I, in thoughtlessness and pride,
Had cross'd the Atlantic Main.

Whatever in those Climes I found
Irregular in sight or sound

Did to my mind impart   75
A kindred impulse, seem'd allied
To my own powers, and justified
The workings of my heart.

Nor less to feed unhallow'd thought
The beauteous forms of nature wrought,   80
Fair trees and lovely flowers;
The breezes their own languor lent;
The stars had feelings which they sent
Into those magic bowers.

Yet, in my worst pursuits, I ween,   85
That often there did intervene
Pure hopes of high intent;
My passions, amid forms so fair
And stately, wanted not their share
Of noble sentiment.   90

So was it then, and so is now:
For, Ruth! with thee I know not how
I feel my spirit burn
Even as the east when day comes forth;
And to the west, and south, and north,   95
The morning doth return.

It is a purer better mind:
O Maiden innocent and kind
What sights I might have seen!
Even now upon my eyes they break!'   100
—And he again began to speak
Of Lands where he had been.°

He told of the Magnolia,* spread°
High as a cloud, high over head!
The Cypress and her spire,   105
—Of † flowers that with one scarlet gleam

---

* Magnolia grandiflora
  † The splendid appearance of these scarlet flowers, which are scattered with such profusion over the Hills in the Southern parts of North America is frequently mentioned by Bartram in his Travels.

Cover a hundred leagues and seem
To set the hills on fire.°

The Youth of green Savannahs spake,°
And many an endless, endless lake,   110
With all its fairy crowds
Of islands, that together lie
As quietly as spots of sky
Among the evening clouds.

And then he said 'How sweet it were°   115
A fisher or a hunter there,
A gardener in the shade,
Still wandering with an easy mind
To build a household fire, and find
A home in every glade.   120

What days and what sweet years! Ah me!
Our life were life indeed, with thee
So pass'd in quiet bliss,
And all the while' said he 'to know
That we were in a world of woe,°   125
On such an earth as this!'

And then he sometimes interwove
Dear thoughts about a Father's love,
'For there,' said he, 'are spun
Around the heart such tender ties,   130
That our own children to our eyes
Are dearer than the sun.

Sweet Ruth! and could you go with me
My helpmate in the woods to be,
Our shed at night to rear;   135
Or run, my own adopted Bride,
A sylvan Huntress at my side
And drive the flying deer.

Beloved Ruth!' No more he said.
Sweet Ruth alone at midnight shed   140
A solitary tear,

She thought again—and did agree
With him to sail across the sea,
And drive the flying deer.

'And now, as fitting is and right,   145
We in the Church our faith will plight,
A Husband and a Wife.'
Even so they did; and I may say
That to sweet Ruth that happy day
Was more than human life.   150

Through dream and vision did she sink,
Delighted all the while to think
That, on those lonesome floods,
And green Savannahs, she should share
His board with lawful joy, and bear   155
His name in the wild woods.°

But, as you have before been told,
This Stripling, sportive, gay, and bold,
And, with his dancing crest,
So beautiful, through savage lands   160
Had roam'd about with vagrant bands
Of Indians in the West.

The wind, the tempest roaring high,
The tumult of a tropic sky
Might well be dangerous food
For him, a Youth to whom was given   165
So much of earth so much of Heaven,
And such impetuous blood.°

Ill did he live, much evil saw
With men to whom no better law   170
Nor better life was known;
Deliberately and undeceiv'd
Those wild men's vices he receiv'd,
And gave them back his own.

His genius and his moral frame   175
Were thus impair'd, and he became

The slave of low desires:
A Man who without self-controul°
Would seek what the degraded soul
Unworthily admires.   180

And yet he with no feign'd delight
Had woo'd the maiden, day and night
Had lov'd her, night and morn:
What could he less than love a Maid
Whose heart with so much nature play'd?   185
So kind and so forlorn!°

But now the pleasant dream was gone;
No hope, no wish remain'd, not one,
They stirr'd him now no more;
New objects did new pleasure give,   190
And once again he wish'd to live
As lawless as before.

Meanwhile, as thus with him it fared,
They for the voyage were prepared
And went to the sea-shore;   195
But, when they thither came, the Youth
Deserted his poor Bride, and Ruth
Could never find him more.

God help thee Ruth!—Such pains she had
That she in half a year was mad   200
And in a prison hous'd;
And there, exulting in her wrongs,
Among the music of her songs.
She fearfully carous'd.

Yet sometimes milder hours she knew,   205
Nor wanted sun, nor rain, nor dew,
Nor pastimes of the May,
—They all were with her in her cell;
And a wild brook with chearful knell
Did o'er the pebbles play.   210

When Ruth three seasons thus had lain
There came a respite to her pain,

She from her prison fled;
But of the Vagrant none took thought;
And where it liked her best she sought   215
Her shelter and her bread.

Among the fields she breath'd again:
The master-current of her brain
Ran permanent and free;
And, coming to the Banks of Tone,*   220
There did she rest; and dwell alone
Under the greenwood tree.°

The engines of her pain, the tools
That shap'd her sorrow, rocks and pools,
And airs that gently stir   225
The vernal leaves, she loved them still,
Nor ever tax'd them with the ill
Which had been done to her.

A Barn her *winter* bed supplies;
But till the warmth of summer skies   230
And summer days is gone,
(And in this tale we all agree)
She sleeps beneath the greenwood tree,
And other home hath none.

The neighbours grieve for her, and say   235
That she will, long before her day,
Be broken down and old.
Sore aches she needs must have! but less
Of mind, than body's wretchedness,
From damp, and rain, and cold.°   240

If she is press'd by want of food
She from her dwelling in the wood
Repairs to a road-side;
And there she begs at one steep place,

---

* The Tone is a River of Somersetshire at no great distance from the Quantock Hills.
These Hills, which are alluded to a few Stanzas below, are extremely beautiful, and in
most places richly covered with Coppice woods.

Where up and down with easy pace   245
The horsemen-travellers ride.

That oaten Pipe of hers is mute,
Or thrown away; but with a flute
Her loneliness she cheers:
This flute made of a hemlock stalk°   250
At evening in his homeward walk
The Quantock Woodman hears.°

I, too, have pass'd her on the hills
Setting her little water-mills
By spouts and fountains wild—   255
Such small machinery as she turn'd
Ere she had wept, ere she had mourn'd,
A young and happy Child!

Farewel! and when thy days are told
Ill-fated Ruth! in hallow'd mold   260
Thy corpse shall buried be;
For thee a funeral bell shall ring,
And all the congregation sing
A Christian psalm for thee.

LINES

*Written with a Slate-pencil, upon a Stone, the largest of a heap lying
near a deserted Quarry, upon one of the Islands at Rydale*

Stranger! this hillock of misshapen stones
Is not a ruin of the ancient time,
Nor, as perchance, thou rashly deem'st, the Cairn
Of some old British Chief: 'tis nothing more°
Than the rude embryo of a little Dome   5
Or Pleasure-house, once destin'd to be built
Among the birch-trees of this rocky isle.
But, as it chanc'd, Sir William having learn'd°
That from the shore a full-grown man might wade,
And make himself a freeman of this spot   10
At any hour he chose, the Knight forthwith

Desisted, and the quarry and the mound
Are monuments of his unfinish'd task.—
The block on which these lines are trac'd, perhaps,
Was once selected as the corner-stone   15
Of the intended Pile, which would have been
Some quaint odd play-thing of elaborate skill,
So that, I guess, the linnet and the thrush,
And other little Builders who dwell here,
Had wonder'd at the work. But blame him not,   20
For old Sir William was a gentle Knight
Bred in this vale, to which he appertain'd°
With all his ancestry. Then peace to him,
And for the outrage which he had devis'd
Entire forgiveness!—But if thou art one   25
On fire with thy impatience to become
An inmate of these mountains, if disturb'd
By beautiful conceptions, thou hast hewn
Out of the quiet rock the elements
Of thy trim mansion destin'd soon to blaze   30
In snow-white glory, think again, and taught°
By old Sir William and his quarry, leave
Thy fragments to the bramble and the rose;
There let the vernal Slow-worm sun himself,
And let the Red-breast hop from stone to stone.   35

LINES

Written on a Tablet in a School

*In the School of —— is a Tablet, on which are inscribed, in gilt let-
ters, the names of the several persons who have been Schoolmasters
there since the foundation of the School, with the time at which they
entered upon, and quitted their office. Opposite one of those names the
Author wrote the following lines.*

If Nature, for a favorite Child°
In thee hath temper'd so her clay,
That every hour thy heart runs wild
Yet never once doth go astray,

Read o'er these lines; and then review   5
This tablet, that thus humbly rears

In such diversity of hue°
Its history of two hundred years.

—When through this little wreck of fame,
Cypher and syllable! thine eye   10
Has travell'd down to Matthew's name,
Pause with no common sympathy.

And, if a sleeping tear should wake,
Then be it neither check'd nor stay'd:
For Matthew a request I make   15
Which for himself he had not made.

Poor Matthew, all his frolics o'er,
Is silent as a standing pool;
Far from the chimney's merry roar,
And murmur of the village school.   20

The sighs which Matthew heav'd were sighs
Of one tir'd out with fun and madness;
The tears which came to Matthew's eyes
Were tears of light, the oil of gladness.°

Yet, sometimes, when the secret cup   25
Of still and serious thought went round,
It seem'd as if he drank it up—
He felt with spirit so profound.

—Thou soul of God's best earthly mould!
Thou happy soul! and can it be   30
That these two words of glittering gold°
Are all that must remain of thee?

THE TWO APRIL MORNINGS

We walk'd along, while bright and red
Uprose the morning sun;
And Matthew stopp'd, he look'd, and said,
'The will of God be done!'

A village Schoolmaster was he,°   5
With hair of glittering grey;
As blithe a man as you could see
On a spring holiday.

And on that morning, through the grass,
And by the steaming rills,   10
We travell'd merrily, to pass
A day among the hills.

'Our work,' said I, 'was well begun;
Then, from thy breast what thought,
Beneath so beautiful a sun,   15
So sad a sigh has brought?'

A second time did Matthew stop;
And, fixing still his eye
Upon the eastern mountain-top,
To me he made reply.   20

'Yon cloud with that long purple cleft
Brings fresh into my mind
A day like this which I have left
Full thirty years behind.

And just above yon slope of corn   25
Such colours, and no other
Were in the sky, that April morn,
Of this the very brother.

With rod and line my silent sport
I plied by Derwent's wave;°   30
And, coming to the church, stopp'd short
Beside my daughter's grave.

Nine summers had she scarcely seen,
The pride of all the vale;
And then she sung;—she would have been   35
A very nightingale.

Six feet in earth my Emma lay;
And yet I lov'd her more,

For so it seem'd, than till that day
I e'er had lov'd before.   40

And, turning from her grave, I met
Beside the church-yard Yew
A blooming Girl, whose hair was wet
With points of morning dew.

A basket on her head she bare;   45
Her brow was smooth and white:
To see a Child so very fair,
It was a pure delight!

No fountain from its rocky cave
E'er tripp'd with foot so free;   50
She seem'd as happy as a wave
That dances on the sea.

There came from me a sigh of pain
Which I could ill confine;
I look'd at her and look'd again: 55
—And did not wish her mine.'

Matthew is in his grave, yet now
Methinks I see him stand,
As at that moment, with his bough
Of wilding in his hand.°   60

THE FOUNTAIN, *a conversation*

We talk'd with open heart, and tongue
Affectionate and true;
A pair of Friends, though I was young,
And Matthew seventy-two.

We lay beneath a spreading oak,°   5
Beside a mossy seat;
And from the turf a fountain broke,
And gurgled at our feet.

'Now, Matthew! let us try to match
This water's pleasant tune   10

With some old Border-song, or Catch°
That suits a summer's noon.

Or of the Church-clock and the chimes
Sing here beneath the shade,
That half-mad thing of witty rhymes   15
Which you last April made!'

In silence Matthew lay, and eyed
The spring beneath the tree;
And thus the dear old Man replied,
The gray-hair'd Man of glee.   20

'Down to the vale this water steers,
How merrily it goes!
'Twill murmur on a thousand years,
And flow as now it flows.

And here on this delightful day,   25
I cannot chuse but think
How oft, a vigorous Man, I lay
Beside this Fountain's brink.

My eyes are dim with childish tears,
My heart is idly stirr'd,   30
For the same sound is in my ears,
Which in those days I heard.

Thus fares it still in our decay:
And yet the wiser mind
Mourns less for what age takes away   35
Than what it leaves behind.

The Blackbird in the summer trees,
The Lark upon the hill,
Let loose their carols when they please,
Are quiet when they will.   40

With Nature never do *they* wage
A foolish strife; they see
A happy youth, and their old age
Is beautiful and free:

But we are press'd by heavy laws;   45
And often, glad no more,
We wear a face of joy, because
We have been glad of yore.

If there is one who need bemoan
His kindred laid in earth,   50
The houshold hearts that were his own,
It is the man of mirth.

My days, my Friend, are almost gone,
My life has been approv'd,
And many love me; but by none   55
Am I enough belov'd.'

'Now both himself and me he wrongs,
The man who thus complains!
I live and sing my idle songs
Upon these happy plains,   60

And, Matthew, for thy Children dead
I'll be a son to thee!'
At this he grasp'd his hands, and said
'Alas! that cannot be.'

We rose up from the fountain-side;   65
And down the smooth descent
Of the green sheep-track did we glide;
And through the wood we went;

And, ere we came to Leonard's Rock,
He sang those witty rhymes   70
About the crazy old church-clock
And the bewilder'd chimes.°

NUTTING

— It seems a day,
(I speak of one from many singled out)
One of those heavenly days which cannot die,

When forth I sallied from our Cottage-door,* °
And with a wallet o'er my shoulder slung,
A nutting crook in hand, I turn'd my steps   5
Towards the distant woods, a Figure quaint,
Trick'd out in proud disguise of Beggar's weeds°
Put on for the occasion, by advice
And exhortation of my frugal Dame.°
Motley accoutrement! of power to smile   10
At thorns, and brakes, and brambles, and, in truth,
More ragged than need was. Among the woods,
And o'er the pathless rocks, I forc'd my way
Until, at length, I came to one dear nook
Unvisited, where not a broken bough   15
Droop'd with its wither'd leaves, ungracious sign
Of devastation, but the hazels rose
Tall and erect, with milk-white clusters hung,
A virgin scene!—A little while I stood,
Breathing with such suppression of the heart   20
As joy delights in; and with wise restraint
Voluptuous, fearless of a rival, eyed
The banquet, or beneath the trees I sate
Among the flowers, and with the flowers I play'd;
A temper known to those, who, after long   25
And weary expectation, have been bless'd
With sudden happiness beyond all hope.—
—Perhaps it was a bower beneath whose leaves
The violets of five seasons re-appear
And fade, unseen by any human eye;°   30
Where fairy water-breaks do murmur on
For ever, and I saw the sparkling foam,
And with my cheek on one of those green stones
That, fleec'd with moss, beneath the shady trees,
Lay round me, scatter'd like a flock of sheep,   35
I heard the murmur and the murmuring sound,
In that sweet mood when pleasure loves to pay
Tribute to ease; and, of its joy secure,
The heart luxuriates with indifferent things,
Wasting its kindliness on stocks and stones,   40
And on the vacant air. Then up I rose,

* The house at which I was boarded during the time I was at School.

And dragg'd to earth both branch and bough, with crash
And merciless ravage; and the shady nook
Of hazels, and the green and mossy bower,
Deform'd and sullied, patiently gave up   45
Their quiet being: and, unless I now
Confound my present feelings with the past,°
Even then, when from the bower I turn'd away
Exulting, rich beyond the wealth of kings,
I felt a sense of pain when I beheld   50
The silent trees and the intruding sky.—

Then, dearest Maiden! move along these shades
In gentleness of heart; with gentle hand
Touch,——for there is a Spirit in the woods.

'Three years she grew in sun and shower'

Three years she grew in sun and shower,
Then Nature said, 'A lovelier flower
On earth was never sown;
This Child I to myself will take;
She shall be mine, and I will make   5
A Lady of my own.

Her Teacher I myself will be,
She is my darling;—and with me
The Girl, in rock and plain,
In earth and heaven, in glade and bower,   10
Shall feel an overseeing power
To kindle or restrain.

She shall be sportive as the Fawn
That wild with glee across the lawn
Or up the mountain springs;   15
And hers shall be the breathing balm,
And hers the silence and the calm
Of mute insensate things.

The floating Clouds their state shall lend
To her; for her the willow bend;   20

Nor shall she fail to see
Even in the motions of the Storm
Grace that shall mould the Maiden's form
By silent sympathy.

The Stars of midnight shall be dear   25
To her; and she shall lean her ear
In many a secret place
Where Rivulets dance their wayward round,
And beauty born of murmuring sound
Shall pass into her face.   30

And vital feelings of delight
Shall rear her form to stately height,
Her virgin bosom swell;
Such thoughts to Lucy I will give
While she and I together live   35
Here in this happy Dell.'

Thus Nature spake—The work was done—
How soon my Lucy's race was run!
She died and left to me
This heath, at his calm and quiet scene;   40
The memory of what has been,
And never more will be.

THE PET-LAMB,

A PASTORAL

The dew was falling fast, the stars began to blink;
I heard a voice; it said, 'Drink, pretty Creature, drink!'
And, looking o'er the hedge, before me I espied,
A snow white mountain Lamb with a Maiden at its side.

No other sheep were near, the Lamb was all alone,   5
And by a slender cord was tether'd to a stone;
With one knee on the grass did the little Maiden kneel
While to that Mountain Lamb she gave its evening meal.

The Lamb while from her hand he thus his supper took
Seem'd to feast with head and ears; and his tail with pleasure
   shook.   10
'Drink, pretty Creature, drink,' she said in such a tone
That I almost receiv'd her heart into my own.

'Twas little Barbara Lewthwaite, a Child of beauty rare!
I watch'd them with delight, they were a lovely pair.
Now with her empty Can the Maiden turn'd away;   15
But ere ten yards were gone her footsteps did she stay.

Towards the Lamb she look'd; and from that shady place
I unobserv'd could see the workings of her face:
If Nature to her tongue could measur'd numbers bring
Thus, thought I, to her Lamb that little Maid might sing.   20

'What ails thee, Young One? What? Why pull so at thy cord?
Is it not well with thee? Well both for bed and board?
Thy plot of grass is soft, and green as grass can be;
Rest little Young One, rest; what is't that aileth thee?

What is it thou would'st seek? What is wanting to thy heart?   25
Thy limbs are they not strong? And beautiful thou art:
This grass is tender grass; these flowers they have no peers;
And that green corn all day is rustling in thy ears!

If the Sun be shining hot, do but stretch thy woollen chain,
This beech is standing by, its covert thou canst gain;   30
For rain and mountain storms! the like thou need'st not fear—
The rain and storm are things which scarcely can come here.

Rest, little Young One, rest; thou hast forgot the day
When my Father found thee first in places far away:
Many flocks were on the hills, but thou wert own'd by none;   35
And thy Mother from thy side for evermore was gone.

He took thee in his arms, and in pity brought thee home:
A blessed day for thee! then whither would'st thou roam?
A faithful Nurse thou hast, the Dam that did thee yean°
Upon the mountain tops no kinder could have been.   40

Thou know'st that twice a day I have brought thee in this Can
Fresh water from the brook as clear as ever ran:
And twice in the day when the ground is wet with dew
I bring thee draughts of milk, warm milk it is and new.

Thy limbs will shortly be twice as stout as they are now,   45
Then I'll yoke thee to my cart like a pony in the plough;
My Playmate thou shalt be; and when the wind is cold
Our hearth shall be thy bed, our house shall be thy fold.

It will not, will not rest!—poor Creature can it be
That 'tis thy Mother's heart which is working so in thee?   50
Things that I know not of belike to thee are dear,
And dreams of things which thou can'st neither see nor hear.

Alas, the mountain tops that look so green and fair!
I've heard of fearful winds and darkness that come there;
The little Brooks, that seem all pastime and all play,   55
When they are angry, roar like Lions for their prey.

Here thou need'st not dread the raven in the sky;
Night and day thou art safe,--our Cottage is hard by.
Why bleat so after me? Why pull so at thy chain?
Sleep—and at break of day I will come to thee again!'   60

--As homeward through the lane I went with lazy feet,
This song to myself did I oftentimes repeat;
And it seem'd, as I retrac'd the ballad line by line,
That but half of it was hers, and one half of it was mine.

Again, and once again did I repeat the song;   65
'Nay,' said I, 'more than half to the Damsel must belong,
For she look'd with such a look, and she spake with such a tone,
That I almost receiv'd her heart into my own.'

WRITTEN IN GERMANY,

On one of the coldest days of the Century

I must apprize the Reader that the stoves in North Germany gener-
ally have the impression of a galloping Horse upon them, this being
part of the Brunswick Arms.

A fig for your languages, German and Norse!
Let me have the song of the Kettle;
And the tongs and the poker, instead of that Horse
That gallops away with such fury and force
On this dreary dull plate of black metal.　　　　　　　　　　5

Our earth is no doubt made of excellent stuff;
But her pulses beat slower and slower:
The weather in Forty was cutting and rough,
And then, as Heaven knows, the Glass stood low enough;°
And *now* it is four degrees lower.　　　　　　　　　　10

Here's a Fly, a disconsolate creature, perhaps
A child of the field, or the grove;
And, sorrow for him! this dull treacherous heat
Has seduc'd the poor fool from his winter retreat,
And he creeps to the edge of my stove.　　　　　　　　　　15

Alas! how he fumbles about the domains
Which this comfortless oven environ;
He cannot find out in what track he must crawl,
Now back to the tiles, and now back to the wall,
And now on the brink of the iron.　　　　　　　　　　20

Stock-still there he stands like a traveller bemaz'd;
The best of his skill he has tried;
His feelers methinks I can see him put forth
To the East and the West, and the South and the North;
But he finds neither Guide-post nor Guide.　　　　　　　　　　25

See! his spindles sink under him, foot, leg and thigh;
His eyesight and hearing are lost;
Between life and death his blood freezes and thaws;

And his two pretty pinions of blue dusky gauze
Are glued to his sides by the frost.   30

No Brother, no Friend has he near him—while I
Can draw warmth from the cheek of my Love;
As blest and as glad in this desolate gloom,
As if green summer grass were the floor of my room,
And woodbines were hanging above.   35

Yet, God is my witness, thou small helpless Thing!
Thy life I would gladly sustain
Till summer comes up from the South, and with crowds
Of thy brethrcn a march thou should'st sound through the clouds,
And back to the forests again.   40

THE CHILDLESS FATHER

'Up, Timothy, up with your Staff and away!
Not a soul in the village this morning will stay;
The Hare has just started from Hamilton's grounds,
And Skiddaw is glad with the cry of the hounds.'°

—Of coats and of jackets grey, scarlet and green,   5
On the slopes of the pastures all colours were seen;
With their comely blue aprons, and caps white as snow,
The Girls on the hills made a holiday show.

The bason of box-wood,* just six months before,
Had stood on the table at Timothy's door;   10
A Coffin through Timothy's threshold had pass'd;
One Child did it bear and that Child was his last.

Now fast up the dell came the noise and the fray,
The horse and the horn, and the hark! hark away!
Old Timothy took up his staff, and he shut   15
With a leisurely motion the door of his hut.

---

* In several parts of the North of England, when a funeral takes place, a bason full of
Sprigs of Box-wood is placed at the door of the house from which the Coffin is taken up,
and each person who attends the funeral ordinarily takes a Sprig of this Box-wood, and
throws it into the grave of the deceased.

Perhaps to himself at that moment he said,
'The key I must take, for my Ellen is dead.'
But of this in my ears not a word did he speak,
And he went to the chase with a tear on his cheek.   20

THE OLD CUMBERLAND BEGGAR,

A DESCRIPTION

*The class of Beggars to which the Old Man here described belongs,
will probably soon be extinct. It consisted of poor, and, mostly, old and
infirm persons, who confined themselves to a stated round in their
neighbourhood, and had certain fixed days, on which, at different
houses, they regularly received alms, sometimes in money, but mostly
in provisions.*

I saw an aged beggar in my walk,
And he was seated by the highway side
On a low structure of rude masonry
Built at the foot of a huge hill, that they
Who lead their horses down the steep rough road   5
May thence remount at ease. The aged Man
Had placed his staff across the broad smooth stone
That overlays the pile, and from a bag
All white with flour the dole of village dames,
He drew his scraps and fragments, one by one,   10
And scann'd them with a fix'd and serious look
Of idle computation. In the sun
Upon the second step of that small pile,
Surrounded by those wild unpeopled hills,
He sate, and eat his food in solitude: 15
And ever, scattered from his palsied hand,
That, still attempting to prevent the waste,
Was baffled still, the crumbs in little showers
Fell on the ground, and the small mountain birds,
Not venturing yet to peck their destin'd meal,   20
Approach'd within the length of half his staff.

Him from my childhood have I known; and then
He was so old, he seems not older now;
He travels on, a solitary Man,
So helpless in appearance, that for him   25

The sauntering Horseman-traveller does not throw
With careless hand his alms upon the ground,
But stops, that he may safely lodge the coin
Within the old Man's hat; nor quits him so,
But still when he has given his horse the rein   30
Towards the aged Beggar turns a look,
Sidelong and half-reverted. She who tends
The Toll-gate, when in summer at her door
She turns her wheel, if on the road she sees°
The aged Beggar coming, quits her work,   35
And lifts the latch for him that he may pass.
The Post-boy when his rattling wheels o'ertake
The aged Beggar, in the woody lane,
Shouts to him from behind, and, if perchance
The old Man does not change his course, the Boy   40
Turns with less noisy wheels to the road-side,
And passes gently by, without a curse
Upon his lips, or anger at his heart.
He travels on, a solitary Man,
His age has no companion. On the ground   45
His eyes are turn'd, and, as he moves along,
They move along the ground; and, evermore,
Instead of common and habitual sight
Of fields with rural works, of hill and dale,
And the blue sky, one little span of earth   50
Is all his prospect. Thus, from day to day,
Bowbent, his eyes for ever on the ground,°
He plies his weary journey; seeing still,
And never knowing that he sees, some straw,
Some scatter'd leaf, or marks which, in one track,   55
The nails of cart or chariot wheel have left
Impress'd on the white road, in the same line,°
At distance still the same. Poor Traveller!
His staff trails with him; scarcely do his feet
Disturb the summer dust; he is so still   60
In look and motion, that the cottage curs,
Ere he have pass'd the door, will turn away,
Weary of barking at him. Boys and Girls,
The vacant and the busy, Maids and Youths,
And Urchins newly breech'd all pass him by: 65
Him even the slow-pac'd Waggon leaves behind.

But deem not this Man useless.—Statesmen! ye°
Who are so restless in your wisdom, ye
Who have a broom still ready in your hands
To rid the world of nuisances; ye proud,　　　　　　70
Heart-swoln, while in your pride ye contemplate
Your talents, power, and wisdom, deem him not
A burthen of the earth. 'Tis Nature's law
That none, the meanest of created things,
Of forms created the most vile and brute,　　　　　　75
The dullest or most noxious, should exist
Divorced from good—a spirit and pulse of good,
A life and soul to every mode of being
Inseparably link'd. While thus he creeps
From door to door, the Villagers in him　　　　　　80
Behold a record which together binds
Past deeds and offices of charity
Else unremember'd, and so keeps alive
The kindly mood in hearts which lapse of years,
And that half-wisdom half-experience gives　　　　　　85
Make slow to feel, and by sure steps resign
To selfishness and cold oblivious cares.
Among the farms and solitary huts,
Hamlets and thinly-scatter'd villages,
Where'er the aged Beggar takes his rounds,　　　　　　90
The mild necessity of use compels
To acts of love; and habit does the work
Of reason; yet prepares that after joy
Which reason cherishes. And thus the soul,
By that sweet taste of pleasure unpursu'd,　　　　　　95
Doth find itself insensibly dispos'd
To virtue and true goodness. Some there are,
By their good works exalted, lofty minds
And meditative, authors of delight
And happiness, which to the end of time　　　　　　100
Will live, and spread, and kindle; minds like these,
In childhood, from this solitary Being,
This helpless Wanderer, have perchance receiv'd,
(A thing more precious far than all that books
Or the solicitudes of love can do!)　　　　　　105
That first mild touch of sympathy and thought,
In which they found their kindred with a world

Where want and sorrow were. The easy Man
Who sits at his own door, and like the pear
Which overhangs his head from the green wall,   110
Feeds in the sunshine; the robust and young,
The prosperous and unthinking, they who live
Shelter'd, and flourish in a little grove
Of their own kindred, all behold in him
A silent monitor, which on their minds   115
Must needs impress a transitory thought
Of self-congratulation, to the heart
Of each recalling his peculiar boons,
His charters and exemptions; and, perchance,
Though he to no one give the fortitude   120
And circumspection needful to preserve
His present blessings, and to husband up
The respite of the season, he, at least,°
And 'tis no vulgar service, makes them felt.

Yet further.—Many, I believe, there are   125
Who live a life of virtuous decency,
Men who can hear the Decalogue and feel
No self-reproach; who of the moral law
Establish'd in the land where they abide
Are strict observers; and not negligent,   130
Meanwhile, in any tenderness of heart
Or act of love to those with whom they dwell,
Their kindred, and the children of their blood.
Praise be to such, and to their slumbers peace!
—But of the poor man ask, the abject poor,   135
Go and demand of him, if there be here
In this cold abstinence from evil deeds,
And these inevitable charities,
Wherewith to satisfy the human soul.
No—man is dear to man: the poorest poor   140
Long for some moments in a weary life
When they can know and feel that they have been
Themselves the fathers and the dealers out
Of some small blessings, have been kind to such
As needed kindness, for this single cause,   145
That we have all of us one human heart.
—Such pleasure is to one kind Being known

My Neighbour, when with punctual care, each week
Duly as Friday comes, though press'd herself
By her own wants, she from her chest of meal   150
Takes one unsparing handful for the scrip°
Of this old Mendicant, and, from her door°
Returning with exhilarated heart,
Sits by her fire and builds her hope in heav'n.

Then let him pass, a blessing on his head!   155
And while in that vast solitude to which
The tide of things has led him, he appears
To breathe and live but for himself alone,
Unblam'd, uninjur'd, let him bear about
The good which the benignant law of heaven   160
Has hung around him; and, while life is his,
Still let him prompt the unletter'd Villagers
To tender offices and pensive thoughts.
Then let him pass, a blessing on his head!
And, long as he can wander, let him breathe   165
The freshness of the vallies; let his blood
Struggle with frosty air and winter snows;
And let the charter'd wind that sweeps the heath°
Beat his grey locks against his wither'd face.
Reverence the hope whose vital anxiousness   170
Gives the last human interest to his heart.
May never HOUSE, misnamed of INDUSTRY!
Make him a captive; for that pent-up din,
Those life-consuming sounds that clog the air,
Be his the natural silence of old age.   175
Let him be free of mountain solitudes;
And have around him, whether heard or not,
The pleasant melody of woodland birds.
Few are his pleasures; if his eyes, which now
Have been so long familiar with the earth,   180
No more behold the horizontal sun
Rising or setting, let the light at least
Find a free entrance to their languid orbs.
And let him, *where* and *when* he will, sit down
Beneath the trees, or by the grassy bank   185
Of high-way side, and with the little birds
Share his chance-gather'd meal: and, finally,

As in the eye of Nature he has liv'd,
So in the eye of Nature let him die.

RURAL ARCHITECTURE

There's George Fisher, Charles Fleming, and Reginald Shore,
Three rosy-cheek'd School-boys, the highest not more
Than the height of a Counsellor's bag;°
To the top of GREAT HOW* did it please them to climb;
And there they built up without mortar or lime   5
A Man on the peak of the crag.

They built him of stones gather'd up as they lay;
They built him and christen'd him all in one day,
An Urchin both vigorous and hale;
And so without scruple they call'd him Ralph Jones.   10
Now Ralph is renown'd for the length of his bones;
The Magog of Legberthwaite dale.°

Just half a week, after the wind sallied forth,
And, in anger or merriment, out of the North
Coming on with a terrible pother,   15
From the peak of the crag blew the Giant away.
And what did these School-boys?—The very next day
They went and they built up another.

—Some little I've seen of blind boisterous works
In Paris and London, 'mong Christians or Turks,   20
Spirits busy to do and undo:
At remembrance whereof my blood sometimes will flag.
—Then, light-hearted Boys, to the top of the Crag!
And I'll build up a Giant with you.

* GREAT HOW is a single and conspicuous hill, which rises towards the foot of
Thirl-mere, on the western side of the beautiful dale of Legberthwaite, along the high
road between Keswick and Ambleside.

A POET'S EPITAPH

Art thou a Statesman, in the van
Of public business train'd and bred,
—First learn to love one living man;
Then may'st thou think upon the dead.

A Lawyer art thou?—draw not nigh;   5
Go, carry to some other place
The hardness of thy coward eye,
The falshood of thy sallow face.

Art thou a Man of purple cheer?
A rosy Man, right plump to see?   10
Approach; yet Doctor, not too near:°
This grave no cushion is for thee.

Art thou a man of gallant pride,
A Soldier, and no man of chaff?
Welcome!—but lay thy sword aside,   15
And lean upon a Peasant's staff.

Physician art thou? One, all eyes,
Philosopher! a fingering slave,°
One that would peep and botanize
Upon his mother's grave?   20

Wrapp'd closely in thy sensual fleece
O turn aside, and take, I pray,
That he below may rest in peace,
Thy pin-point of a soul away!

—A Moralist perchance appears;°   25
Led, Heaven knows how! to this poor sod:
And He has neither eyes nor ears;
Himself his world, and his own God;

One to whose smooth-rubb'd soul can cling
Nor form nor feeling great nor small;   30
A reasoning, self-sufficient thing,
An intellectual All in All!

Shut close the door! press down the latch:
Sleep in thy intellectual crust!
Nor lose ten tickings of thy watch,   35
Near this unprofitable dust.

But who is He, with modest looks,
And clad in homely russet brown?
He murmurs near the running brooks
A music sweeter than their own.°   40

He is retired as noontide dew,
Or fountain in a noonday grove;
And you must love him, ere to you
He will seem worthy of your love.

The outward shews of sky and earth,   45
Of hill and valley he has view'd;
And impulses of deeper birth
Have come to him in solitude.

In common things that round us lie
Some random truths he can impart,   50
—The harvest of a quiet eye
That broods and sleeps on his own heart.

But he is weak, both Man and Boy,
Hath been an idler in the land;
Contented if he might enjoy   55
The things which others understand.

—Come hither in thy hour of strength;
Come, weak as is a breaking wave!
Here stretch thy body at full length;
Or build thy house upon this grave.—°   60

A FRAGMENT

Between two sister moorland rills
There is a spot that seems to lie
Sacred to flowrets of the hills,
And sacred to the sky.

And in this smooth and open dell　　　　　　5
There is a tempest-stricken tree;
A corner-stone by lightning cut,
The last stone of a cottage hut;
And in this dell you see
A thing no storm can e'er destroy,　　　　　10
The shadow of a Danish Boy.

In clouds above, the Lark is heard,
He sings his blithest and his best;
But in this lonesome nook the Bird
Did never build his nest.　　　　　　　15
No Beast, no Bird hath here his home;
The Bees borne on the breezy air
Pass high above those fragrant bells
To other flowers, to other dells,
Nor ever linger there.　　　　　　　20
The Danish Boy walks here alone:
The lovely dell is all his own.

A spirit of noon day is he,
He seems a Form of flesh and blood;
Nor piping Shepherd shall he be,　　　　25
Nor Herd-boy of the wood.
A regal vest of fur he wears,
In colour like a raven's wing;
It fears not rain, nor wind, nor dew;
But in the storm 'tis fresh and blue　　　30
As budding pines in Spring;
His helmet has a vernal grace,
Fresh as the bloom upon his face.

A harp is from his shoulder slung:
He rests the harp upon his knee;　　　　35
And there in a forgotten tongue
He warbles melody.
Of flocks upon the neighbouring hills
He is the darling and the joy;
And often, when no cause appears,　　　40
The mountain ponies prick their ears,
They hear the Danish Boy,

While in the dell he sits alone
Beside the tree and corner-stone.

There sits he: in his face you spy   45
No trace of a ferocious air,
Nor ever was a cloudless sky
So steady or so fair.
The lovely Danish Boy is blest
And happy in his flowery cove: 50
From bloody deeds his thoughts are far;
And yet he warbles songs of war;
They seem like songs of love,
For calm and gentle is his mien;
Like a dead Boy he is serene.   55

POEMS on the NAMING of PLACES

ADVERTISEMENT

By Persons resident in the country and attached to rural objects,
many places will be found unnamed or of unknown names, where little
Incidents will have occurred, or feelings been experienced, which will
have given to such places a private and peculiar interest. From a wish
to give some sort of record to such Incidents or renew the gratification
of such Feelings, Names have been given to Places by the Author and
some of his Friends, and the following Poems written in consequence.

I

It was an April morning: fresh and clear
The Rivulet, delighting in its strength,
Ran with a young man's speed; and yet the voice
Of waters which the winter had supplied
Was soften'd down into a vernal tone.   5
The spirit of enjoyment and desire,
And hopes and wishes, from all living things
Went circling, like a multitude of sounds.
The budding groves appear'd as if in haste
To spur the steps of June; as if their shades   10
Of *various* green were hindrances that stood
Between them and their object: yet, meanwhile,
There was such deep contentment in the air
That every naked ash, and tardy tree

Yet leafless, seem'd as though the countenance   15
With which it look'd on this delightful day
Were native to the summer.—Up the brook
I roam'd in the confusion of my heart,
Alive to all things and forgetting all.
At length I to a sudden turning came   20
In this continuous glen, where down a rock
The stream, so ardent in its course before,
Sent forth such sallies of glad sound, that all
Which I till then had heard, appear'd the voice
Of common pleasure: beast and bird, the Lamb,   25
The Shepherd's Dog, the Linnet and the Thrush
Vied with this Waterfall, and made a song
Which, while I listen'd, seem'd like the wild growth,
Or like some natural produce of the air
That could not cease to be. Green leaves were here,   30
But 'twas the foliage of the rocks, the birch,
The yew, the holly, and the bright green thorn,
With hanging islands of resplendant furze:
And on a summit, distant a short space,
By any who should look beyond the dell,   35
A single mountain Cottage might be seen.
I gaz'd and gaz'd, and to myself I said,
'Our thoughts at least are ours; and this wild nook,
My EMMA, I will dedicate to thee.'
——Soon did the spot become my other home,   40
My dwelling, and my out-of-doors abode.
And, of the Shepherds who have seen me there,
To whom I sometimes in our idle talk
Have told this fancy, two or three, perhaps,
Years after we are gone and in our graves,   45
When they have cause to speak of this wild place,
May call it by the name of EMMA'S DELL.

II

TO JOANNA

Amid the smoke of cities did you pass
Your time of early youth; and there you learn'd,
From years of quiet industry, to love
The living Beings by your own fire-side,

With such a strong devotion, that your heart   5
Is slow towards the sympathies of them
Who look upon the hills with tenderness,
And make dear friendships with the streams and groves.
Yet we, who are transgressors in this kind,
Dwelling retired in our simplicity   10
Among the woods and fields, we love you well,
Joanna! and I guess, since you have been
So distant from us now for two long years,
That you will gladly listen to discourse
However trivial, if you thence are taught   15
That they, with whom you once were happy, talk
Familiarly of you and of old times.

While I was seated, now some ten days past,
Beneath those lofty firs, that overtop
Their ancient neighbour, the old Steeple tower,   20
The Vicar from his gloomy house hard by
Came forth to greet me, and when he had ask'd,
'How fares Joanna, that wild-hearted Maid!
And when will she return to us?' he paus'd;
And, after short exchange of village news,   25
He with grave looks demanded, for what cause,
Reviving obsolete Idolatry,
I, like a Runic Priest, in characters°
Of formidable size, had chisel'd out
Some uncouth name upon the native rock,   30
Above the Rotha, by the forest side.°
—Now, by those dear immunities of heart
Engender'd betwixt malice and true love,
I was not loth to be so catechiz'd,
And this was my reply.—'As it befel,   35
One summer morning we had walk'd abroad
At break of day, Joanna and myself.
—'Twas that delightful season, when the broom,
Full flower'd, and visible on every steep,
Along the copses runs in veins of gold.   40
Our pathway led us on to Rotha's banks;
And when we came in front of that tall rock
Which looks towards the East, I there stopp'd short,
And trac'd the lofty barrier with my eye

From base to summit; such delight I found   45
To note in shrub and tree, in stone and flower,
That intermixture of delicious hues,
Along so vast a surface, all at once,
In one impression, by connecting force
Of their own beauty, imag'd in the heart.   50
—When I had gaz'd perhaps two minutes' space,
Joanna, looking in my eyes, beheld
That ravishment of mine, and laugh'd aloud.
The rock, like something starting from a sleep,
Took up the Lady's voice, and laugh'd again: 55
That ancient Woman seated on Helm-crag
Was ready with her cavern; Hammar-Scar,
And the tall Steep of Silver-How sent forth
A noise of laughter; southern Loughrigg heard
And Fairfield answer'd with a mountain tone: 60
Helvellyn far into the clear blue sky
Carried the Lady's voice,—old Skiddaw blew
His speaking trumpet;—back out of the clouds
Of Glaramara southward came the voice;
And Kirkstone toss'd it from his misty head.°   65
Now whether,' (said I to our cordial Friend
Who in the hey-day of astonishment
Smil'd in my face) 'this were in simple truth
A work accomplish'd by the brotherhood
Of ancient mountains, or my ear was touch'd   70
With dreams and visionary impulses,
Is not for me to tell; but sure I am
That there was a loud uproar in the hills.
And, while we both were listening, to my side
The fair Joanna drew, as if she wish'd   75
To shelter from some object of her fear.
—And hence, long afterwards, when eighteen moons
Were wasted, as I chanc'd to walk alone
Beneath this rock, at sun-rise, on a calm
And silent morning, I sate down, and there,   80
In memory of affections old and true,
I chissel'd out in those rude characters
Joanna's name upon the living stone.
And I, and all who dwell by my fire-side
Have call'd the lovely rock, JOANNA'S ROCK.'   85

NOTE

In Cumberland and Westmoreland are several Inscriptions, upon the native rock, which, from the wasting of time, and the rudeness of the Workmanship had been mistaken for Runic. They are without doubt Roman.

The Rotha, mentioned in this poem, is the River which, flowing through the Lakes of Grasmere and Rydale, falls into Wyndermere. On Helm-Crag, that impressive single Mountain at the head of the Vale of Grasmere, is a Rock which from most points of view bears a striking resemblance to an Old Woman cowering. Close by this rock is one of those Fissures or Caverns, which in the language of the Country are called Dungeons. Most of the Mountains here mentioned immediately surround the vale of Grasmere; of the others, some are at a considerable distance, but they belong to the same cluster.

III

There is an Eminence,—of these our hills
The last that parleys with the setting sun.
We can behold it from our Orchard-seat;°
And, when at evening we pursue our walk
Along the public way, this Cliff, so high   5
Above us, and so distant in its height,
Is visible, and often seems to send
Its own deep quiet to restore our hearts.
The meteors make of it a favorite haunt:
The star of Jove, so beautiful and large   10
In the mid heav'ns, is never half so fair
As when he shines above it. 'Tis in truth
The loneliest place we have among the clouds.
And She who dwells with me, whom I have lov'd
With such communion, that no place on earth°   15
Can ever be a solitude to me,
Hath said, this lonesome Peak shall bear my Name.

IV

A narrow girdle of rough stones and crags,
A rude and natural causeway, interpos'd
Between the water and a winding slope
Of copse and thicket, leaves the eastern shore
Of Grasmere safe in its own privacy.   5
And there, myself and two beloved Friends,
One calm September morning, ere the mist
Had altogether yielded to the sun,
Saunter'd on this retir'd and difficult way.

——Ill suits the road with one in haste, but we   10
Play'd with our time; and, as we stroll'd along,
It was our occupation to observe
Such objects as the waves had toss'd ashore,
Feather, or leaf, or weed, or wither'd bough,
Each on the other heap'd along the line   15
Of the dry wreck. And, in our vacant mood,
Not seldom did we stop to watch some tuft
Of dandelion seed or thistle's beard,
Which, seeming lifeless half, and half impell'd
By some internal feeling, skimm'd along   20
Close to the surface of the lake that lay
Asleep in a dead calm—ran closely on
Along the dead calm lake, now here, now there,
In all its sportive wanderings all the while
Making report of an invisible breeze   25
That was its wings, its chariot, and its horse,
Its very playmate, and its moving soul.
——And often, trifling with a privilege
Alike indulg'd to all, we paus'd, one now,
And now the other, to point out, perchance   30
To pluck, some flower or water-weed, too fair
Either to be divided from the place
On which it grew, or to be left alone
To its own beauty. Many such there are,
Fair Ferns and Flowers, and chiefly that tall Fern   35
So stately, of the Queen Osmunda nam'd;°
Plant lovelier in its own retir'd abode
On Grasmere's beach, than Naiad by the side
Of Grecian brook, or Lady of the Mere
Sole-sitting by the shores of old Romance.   40
——So fared we that sweet morning: from the fields,
Meanwhile, a noise was heard, the busy mirth
Of Reapers, Men and Women, Boys and Girls.
Delighted much to listen to those sounds,
And, in the fashion which I have describ'd,   45
Feeding unthinking fancies, we advanc'd
Along the indented shore; when suddenly,
Through a thin veil of glittering haze, we saw
Before us on a point of jutting land
The tall and upright figure of a Man   50

Attir'd in peasant's garb, who stood alone
Angling beside the margin of the lake.
That way we turn'd our steps; nor was it long,
Ere, making ready comments on the sight
Which then we saw, with one and the same voice   55
We all cried out, that he must be indeed
An idle man, who thus could lose a day
Of the mid harvest, when the labourer's hire
Is ample, and some little might be stor'd
Wherewith to cheer him in the winter time.   60
Thus talking of that Peasant we approach'd
Close to the spot where with his rod and line
He stood alone; whereat he turn'd his head
To greet us—and we saw a Man worn down
By sickness, gaunt and lean, with sunken cheeks   65
And wasted limbs, his legs so long and lean
That for my single self I look'd at them,
Forgetful of the body they sustain'd.—
Too weak to labour in the harvest field,
The Man was using his best skill to gain   70
A pittance from the dead unfeeling lake
That knew not of his wants. I will not say
What thoughts immediately were ours, nor how
The happy idleness of that sweet morn,
With all its lovely images, was chang'd   75
To serious musing and to self-reproach.
Nor did we fail to see within ourselves
What need there is to be reserv'd in speech,
And temper all our thoughts with charity.
—Therefore, unwilling to forget that day,   80
My Friend, Myself, and She who then receiv'd
The same admonishment, have call'd the place
By a memorial name, uncouth indeed
As e'er by Mariner was given to Bay
Or Foreland on a new-discover'd coast,
And, POINT RASH-JUDGMENT is the Name it bears.   85

V
To M. H.

Our walk was far among the ancient trees;
There was no road nor any wood-man's path;
But the thick umbrage, checking the wild growth
Of weed and sapling, on the soft green turf
Beneath the branches of itself had made   5
A track which brought us to a slip of lawn,
And a small bed of water in the woods.
All round this pool both flocks and herds might drink
On its firm margin, even as from a Well,
Or some Stone-bason which the Herdsman's hand   10
Had shap'd for their refreshment; nor did sun
Or wind from any quarter ever come,
But as a blessing, to this calm recess,
This glade of water and this one green field,
The spot was made by Nature for herself: 15
The travellers know it not, and 'twill remain
Unknown to them; but it is beautiful,
And if a man should plant his cottage near,
Should sleep beneath the shelter of its trees,
And blend its waters with his daily meal,
He would so love it that in his death hour   20
Its image would survive among his thoughts:
And, therefore, my sweet MARY, this still nook
With all its beeches we have named for You.

LINES
Written when sailing in a Boat at Evening

How rich the wave, in front, imprest
With evening twilight's summer hues,
While, facing thus the crimson west,
The Boat her silent course pursues!
And see how dark the backward stream!   5
A little moment past, so smiling!
And still, perhaps, with faithless gleam,
Some other Loiterer beguiling.

Such views the youthful Bard allure;
But, heedless of the following gloom,   10
He deems their colours shall endure
'Till peace go with him to the tomb.
—And let him nurse his fond deceit,
And what if he must die in sorrow!
Who would not cherish dreams so sweet,   15
Though grief and pain may come to-morrow?

REMEMBRANCE of COLLINS,

Written upon the Thames, near Richmond.

Glide gently, thus for ever glide
O Thames! that other Bards may see
As lovely visions by thy side
As now, fair River! come to me.
Oh glide, fair Stream! for ever so;   5
Thy quiet soul on all bestowing,
'Till all our minds for ever flow,
As thy deep waters now are flowing.

Vain thought! yet be as now thou art,
That in thy waters may be seen   10
The image of a poet's heart,
How bright, how solemn, how serene!
Such as did once the Poet bless,
Who, pouring here a* later ditty,
Could find no refuge from distress,   15
But in the milder grief of pity.

Now let us, as we float along,
For *him* suspend the dashing oar;
And pray that never child of Song
May know that Poet's sorrows more.   20
How calm! how still! the only sound,
The dripping of the oar suspended!
—The evening darkness gathers round
By virtue's holiest Powers attended.

* Collins's Ode on the death of Thompson, the last written, I believe, of the poems which were published during his life-time. This Ode is also alluded to in the next stanza.

THE TWO THIEVES,
or the last stage of Avarice

Oh now that the genius of Bewick were mine,
And the skill which he learn'd on the Banks of the Tyne!°
Then the Muses might deal with me just as they chose,
For I'd take my last leave both of verse and of prose.

What feats would I work with my magical hand!   5
Book learning and books should be banish'd the land:
And for hunger and thirst and such troublesome calls!
Every Ale-house should then have a feast on its walls.

The Traveller would hang his wet clothes on a chair;
Let them smoke, let them burn, not a straw would he care;   10
For the Prodigal Son, Joseph's Dream and his Sheaves,°
Oh what would they be to my tale of two Thieves!

Little Dan is unbreech'd, he is three birth-days old;°
His Grandsire that age more than thirty times told;
There are ninety good seasons of fair and foul weather   15
Between them, and both go a stealing together.

With chips is the Carpenter strewing his floor?
Is a cart-load of peats at an old Woman's door?
Old Daniel his hand to the treasure will slide;
And his Grandson's as busy at work by his side.   20

Old Daniel begins, he stops short—and his eye
Through the lost look of dotage is cunning and sly.
'Tis a look which at this time is hardly his own,
But tells a plain tale of the days that are flown.

Dan once had a heart which was mov'd by the wires   25
Of manifold pleasures and many desires:
And what if he cherish'd his purse? 'Twas no more
Than treading a path trod by thousands before.

'Twas a path trod by thousands; but Daniel is one
Who went something farther than others have gone: 30

And now with old Daniel you see how it fares;
You see to what end he has brought his grey hairs.

The Pair sally forth hand in hand: ere the sun
Has peer'd o'er the beeches their work is begun:
And yet, into whatever sin they may fall,   35
This Child but half knows it and that not at all.

They hunt through the street with deliberate tread,
And each in his turn is both leader and led;
And, wherever they carry their plots and their wiles,
Every face in the village is dimpled with smiles.   40

Neither check'd by the rich nor the needy they roam;
For grey-headed Dan has a daughter at home,
Who will gladly repair all the damage that's done;
And three, were it ask'd, would be render'd for one.

Old Man! whom so oft I with pity have ey'd,   45
I love thee and love the sweet Boy at thy side:
Long yet may'st thou live, for a teacher we see
That lifts up the veil of our nature in thee.

'A whirl-blast from behind the Hill'

A whirl-blast from behind the hill
Rush'd o'er the wood with startling sound:
Then all at once the air was still,
And showers of hail-stones patter'd round.
Where leafless Oaks tower'd high above,   5
I sate within an undergrove
Of tallest hollies, tall and green;
A fairer bower was never seen.
From year to year the spacious floor
With wither'd leaves is cover'd o'er,   10
You could not lay a hair between:
And all the year the bower is green.
But see! where'er the hailstones drop
The wither'd leaves all skip and hop,
There's not a breeze—no breath of air—   15

Yet here, and there, and every where
Along the floor, beneath the shade
By those embowering hollies made,
The leaves in myriads jump and spring,
As if with pipes and music rare   20
Some Robin Good-fellow were there,°
And all those leaves, that jump and spring,
Were each a joyous, living thing.

Oh! grant me Heaven a heart at ease,
That I may never cease to find,   25
Even in appearances like these
Enough to nourish and to stir my mind!

SONG FOR THE WANDERING JEW

Though the torrents from their fountains
Roar down many a craggy steep,
Yet they find among the mountains
Resting-places calm and deep.

Though almost with eagle pinion   5
O'er the rocks the Chamois roam,°
Yet he has some small dominion
Which, no doubt, he calls his home.

If on windy days the Raven
Gambol like a dancing skiff,   10
Not the less he loves his haven
On the bosom of the cliff.

Though the Sea-horse in the ocean
Own no dear domestic cave;
Yet he slumbers without motion   15
On the calm and silent wave.

Day and night my toils redouble!
Never nearer to the goal,
Night and day, I feel the trouble
Of the Wanderer in my soul.

MICHAEL,

A PASTORAL POEM

If from the public way you turn your steps
Up the tumultuous brook of Green-head Gill,°
You will suppose that with an upright path
Your feet must struggle; in such bold ascent
The pastoral Mountains front you, face to face.   5
But, courage! for beside that boisterous Brook
The mountains have all open'd out themselves,
And made a hidden valley of their own.
No habitation there is seen; but such
As journey thither find themselves alone   10
With a few sheep, with rocks and stones, and kites°
That overhead are sailing in the sky.
It is in truth an utter solitude,
Nor should I have made mention of this Dell
But for one object which you might pass by,   15
Might see and notice not. Beside the brook
There is a straggling heap of unhewn stones!
And to that place a story appertains,
Which, though it be ungarnish'd with events,°
Is not unfit, I deem, for the fire-side,   20
Or for the summer shade. It was the first,
The earliest of those tales that spake to me
Of Shepherds, dwellers in the vallies, men
Whom I already lov'd, not verily
For their own sakes, but for the fields and hills   25
Where was their occupation and abode.
And hence this Tale, while I was yet a Boy
Careless of books, yet having felt the power
Of Nature, by the gentle agency
Of natural objects led me on to feel   30
For passions that were not my own, and think
(At random and imperfectly indeed)
On man, the heart of man, and human life.
Therefore, although it be a history
Homely and rude, I will relate the same   35
For the delight of a few natural hearts,
And with yet fonder feeling, for the sake

Of youthful Poets, who among these Hills
Will be my second self when I am gone.

Upon the Forest-side in Grasmere Vale°   40
There dwelt a Shepherd, Michael was his name,
An Old Man, stout of heart, and strong of limb.
His bodily frame had been from youth to age
Of an unusual strength: his mind was keen
Intense and frugal, apt for all affairs,   45
And in his Shepherd's calling he was prompt
And watchful more than ordinary men.
Hence he had learn'd the meaning of all winds,
Of blasts of every tone; and, oftentimes,
When others heeded not, He heard the South   50
Make subterraneous music, like the noise
Of Bagpipers on distant Highland hills;
The Shepherd, at such warning, of his flock
Bethought him, and he to himself would say,
'The winds are now devising work for me!'   55
And, truly, at all times the storm, that drives
The Traveller to a shelter, summon'd him
Up to the mountains: he had been alone
Amid the heart of many thousand mists,
That came to him and left him on the heights.   60
So liv'd he till his eightieth year was pass'd.

And grossly that man errs, who should suppose
That the green Valleys, and the Streams and Rocks
Were things indifferent to the Shepherd's thoughts.
Fields, where with chearful spirits he had breath'd   65
The common air; the hills, which he so oft
Had climb'd with vigorous steps; which had impress'd
So many incidents upon his mind
Of hardship, skill or courage, joy or fear;
Which like a book preserv'd the memory   70
Of the dumb animals, whom he had sav'd,
Had fed or shelter'd, linking to such acts,
So grateful in themselves, the certainty
Of honorable gains; these fields, these hills,
Which were his living Being, even more°   75
Than his own blood—what could they less? had laid

Strong hold on his affections, were to him
A pleasurable feeling of blind love,
The pleasure which there is in life itself.

He had not passed his days in singleness.   80
He had a Wife, a comely Matron, old
Though younger than himself full twenty years.
She was a woman of a stirring life
Whose heart was in her house: two wheels she had
Of antique form, this large for spinning wool,   85
That small for flax, and if one wheel had rest,°
It was because the other was at work.
The Pair had but one Inmate in their house,
An only Child, who had been born to them
When Michael telling o'er his years began   90
To deem that he was old, in Shepherd's phrase,
With one foot in the grave. This only Son,
With two brave Sheep-dogs tried in many a storm,
The one of an inestimable worth,
Made all their Household. I may truly say,   95
That they were as a proverb in the vale
For endless industry. When day was gone,°
And from their occupations out of doors
The Son and Father were come home, even then
Their labour did not cease; unless when all   100
Turn'd to their cleanly supper-board, and there,
Each with a mess of pottage and skimm'd milk,
Sate round their basket pil'd with oaten cakes,
And their plain home-made cheese. Yet when their meal
Was ended, LUKE (for so the Son was nam'd)   105
And his old Father, both betook themselves
To such convenient work, as might employ
Their hands by the fire-side; perhaps to card
Wool for the House-wife's spindle, or repair
Some injury done to sickle, flail, or scythe,   110
Or other implement of house or field.

Down from the cieling by the chimney's edge,
Which in our ancient uncouth country style°
Did with a huge projection overbrow
Large space beneath, as duly as the light   115

Of day grew dim, the House-wife hung a Lamp;
An aged utensil, which had perform'd
Service beyond all others of its kind.
Early at evening did it burn and late,
Surviving Comrade of uncounted Hours   120
Which going by from year to year had found
And left the couple neither gay perhaps
Nor chearful, yet with objects and with hopes,
Living a life of eager industry.
And now, when Luke was in his eighteenth year,   125
There by the light of this old Lamp they sate,
Father and Son, while late into the night
The House-wife plied her own peculiar work,
Making the cottage thro' the silent hours
Murmur as with the sound of summer flies.   130
Not with a waste of words, but for the sake
Of pleasure, which I know that I shall give
To many living now, I of this Lamp
Speak thus minutely: for there are no few
Whose memories will bear witness to my tale.   135
The Light was famous in its neighbourhood,
And was a public Symbol of the life,
The thrifty Pair had liv'd. For, as it chanc'd,
Their Cottage on a plot of rising ground
Stood single, with large prospect, North and South,   140
High into Easedale, up to Dunmal-Raise,°
And Westward to the village near the Lake,
And, from this constant light so regular
And so far seen, the House itself, by all
Who dwelt within the limits of the vale,   145
Both old and young, was nam'd The EVENING STAR.°

Thus living on through such a length of years,
The Shepherd, if he lov'd himself, must needs
Have lov'd his Help-mate; but to Michael's heart°
This Son of his old age was yet more dear——°   150
Effect which might perhaps have been produc'd
By that instinctive tenderness, the same
Blind Spirit, which is in the blood of all——
Or that a child, more than all other gifts,
Brings hope with it, and forward-looking thoughts,   155

And stirrings of inquietude, when they
By tendency of nature needs must fail.
From such, and other causes, to the thoughts
Of the old Man his only Son was now
The dearest object that he knew on earth.   160
Exceeding was the love he bare to him,
His Heart and his Heart's joy! For oftentimes
Old Michael, while he was a babe in arms,
Had done him female service, not alone
For dalliance and delight, as is the use   165
Of Fathers, but with patient mind enforc'd
To acts of tenderness; and he had rock'd
His cradle with a woman's gentle hand.

And, in a later time, ere yet the Boy
Had put on Boy's attire, did Michael love,   170
Albeit of a stern unbending mind,
To have the young one in his sight, when he
Had work by his own door, or when he sate
With sheep before him on his Shepherd's stool,
Beneath that large old Oak, which near their door°   175
Stood, and from its enormous breadth of shade
Chosen for the Shearer's covert from the sun,
Thence in our rustic dialect was call'd
The CLIPPING TREE,* a name which yet it bears.
There, while they two were sitting in the shade,   180
With others round them, earnest all and blithe,
Would Michael exercise his heart with looks
Of fond correction and reproof bestow'd
Upon the Child, if he disturb'd the sheep
By catching at their legs, or with his shouts   185
Scar'd them, while they lay still beneath the shears.

And when by Heaven's good grace the Boy grew up
A healthy Lad, and carried in his cheek
Two steady roses that were five years old,
Then Michael from a winter coppice cut   190
With his own hand a sapling, which he hoop'd

---

* Clipping is the word used in the North of England for shearing.

With iron, making it throughout in all
Due requisites a perfect Shepherd's Staff,
And gave it to the Boy; wherewith equipp'd
He as a Watchman oftentimes was plac'd   195
At gate or gap, to stem or turn the flock;
And to his office prematurely call'd
There stood the Urchin, as you will divine,
Something between a hindrance and a help,
And for this cause not always, I believe,   200
Receiving from his Father hire of praise.
Though nought was left undone which staff or voice,
Or looks, or threatening gestures could perform.
But soon as Luke, full ten years old, could stand
Against the mountain blasts, and to the heights,   205
Not fearing toil, nor length of weary ways,
He with his Father daily went, and they
Were as companions, why should I relate
That objects which the Shepherd lov'd before
Were dearer now? that from the Boy there came   210
Feelings and emanations, things which were
Light to the sun and music to the wind;
And that the Old Man's heart seem'd born again.
Thus in his Father's sight the Boy grew up:
And now when he had reach'd his eighteenth year,   215
He was his comfort and his daily hope.°

While in the fashion which I have described
This simple Household thus were living on
From day to day, to Michael's ear there came
Distressful tidings. Long before the time
Of which I speak, the Shepherd had been bound   220
In surety for his Brother's Son, a man
Of an industrious life, and ample means,
But unforeseen misfortunes suddenly
Had press'd upon him, and old Michael now
Was summon'd to discharge the forfeiture,   225
A grievous penalty, but little less
Than half his substance. This unlook'd for claim,
At the first hearing, for a moment took
More hope out of his life than he supposed
That any old man ever could have lost.   230

As soon as he had gathered so much strength
That he could look his trouble in the face,
It seem'd that his sole refuge was to sell
A portion of his patrimonial fields.
Such was his first resolve; he thought again,   235
And his heart fail'd him. 'Isabel,' said he,
Two evenings after he had heard the news,
'I have been toiling more than seventy years,
And in the open sun-shine of God's love
Have we all liv'd, yet if these fields of ours   240
Should pass into a Stranger's hand, I think
That I could not lie quiet in my grave.
Our lot is a hard lot; the Sun itself
Has scarcely been more diligent than I,
And I have liv'd to be a fool at last   245
To my own family. An evil Man
That was, and made an evil choice, if he
Were false to us; and if he were not false,
There are ten thousand to whom loss like this
Had been no sorrow. I forgive him—but   250
'Twere better to be dumb than to talk thus.
When I began, my purpose was to speak
Of remedies and of a chearful hope.
Our Luke shall leave us, Isabel; the land
Shall not go from us, and it shall be free;   255
He shall possess it, free as is the wind°
That passes over it. We have, thou knowest,
Another Kinsman—he will be our friend
In this distress. He is a prosperous man,
Thriving in trade—and Luke to him shall go,   260
And with his Kinsman's help and his own thrift
He quickly will repair this loss, and then
May come again to us. If here he stay,
What can be done? Where every one is poor
What can be gain'd?' At this, the old man paus'd,   265
And Isabel sate silent, for her mind
Was busy, looking back into past times.
There's Richard Bateman, thought she to herself,
He was a Parish-boy—at the Church-door
They made a gathering for him, shillings, pence,   270
And halfpennies, wherewith the neighbours bought

A Basket, which they fill'd with Pedlar's wares;
And with this Basket on his arm, the Lad
Went up to London, found a Master there,
Who out of many chose the trusty Boy   275
To go and overlook his merchandise
Beyond the seas, where he grew wond'rous rich,
And left estates and monies to the poor,
And at his birth-place built a Chapel, floor'd
With Marble, which he sent from foreign lands.°   280
These thoughts, and many others of like sort,
Pass'd quickly through the mind of Isabel,
And her face brighten'd. The Old Man was glad,
And thus resum'd. 'Well! Isabel, this scheme
These two days has been meat and drink to me.   285
Far more than we have lost is left us yet.
—We have enough—I wish indeed that I
Were younger, but this hope is a good hope.
—Make ready Luke's best garments, of the best
Buy for him more, and let us send him forth   290
To-morrow, or the next day, or to-night:
—If he could go, the Boy should go to-night.'
Here Michael ceas'd, and to the fields went forth
With a light heart. The House-wife for five days
Was restless morn and night, and all day long   295
Wrought on with her best fingers to prepare
Things needful for the journey of her Son.
But Isabel was glad when Sunday came
To stop her in her work: for, when she lay
By Michael's side, she for the two last nights   300
Heard him, how he was troubled in his sleep:
And when they rose at morning she could see
That all his hopes were gone. That day at noon
She said to Luke, while they two by themselves
Were sitting at the door, 'Thou must not go,   305
We have no other child but thee to lose,
None to remember—do not go away,
For if thou leave thy Father he will die.'
The Lad made answer with a jocund voice;
And Isabel, when she had told her fears,   310
Recover'd heart. That evening her best fare
Did she bring forth, and all together sate,

Like happy people round a Christmas fire.
Next morning Isabel resum'd her work;
And all the ensuing week the house appear'd   315
As cheerful as a grove in Spring: at length
The expected letter from their Kinsman came,
With kind assurances that he would do
His utmost for the welfare of the Boy,
To which requests were added that forthwith   320
He might be sent to him. Ten times or more
The letter was read over; Isabel
Went forth to shew it to the neighbours round
Nor was there at that time on English Land
A prouder heart than Luke's. When Isabel   325
Had to her house return'd, the Old Man said,
'He shall depart to-morrow.' To this word
The House-wife answered, talking much of things
Which, if at such short notice he should go,
Would surely be forgotten. But at length   330
She gave consent, and Michael was at ease.

Near the tumultuous brook of Green-head Gill,
In that deep Valley, Michael had design'd
To build a sheep-fold; and, before he heard
The tidings of his melancholy loss,   335
For this same purpose he had gather'd up
A heap of stones, which close to the brook side
Lay thrown together, ready for the work.
With Luke that evening thitherward he walk'd;
And soon as they had reach'd the place he stopp'd,°   340
And thus the Old Man spake to him. 'My Son,
To-morrow thou wilt leave me: with full heart
I look upon thee, for thou art the same
That wert a promise to me ere thy birth,
And all thy life hast been my daily joy.   345
I will relate to thee some little part
Of our two histories; 'twill do thee good
When thou art from me, even if I should speak
Of things thou canst not know of.——After thou
First cam'st into the world, as it befalls   350
To new-born infants, thou didst sleep away
Two days, and blessings from thy Father's tongue

Then fell upon thee. Day by day pass'd on,
And still I lov'd thee with encreasing love.
Never to living ear came sweeter sounds   355
Than when I heard thee by our own fire-side
First uttering, without words, a natural tune,
When thou, a feeding babe, didst in thy joy
Sing at thy Mother's breast. Month follow'd month,
And in the open fields my life was pass'd   360
And in the mountains, else I think that thou
Hadst been brought up upon thy Father's knees.
—But we were playmates, Luke; among these hills,
As well thou know'st, in us the old and young
Have play'd together, nor with me didst thou   365
Lack any pleasure which a boy can know.'
Luke had a manly heart; but at these words
He sobb'd aloud; the Old Man grasp'd his hand,
And said, 'Nay do not take it so—I see
That these are things of which I need not speak.   370
—Even to the utmost I have been to thee
A kind and a good Father: and herein
I but repay a gift which I myself
Receiv'd at others hands; for, though now old
Beyond the common life of man, I still   375
Remember them who lov'd me in my youth.
Both of them sleep together: here they liv'd,
As all their Forefathers had done, and when
At length their time was come, they were not loth
To give their bodies to the family mold.   380
I wish'd that thou should'st live the life they liv'd.
But 'tis a long time to look back, my Son,
And see so little gain from sixty years.
These fields were burthen'd when they came to me;
'Till I was forty years of age, not more   385
Than half of my inheritance was mine,
I toil'd and toil'd; God bless'd me in my work,
And 'till these three weeks past the land was free.
—It looks as if it never could endure
Another Master. Heaven forgive me, Luke,   390
If I judge ill for thee, but it seems good
That thou shouldst go.' At this the Old Man paus'd;
Then, pointing to the Stones near which they stood,

Thus, after a short silence, he resum'd:
'This was a work for us; and now, my Son,   395
It is a work for me. But, lay one Stone—
Here, lay it for me, Luke, with thine own hands.
Nay, Boy, be of good hope:—we both may live
To see a better day. At eighty-four   400
I still am strong and stout;—do thou thy part,
I will do mine.—I will begin again
With many tasks that were resign'd to thee;
Up to the heights, and in among the storms,
Will I without thee go again, and do   405
All works which I was wont to do alone,
Before I knew thy face.——Heaven bless thee, Boy!
Thy heart, these two weeks has been beating fast
With many hopes—it should be so—yes—yes—
I knew that thou could'st never have a wish   410
To leave me, Luke, thou hast been bound to me
Only by links of love, when thou art gone
What will be left to us!—But, I forget
My purposes. Lay now the corner-stone,
As I requested, and hereafter, Luke,   415
When thou art gone away, should evil men
Be thy companions think of me, my Son,
And of this moment; hither turn thy thoughts
And God will strengthen thee: amid all fear
And all temptation, Luke, I pray that thou°   420
May'st bear in mind the life thy Fathers liv'd,
Who, being innocent, did for that cause
Bestir them in good deeds. Now, fare thee well—
When thou return'st thou in this place wilt see
A work which is not here; a covenant°   425
'Twill be between us—— but whatever fate
Befal thee, I shall love thee to the last,
And bear thy memory with me to the grave.'

The Shepherd ended here: and Luke stoop'd down,
And as his Father had requested, laid   430
The first stone of the Sheep-fold; at the sight
The Old Man's grief broke from him, to his heart
He press'd his Son, he kissed him and wept;
And to the House together they return'd.

Next morning, as had been resolv'd, the Boy   435
Began his journey, and when he had reach'd
The public Way, he put on a bold face;
And all the Neighbours as he pass'd their doors
Came forth, with wishes and with farewell pray'rs,
That follow'd him 'till he was out of sight.   440

A good report did from their Kinsman come,
Of Luke and his well-doing: and the Boy
Wrote loving letters, full of wond'rous news,
Which, as the House-wife phrased it, were throughout
The prettiest letters that were ever seen.   445
Both parents read them with rejoicing hearts.
So, many months pass'd on: and once again
The Shepherd went about his daily work
With confident and cheerful thoughts; and now
Sometimes when he could find a leisure hour   450
He to that valley took his way, and there
Wrought at the Sheep-fold. Meantime Luke began
To slacken in his duty; and at length
He in the dissolute city gave himself°
To evil courses: ignominy and shame   455
Fell on him, so that he was driven at last
To seek a hiding-place beyond the seas.

There is a comfort in the strength of love;
'Twill make a thing endurable, which else
Would break the heart:—Old Michael found it so.   460
I have convers'd with more than one who well
Remember the Old Man, and what he was
Years after he had heard this heavy news.
His bodily frame had been from youth to age
Of an unusual strength. Among the rocks   465
He went, and still look'd up upon the sun,
And listen'd to the wind; and as before
Perform'd all kinds of labour for his Sheep,
And for the land his small inheritance.
And to that hollow Dell from time to time   470
Did he repair, to build the Fold of which
His flock had need. 'Tis not forgotten yet
The pity which was then in every heart

For the Old Man—and 'tis believ'd by all
That many and many a day he thither went,   475
And never lifted up a single stone.

There, by the Sheep-fold, sometimes was he seen
Sitting alone, with that his faithful Dog,
Then old, beside him, lying at his feet.
The length of full seven years from time to time   480
He at the building of this Sheep-fold wrought,
And left the work unfinished when he died.

Three years, or little more, did Isabel,
Survive her Husband: at her death the estate
Was sold, and went into a Stranger's hand.   485
The Cottage which was nam'd The EVENING STAR
Is gone—the ploughshare has been through the ground
On which it stood; great changes have been wrought
In all the neighbourhood;—yet the Oak is left
That grew beside their Door; and the remains   490
Of the unfinished Sheep-fold may be seen
Beside the boisterous brook of Green-head Gill.

APPENDIX.

'WHAT IS USUALLY CALLED POETIC DICTION.'

As perhaps I have no right to expect from a Reader of an Introduction to a volume of Poems that attentive perusal without which it is impossible, imperfectly as I have been compelled to express my meaning, that what I have said in the Preface should throughout be fully understood, I am the more anxious to give an exact notion of the sense in which I use the phrase *poetic diction*; and for this purpose I will here add a few words concerning the origin of the phraseology which I have condemned under that name.—The earliest Poets of all nations generally wrote from passion excited by real events; they wrote naturally, and as men: feeling powerfully as they did, their language was daring, and figurative. In succeeding times, Poets, and men ambitious of the fame of Poets, perceiving the influence of such language, and desirous of producing the same effect, without having the same animating passion, set themselves to a mechanical adoption of those figures of speech, and made use of them, sometimes with propriety, but much more frequently applied them to feelings and ideas with which they had no natural connection whatsoever. A language was thus insensibly produced, differing materially from the real language of men in *any situation*. The Reader or Hearer of this distorted language found himself in a perturbed and unusual state of mind: when affected by the genuine language of passion he had been in a perturbed and unusual state of mind also: in both cases he was willing that his common judgment and understanding should be laid asleep, and he had no instinctive and infallible perception of the true to make him reject the false; the one served as a passport for the other. The agitation and confusion of mind were in both cases delightful, and no wonder if he confounded the one with the other, and believed them both to be produced by the same, or similar causes. Besides, the Poet spake to him in the character of a man to be looked up to, a man of genius and authority. Thus, and from a variety of other causes, this distorted language was received with admiration; and Poets, it is probable, who had before contented themselves for the most part with misapplying only expressions which at first had been dictated by real passion, carried the abuse still further, and introduced phrases composed apparently in the spirit of the original figurative language of passion, yet altogether of their own invention, and distinguished by various degrees of wanton deviation from good sense and nature.

It is indeed true that the language of the earliest Poets was felt to differ materially from ordinary language, because it was the language of extraordinary occasions; but it was really spoken by men, language which the Poet himself had uttered when he had been affected by the events which he described, or which he had heard uttered by those around him. To this language it is probable that metre of some sort or other was early superadded. This separated the genuine language of Poetry still further from common life, so that whoever read or heard the poems of these earliest Poets felt himself moved in a way in which he had not been accustomed to be moved in real life, and by causes manifestly different from those which acted upon him in real life. This was the great temptation to all the corruptions which have followed: under the protection of this feeling succeeding Poets constructed a phraseology which had one thing, it is true, in common with the genuine language of poetry, namely, that it was not heard in ordinary conversation; that it was unusual. But the first Poets, as I have said, spake a language which though unusual, was still the language of men. This circumstance, however, was disregarded by their successors; they found that they could please by easier means: they became proud of a language which they themselves had invented, and which was uttered only by themselves; and, with the spirit of a fraternity, they arrogated it to themselves as their own. In process of time metre became a symbol or promise of this unusual language, and whoever took upon him to write in metre, according as he possessed more or less of true poetic genius, introduced less or more of this adulterated phraseology into his compositions, and the true and the false became so inseparably interwoven that the taste of men was gradually perverted; and this language was received as a natural language; and, at length, by the influence of books upon men, did to a certain degree really become so. Abuses of this kind were imported from one nation to another, and with the progress of refinement this diction became daily more and more corrupt, thrusting out of sight the plain humanities of nature by a motley masquerade of tricks, quaintnesses, hieroglyphics, and enigmas.

It would be highly interesting to point out the causes of the pleasure given by this extravagant and absurd language; but this is not the place; it depends upon a great variety of causes, but upon none perhaps more than its influence in impressing a notion of the peculiarity and exaltation of the Poet's character, and in flattering the Reader's self-love by bringing him nearer to a sympathy with that character; an effect which is accomplished by unsettling ordinary habits of thinking, and thus assisting the Reader to approach to that perturbed and dizzy state of mind in which if he does not find himself, he imagines that he is *balked* of a peculiar enjoyment which poetry can, and ought to bestow.

The sonnet which I have quoted from Gray, in the Preface, except the lines printed in Italics, consists of little else but this diction, though not of the worst kind; and indeed, if I may be permitted to say so, it is far too common in the best writers, both antient and modern. Perhaps I can in no way, by positive example, more easily give my Reader a notion of what I mean by the phrase *poetic diction* than by referring him to a comparison between the metrical paraphrases which we have of passages in the old and new Testament, and those passages as they exist in our common Translation. See Pope's 'Messiah' throughout, Prior's 'Did sweeter sounds adorn my flowing tongue,' &c. &c. 'Though I speak with the tongues of men and of angels,' &c. &c. See 1st Corinthians Chapter 13th. By way of immediate example, take the following of Dr. Johnson.

> 'Turn on the prudent Ant thy heedless eyes,
> Observe her labours, Sluggard, and be wise;
> No stern command, no monitory voice,
> Prescribes her duties, or directs her choice;
> Yet timely provident she hastes away,
> To snatch the blessings of a plenteous day;
> When fruitful Summer loads the teeming plain,
> She crops the harvest and she stores the grain.
> How long shall sloth usurp thy useless hours,
> Unnerve thy vigour, and enchain thy powers?
> While artful shades thy downy couch enclose,
> And soft solicitation courts repose,
> Amidst the drowsy charms of dull delight,
> Year chases year with unremitted flight,
> Till want now following, fraudulent and slow,
> Shall spring to seize thee, like an ambushed foe.'°

From this hubbub of words pass to the original. 'Go to the Ant, thou Sluggard, consider her ways, and be wise: which having no guide, overseer, or ruler, provideth her meat in the summer, and gathereth her food in the harvest. How long wilt thou sleep, O Sluggard? when wilt thou arise out of thy sleep? Yet a little sleep, a little slumber, a little folding of the hands to sleep. So shall thy poverty come as one that travaileth, and thy want as an armed man.' Proverbs, chap. 6th.

One more quotation and I have done. It is from Cowper's verses supposed to be written by Alexander Selkirk.

> 'Religion! What treasure untold
> Resides in that heavenly word!
> More precious than silver and gold,
> Or all that this earth can afford.
> But the sound of the church-going bell
> These valleys and rocks never heard
> Ne'er sigh'd at the sound of a knell,
> Or smiled when a sabbath appear'd.
>
> Ye winds, that have made me your sport,
> Convey to this desolate shore
> Some cordial endearing report
> Of a land I must visit no more.
> My Friends, do they now and then send
> A wish or a thought after me?
> O tell me I yet have a friend
> Though a friend I am never to see.'°

I have quoted this passage as an instance of three different styles of composition. The first four lines are poorly expressed; some Critics would call the language prosaic; the fact is, it would be bad prose, so bad, that it is scarcely worse in metre. The epithet 'church-going' applied to a bell, and that by so chaste a writer as Cowper, is an instance of the strange abuses which Poets have introduced into their language till they and their Readers take them as matters of course, if they do not single them out expressly as objects of admiration. The two lines 'Ne'er sigh'd at the sound,' &c. are, in my opinion, an instance of the language of passion wrested from its proper use, and, from the mere circumstance of the composition being in metre, applied upon an occasion that does not justify such violent expressions, and I should condemn the passage, though perhaps few Readers will agree with me, as vicious poetic diction. The last stanza is throughout admirably expressed: it would be equally good whether in prose or verse, except that the Reader has an exquisite pleasure in seeing such natural language so naturally connected with metre. The beauty of this stanza tempts me here to add a sentiment which ought to be the pervading spirit of a system, detached parts of which have been imperfectly explained in the Preface, namely, that in proportion as ideas and feelings are valuable, whether the composition be in prose or in verse, they require and exact one and the same language.

WORDSWORTH'S ENDNOTES

THE BROTHERS

'There were two springs which bubbled side by side.' The impressive circumstance here described, actually took place some years ago in this country, upon an eminence called Kidstow Pike, one of the highest of the mountains that surround Hawes-water. The summit of the pike was stricken by lightning; and every trace of one of the fountains disappeared, while the other continued to flow as before.

'The thought of death sits easy on the man,' &c. There is not any thing more worthy of remark in the manners of the inhabitants of these mountains, than the tranquillity, I might say indifference, with which they think and talk upon the subject of death. Some of the country church-yards, as here described, do not contain a single tomb-stone, and most of them have a very small number.

MICHAEL

'There's Richard Bateman,' &c. The story alluded to here is well known in the country. The chapel is called Ings Chapel; and is on the right hand side of the road leading from Kendal to Ambleside.

'—had design'd to build a sheep-fold,' &c. It may be proper to inform some readers, that a sheep-fold in these mountains is an unroofed building of stone walls, with different divisions. It is generally placed by the side of a brook, for the convenience of washing the sheep; but it is also useful as a shelter for them, and as a place to drive them into, to enable the shepherds conveniently to single out one or more for any particular purpose.

APPENDIX 1

COLERIDGE'S MARGINAL GLOSSES TO 'THE ANCIENT MARINER'

These were added in 1817 when the poem was published in *Sibylline Leaves*. Line references are closer to 1802 than 1798.

l. 1   An ancient Mariner meeteth three Gallants bidden to a wedding-feast, and detaineth one.

l. 13   The Wedding-Guest is spellbound by the eye of the old seafaring man, and constrained to hear his tale.

l. 25   The Mariner tells how the ship sailed southward with a good wind and fair weather, till it reached the line.

l. 33   The Wedding-Guest heareth the bridal music; but the Mariner continueth his tale.

l. 41   The ship driven by a storm toward the south pole.

l. 55   The land of ice, and of fearful sounds where no living thing was seen.

l. 63   Till a great sea-bird called the Albatross, came through the snow-fog, and was received with great joy and hospitality.

l. 71   And lo! The Albatross proveth a bird of good omen, and followeth the ship as it returned northward through fog and floating ice.

l. 79   The ancient Mariner inhospitably killeth the pious bird of good omen.

l. 91   His shipmates cry out against the ancient Mariner, for killing the bird of good luck.

l. 97   But when the fog cleared off, they justify the same and thus make themselves accomplices in the crime.

l. 103   The fair breeze continues; the ship enters the Pacific Ocean and sails northward, even till it reaches the Line.

l. 108   The ship hath been suddenly becalmed.

l. 119   And the Albatross begins to be avenged.

l. 131   A Spirit had followed them; one of the invisible inhabitants of this planet, neither departed souls nor angels; concerning whom the learned Jew, Josephus, and the Platonic Constantinopolitan, Michael Psellus, may be consulted. They are very numerous and there is no climate or element without one or more.

l. 139   The shipmates, in their sore distress, would fain throw the whole guilt on the ancient Mariner; in sign whereof they hang the dead sea-bird round his neck.

l. 147 The ancient Mariner beholdeth a sign in the element afar off.

l. 157 At its nearer approach, it seemeth him to be a ship; and at a dear ransom he freeth his speech from the bonds of thirst.

l. 164 A flash of joy;

l. 167 And horror follows. For can it be a ship that comes onward without wind or tide?

l. 177 It seemeth him but the skeleton of a ship.

l. 183 And its ribs are seen as bars on the face of the setting Sun.

l. 185 The Spectre-Woman and her Death-mate, and no other on board the skeleton ship.

l. 190 Like vessel, like crew!

l. 192 Death and Life-in-Death have diced for the ship's crew and she (the latter) winneth the ancient Mariner.

l. 198 No twilight within the courts of the Sun.

l. 203 At the rising of the Moon,

l. 212 One after another,

l. 216 His shipmates drop down dead.

l. 220 But Life-in-Death begins her work on the ancient Mariner.

l. 224 The Wedding-Guest feareth that a Spirit is talking to him;

l. 230 But the ancient Mariner assureth him of his bodily life, and proceedeth to relate his horrible penance.

l. 236 He despiseth the creatures of the calm,

l. 240 And envieth that *they* should live and so many lie dead.

l. 253 But the curse liveth for him in the eye of the dead men.

l. 263 In his loneliness and fixedness he yearneth towards the journeying Moon, and the stars that still sojourn, yet still move onward; and every where the blue sky belongs to them, and is their appointed rest, and their native country and their own natural homes, which they enter unannounced as lords that are certainly expected and yet there is a silent joy at their arrival.

l. 272 By the light of the Moon he beholdeth God's creatures of the great calm.

l. 281 Their beauty and their happiness.

l. 285 He blesseth them in his heart.

l. 288 The spell begins to break.

l. 297 By the grace of the holy Mother, the ancient Mariner is refreshed with rain.

l. 308 He heareth sounds and seeth strange sights and commotions in the sky and the element.

l. 327 The bodies of the ship's crew are inspirited and the ship moves on

l. 346 But not by the souls of the men, nor by dæmons of earth or middle air, but by a blessed troop of angelic spirits sent down by the invocation of the guardian saint.

l. 377 The lonesome Spirit from the south-pole carries on the ship as far as the Line, in obedience to the angelic troop, but still requireth vengeance.

l. 393 The Polar Spirit's fellow dæmons, the invisible inhabitants of the element, take part in his wrong; and two of them relate, one to the other, that penance long and heavy for the ancient Mariner hath been accorded to the Polar Spirit, who returneth southward.

l. 422 The Mariner hath been cast into a trance; for the angelic power causeth the vessel to drive northward faster than human life could endure.

l. 430 The supernatural motion is retarded; the Mariner awakes, and his penance begins anew.

l. 442 The curse is finally expiated.

l. 464 And the ancient Mariner beholdeth his native country.

l. 482 The angelic spirits leave the dead bodies,

l. 484 And appear in their own forms of light.

l. 514 The Hermit of the Wood,

l. 527 Approacheth the ship with wonder.

l. 546 The ship suddenly sinketh.

l. 550 The ancient Mariner is saved in the Pilot's boat.

l. 574 The ancient Mariner earnestly entreateth the Hermit to shrieve him; and the penance of life falls on him.

l. 582 And ever and anon throughout his future life, an agony constraineth him to travel from land to land;

l. 610 And to teach by his own example, love and reverence to all things that God made and loveth.

APPENDIX 2

WORDSWORTH'S LETTER TO CHARLES JAMES FOX

Grasmere, Westmoreland; 14 January 1801

Sir,

It is not without much difficulty, that I have summoned the courage to request your acceptance of these Volumes. Should I express my real feelings, I am sure that I should seem to make a parade of diffidence and humility.

Several of the poems contained in these Volumes are written upon subjects, which are the common property of all Poets, and which, at some period of your life, must have been interesting to a man of your sensibility, and perhaps may still continue to be so. It would be highly gratifying to me to suppose that even in a single instance the manner in which I have treated these general topics should afford you any pleasure; but such a hope does not influence me upon the present occasion; in truth I do not feel it. Besides, I am convinced that there must be many things in this collection, which may impress you with an unfavorable idea of my intellectual powers. I do not say this with a wish to degrade myself; but I am sensible that this must be the case, from the different circles in which we have moved, and the different objects with which we have been conversant.

Being utterly unknown to you as I am, I am well aware, that if I am justified in writing to you at all, it is necessary, my letter should be short; but I have feelings within me which I hope will so far shew themselves in this letter, as to excuse the trespass which I am afraid I shall make. In common with the whole of the English people I have observed in your public character a constant predominance of sensibility of heart. Necessitated as you have been from your public situation to have much to do with men in bodies, and in classes, and accordingly to contemplate them in that relation, it has been your praise that you have not thereby been prevented from looking upon them as individuals, and that you have habitually left your heart open to be influenced by them in that capacity. This habit cannot but have made you dear to Poets; and I am sure that, if since your first entrance into public life there has been a single true poet living in England, he must have loved you.

But were I assured that I myself had a just claim to the title of a Poet, all the dignity being attached to the word which belongs to it, I do not think that I should have ventured for that reason to offer these volumes to you: at present it is solely on account of two poems in the second volume, the one entitled 'The Brothers', and the other 'Michael', that I have been emboldened to take this liberty.

It appears to me that the most calamitous effect, which has followed the measures which have lately been pursued in this country, is a rapid decay of the domestic affections among the lower orders of society. This effect the present Rulers of this country are not conscious of, or they disregard it. For many years past, the tendency of society amongst almost all the nations of Europe has been to produce it. But recently by the spreading of manufactures through every part of the country, by the heavy taxes upon postage, by workhouses, Houses of Industry, and the invention of Soup-shops &c, &c superadded to the encreasing disproportion between the price of labour and that of the necessaries of life, the bonds of domestic feeling among the poor, as far as the influence of these things has extended, have been weakened, and in innumerable instances entirely destroyed. The evil would be the less to be regretted, if these institutions were regarded only as palliatives to a disease; but the vanity and pride of their promoters are so subtly interwoven with them, that they are deemed great discoveries and blessings to humanity. In the mean time parents are separated from their children, and children from their parents; the wife no longer prepares with her own hands a meal for her husband, the produce of his labour; there is little doing in his house in which his affections can be interested, and but little left in it which he can love. I have two neighbours, a man and his wife, both upwards of eighty years of age; they live alone; the husband has been confined to his bed many months and has never had, nor till within these few weeks has ever needed, any body to attend to him but his wife. She has recently been seized with a lameness which has often prevented her from being able to carry him his food to his bed; the neighbours fetch water for her from the well, and do other kind offices for them both, but her infirmities encrease. She told my Servant two days ago that she was afraid they must both be boarded out among some other Poor of the parish (they have long been supported by the parish) but she said, it was hard, having kept house together so long, to come to this, and she was sure that 'it would burst her heart'. I mention this fact to shew how deeply the spirit of independence is, even yet, rooted in some parts of the country. These people could not express themselves in this way without an almost sublime conviction of the blessings of independent domestic life. If it is true, as I believe, that this spirit is rapidly disappearing, no greater curse can befal a land.

I earnestly entreat your pardon for having detained you so long. In the two Poems, 'The Brothers' and 'Michael' I have attempted to draw a picture of the domestic affections as I know they exist amongst a class of men who are now almost confined to the North of England. They are small independent *proprietors* of land here called statesmen, men of respectable education who daily labour on their own little properties. The domestic affections will always be strong amongst men who live in a country not crowded with population, if these men are placed above poverty. But if they are proprietors of small estates, which have descended to them from their ancestors, the power which these affections will acquire amongst such men is inconceivable by those who have only had an opportunity of observing hired labourers, farmers, and the manufacturing Poor. Their little tract of land serves as a kind of permanent rallying point for their domestic feelings, as a tablet upon which they are written which makes them objects of memory in a thousand instances when they would otherwise be forgotten. It is a fountain fitted to the nature of social man from which supplies of affection, as pure as his heart was intended for, are daily drawn. This class of men is rapidly disappearing. You, Sir, have a consciousness, upon which every good man will congratulate you, that the whole of your public conduct has in one way or other been directed to the preservation of this class of men, and those who hold similar situations. You have felt that the most sacred of all property is the property of the Poor. The two poems which I have mentioned were written with a view to shew that men who do not wear fine cloaths can feel deeply. 'Pectus enim est quod disertos facit, et vis mentis. Ideoque imperitis quoque, si modo sint aliquo affectu concitati, verba non desunt'[1] The poems are faithful copies from nature; and I hope, whatever effect they may have upon you, you will at least be able to perceive that they may excite profitable sympathies in many kind and good hearts, and may in some small degree enlarge our feelings of reverence for our species, and our knowledge of human nature, by shewing that our best qualities are possessed by men whom we are too apt to consider, not with reference to the points in which they resemble us, but to those in which they manifestly differ from us. I thought, at a time when these feelings are sapped in so many ways that the two poems might co-operate, however feebly, with

---

[1] *Editor's note:* The Latin quotation, from Quintilian, became an additional epigraph for the 1802 edition of *Lyrical Ballads*, see p. 93 and note.

the illustrious efforts which you have made to stem this and other evils with which the country is labouring, and it is on this account alone that I have taken the liberty of thus addressing you.

Wishing earnestly that the time may come when the country may perceive what it has lost by neglecting your advice, and hoping that your latter days may be attended with health and comfort.

I remain, with the highest respect and admiration,
Your most obedient and humble Servt
W Wordsworth

APPENDIX 3

JOHN WILSON'S LETTER TO WORDSWORTH, 24 MAY 1802

From Dove Cottage Manuscript. Accession number: WLMS A / Wilson, John / 1

My Dear Sir

You may perhaps be surprised to see yourself addressed in this manner by one who never had the happiness of being in company with you, and whose knowledge of your Character is drawn solely from the perusal of your Poems. But Sir, though I am not personally acquainted with you, I may almost venture to affirm that the qualities of your Soul are not unknown to me—In your Poems I discovered such marks of delicate feeling, such benevolence of disposition, and such knowledge of human nature, as made an impression on my mind that nothing will ever efface—and while I felt my Soul refined by the Sentiments contained in them, and filled with those delightful emotions which it would be almost impossible to describe, I entertained for you an attachment made up of Love, and admiration. Reflection upon that delight which I enjoyed from reading your Poems, will ever make me regard you with gratitude, and the consciousness of feeling those emotions you delineate, makes me proud to regard your character with esteem and admiration. In whatever view you regard my behavior in writing this letter—whether you consider it as the effect of ignorance and conceit, or correct taste and refined feeling, I will in my own mind be satisfied with your opinion. To receive a letter from you would afford me more happiness than any occurrence in this world, save the happiness of my friends—and greatly enhance the pleasure I receive from reading your Lyrical ballads. Your silence would certainly distress me— but still I would have the happiness to think that the neglect even of the virtuous cannot extinguish the sparks of sensitivity, or diminish the luxury arising from refined emotions. That luxury, Sir, I have enjoyed that luxury your Poems have afforded me—and for this reason do I now address you. Accept my thanks for the raptures you have occasioned me, and however much you may be inclined to despise me, know at least that these thanks are sincere & fervent.—

To you Sir, Mankind are indebted for a species of Poetry, which will continue to afford pleasure, while respect is paid to virtuous feelings—and while sensibility continues to pour forth tears of rapture. The flimsy ornaments of language used to conceal meaness of thought, and want of feeling, may captivate for a short time the ignorant and the unwary—but true taste will discover the imposture and expose the authors of it to merited contempt. The real feelings of human nature, expressed in simple *and* forcible language, will on the contrary, please those only who are capable of entertaining them—and in proportion to the attention which we pay to the faithful delineation of such feelings, will be the enjoyment derived from them. That Poetry therefore which is the language of Nature, is certain of immortality, provided circumstances do not occur, to pervert the feelings of humanity, and occasion a complete revolution in the government of the Mind.—That your Poetry is the language of Nature, in my opinion, admits of no doubt. Both the thoughts and expressions may be tried by that Standard. You have seized upon those feelings that most deeply interest the heart—and that also come within the Sphere of common observation. You do not write merely for the pleasure, of philosophers and men of improved taste, but for all who think,—for all who feel.—If we have ever known the happiness arising from parental or fraternal love—but if we have ever known that delightful sympathy of Souls connecting persons of different Sexes,—if we have ever dropped a tear at the death of friends,—or grieved for the misfortunes of others—if in short we have ever felt the more amiable emotions of human nature—it is impossible to read your Poems without being greatly interested, and frequently in raptures. Your sentiments, feelings and thoughts are therefore exactly such as ought to constitute the subject of Poetry and cannot fail of exciting interest in every heart.——

But Sir, your merit does not solely consist in delineating the real features of the human mind, under those different aspects it assumes when under the influence of various passions, and feelings—you have in a manner truly admirable, explained a circumstance very important in its effects upon the Soul when agitated, that has indeed been frequently alluded to, but never generally adopted by any author, in tracing the progress of emotions.—I mean that wonderful effect which the appearances of external nature, have upon the mind when in a State of strong feeling. We must all have been sensible, that when under the influence of grief, nature when arrayed in her gayest attire, appears to us dull and gloomy—and that when our hearts bound with joy, her most deformed prospects seldom fail of pleasing. This disposition of the mind to assimilate the appearances of external nature to its own situation is a fine subject for poetical allusion, and in several Poems you have employed it with a most electrifying Effect. But you have not stopped here. You have shown the effect which the qualities of external nature have, in forming the human mind—and have presented us with several characters whose particular biass arose from that situation in which they were places with respect to the Scenery of nature. This Idea is inexpressibly beautiful, and though I confess that to me it appeared to border upon fiction when I first considered it, yet at this moment I am convinced of its foundation on nature, and its great importance in accounting for various phenomena in the human Mind. It serves to explain those diversities in the structure of the mind, which have baffled all the ingenuity of philosophers to account for. It serves to overturn the Theories of men who have attempted to write on human nature, without a knowledge of the causes that affect it, and who have discovered greater eagerness to show their own subtlety than arrive at the acquisition of truth. May not the face of external nature through different quarters of the globe, account for the dispositions of different nations? May not mountains forests, plains, groves, and lakes, as much as the temperature of the Atmosphere, or the form of government, produce important effects upon the human Soul, and may not the difference subsisting between the former of these in different countries, produce as much diversity among the inhabitants as any varieties among the latter? The effect you have shown to take place in particular cases so much to my satisfaction most certainly may be extended so far as to authorise general inferences. This Idea has no doubt struck you—and I trust that if it be founded on nature, your mind so long accustomed to the philosophical investigation will perceive how far it may be carried, and what consequences are likely to result from it.—Your Poems, Sir, are of very great advantage to the world, from containing in them a system of philosophy, that regards one of the most curious subjects of investigation—and at the same time one of the most important. But your Poems may not be considered merely in a philosophical light, or even as containing refined and natural feelings—they present us with a body of morality of the purest kind. They represent the enjoyment resulting from the cultivation of the social affections of our nature;—they inculcate a conscientious regard to the rights of our fellow men—they show that every creature on the face of the Earth is entitled in some measure to our kindness;—they prove that in every mind however depraved there exist some qualities deserving our esteem—they point out the proper way to happiness—they show that such a thing as perfect misery does not exist—they flash on our Souls conviction of immortality—Considered therefore in this view, Lyrical ballads is, to use your own words, the book which I value next to my bible—and though I may perhaps never have the happiness of seeing you, yet I will always consider you as a friend who has by his instructions done me a Service which it never can be in my power to repay. Your instructions have afforded me inexpressible pleasure,— it will be my own fault if I do not reap from them much advantage.

I have said, Sir, that in all your Poems you have adhered strictly to natural feelings, and described what comes within the range of every person's observation. It is from following out this plan that in my esti-mation you have surpassed every Poet both of ancient and modern times. But to me it appears that in the execution of this design, you have inadvertently fallen into an Error, the effects of which are how-ever exceedingly trivial. No feeling, no State of mind, ought in my opinion to become the Subject of Poetry, that does not please. Pleasure may indeed be produced in many ways, and by means that at first sight appear calculated to accomplish a very different end. Tragedy of the deepest kind produces pleasure of a high Nature. To point out the causes of this would be foreign to the purpose. But we may lay this down as a general rule, that no description can please, where the Sympathies of our Soul are not excited, and no narration interest, where we do not enter into the feelings of some of the parties con-cerned. On this principle many feelings which are undoubtedly nat ural, are improper subjects of Poetry, and many situations no less natural, incapable of being described so as to produce the grand effect of poetical composition. This, Sir, I would apprehend is reason-able—and founded on the constitution of the human mind. There are a thousand occurrences happening every day, which do not in the least interest an unconcerned Spectator—though they no doubt occasion various emotions in the breast of those to whom they immediately relate. To describe these in poetry would be improper.—Now Sir, I think that in several cases you have fallen into this Error. You have described feelings with which I cannot sympathise—and situations in which I take no interest. I know that I can relish your beauties— and that makes me think that I can also perceive your faults. But in this matter I have not trusted wholly to my own Judgement, but heard the sentiments of men whose feelings I admired and whose under-standing I respected. In a few cases then, I think that even you have failed to excite interest.—in the poem entitled the Idiot Boy, your intention, as you inform us in your preface, was to trace the maternal passion through its more subtle windings. This design is no doubt accompanied with much difficulty, but if properly executed, cannot fail of interesting the heart. But Sir in my opinion, the manner in which you have executed this plan, has frustrated the end you intended to produce by it. The affection of Betty Foy has nothing in it, to excite interest. It exhibits merely the effects of that instinctive feeling inherent in the constitution of every animal. The excessive fondness of the mother disgusts us—and prevents us from sympathising with her. We are unable to enter into her feelings, and consequently take little or no interest in her Situation. The object of her affection is indeed her Son—and in that relation much consists—but then he is represented as totally destitute of any attachment towards her—the State of his mind is represented as perfectly deplorable—and in short to me it appears almost unnatural that a person in a State of complete ideotism, should excite the warmest feelings of attachment in the breast even of his Mother. This much I know, that among all the people I ever knew to have read this poem, I never met one who did not rise rather displeased from the perusal of it—and the only cause I could assign for it was the one now mentioned. This inability to receive pleasure from descriptions such as that of the Idiot boy, is I am convinced founded upon established feelings of human nature, and the principle of it constitutes as I daresay you recollect, the leading feature of Smith's Theory of moral Sentiments. I therefore think that in the choice of this Subject, you have committed an Error. You never deviate from Nature,—in you that it [sic] would be impossible but in this case you have delineated feelings which though natural do not please—but which create a certain degree of disgust and contempt. With regard to the manner in which you have executed your plan, I think too great praise cannot be bestowed upon your talents. You have most admirably delineated the ideotism of the boy's mind—and the situations in which you place him are perfectly calculated to display it. The curious thoughts that pass through the mother's mind, are highly descriptive of her foolish fondness—her extravagant fears—and her ardent hopes. The manner in which you show how bodily sufferings are frequently removed by mental anxieties or pleasures, in the description of the cure of Betty Foy's female friend, is excessively well managed—and serves to establish a very curious and important Truth. In short every thing you proposed to execute has been executed in a masterly manner. The fault, if there be one, lies in the plan, not in the execution. This poem I have heard recommended as one in your best manner, and accordingly it is frequently read under this belief. The judgement formed of it, is consequently erroneous. Many people are displeased with the performance—but they are not careful to distinguish faults in the plan, from faults in the execution—and the consequence is that they form an improper opinion of your genius. In reading any composition, most certainly the pleasure we receive arises almost wholly from the Sentiments, thoughts, & descriptions contained in it. A secondary pleasure arises from admiration of those talents requisite to the production of it. In reading the Idiot boy, all persons who allow themselves to think must admire your talents. But they regret that they have been so employed—and while they esteem the author, they cannot help being displeased with his performance. I have seen a most excellent painting of an Ideot—but it created in me inexpressible disgust. I was struck with the excellence of the picture—I admired the talents of the artist—but I had no other source of pleasure. The Poem of the Ideot boy produced upon me an effect in every respect similar. I find that my remarks upon several of your other Poems must be reserved for another Letter. If you think this one deserves an answer—a letter from Wordsworth would be to me a treasure. If your silence tells me that my letter was beneath your notice, you will never again be troubled by one whom you consider as an ignorant admirer. But if your mind be as amiable as it is reflected in your Poems—you will make allowance for defects that age may supply and make a fellow creature happy, by dedicating a few moments to the instructions of an admirer and sincere friend

John Wilson

Professor Jardine's College, Glasgow
May 24. 1802

APPENDIX 4

WORDSWORTH'S LETTER TO JOHN WILSON

Grasmere, Westmoreland; 7 June 1802

My dear Sir,

Had it not been for a very amiable modesty you could not have imagined that your letter could give me any offence. It was on many accounts highly grateful to me. I was pleas'd to find that I had given so much pleasure to an ingenuous and able mind and I further considered the enjoyment which you had had from my poems as an earnest that others might be delighted with them in the same or a like manner. It is plain from your letter that the pleasure which I have given you has not been blind or unthinking you have studied the poems and prove that you have entered into the spirit of them. They have not given you a cheap or vulgar pleasure therefore I feel that you are entitled to my kindest thanks for having done some violence to your natural diffidence in the communication which you have made to me.

There is scarcely any part of your letter that does not deserve particular notice, but partly from a weakness in my stomach and digestion and partly from certain habits of mind I do not write any letters unless upon business not even to my dearest Friends. Except during absence from my own family I have not written five letters of friendship during the last five years. I have mentioned this in order that I may retain your good opinion should my letter be less minute than you are entitled to expect. You seem to be desirous of my opinion on the influence of natural objects in forming the character of nations. This cannot be understood without first considering their influence upon men in general first with references to such subjects as are common to all countries: and next such as belong exclusively to any particular country or in a greater degree to it than to another. Now it is manifest that no human being can be so besotted and debased by oppression, penury or any other evil which unhumanizes man as to be utterly insensible to the colours, forms, or smell of flowers, the voices and motions of birds and beasts, the appearances of the sky and heavenly bodies, the genial warmth of a fine day, the terror and uncomfortableness of a storm, &c &c. How dead soever many full-grown men may outwardly seem to these things they all are more or less affected by them, and in childhood, in the first practice and exercise of their senses, they must have been not the nourishers merely, but often the fathers of their passions. There cannot be a doubt that in tracts of country where images of danger, melancholy, grandeur, or loveliness, softness, and ease prevail, that they will make themselves felt power-fully in forming the characters of the people, so as to produce a uni-formity of national character, where the nation is small and is not made up of men who, inhabiting different soils, climates, &c by their civil usages, and relations materially interfere with each other. It was so for-merly, no doubt, in the Highlands of Scotland but we cannot perhaps observe much of it in our own island at the present day, because, even in the most sequestered places, by manufactures, traffic, religion, Law, interchange of inhabitants &c distinctions are done away which would otherwise have been strong and obvious. This complex state of society does not, however, prevent the characters of individuals from fre-quently receiving a strong bias not merely from the impressions of general nature, but also from local objects and images. But it seems that to produce these effects in the degree in which we frequently find them to be produced there must be a peculiar sensibility of original organization combining with moral accidents, as is exhibited in *The Brothers* and in *Ruth*—I mean, to produce this in a marked degree not that I believe that any man was ever brought up in the country without loving it, especially in his better moments, or in a district of particular grandeur or beauty without feeling some stronger attachment to it on that account than he would otherwise have felt. I include, you will observe, in these considerations the influence of climate, changes in the atmosphere and elements and the labours and occupations which particular districts require.

You begin what you say upon the Idiot Boy with this observation, that nothing is a fit subject for poetry which does not please. But here follows a question, Does not please whom? Some have little knowledge of natural imagery of any kind, and, of course, little relish for it, some are disgusted with the very mention of the words pastoral poetry, sheep or shepherds, some cannot tolerate a poem with a ghost or any super-natural agency in it, others would shrink from an animated description of the pleasures of love, as from a thing carnal and libidinous, some cannot bear to see delicate and refined feelings ascribed to men in low conditions of society, because their vanity and self-love tell them that these belong only to themselves and men like themselves in dress, sta-tion, and way of life; others are disgusted with the naked language of some of the most interesting passions of men, because either it is indeli-cate, or gross, or vulgar, as many fine ladies could not bear certain

expressions in The Mad Mother and the Thorn, and, as in the instance
of Adam Smith, who, we are told, could not endure the Ballad of
Clym of the Clough, because the author had not written like a gentle-
man; then there are professional local and national prejudices forever-
more; some take no interest in the description of a particular passion or
quality, as love of solitariness, we will say genial activity of fancy, love
of nature, religion, and so forth, because they have little or nothing of
it in themselves, and so on without end. I return then to the question,
please whom? or what? I answer, human nature, as it has been and ever
will be. But where are we to find the best measure of this? I answer,
from within; by stripping our own hearts naked, and by looking out of
ourselves towards men who lead the simplest lives most according to
nature men who [ha]ve never known false refinements, wayward and
artificial desires, false criticisms, effeminate habits of thinking and feel-
ing, or who, having known these things, have outgrown them. This
latter class is the most to be depended upon, but it is very small in
number. People in our rank in life are perpetually falling into one sad
mistake, namely, that of supposing that human nature and the persons
they associate with are one and the same thing. Whom do we generally
associate with? Gentlemen, persons of fortune, professional men,
ladies, persons who can afford to buy or can easily procure books of half
a guinea price, hot-pressed, and printed upon superfine paper. These
persons are, it is true, a part of human nature, but we err lamentably if
we suppose them to be fair representatives of the vast mass of human
existence. And yet few ever consider books but with reference to their
power of pleasing these persons and men of a higher rank; few descend
lower among cottages and fields and among children. A man must have
done this habitually before his judgment upon the Idiot Boy would be
in any way decisive with me. I *know* I have done this myself habitually;
I wrote the poem with exceeding delight and pleasure, and whenever
I read it I read it with pleasure. You have given me praise for having
reflected faithfully in my poems the feelings of human nature I would
fain hope that I have done so. But a great Poet ought to do more than
this, he ought to a certain degree to rectify men's feelings, to give them
new compositions of feeling, to render their feelings more sane pure
and permanent, in short, more consonant to nature, that is, to eternal
nature, and the great moving spirit of things. He ought to travel before
men occasionally as well as at their sides. I may illustrate this by a refer-
ence to natural objects. What false notions have prevailed from gener-
ation to generation as to the true character of the nightingale. As far as
my Friend's Poem in the Lyrical Ballads is read it will contribute

greatly to rectify these. You will recollect a passage in Cowper where, speaking of rural sounds, he says—

> 'and *even* the boding Owl
> That hails the rising moon has charms for me'

Cowper was passionately fond of natural objects yet you see he mentions it as a marvellous thing that he could connect pleasure with the cry of the owl. In the same poem he speaks in the same manner of that beautiful plant, the gorse; making in some degree an amiable boast of his loving it, '*unsightly* and unsmooth' as it is. There are many aversions of this kind, which, though they have some foundation in nature, have yet so slight a one, that though they may have prevailed hundreds of years, a philosopher will look upon them as accidents. So with respect to many moral feelings, either of love or dislike, what excessive admiration was payed in former times to personal prowess and military success (it is so with the latter even at the present day) but surely not nearly so much as heretofore. So with regard to birth, and innumerable other modes of sentiment, civil and religious. But you will be inclined to ask by this time how all this applies to the Idiot Boy. To this I can only say that the loathing and disgust which many people have at the sight of an Idiot, is a feeling which, though having some foundation in human nature is not necessarily attached to it in any virtuous degree, but is owing, in a great measure to a false delicacy, and, if I may say it without rudeness, a certain want of comprehensiveness of thinking and feeling. Persons in the lower classes of society have little or nothing of this; if an Idiot is born in a poor man's house, it must be taken care of and cannot be boarded out, as it would be by gentlefolks, or sent to a public or private receptacle for such unfortunate beings. Poor people seeing frequently among their neighbours such objects, easily forget whatever there is of natural disgust about them, and have therefore a sane state, so that without pain or suffering they perform their duties towards them. I could with pleasure pursue this subject, but I must now strictly adopt the plan which I proposed to myself when I began to write this letter, namely that of setting down a few hints or memorandums, which you will think of for my sake.

I have often applied to Idiots, in my own mind, that sublime expression of scripture that, '*their life is hidden with God*'. They are worshipped, probably from a feeling of this sort, in several parts of the East. Among the Alps where they are numerous, they are considered, I believe, as a blessing to the family to which they belong. I have indeed often looked upon the conduct of fathers and mothers of the lower classes of society towards Idiots as the great triumph of the human heart. It is there that we see the strength, disinterestedness, and grandeur of love, nor have I ever been able to contemplate an object that calls out so many excellent and virtuous sentiments without finding it hallowed thereby and having something in me which bears down before it, like a deluge, every feeble sensation of disgust and aversion.

There are in my opinion, several important mistakes in the latter part of your letter which I could have wished to notice; but I find myself much fatigued. These refer both to the Boy and the Mother. I must content myself simply with observing that it is probable that the principle cause of your dislike to this particular poem lies in the *word* Idiot. If there had been any such word in our language, *to which we had attached passion,* as lack-wit, half-wit, witless &c I should have certainly employed it in preference, but there is no such word. Observe, (this is entirely in reference to this particular poem) my Idiot is not one of those who cannot articulate and such as are usually disgusting in their persons—

> 'Whether in cunning or in joy
> And then his words were not a few' &c

and the last speech at the end of the poem. The Boy whom I had in my mind was, by no means disgusting in his appearance, quite the contrary, and I have known several with imperfect faculties who are handsome in their persons and features. There is one, at present, within a mile of my own house remarkably so, though there is something of a stare and vacancy in his countenance. A Friend of mine, knowing that some persons had a dislike to the poem such as you have expressed advised me to add a stanza describing the person of the Boy so as entirely to separate him in the imaginations of my Readers from that class of idiots who are disgusting in their persons, but the narration in the poem is so rapid and impassioned that I could not find a place in which to insert the stanza without checking the progress of it, and so leaving a deadness upon the feeling. This poem has, I know, frequently produced the same effect as it did upon you and your Friends but there are many people also to whom it affords exquisite delight, and who indeed, prefer it to any other of my Poems. This proves that the feelings there delineated are such as all men *may* sympathize with. This is enough for my purpose. It is not enough for me as a poet, to delineate merely such feelings as all men *do* sympathise with but, it is also highly desirable to add to these others, such as all men *may* sympathize with, and such as there is reason to believe they would be better and more moral beings if they did sympathize with.

I conclude with regret, because I have not said one half of what I intended to say: but I am sure you will deem my excuse sufficient when I inform you that my head aches violently, and I am, in other respects, unwell. I must, however, again give you my warmest thanks for your kind letter. I shall be happy to hear from you again and do not think it unreasonable that I should request a letter from you when I feel that the answer which I may make to it will not perhaps, be above three or four lines. This I mention to you with frankness, and you will not take it ill after what I have before said of my remissness in writing letters.

> I am, dear Sir
> > With great Respect
> > > Your sincerely W Wordsworth

EXPLANATORY NOTES

LYRICAL BALLADS, WITH A FEW OTHER POEMS, 1798

Lyrical Ballads was originally printed in Bristol in August 1798 by Coleridge's publisher, Joseph Cottle, but although 500 copies were printed and a few copies assembled, with a title page giving the publisher as T. N. Longman, of Paternoster Row, in London, the planned publication did not take place. After Wordsworth offered the book to the publisher of his own first volumes of poetry, Joseph Johnson, Cottle appears to have sold his stock of *Lyrical Ballads* to the London firm J. and A. Arch, who finally brought out the volume on 4 October 1798 at a price of 5 shillings. Late additions to the volume included 'The Nightingale' (substituted for 'Lewti', probably in an attempt to preserve the anonymity of *Lyrical Ballads*, since Coleridge was known to be the author of 'Lewti' following its publication in the *Morning Post*); and 'Lines written a few miles above Tintern Abbey', which Wordsworth wrote on his July walking tour and took straight to Cottle on his return to Bristol. For detailed accounts of the complicated publication process, see D. F. Foxon, 'The Printing of *Lyrical Ballads*', *The Library*, 5th ser. 9 (1954), 221–41; John E. Jordan, *Why the Lyrical Ballads?* (Berkeley, Los Angeles, and London, 1976).

3 *ADVERTISEMENT*: *Reynolds.* Sir Joshua Reynolds (1723–92), leading British artist and first president of the Royal Academy of Art, whose *Discourses on Art* were a major influence on late-eighteenth-century aesthetic ideas. In 'Discourse VII', Reynolds argued that taste, in all the arts, was 'acquired by a laborious and diligent investigation of nature', an argument that developed from his earlier Discourses (II, VI) on the importance of studying 'the great works of the great masters', *Discourses on Art*, ed. R. Wark (New Haven and London, 1997), 134, 113.

4 *elder poets.* Poets writing before the Restoration.

a friend. Probably William Hazlitt (1778–1830), the essayist and critic, who recalled his memorable first meeting and conversations with Wordsworth and Coleridge in 1797 in 'My First Acquaintance with the Poets' (Hazlitt, xvii. 119).

5 *The Rime of the Ancyent Marinere.* Composed 1797–8 and frequently revised—see 1802 version included in this volume. Coleridge revised the poem for successive editions, adding extensive marginal glosses when it was included in *Sibylline Leaves* in 1817 (see Appendix 1). For full details of the revisions, see Jack Stillinger, *Coleridge and Textual Instability* (Oxford, 1994), 60–72, 158–84; and *CP* I. i. 365–419.

Coleridge started composing the poem on 12 November 1797 when he embarked on a tour of the Somerset coast with William and Dorothy Wordsworth. His own account of its origins was published in *Biographia Literaria* (see Introduction, p. xxvii). Wordsworth offered a slightly different account, recalling that the poem was 'founded on a dream, as Mr Coleridge said, of his friend Mr Cruikshank. Much the greatest part of the story was Mr Coleridge's invention; but certain parts I myself suggested, for example some crime was to be committed, which would bring on the Old Navigator, as Coleridge afterwards delighted to call him, the spectral persecution, as a consequence of that crime and his own wanderings. I had been reading in Shelvocke's Voyages a day or two before that while doubling Cape Horn they frequently saw albatrosses, in that latitude the largest sort of seafowl, some extending their wings 12 or 13 feet. "Suppose" said I, "you represent him as having killed one of these birds on entering the South Sea, and that the tutelary Spirits of these regions take upon them to avenge the crime." The incident was thought fit for purpose and adopted accordingly. I also suggested the navigation of the ship by the dead men, but do not recall that I had anything more to do with the scheme of the poem. The gloss with which it was subsequently accompanied was not thought of by either of us at the time, at least not a hint of it was given to me, & I have no doubt it was a gratuitous afterthought. We began the composition together on that to me memorable evening: I furnished two or three lines at the beginning of the poem, in particular.

> And listened like a three years' child;
> The Mariner had his will.

These trifling contributions all but one (which Mr C. has with unnecessary scrupulosity recorded) slipt out of his mind as they well might. As we endeavoured to proceed conjointly (I am speaking of the same evening) our respective manners proved so widely different that it would have been quite presumptuous in me to do anything but separate from an undertaking upon which I could only have been a clog' (*IF*, 2–3).

The importance of Coleridge's reading to the poem was examined exhaustively by John Livingstone Lowes in *The Road to Xanadu*, 2nd edn. (London, 1927); subsequent scholars have attempted to shed further light on the poem's sources, suggesting a wide range of illuminating contexts, literary, religious, philosophical, archetypal, psychological, biographical, sexual, historical, political, colonial, geographical, ecological. As Mays comments, 'there are debts of every kind and degree of significance, many of them unconscious' (*CP* I. i. 367). Annotation below is necessarily selective.

5 *the Line.* The equator. The ship sails south towards the Antarctic, a region still unexplored in 1798, rounds Cape Horn, and voyages across the Pacific before returning home. In 1800, the reference to the Pacific was dropped, but it is mentioned in the glosses added in 1817 (see Appendix 1).

l. 15. *Loon.* Defined by Johnson as 'A sorry fellow, or scoundrel'. Also a word for a waterbird.

6 l. 27. *Kirk.* Church (northern English and Scots). The Mariner's vocabulary frequently suggests a Scottish or northern background, in his use of Kirk (ll. 27, 471, 636, 638), 'cauld' (l. 50), 'ken' (l. 55), 'an' (l. 63), 'drouth' (l. 131), 'pheere' (l. 180), 'ween' (l. 182), 'sterte' (l. 195), 'eldritch' (l. 234), 'lav'rock' (l. 348), 'een' (l. 445). This may reflect Coleridge's debts to the old Scottish ballads and songs collected by Percy, Herd, and Ritson, though some of the language was also used by Chaucer and Spenser. Many of the older words appear in Percy's Glossary to the *Reliques*.

l. 47. *freaks.* Unexpected changes of mind; capricious tricks.

l. 50. *cauld.* Cold.

l. 55. *Ne . . . ne.* Neither, nor.

l. 55. *ken.* Recognize.

7 l. 60. *swound.* Swoon (arch.). Line altered in 1800 to 'A wild and ceaseless sound', perhaps in response to negative criticism such as the reviewer in the *British Critic*, 14 (Oct. 1799), 364–9, who dismissed 'noises in a swound' as 'nonsense' (Woof, 79). The word occurs in 'Sir Cauline' in Percy.

l. 61. *Albatross.* A very large seabird, with wingspan of up to 12 feet, belonging to the Southern Ocean. See headnote. Wordsworth had been reading George Shelvocke, *A Voyage Round the World, by the way of the Great South Sea* (London, 1726), 72: 'one would think it impossible that any living thing could subsist in so rigid a climate; and, indeed, we all observed, that we had not the sight of one fish of any kind, since we were come to the Southward of the streights of *Le Mair*, nor one seabird, except a disconsolate black *Albitross*, who accompanied us for several days, hovering about as if he had lost himself, till *Hatley* (my second captain) observing, in one of his melancholy fits, that this bird was always hovering near us, imagined, from his colour, that it might be some ill omen. That which I suppose, induced him the more to encourage his superstition, was the continued series of contrary tempestuous winds, which had oppressed us ever since we got into this sea. But be that as it would, he, after some fruitless attempts, at length shot the *Albitross*, not doubting that we should (perhaps) have a fair wind after it.'

l. 63. *an.* And, if.

l. 74. *vespers.* Evenings; normally used in relation to the service of evening prayer.

l. 83. *weft.* A thin line of cloud or mist; or a broad flag on a ship. In 1800 the internal rhyme was sacrificed for the sake of the sense: 'Still hid in mist; and on the left', perhaps in response to remarks in the same negative review noted in l. 60.

9 l. 129. *fathom.* A measurement of 6 feet (180 cm), used for measuring the depth of water.

9 l. 131. *drouth*. Thirst; drought.

l. 135. *Ah wel-a-day!*. Alas. *Romeo and Juliet*, III. ii. 38.

l. 144. *wist*. Knew.

l. 147. *water-sprite*. Spirit that lives in or rules over water, common in Scottish folklore.

ll. 149 and 154. *unslack'd*. Amended in 1800 to 'unslak'd'; unrelaxed, unquenched.

l. 156. *Gramercy!*. Mercy on us (contracted from 'Grant me mercy', according to Johnson).

10 l. 160. *weal*. Good.

l. 176. *gossameres*. Fine cobwebs, which can be seen floating in the air. According to Johnson, 'The down of plants'.

l. 180. *Pheere*. Companion or consort. The word appears in 'Sir Cauline', in Percy.

l. 182. *ween*. Suppose or think. Used similarly in 'The Not Browne Maid', in Percy; see note to p. 238, 'The Idle Shepherd Boys', l. 79.

11 l. 195. *sterte*. Started.

ll. 202 and 204. *horned Moon*. Crescent moon. Dorothy Wordsworth noted on 21 March 1798, after tea at Coleridge's cottage, 'the sky partially shaded with clouds. The horned moon was set' (*Journals*, i. 13). See also Wordsworth's *Peter Bell*, ll. 1–35, composed in 1798, but not published until 1819. Coleridge's continuing preoccupation with the crescent moon can be seen in 'Dejection: An Ode', ll. 9–14, and 'A Soliloquy of the Full Moon'; see also Lowes, *Road to Xanadu*, 159.

l. 206. *ghastly*. a) causing terror; b) death-like or spectre-like.

l. 207. *ee*. Eye. The word occurs memorably in 'Sir Patrick Spens' in Percy.

12 l. 234. *eldritch*. Glossed by Percy as 'wild, hideous, ghostly, lonesome, uninhabited'; a key word in 'Sir Cauline'. Revised in 1800 to 'ghastly'.

13 l. 286. *Mary-queen . . . yeven*. The Mariner's recourse to Mary, mother of Christ may indicate his Catholicism and, perhaps, a pre-Reformation setting for the poem, reinforced by the archaic form of 'given'.

l. 289. *silly*. Simple, homely.

14 l. 302. *anear*. Near as opposed to 'afar'. First recorded usage in English.

15 l. 348. *Lavrock*. Lark, a songbird associated with the dawn. As a land-bird, its sound, like that of the 'hidden brook' (l. 358), suggests that the Mariner is dreaming of being ashore.

l. 351. *jargoning*. Twittering. The word had been obsolete since the fifteenth century when Coleridge revived it for this poem.

16 ll. 362–77. *Listen . . . behold*. Stanzas dropped from the poem in 1800.

ll. 367 and 371. *a man of woman born*. See Job 14: 1; *Macbeth*, IV. i. 80, V. viii. 13.

l. 375. *n'old*. Would not.

17 l. 412. *honey-dew*. Sweet, luscious nectar, often represented in poetry as falling like dew. See 'Kubla Khan', l. 53, also composed in 1798.

l. 419. *a Slave*. Awareness of the plight of slaves may have influenced the poem. In June 1795, Coleridge had denounced the slave trade in a lecture delivered in Bristol, one of the major ports involved in the trade. For useful summary of the critical debate, see Raimonda Modiano, 'Historicist Readings of The Ancient Mariner', in N. Roe (ed.), *Samuel Taylor Coleridge and the Sciences of Life* (Oxford, 2001), 276–83.

18 l. 432. *belated*. Overtaken by the lateness of the night.

l. 445. *een*. Eyes (revised in 1800 to 'eyes').

19 l. 490. *rood*. Cross. Commonly used in exclamations, cf. *Hamlet*, III. iv. 14.

21 l. 527. *Eftsones*. Soon afterwards, again; revised in 1800 to 'But soon'.

l. 528. *pilot*. The helmsman whose local knowledge means that he can steer a ship into harbour.

l. 542. *Hermit*. Solitary man who has retired from society, usually for religious purposes. But see also 'Lines written a few miles above Tintern Abbey', ll. 22–3.

l. 545. *shrieve my soul*. Impose penance, administer absolution, hear a confession.

l. 556. *Skiff-boat*. A small seagoing boat, with oars and sails.

l. 557. *I trow!*. I believe.

22 l. 568. *Ivy-tod*. Ivy-bush. Cf. Spenser, *Shepheardes Calendar*, 'March', 67.

23 l. 610. *What manner man*. See Matthew 8: 27.

ll. 619–20. *pass . . . speech*. Cf. 'The Wandering Jew', ll. 65–70, in Percy.

24 l. 656. *sense forlorn*. Deprived of sense.

25 *The Foster-Mother's Tale*. Coleridge's poem is taken from his tragedy, *Osorio*, IV. ii. 3–83, which was rejected by London theatres in 1797. In its revised version, and under the new title, *Remorse*, it was accepted for production at Drury Lane in 1813. Wordsworth's pervasive influence on the poem is discussed by Newlyn, 24–6.

26 l. 36. *simples*. Medicinal herbs. Cf. *Romeo and Juliet*, V. i. 40.

l. 62. *savannah*. At this time understood to mean a largely treeless plain in the tropical regions of America. See 'Ruth', l. 109.

27 *Lines left upon a seat in a yew-tree*. Wordsworth's poem, begun while he was still at school in Hawkshead, describes a spot on the shore of the nearby lake of Esthwaite. In 1843, he recalled: 'The tree has disappeared, & the slip of common on which it stood, that ran parallel to the lake and lay open to it,

has long been enclosed, so that the road has lost much of its attraction. This spot was my favourite walk in the evenings during the latter part of my School-time. The individual whose habits and character are here given was a gentleman of the neighbourhood, a man of talent and learning who had been educated at one of our Universities, & returned to pass his time in seclusion on his own estate. He died a bachelor in middle age. Induced by the beauty of the prospect, he built a small summerhouse on the rocks above the penninsula on which the ferry-house stands. This property afterwards passed into the hands of the late Mr Curwen. The site was long ago pointed out by Mr West in his Guide, as the pride of the Lakes, and now goes by the name of "The Station". So much used I to be delighted with the view from it, while a little boy, that some years before the first pleasure-house was built I led thither from Hawkshead a youngster about my own age, an Irish boy, who was a servant to an Itinerant Conjuror. My motive was to witness the pleasure I expected the boy would receive from the prospect of the islands below & the intermingling water. I was not disappointed; and I hope the fact, insignificant as it may seem to some, may be thought worthy of note by others who may cast their eye over these notes' (*IF*, 36). The seat under the yew was constructed by Revd William Braithwaite of Satterhow, whose reclusive habits ended in 1787 when he became the vicar of Burton Pedwardine in Lincolnshire (*WH*, 256–65). For the importance of Esthwaite to Wordsworth, see McCracken, 82–8. Wordsworth made minor revisions in 1800, as noted in 1802 version below.

27 l. 1. *Nay, Traveller! rest*. Wordsworth adapts the Latin convention 'siste, viator', commonly found on Roman memorials and in later eighteenth-century poetry—see, for example, Burns, 'Elegy on Captain Matthew Henderson', l. 97; Cowper, 'Inscription for the Tomb of Mr Hamilton', l. 1. See also Wordsworth's *Essay upon Epitaphs*, I, in *Prose*, ii.

l. 24. *stone-chat . . . sand-piper*. British birds, common in the Lake District, but not hitherto, in English poetry. Thomas Bewick's *A History of British Birds* was published in 1797.

29 *The Nightingale*. Composed by Coleridge, April–May 1798 and substituted for 'Lewti'. In 1800, 'a conversational poem' was dropped. Modern scholars have often grouped this poem with other 'conversation poems' composed by Coleridge at this time but not published in *Lyrical Ballads*, including 'Frost at Midnight', 'This Lime-Tree Bower my Prison', and 'Fears in Solitude'. When Coleridge sent the poem to Wordsworth in May 1798, he added the following reflection:

> In stale blank verse a subject stale
> I sent *per post* my *Nightingale*:
> And like an honest bard, dear Wordsworth,
> You'll tell me what you think my Bird's worth.
> My opinion's briefly this—
> His *bill* he opens not amiss;

And when he has sung a stave or so,
His breast, & some small space below,
So throbs & swells, that you might swear
No vulgar music's working there.
So far, so good; but then, 'od rot him!
There's something falls off at his bottom.
Yet, sure, no wonder it should breed,
That my Bird's Tail's a tail indeed
And makes its own inglorious harmony
Aeolio crepitu, non carmine. (*CL* i. 406)

Mays notes the echo of Horace, *Odes*, 4.3.12, and translates Coleridge's
last line thus: 'With Aeolian farting, not with song' (*CP* I. i. 521).

l. 13. *Most musical, most melancholy*. From Milton's 'Il Penseroso', l. 62.
The association had recently been consolidated by the inclusion of Milton's
lines in the section on 'The Nightingale' in Bewick's *British Birds* (1797).

l. 18. *distemper*. Depression; mental disorder or disturbance.

l. 23. *conceit*. Personal or private opinion; fanciful notion or contrived liter-
ary figure; personal pride and vanity.

30 l. 39. *Philomela*. Poetic name for the nightingale, derived from the Greek
myth in which Philomela, having been raped by her brother-in-law,
Tereus, who also cut out her tongue, was turned into a nightingale.

l. 40. *My Friend, and my Friend's Sister!*. William and Dorothy Wordsworth.

l. 41. *lore*. Lesson or teaching.

l. 60. *jug jug*. The traditional representation of the nightingale's call.

ll. 64–9. *On moonlight bushes . . . love-torch*. Deleted in 1800.

l. 68. *glow-worm*. Insect which sheds green light, visible at dusk, and in
English poetry from Shakespeare, *A Midsummer Night's Dream*, III. i. 156,
to Cowper, 'The Nightingale and Glow-Worm', and William Bowles, 'The
Glow Worm'. For full discussion of the glow-worm's associations, see
Lucy Newlyn, 'Wordsworth Among Glow-worms', *Essays in Criticism*,
61 (2011), 249–74.

31 ll. 81–2. *sudden Gale . . . harps*. Aeolian harp, a fashionable, stringed instru-
ment, whose notes were produced by the breeze blowing across the strings,
had already inspired Coleridge's 'The Eolian Harp' in 1796, and would
recur, painfully, in 'Dejection: An Ode', ll. 97–100. The image may owe
something to Macpherson's Ossian, the quintessentially melancholy Celtic
Bard, who was depicted sitting beneath a harp suspended from a ruined
oak-tree.

l. 84. *blosmy*. Blossomy. Coleridge is reviving a word used by Chaucer,
which had been obsolete during the intervening centuries.

l. 90. *That strain again!*. Cf. *Twelfth Night*, I. i. 14.

31 l. 91. *My dear Babe*. Hartley Coleridge was born on 19 September 1796.

l. 104. *undropt*. Coleridge's coinage is the first recorded example in the *Oxford English Dictionary*.

l. 109. *associate Joy*. An idea strongly influenced by the associationist psychological theories of David Hartley, the Yorkshire physician and philosopher, after whom Coleridge named his son. Hartley's *Observations on Man, His Frame, His Duty and His Expectations* was first published in 1749, but enjoyed new success after the publication of a new, shorter edition in 1775, edited by Joseph Priestley.

32 *The Female Vagrant*. Wordsworth's poem was originally part of a long poem, 'Salisbury Plain', begun in 1793, revised into 'Adventures on Salisbury Plain' in 1795 and now abandoned except for this extract. It was finally published in 1842 as *Guilt and Sorrow*. For full details, see William Wordsworth, *The Salisbury Plain Poems*, ed. Stephen Gill (Cornell Wordsworth edn.; Ithaca, NY, and London, 1975), and Stephen Gill, *Wordsworth's Revisitings* (Oxford, 2011), 188–212. Wordsworth later recalled that 'The chief incident of it, more particularly her description of her feelings on the Atlantic are taken from life' (*IF*, 7–8). The poem was revised extensively for 1800—see the 1802 version below.

l. 1. *Derwent's side*. By Derwent Water, which lies between Keswick and Borrowdale in the Lake District.

l. 23. *freaks*. Unpredictable jumps and capers.

33 l. 44. *hereditary nook*. Wordsworth's awareness of the importance of inheritance among small, independent farmers anticipates 'Michael'. See also his letter to Charles James Fox (Appendix 2).

34 l. 74. *artist's trade*. The skilled work of a craftsman or artisan.

l. 89. *empty loom . . . silent wheel*. The loom and spinning wheel were crucial tools of the trade for hand-loom weavers. Wordsworth's dismay over the decline of traditional cottage industries was later expressed in a series of poems on the spinning wheel, included in William Wordsworth, *Shorter Poems*, ed. Carl H. Ketcham (Ithaca, NY, and London, 1989), 108–9, 124–5; and in his related comment, 'I could write a treatise of lamentation upon the changes brought about among the cottages of Westmoreland by the silence of the Spinning Wheel. During long winter nights & wet days, the wheel upon which the wool was spun gave employment to a great part of a family. The old man, however infirm, was able to card the wool, as he sate in the corner by the fire-side; and often, when a boy, have I admired the cylinders of carded wool which were softly laid upon each other by his side. Two wheels were often at work on the same floor, and others of the family, chiefly the little children, were occupied in teasing and cleaning the wool to fit it for the hand of the carder. So that all except the smallest infants were contributing to mutual support. Such was the employment that prevailed in the pastoral vales' (*IF*, 20). See also 'Michael'.

l. 92. *relief.* Assistance given to people in need, administered by the parish. Poor relief was a major issue of the 1790s, and the subject of parliamentary debate and legislation. See also 'The Old Cumberland Beggar' and headnote.

l. 108. *parting signal.* Flag signalling that the ship was embarking.

l. 110. *equinoctial.* Associated with the autumn equinox, a time of gales and storms, but possibly referring also to the regions near the equator.

35 l. 124. *dog-like . . . heels of war. Henry V,* Prologue, 6–7.

37 l. 215. *wild brood.* Gypsies. Revised to 'Travellers' in 1802. Gypsies were considered picturesque by theorists of landscape, such as William Gilpin in his *Observations relative Chiefly to Picturesque Beauty . . . particularly the Mountains, and Lakes of Cumberland and Westmoreland,* 2 vols. (London, 1786), i. 277–8.

38 l. 226. *panniered ass.* Like Gypsies, donkeys with baskets or panniers, were regarded as 'picturesque', as in Gilpin, *Three Essays: On Picturesque Beauty, On Picturesque Travel, On Sketching Landscape* (London, 1792).

l. 230. *bag-pipe.* Musical instrument with reed pipes and an airbag once popular throughout Britain.

39 l. 258. *ruth.* Grief or sorrow, or the prompt for sorrow and regret.

Goody Blake, and Harry Gill. Wordsworth's poem was written in March 1798 and based on a passage from Erasmus Darwin's *Zoonomia; or The Laws of Organic life* (1794–6), which he had requested from Joseph Cottle earlier that month (*EY,* 199). In *Zoonomia,* Darwin devoted a section to 'Diseases of Volition', including 'mania mutabilis' or 'Mutable madness. Where patients are liable to mistake ideas of sensation for those from irritation, that is, imagination for realities' (ii. 356). Several examples of the condition are given, including the following case, spotted in a newspaper: 'A young farmer in Warwickshire, finding his hedges broke, and the sticks carried away during a frosty season, determined to watch for the thief. He lay many cold hours under a haystack, and at length an old woman, like a witch in a play, approached, and began to pull up the hedge; he waited till she had tied up her bottle of sticks, and was carrying them off, that he might convict her of the theft, and then springing from his concealment, he seized his prey with violent threats. After some altercation, in which her load was left upon the ground, she kneeled upon her bottle of sticks, and raising her arms to heaven beneath the bright cold moon then at the full, spoke to the farmer already shivering with cold. "Heaven grant, that thou mayest never know again the blessing to be warm". He complained of cold all the next day, and wore an upper coat, and in a few days another, and in a fortnight took to his bed, always saying nothing made him warm; he covered himself with very many blankets, and had a sieve over his face, as he lay; and from this one insane idea he kept his bed above twenty years for fear of the cold air, till at length he died' (ii. 359). The factual basis of the poem is emphasized in the Preface to *Lyrical Ballads*.

Wordsworth transplanted the characters to Dorset and gave them names that were relatively common locally. 'Goody' is a polite term for a married woman in humble circumstances.

39 l. 17. *drover*. Cattle or sheep farmer.

40 l. 25. *All day she spun*. Spinning was a common, but poorly paid, occupation for cottage workers, already in decline because of the mechanization of the industry (see note to p. 34, 'The Female Vagrant', l. 89). Old women and spinning wheels were also common in fairy tales.

l. 31. *coals are dear*. Dorset was not a mining area, so coal was imported by sea from Wales or the North.

l. 33. *pottage*. Probably a vegetable dish or soup, but possibly referring to the archaic meaning, porridge. In either case, indicative of poverty.

l. 39. *canty*. Lively, cheerful, active. A Scots or northern dialect word, common in traditional songs and used by Burns.

41 l. 60. *old hedge*. The hedge appeals as a source of wood for the fire. Wood-gathering from common land was an ancient right for rural dwellers, but the widespread Enclosure Acts of the later eighteenth century meant that much of the old sources of firewood had become the property of landowners.

l. 66. *trespass*. The criminal act of entering another's property, but also carrying the older, more general meaning of an error, and thus recalling the Lord's Prayer.

l. 76. *stubble-land*. The cornfield after the harvest. Harry Gill is an arable as well as a stock farmer, benefiting from the agricultural improvements associated with the enclosure of fields.

43 *Lines written at a small distance from my House*. Composed by Wordsworth at Alfoxden in March 1798. The little boy was Basil Montagu.

l. 3. *tall larch*. Wordsworth later recorded that 'the larch mentioned in the first stanza was standing when I revisited the place in 1841, more than 40 years after.—I was disappointed that it had not improved in appearance, as to size, nor had it acquired anything of the majesty of age, which, even though less perhaps than any other tree, the larch sometimes does' (*IF*, 37). The larch is a tall, slender deciduous tree.

44 *Simon Lee*. Wordsworth's poem, composed in March–April 1798, was based on a retired huntsman, Christopher Trickey, whose cottage was on the common near the entrance to Alfoxden Park. He later reported having 'after an interval of 45 years, the image of the old man as fresh before my eyes as if I had seen him yesterday. The expression when the hounds were out, "I dearly love their voice" was word for word from his own lips' (*IF*, 37). Simon Lee's career has been transplanted to Wales.

l. 1. *Cardigan.* Ceredigion, the county in mid-Wales bordered by Cardigan Bay, was formerly known as Cardigan.

l. 2. *Ivor-hall.* The lament for the ruined hall of Ivor, 'Llys Ifor Hael', apparently inspired by Ifor ap Llywelyn's estate at Bassaleg in South Wales, was written by the eighteenth-century antiquarian Evan Evans, and became a well-known Welsh song. For discussion, see Peter Bement, 'Simon Lee and Ivor Hall: A Possible Source', *Wordsworth Circle*, 13 (1982), 35–6.

l. 14. *running huntsman.* Simon Lee followed the hounds on foot; cp. 'The Childless Father'.

l. 16. *cheek . . . like a cherry.* This apparently picturesque detail may indicate heart disease, given Simon's other symptoms.

45 l. 35. *ancles . . . swoln and thick.* Simon suffers from oedema, a common sign of congestive cardiac problems.

l. 38. *husbandry or tillage.* As huntsman for a wealthy family, he would not have gained experience of cultivating crops.

l. 44. *reeled . . . stone-blind.* An effect of over-exertion. Collapse during the hunt might also indicate an underlying heart condition (though not the gradual congestive cardiac condition indicated by his thick ankles). I am indebted to Craig Sharp for the medical information relating to Simon Lee.

46 l. 62. *Enclosed.* The series of Enclosure Acts in the later eighteenth century meant that commons and wastelands were converted into private property.

l. 69. *My gentle reader.* A polite address common in older texts, and frequently used by eighteenth-century writers, including Pope, Swift, Fielding, and Sterne, as a playful archaism.

l. 85. *mattock.* Agricultural tool for breaking hard ground or removing trees.

47 *Anecdote for Fathers.* Wordsworth's poem was written at Alfoxden in April–May 1798. Wordsworth later recalled that 'The Boy was a son of my friend Basil Montagu' (*IF*, 4). In a letter of 1826(?) he commented that the poem exposed 'the injurious effects of putting inconsiderate questions to Children, and urging them to give answers upon matters either uninteresting to them, or upon which they had no decided opinion' (*LY* i. 486). Minor but significant revision in 1800, see 1802 version below.

l. 3. *in beauty's mould.* Cf. 'The Children in the Wood', l. 20, in Percy's *Reliques*.

l. 10. *Kilve.* A village on the Bristol Channel, near Alfoxden.

48 l. 24. *Liswyn.* Llyswen, in the Wye Valley near Brecon, was home to John Thelwall, the radical writer and lecturer, who had been tried and acquitted in the notorious Treason Trials of 1794, and invited to Nether Stowey in July 1797. Wordsworth, who visited Llyswen in August 1798, admired Thelwall not only for his commitment to social improvement,

but also as a model of domestic virtue: 'a man of extraordinary talent, an affectionate husband and a good father. Though brought up in the city on a tailor's board he was truly sensible of the beauty of natural objects' (*IF*, 4).

49 *We are Seven*. Composed in the grove at Alfoxden in March–April 1798. The poem was based on a little girl whom Wordsworth met in the ruins of Goodrich Castle, in the Wye Valley, in 1793, on his way from the south coast to visit Robert Jones in North Wales. He revisited the area in 1841, but was unable to track down the woman who had inspired him, because, as he recalled with regret, 'I did not even know her name' (*IF*, 4). Wordsworth also recalled that 'while walking to and fro I composed the last stanza first, having begun with the last line. When it was all but finished I came in, and recited it to Mr Coleridge and my Sister, and said "A prefatory stanza must be added, and I should sit down to our little tea-meal with greater pleasure if my task was finished." I mentioned in substance what I wished to be expressed, and Coleridge immediately threw off the stanza thus:

> A little Child, dear brother Jem,—

I objected to the rhyme, dear brother Jem as being ludicrous, but we all enjoyed the joke of hitching in our friend James Tobin's name who was familiarly called Jem.' Wordsworth's friend, James, was less amused by the joke, but his request for revision went unheeded (*IF*, 3).

l. 19. *Conway*. Town on the coast of North Wales.

50 l. 47. *porringer*. Small bowl suitable for soup or porridge.

51 *Lines written in early spring*. Composed in early March 1798, by the side of a brook in the grounds at Alfoxden, as Wordsworth later recalled: 'The brook fell down a sloping rock so as to make a waterfall considerable for that country, and, across the pool below, had fallen a tree, an ash if I rightly remember, from which rose perpendicularly boughs in search of the light intercepted by the deep shade above. The boughs bore leaves of green that for want of sunshine had faded almost into a lily-white: and, from the underside of this natural sylvan bridge depended long & beautiful tresses of ivy which waved gently in the breeze that might poetically speaking be called the breath of the water-fall. This motion varied of course according to the power of water in the brook' (*IF*, 36–7).

l. 8. *What man has made of man*. See Burns, 'Man was made to Mourn', l. 55.

52 *The Thorn*. Composed by Wordsworth at Alfoxden after a walk with Dorothy and Basil on 19 March 1798, where he saw 'a stunted thorn' (*Journals*, i. 10). Wordsworth recalled that the poem 'arose out of my observing, on the ridge of Quantock Hill, on a stormy day, a thorn which I had often passed in calm and bright weather without noticing it. I said to myself, "Cannot I by some invention do as much to make this thorn permanently an impressive object as the storm has made it to my eyes at

this moment." I began the poem accordingly and composed it with great rapidity' (*IF*, 14). 'A thorn' refers to a hawthorn bush, common across Britain, and characterized by its distinctive red berries. In John Langhorne's *The Country Justice* (1755), 'a solitary thorn' marks the spot where a pregnant woman, driven from town and forced to give birth alone on the heath, died from 'famine, pain, and cold, And anguish' (pt. II, ll. 59–86). In 1800, Wordsworth added a long note to 'The Thorn' (included in this volume, pp. 199–200). His friend and patron Sir George Beaumont was inspired to paint a picture based on the poem, prompting Wordsworth in 1805 to acknowledge 'The Thorn' as 'a favourite' (*EY*, 588).

54 l. 63. *woman . . . scarlet cloak*. Cf. Crazy Kate in Cowper's *The Task*, i. 534–56. Scarlet may be associated with shame, with an offence, or with sin (Isaiah 1: 18; Revelation 17: 1–5).

l. 65. *Oh misery! oh misery!*. Cf. 'Waly, waly, Love be Bonny', in Percy.

55 l. 116. *Martha Ray*. The name is the same as that of Basil Montagu's grandmother, who had been murdered by James Hackman in 1779. The celebrated murder was mentioned by Darwin in his discussion of violent insanity in *Zoonomia*, ii. 365 (see headnote to 'Goody Blake and Harry Gill', p. 331).

l. 119. *blithe and gay*. A phrase common in eighteenth-century songs and pastorals, see John Thelwall, 'Eclogue I'. Also reminiscent of the child born on the Sabbath day in the traditional children's rhyme, 'Monday's Child'.

l. 120. *happy, happy*. See Burns, 'The Cotter's Saturday Night', l. 73.

57 l. 181. *telescope*. In his 1800 'Note to The Thorn' (included in this volume, p. 199), Wordsworth identified the speaker as a sea captain.

58 l. 206. *the pond*. Cf. Bürger, 'The Lass of Fair Wone', stanzas 43–7, repr. in Jacobus, 288.

59 *The Last of the Flock*. Composed by Wordsworth at Alfoxden in March, April, or May 1798. According to Wordsworth, 'the incident occurred in the village of Holford, close by Alfoxden' (*IF*, 9). Minor but significant revision in 1800, see 1802 version.

l. 4. *Weep . . . alone*. In a letter to John Kenyon of September 1836, Wordsworth commented that 'I never in my whole life saw a man weep *alone* in the roads; but a friend of mine *did* see this poor man weeping *alone*, with the Lamb, the last of his flock, in his arms' (*LY* iii. 292).

60 l. 41. *Ten*. Revised to 'Six' in 1800.

l. 44. *parish . . . relief*. See note to p. 34, 'The Female Vagrant', l. 92.

62 *The Dungeon*. Composed April–September 1797. Coleridge's poem was taken from his tragedy, *Osorio* (V. ii. 1–30). See headnote to 'The Foster-Mother's Tale', p. 327. 'The Dungeon' may be indebted to Cowper's *The Task*, i. 436–54 and v. 384–455. The poem was dropped from *Lyrical Ballads* in 1802.

62 l. 11. *mountebanks*. Itinerant charlatans selling remedies.

63 l. 20. *ministrations*. Services, with religious connotations. Cf. 'Frost at Midnight', 1, 72.

l. 21. *distempered*. Disordered, diseased, unbalanced.

The Mad Mother. Composed by Wordsworth in Alfoxden in 1798, and apparently inspired by 'A Lady of Bristol who had seen the poor creature' (*IF*, 11). Butler and Green note the suggestion in Darwin's *Zoonomia* that in order to treat post-natal insanity 'the child should be brought frequently to the mother, and applied to her breast', since maternal feelings were regarded as the cure (ii. 360). The poem may also be indebted to 'The Frantic Lady', in Percy, and 'Lady Anne Bothwell's Lament', which was included in Percy, Herd, and Ritson.

l. 4. *from over the main*. The woman, who speaks 'the English tongue', has arrived after a long sea voyage. In a letter to John Kenyon of 24 September 1836, Wordsworth commented that since English was her native tongue, she was 'either of these Islands, or a North American. On the latter supposition, while the distance removes her from us, the fact of her speaking our language brings us at once into close sympathy with her' (*LY* iii. 293).

65 l. 96. *earth-nuts*. The tubers of certain plants.

66 *The Idiot Boy*. Composed by Wordsworth in 1798, as he recalled, 'The last stanza—"The Cocks did crow & the sun did shine so cold" was the foundation of the whole. The words were reported to me by my dear friend Thomas Poole; but I have since heard the same repeated of other Idiots. Let me add that this long poem was composed in the Groves of Alfoxden almost extempore; not a word, I believe, being corrected, though one stanza was omitted. I mention this in gratitude to those happy moments, for, in truth, I never wrote anything with so much glee' (*IF*, 10). In his letter to John Wilson, Wordsworth defended the poem vigorously, see Appendix 4.

l. 6. *Halloo! halloo!*. Cf. Bürger, 'Lenora', ll. 105, 129; see Jacobus, 281–2.

67 l. 60. *hurly-burly*. Commotion, noisy excitement. See *Macbeth*, I. i. 3; *Henry IV pt I*, V. i. 78.

69 l. 116. *beneath the moon*. Cf. *King Lear*, IV. vi. 26–7.

ll. 125–6. *he cannot tell . . . back*. Cf. Cowper, 'The Diverting History of John Gilpin', ll. 95–6.

70 l. 139. *porringer*. Small bowl suitable for soup or porridge.

72 l. 220. *bush and brake*. Cf. Shakespeare, *Midsummer Night's Dream*, III. i. 97.

l. 225. *the moon . . . brook*. The detail may be informed by the Wiltshire legend of the 'moonrakers', who attempted to catch the moon they could see in the pond; it was recorded by Francis Grose in his *Provincial Glossary* (1787).

73 l. 247. *distemper*. Mental disturbance or unbalance.

74 ll. 303 and 318. *deadly sin*. Suicide.

75 l. 335. *horseman-ghost*. Cf. Bürger, 'Lenora', ll. 115–24; in Jacobus, 282.

79 l. 462. *glory*. Triumph, but with possible suggestion of divine manifestation or a halo.

Lines written near Richmond. Wordsworth began the poem as a student in Cambridge, as he later recalled, 'It was during a solitary walk on the banks of the Cam that I was first struck with this appearance, & applied it to my own feelings in the manner here expressed, changing the scene to the Thames near Windsor' (*IF*, 36). In 1800, following advice from Coleridge, the poem was divided into two separate poems, 'Lines written when sailing in a Boat at Evening' and 'Lines written near Richmond upon the Thames' (see 1802 versions).

80 l. 30. *a later ditty*. William Collins elegized James Thomson (1700–48), author of *The Seasons*, who was buried at Richmond on Thames, in his 'Ode on the Death of Mr. Thomson'. For full discussion, see E. Stein, *Wordsworth's Art of Allusion* (University Park, Penn., 1988).

l. 34. *suspend the dashing oar*. See Collins's 'Ode on . . . Thomson', 15. Collins died in 1759. Wordsworth also echoed the line when describing William Tell's monument in *Descriptive Sketches*, 349.

Expostulation and Reply. Composed by Wordsworth at Alfoxden in spring 1798. See the Advertisement and note to p. 4. An expostulation is a friendly remonstrance.

81 l. 13. *Esthwaite lake*. Near Hawkshead. See 'Lines left upon a Seat in a Yew-tree'.

l. 15. *Matthew*. The friend mentioned in the 1798 Advertisement was identified by Wordsworth as William Hazlitt, but since the friend in the poem is called Matthew, this poem and its companion may be connected with the later sequence, 'If Nature . . .', 'The Two April Mornings', 'The Fountain'. See headnote to 'Lines written on a Tablet'.

The Tables turned. The companion poem to 'Expostulation and Reply', composed by Wordsworth at Alfoxden in 1798. The reversal of positions suggested by the title recalls the reversal of the board in games such as draughts.

82 l. 25. *lore*. Teaching or creed (with play on its homonym, 'law').

l. 28. *murder to dissect*. Though the line is metaphorical, at this period animals and birds were frequently hunted for the purposes of dissection.

l. 30. *barren leaves*. Bare, unfruitful leaves of the book, rather than the living leaves of fertile plants and trees.

Old Man travelling. Composed by Wordsworth 1796–7, and regarded as 'an overflowing from the old Cumberland Beggar' (*IF*, 57). Minor but significant revision in 1800—see 1802 version.

83 l. 19. *sea-fight . . . Falmouth.* The Merchants' Hospital for maimed and disabled seamen was founded in 1750 in the Cornish port of Falmouth. With its deep harbour and situation on the south-west peninsula, Falmouth was often the first port of call for naval vessels returning to Britain.

The Complaint of a forsaken Indian Woman. Composed by Wordsworth at Alfoxden in March–May 1798, and based on an incident in Samuel Hearne's *A Journey from Prince of Wales's Fort in Hudson Bay to the Northern Ocean, 1769–1772* (London, 1795), 203, which he had 'read with deep interest' (*IF*, 9). Hearne wrote that 'One of the Indian's wives, who for some time had been in a consumption, had for a few days past become so weak as to be incapable of travelling, which, among those people, is the most deplorable state to which a human being can possibly be brought. Whether she had been given over by the doctors, or that it was for want of friends among them, I cannot tell, but certain it is, that no expedients were taken for her recovery; so that, without much ceremony, she was left unassisted to perish above ground.

'Though this was the first instance of the kind I had seen, it is the common, and indeed the constant practice of those Indians; for when a grown person is so ill, especially in the summer, as not to be able to walk, and too heavy to be carried, they say it is better to leave one who is past recovery, than for the whole family to sit down by them and starve to death, well knowing that it cannot be of any service to the afflicted. On those occasions, therefore, the friends or relations of the sick generally leave them some victuals and water; and if the situation of the place will afford it, a little firing. When those articles are provided, the person to be left is to be acquainted with the road which the others intend to go; and then, after covering them well up with deer skins etc. they take their leave, and walk away crying.

'Sometimes persons thus left, recover; and come up with their friends, or wander about till they meet with other Indians, whom they accompany till they again join their relations. Instances of this kind are seldom known. The poor woman above mentioned, however, came up with us three several times, after having been left in the manner described. At length, poor creature! She dropped behind, and no one attempted to go back in search of her' (pp. 202–3).

The songs of Native Americans had interested scholars such as Blair and Ritson and inspired poets from Warton and Gray to Bowles and Southey. For discussion, see Tim Fulford, *Romantic Indians* (Oxford, 2006), 141–55.

In the title, *Complaint* is a word with several meanings, historically: an expression of grief; a plaintive poem; an outcry against injury; a statement of injustice. *Forsaken* means deserted, left solitary, a word with strong biblical associations (Psalms 22: 1, 71: 9, 11, 18; Matthew 27: 46; Mark 15: 34).

l. 3. *northern gleams.* Northern Lights or aurora borealis.

84 l. 24. *heartless.* Disheartened, dejected. Cf. *Prelude*, ix. 517.

85 l. 65. *forsaken.* The dying Mother expresses guilt over abandoning her child, recalling the title of the poem.

The Convict. Wordsworth's poem was first published in the *Morning Post* on 14 December 1797, with the pseudonym 'Mortimer', the name of a leading character in *The Borderers*. It was dropped from *Lyrical Ballads* in 1800.

86 l. 25. *synod.* Assembly or council, usually ecclesiastical.

l. 37. *jail-mastiff.* Cf. Pope, *Moral Essays, Epistle III, To Bathurst*, ll. 197–8. See also 'Christabel', l. 7, composed in 1798 but not published until 1816.

l. 46. *complacence.* Pleasure in one's own doings.

87 *Lines written a few miles above Tintern Abbey.* Composed July 1798. Wordsworth looked back on this poem fondly: 'No poem of mine was ever composed under circumstances more pleasant for me to remember than this: I began it upon leaving Tintern, after crossing the Wye, and concluded it just as I was entering Bristol in the evening, after a ramble of 4 or 5 days, with my sister. Not a line of it was altered, and not any part written down till I reached Bristol. It was published almost immediately after' (*IF*, 15). The date of composition, included in the subtitle, probably refers to the last day of the tour, when the Wordsworths returned to Bristol. Although the abbey does not appear in the poem, it was a very familiar landmark for contemporary readers. Works such as Thomas Whatley's *Observations on Modern Gardening* (1770) and William Gilpin's *Observations on the River Wye, and several parts of South Wales, etc., relative chiefly to Picturesque Beauty* (London, 1782), had encouraged tourists to visit the Wye and by the 1790s, the numerous guides, poems, essays, and landscape paintings ensured that features such as the garden at Piercefield, the New Weir at Symonds Yat, the ironworks and ruined abbey at Tintern were all very well known. Wordsworth met Richard Warner in Bristol and took his recently published guidebook, *A Walk Through Wales, in August 1797*, with him on the tour, drawing on it for some of the poem's details (see Jacobus, 104–30). For the importance of the picturesque theorists Uvedale Price and Richard Knight who both had estates in the Wye Valley, see Stephen Daniels and Charles Watkins, 'Picturesque Landscaping and Estate Management: Uvedale Price and Nathaniel Kent at Foxley', in Stephen Copley and Peter Garside (eds.), *The Politics of the Picturesque* (Cambridge, 1994), 13–41. The 'Banks of Wye' were also famous from Shakespeare's *Henry IV, Part I*, III. i. 61, and *Henry V*, IV. vii. 110; John of Gaunt's castle at nearby Monmouth was the birthplace of Henry V. No exact location for the composition of the poem has been identified.

l. 1. *Five years have passed.* Wordsworth first visited the Wye in 1793 on his way from the Isle of Wight to North Wales. His memorable journey across Salisbury Plain is recalled in *The Prelude*, xii. 312–53, as well as in the

'Salisbury Plain Poems', from which 'The Female Vagrant' was extracted for *Lyrical Ballads* (see headnote to 'The Female Vagrant').

87 l. 4. *sweet*. May refer to fresh rather than salt water. The absence of tides, noted by Wordsworth, indicates considerable distance from the Severn estuary; see Damian Walford Davies, 'Romantic Hydrography: Tide and Transit in Tintern Abbey', in N. Roe (ed.), *English Romantic Writers and the West Country* (Basingstoke, 2010), 218–36.

l. 5. *steep and lofty cliffs*. Cf. Gilpin's *Observations on the River Wye*, 7–8.

l. 10. *sycamore*. See Izaak Walton, *The Compleat Angler*, ed. John Buxton (Oxford, 1930), 113; Virgil, *Eclogues*, i. 1–2. See also 'Willow, willow, willow', in Percy.

l. 17. *pastoral*. A reference to the grazing livestock of these farms, but recalling the ancient literary tradition celebrating simple, rural lifestyles and values.

l. 18. *smoke*. Gilpin described the smoke from the furnaces in the Wye Valley in his *Observations on the River Wye*, 12. Vigorous debate over the Wye industries and Wordsworth's (non-)representation of these details was sparked by Marjorie Levinson in *Wordsworth's Great Period Poems* (Cambridge, 1986); see Thomas Mcfarland, *William Wordsworth: Intensity and Achievement* (Oxford, 1992); Charles Rzepka, 'Pictures of the Mind: Iron and Charcoal, "Ouzy" Tides and "Vagrant Dwellers" at Tintern 1798', *Studies in Romanticism*, 42 (2003), 155–86.

l. 19. In 1798, the poem included an additional line, 'And the low copses, coming from the trees', but an errata slip at the end of the volume directed readers to omit it.

l. 23. *hermit*. See 'The Rime of the Ancyent Marinere', l. 542 and note.

l. 25. *landscape to a blind man's eye*. Often read in the light of eighteenth-century theories on blindness, such as the 'Molyneux problem', which examined the experience of a blind man suddenly able to see, as discussed by Heather Glen, *Vision and Enchantment: Blake's Songs and Wordsworth's Lyrical Ballads* (Cambridge, 1983), 253–4; Alan Bewell, *Wordsworth and the Enlightenment* (New Haven and London, 1989), 26–8. The line may simply contrast the speaker's temporary deprivation of the sight of the Wye Valley and the blind man's permanent inability to see. Uvedale Price referred to Milton's dreadful deprivation of sight, quoting *Paradise Lost*, iii. 45–50, in his *Essay on the Picturesque* (London, 1796), 302–3. See also Wordsworth's *Essay, Supplementary to the Preface* of 1815, in *Prose*, ii.

88 l. 34. *good man's life*. Cf. Preface to Milton's *The Judgment of Martin Bucer concerning Divorce*. Wordsworth may also be recalling one of the Wye's most famous residents, John Kyrle, 'The Man of Ross', described by Pope in the *Moral Essays, Epistle III: To Bathurst*, ll. 249–74, and mentioned in many Tours of the Wye, including those of Gilpin, Warner, and Joseph Hucks.

ll. 46–7. *laid asleep . . . living soul.* See Genesis 2: 7; Milton, *Paradise Lost*, vii. 528; viii. 453–64, 528.

l. 50. *We see . . . life of things.* Gill notes Coleridge's Notebook entry 921, in relation to this line.

ll. 56 and 58. *How oft, in spirit . . . How often has my spirit.* Cf. Coleridge, 'Frost at Midnight', 28. For full discussion, see Newlyn, 53–6.

l. 57. *O sylvan . . . woods.* The apostrophe to the wooded (sylvan) Wye may recall Virgil, *Eclogues*, iv. 1–3. See also Michael Bruce, 'Lochleven', l. 214, from *Poems on Several Occasions* (London, 1796).

89 l. 68. *a roe.* A small deer, now common throughout Britain, but in 1798 almost extinct, as noted by contemporary natural histories such as Goldsmith's popular *Animated Nature.* See also Song of Solomon 2: 9.

l. 74. *The coarser . . . boyish days.* As described in *The Prelude*, i and ii, and noted by Gill.

l. 76. *I cannot paint.* Unlike Gilpin and other picturesque tourists, Wordsworth avoids the fashionable impulse to pictorialize the scene in his memory.

l. 89. *Abundant recompence.* Cf. Milton, 'Lycidas', l. 184; Burns, 'Man was made to Mourn', l. 79.

90 ll. 107–8. *half-create . . . perceive.* Wordsworth directs attention to Young's *Night Thoughts*, which recommends imaginative cooperation with the senses: 'Take in, at once, the Landscape of the world, | At a small Inlet, which a Grain might close, | And half create the wonderous World, they see' (Night VI, ll. 425–7). But see also Cowper, *The Task*, iv. 290.

l. 114. *genial spirits.* Milton, *Samson Agonistes*, 594.

l. 115. *For thou art with me.* Psalm 23: 4.

l. 123. *Nature never did betray.* Mason suggests an echo of Samuel Daniel, *The Civil Wars*, ii. 29–30, 'Here have you craggie Rocks to take your part; | That never will betray their faith to you'. Butler and Green point to Coleridge, 'This Lime-Tree Bower my Prison', ll. 59–60.

l. 129. *evil tongues.* Milton, *Paradise Lost*, vii. 26.

l. 135. *Therefore let the moon.* See 'Frost at Midnight', ll. 65–74.

LYRICAL BALLADS, WITH PASTORAL AND OTHER POEMS, 1802

In 1800 the collection was published in two volumes, under Wordsworth's name and the title, *Lyrical Ballads, with Other Poems.* The Latin epigraph, added to the title page in 1800, means 'How utterly unsuited to your taste, Papinianus'. It appears in the foreword to Drayton's *Poly-Olbion*, which Wordsworth read in Robert Anderson's edition of *The Works of the British Poets.* Papinianus was a distinguished Roman jurist—or judge—so the motto is probably a light-hearted address to the reviewers or unsympathetic readers who might pass judgement on the volume. The 1800 edition included forty-one new poems by Wordsworth, and one by Coleridge ('Love'). 'The Convict' was dropped and 'Lines written near Richmond' divided into two poems; other poems were reordered and revised, notably 'The Rime of the Ancyent Marinere'. The Advertisement was replaced by the Preface. Some early copies of the 1800 edition included a reference to 'Christabel' and omitted fourteen lines of 'Michael'. These were rapidly corrected. Fewer copies of Volume I were published in 1800, because most of the poems had already appeared as *Lyrical Ballads* in 1798. Readers who bought only Volume II would not have had the Preface, nor the revised and reordered versions of 'The Ancient Mariner' and some of the other poems.

In 1802, the addition of *'Pastoral and'* to the title drew attention to poems such as 'The Brothers' and 'Michael', which Wordsworth especially singled out for notice in his letter of 14 January 1801, to Charles James Fox (see Appendix 2). A further Latin quotation from Quintilian, which Wordsworth had quoted in the letter to Fox, was added as an epigraph (originally placed after the Preface): 'Pectus enim id est quod disertos facit . . . verba non desunt' (It is feeling and force of imagination that makes us eloquent. It is for this reason that even the uneducated have no difficulty in finding words to express their meaning, if only they are stirred by some strong emotion). Wordsworth also made substantial additions to the 1800 Preface, and added an appendix on 'Poetic Diction', included after the last poem. He made minor revisions to some poems, though 'Ruth' was altered more extensively, with new stanzas added. The sequence of poems was reorganized and 'A Character', added in 1800, was dropped. In 1805, a fourth edition was prepared, but revisions were not extensive or particularly significant and the arrangement of the poems was unchanged from 1802. In later, collected editions, Wordsworth reorganized poems published in *Lyrical Ballads*, grouping them with other work under various thematic headings.

PREFACE

Composed September–October 1800, revised 1802, as discussed in the Introduction, pp. xxxix–xli. Since the contents reflect numerous eighteenth-century currents of thought, full annotation is not appropriate here. For full detail, readers should consult W. J. B. Owen's annotated edition in *Prose*, i, and his companion volume, *Wordsworth's Literary Criticism*; and Mason. Important sources range from classical authorities such as Aristotle and Quintilian to modern critics such as John Dennis, Samuel Johnson, Hugh Blair, and James Currie. Coleridge analysed the Preface in detail in *Biographia Literaria*, chs. 14–20 (*BL* ii. 5–106), though his retrospective account reflects his divergence from Wordsworth in the intervening years.

95 *difference . . . coincide.* On 29 July 1802, Coleridge wrote to Southey: 'altho' Wordworth's Preface is half a child of my own Brain & so arose out of Conversations, so frequent, that with few exceptions we could scarcely

either of us perhaps positively say, which first started any particular Thought—I am speaking of the Preface as it stood in the second Volume—yet I am far from going all lengths with Wordsworth He has written lately a number of Poems (32 in all) some of them of considerable Length (the longest 160 Lines) the greater number of these to my feelings very excellent Compositions but here & there a daring Humbleness of Language & Versification, and a strict adherence to matter of fact, even to prolixity, that startled me his alterations likewise in Ruth perplexed me and I have thought & thought again & have not had my doubts resolved by Wordsworth On the contrary, I rather suspect that some where or other there is a radical Difference in our theoretical opinions respecting Poetry' (*CL* ii. 830). The radical difference became apparent to everyone after the publication of *Biographia Literaria*.

96 *Catullus . . . Pope.* A parallel is being drawn between two distinct phases of classical literature and corresponding phases of English literature. Catullus, Terence, and Lucretius were great writers of the late Roman Republic, working in the first and second centuries BC, Statius and Claudian were later poets of imperial Rome, often regarded as the 'Silver Age' of Latin literature. Shakespeare, Beaumont, and Fletcher were early modern dramatists and regarded in Wordsworth's times as part of the 'Golden Age' of English literature; the post-Restoration poetry of Dryden, Cowley, and Pope was increasingly considered correct and polished, but lacking in originality and imagination: a 'Silver Age'.

if they persist . . . that title. Adapted from the 1798 Advertisement.

97 *situations interesting.* Revised from 'of common life interesting' of 1800.

condition. Revised from 'situation' of 1800.

99 *great national events . . . gratifies.* The rapidly shifting news relating to the war with France. In 1800 Napoleon's successes were causing widespread alarm, by 1802 when the third edition of *Lyrical Ballads* appeared, the Treaty of Amiens had been signed, bringing a short-lived peace, on terms that caused fresh anxieties to many, including Wordsworth.

100 *frantic novels . . . in verse.* The rage for Gothic fiction, drama, and poetry was at its height in the 1790s, with numerous new titles and productions. The German tragedies may refer to those of Kotzebue, whose *Die Spanier in Peru* was adapted by Richard Brinsley Sheridan as the basis of his extraordinarily successful *Pizarro*, in 1799. The contemporary enthusiasm is brilliantly caught by Jane Austen in *Northanger Abbey*, which was drafted in *c*.1797, and sold to a publisher in 1803, though it did not appear.

never attempted. The following words of the next sentence of 1800 were dropped from 1802: 'Except in a very few instances'.

102 *In vain . . . in vain.* Thomas Gray did not publish his 'Sonnet on the Death of Richard West', but it had appeared in William Mason's edition

of *The Poems of Mr Gray*, 1775. Wordsworth's remarks on 'poetic diction' are further amplified in his appendix, included on pp. 298–301.

102 *Poetry . . . Sisters*. Known as the 'Sister Arts', the relationship between poetry and painting was the subject of considerable aesthetic discussion, which went back to Horace's *ars poetica*.

Angels weep . . . them both. *Paradise Lost*, i. 620. The major additional passage of 1802 begins here, leading into the passage on metre.

105 *Frontiniac or Sherry*. Frontignac is a dessert wine from the Languedoc. Wordsworth is mocking contemporary conversations about 'Taste' which have the tendency to reduce poetry to a fashion item or matter of personal preference.

Aristotle . . . writing. Probably a reference to the *Poetics*, 1451b5–7, perhaps via Coleridge, but see W. J. B. Owen, *Wordsworth as Critic* (Toronto, 1969), 88–91 for full discussion.

106 *before and after*. *Hamlet*, IV. iv. 37.

108 *the distinction of metre*. Wordsworth's practical interest in metre is evident in numerous comments on other poets as well as in his own experimentation; see also his transcriptions from Richard Payne Knight's *The Progress of Civil Society* , in Wu, i. 81, or the letter to Thelwall of January 1804 (*EY*, 434). For critical discussion, see Owen, *Wordsworth as Critic*, 27–36; J. W. Page, 'Wordsworth and the Psychology of Metre', *Papers on Language and Literature*, 21 (1985), 275–94; Susan Wolfson, 'Romanticism and the Measures of Meter', *Eighteenth-Century Life* (1992), 162–80; Brennan O'Donnell, *The Passion of Meter* (Kent, OH, 1995).

110 *Clarissa . . . Gamester*. Samuel Richardson's novel, *Clarissa* (1748); Edward Moore's tragedy, *The Gamester* (1753).

111 *construction*. The clauses following, up to 'so widely', were added in 1802.

112 *Pope . . . passion*. Probably referring to *An Essay on Criticism*.

113 *'I put my hat . . . in his hand'*. Johnson's parody of the well-known ballad, 'The Babes in the Wood', published in the *London Magazine* (April 1785), 254.

'These pretty Babes . . . the Town'. From 'The Children in the Wood', in Percy and widely reprinted.

114 *Reynolds*. See Advertisement to 1798 and note to p. 3.

POEMS, VOLUME I

For the poems in Volume I, see the notes to 1798 edition, except where additional detail is included below. Revisions to the poems can be seen by comparing the 1802 texts with the 1798 edition, above, but significant alterations are highlighted in the notes below.

119 *Animal Tranquillity and Decay.* Title revised from *Old Man travelling.* ll. 16–20 put into reported rather than direct speech.

123 *The Last of the Flock.* l. 41 revised from 'Ten' to 'Six', perhaps to avoid confusion at l. 92.

126 *Lines left upon a seat in a YEW-TREE.* l. 13. 'science' replaces 'genius'. ll. 14–15 and ll. 20–1 considerably altered. l. 30. 'downcast' replaces 'downward' of 1798; l. 38 added.

128 *The Foster-Mother's Tale.* See the longer version, with shorter title, published in 1798; sixteen opening lines of 1798 dropped in 1800. l. 21. 'sought for' replaces 'gathered' of 1798. l. 42. 'cell' replaces 'hole'of 1798. l. 44. 'near the cell' replaces 'in the cellar'. l. 53. two lines of 1798 version dropped.

129 *The Thorn.* Wordsworth's own 'Note to The Thorn' is reprinted at the end of Volume I, as in the original edition.

139 *Anecdote for Fathers.* Revision to ll. 45–7.

142 *The Female Vagrant.* Revisions in 1800 extensive enough to merit careful comparison of 1798 and 1802 poems. Changes include deletion of some 1798 stanzas ll. 1–9, 19–36, 118–26; and extensive rewording throughout.

150 *Simon Lee.* Fourth stanza of 1798 moved to become the sixth stanza in 1800.

153 *The Nightingale.* Revised in 1800, when ll. 64–9 were removed.

169 *Love.* Composed by Coleridge November–December 1799 and added to *Lyrical Ballads* in 1800. A longer version was published in the *Morning Post*, 21 December 1799, with Coleridge's name, as 'Introduction to the Tale of the Dark Ladie'. Apparently inspired by visiting Sockburn and falling in love with Sara Hutchinson. The poem was admired by Walter Scott, and according to John Gibson Lockhart, was 'better known than any of it's author's productions' and known by heart to many readers, as Mays notes (*CP* I. ii. 605).

l. 5. *waking dreams.* A state in which the conscious mind experiences dreamlike images, fascinating to eighteenth-century philosophers and poets, and analysed by Henry Home, Lord Kames in his influential *Elements of Criticism*, 3 vols. (Edinburgh, 1762), i. 116–22.

ll. 9–10. *Moonshine . . . Eve.* Mays notes the similarity to a letter to Sara Coleridge, 17 May 1799, *CL* i. 499.

175 *The Ancient Mariner.* Title and numerous spellings revised in 1800, to the dismay of admirers such as Charles Lamb. Wordsworth wrote to Cottle on 24 June 1799, 'From what I can gather it seems that The Ancyent Mariner has upon the whole been an injury to the volume, I mean that the old words and the strangeness of it have deterred readers from going on' (*EY*, 264). Wordsworth added a note in 1800, which was removed in 1802: 'I cannot refuse myself the gratification of informing such Readers as may have been pleased with this Poem, or with any part of it, that they owe

their pleasure in some sort to me; as the Author was himself very desirous that it should be suppressed. This wish had arisen from a consciousness of the defects of the Poem, and from a knowledge that many persons had been much displeased with it. The Poem of my Friend has indeed great defects; first, that the principal person has no distinct character, either in his profession of Mariner, or as a human being who having been long under the control of supernatural impressions might be supposed to partake of something supernatural: secondly that he does not act, but is continually acted upon: thirdly, that the events having no necessary connection do not produce each other: and lastly, that the imagery is somewhat too laboriously accumulated. Yet the Poem contains many delicate touches of passion, and indeed the passion is everywhere true to nature; a great number of the stanzas present beautiful images, and are expressed with unusual felicity of language; and the versification, though the metre is itself unfit for long poems, is harmoniously and artfully varied, exhibiting the utmost powers of that metre, and every variety of which it is capable. It therefore appeared to me that these several merits (the first of which, namely that of the passion, is of the highest kind) gave to the Poem a value which is not often possessed by better Poems. On this account I requested my Friend to permit me to republish it.'

175   'Argument' revised in 1800 to read 'How a ship, having first sailed to the Equator, was driven by Storms, to the cold Country towards the South Pole; how the Ancient Mariner cruelly, and in contempt of the laws of hospitality, killed a Sea-bird; and how he was followed by many and strange Judgements; and in what manner he came back to his own Country'.

Coleridge revised the archaic spellings throughout, as can be seen most easily by comparing the 1798 version with that of 1802. The notes below draw attention to the more substantial alterations and excisions.

ll. 45–7. Revised from 1798 'Listen Stranger! Storm and Wind, A Wind and Tempest strong! | For days and weeks it played us freaks'.

l. 60. Revised from 1798 'Like noises of a swound'.

l. 83. Revised from 1798 'And broad as a weft upon the left'.

ll. 139–42. Expanded into a separate stanza in 1800, and lines altered accordingly.

l. 161. Revised from 1798.

ll. 179–82. Entire stanza revised from 1798.

l. 262. Revised from 1798, 'Like morning frosts yspread'.

l. 303. Revised from 1798, 'The roaring wind! It roar'd far off'.

l. 311. Revised from 1798, 'The stars danced on between'.

l. 316. Revised from 1798, 'Hark! Hark! The thick black cloud is cleft'.

ll. 321–2. Revised from 1798, 'The strong wind reach'd the ship: it roar'd | And dropp'd down like a stone!'

ll. 339–43. Added in 1800, while two lines of 1798 (ll. 337–8) dropped.

l. 366. Four stanzas dropped from 1798 (ll. 362–77).

ll. 437–8. Revised from 1798, 'And in its time the spell was snapp'd | And I could move my een.'

l. 469. Five stanzas dropped from 1798 (ll. 481–502).

l. 474. Revised from 1798 'The moonlight bay was white all o'er'.

ll. 576–9. Entire stanza revised from 1798.

199 *Note to The Thorn*. Added in 1800, and forming the last pages of Volume I.

superstition . . . mind. Wordsworth's note suggests a link to 'Goody Blake and Harry Gill' and the influence of Darwin's *Zoonomia*.

imagination . . . fancy. The distinction became increasingly important to Wordsworth and Coleridge, forming a major focus of *Biographia Literaria* (i. 295–305) and the Preface to Wordsworth's *Poems*, 1815.

200 *Bible*. The Bible, and especially the prophetic books of the Old Testament, had been regarded as a source of sublime poetry since the publication of Robert Lowth's influential *Lectures on the Sacred Poetry of the Hebrews*, published in Latin in 1753 and translated into English by George Gregory in 1787.

POEMS, VOLUME TWO

203 *Hart-leap Well*. Wordsworth wrote the poem in January 1800, soon after he moved to Grasmere, as he later recalled, 'The first eight stanzas were composed extempore one winter evening in the cottage; when, after having tired and disgusted myself with labouring at an awkward passage in "The Brothers", I started with a sudden impulse to this to get rid of the other, and finished it in a day or two. My Sister and I had passed the place a few weeks before in our wild winter journey from Sockburn on the banks of the Tees to Grasmere. A peasant whom we met near the spot told us the story so far as concerned the name of the well, and the hart; and pointed out the stones. Both the stones and the well are objects that may easily be missed: the tradition by this time may be extinct in the neighbourhood: the man who related it to us was very old' (*IF*, 15). The poem is indebted to traditional ballads in Percy, Ritson, and Herd, and to Bürger, 'The Wild Horseman', but see also Psalm 42: 1. On the biographical significance for Wordsworth, see Gill, and James Butler, 'Tourist or Native Son: Wordsworth's Homecomings of 1799–1800', *Nineteenth-Century Literature*, 51/1 (1996), 1–15.

l. 1. *Wensley*. Wensleydale is part of the Yorkshire Dales, now a National Park. The road from Richmond to Hawes runs through Wensleydale.

204 l. 28. *Hart*. A mature male deer or stag, usually a red deer, the largest of the British native species; but with obvious play on 'heart'.

l. 50. *roods*. A measurement of length, 8 yards, or *c*.7.5 m.

l. 56. *fountain*. A natural spring.

205 ll. 75–6. *Swale . . . Ure.* Rivers in North Yorkshire, running into the Great Ouse.

206 l. 97. *moving accident.* See *Othello*, I. iii. 135.

l. 98. *freeze the blood.* Revised from the curious 'curl the blood' of 1800. Cf. *Hamlet*, I. v. 15–16.

l. 101. *Hawes to Richmond.* Yorkshire towns at either end of Wensleydale.

l. 103. *Aspins.* A kind of poplar, with grey trunk and leaves that appear to tremble in the breeze. Butler and Green note the folklore tradition that the cross at the Crucifixion was made of aspen wood.

208 *There was a Boy.* Composed in Goslar in October–November 1798. Later incorporated into *The Prelude*, v. 389–422. Wordsworth commented, 'This is an extract from the Poem on my own poetical education. This practise of making an instrument of their own fingers is known to most boys, though some are more skilful at it than others. William Raincock of Rayrigg, a fine spirited lad, took the lead of all my schoolfellows in this art' (*IF*, 13). See also *Poems*, 1815: 'Guided by one of my primary conscious-nesses, I have represented a commutation and transfer of internal feelings, co-operating with external accidents, to plant, for immortality, images of sound and sight, in the celestial soil of the Imagination. The Boy, there introduced, is listening with something of a feverish and restless anxiety for the recurrence of sounds which he had previously excited; and, at the moment when the intenseness of his mind is beginning to remit, he is sur-prised into the solemn and tranquillizing images which the Poem describes' (Preface). The later version in *The Prelude* is associated with the grave of a boy in Hawkshead churchyard, discussed by Thompson, in *WH*, 55–6; for William Raincock's bird's nesting, see *WH*, 211–13.

l. 2. *Winander.* Archaic name for Windermere, the largest of the English Lakes, 3 miles south of Grasmere. Described in *Guide*, 29–30, where Wordsworth recommends viewing its grandeur from 'the bosom of the Lake'.

l. 10. *mimic hootings.* Jonathan Wordsworth in *Ancestral Voices* (Spelsbury, 1991), 96–7, notes the echo of Joanna Baillie's play *De Montfort*, IV. i. 32–57, *A Series of Plays*, i (1798), 378–9.

209 *The Brothers.* Composed December 1799–April 1800. Wordsworth and Coleridge visited Ennerdale on their walking tour in 1799 though the poem was composed later, in 'a grove at the north-eastern end of Grasmere Lake' (*IF*, 8); in Ennerdale, they heard about the death of Jerome Bowman, who broke his leg and died on the fells, and his son who had perished on The Pillar, as Coleridge recorded: he was 'supposed to have layed down & slept—but walked in his sleep, & so came to this crag, & fell off . . . his Pike staff stuck midway & stayed there till it rotted away' (Notebook entry 541). The poem also drew on the incident noted by Wordsworth, when one of the two mountain springs at Kidstow Pike, near Hawes-water,

disappeared after a lightning strike. As emphasized by the subtitle, this is one of the Pastorals highlighted in the revised title of the 1802 *Lyrical Ballads*. Wordsworth's sense of its value is evident in his letter to Fox (see Appendix 3).

l. 1. *Tourists*. The Lake District had become a popular destination for tourists since the publication of Thomas West's *A Guide to the Lakes* (1778) and William Gilpin's *Observations relative chiefly to Picturesque Beauty, made in the year 1772, on Several Parts of England; especially the Mountains and Lakes* (1786).

210 l. 13. *neither epitaph nor monument*. See the three *Essays on Epitaphs* (*Prose*, i) for extended discussion on memorialization, and especially the second essay, on country churchyards.

l. 16. *Ennerdale*. A valley in the western Lakes, described by Wordsworth in *Guide*, 42–4, 109–10.

ll. 21–3. *teasing . . . spindle*. See note to p. 34, 'The Female Vagrant', l. 89.

l. 39. *mariners*. Wordsworth's own brother, John, was a sea captain. His arrival in Grasmere in January 1800 may have influenced the poem. Wordsworth's 'When first I journeyed hither' treats fraternal separation and reunion more personally.

211 ll. 50–62 and footnote. *Calenture*. An illness afflicting sailors, causing the illusion that the sea was a green field and therefore encouraging them to leap overboard. Cf. 'Poor Susan'. Wordsworth's note refers to William Gilbert, whom he had met in Bristol through Joseph Cottle and whose best known work, *The Hurricane*, was published in 1796. See Paul Cheshire, 'William Gilbert and his Bristol Circle, 1788–1798', in Roe (ed.), *English Romantic Writers and the West Country*, 79–98.

l. 73. *last of all their race*. This resonant phrase had become commonplace since the success of Macpherson's *Ossian*.

212 l. 100. *complacency*. Pleasure, perhaps with overtones of self-satisfaction.

213 ll. 138–43. *two Springs . . . flowing still*. Wordsworth's note on the factual basis for these lines is reprinted on p. 302.

214 l. 173. *Stone-cutters*. One of the principle jobs for stone-cutters, or masons, was inscribing gravestones.

ll. 180–1. *thought of death . . . mountains*. Wordsworth's note on these lines appeared at the end of the volume and is reprinted accordingly in this edition. For later reflections on memorialization and country churchyards, see his three *Essays Upon Epitaphs*.

ll. 187–8. *winter's evening . . . chimney's nook*. Traditional time and place for rural storytelling or Bible-reading, as celebrated by Robert Fergusson in 'The Farmer's Ingle' and Burns in 'The Cotter's Saturday Night'. See also Burns, 'Written in Friar's Carse Hermitage', l. 28.

215 l. 211. *kept up*. Revised from 1800 which read 'Preserv'd'.

216 l. 262. *great book of the world*. Finding evidence of God's plenitude in the book of nature was a commonplace of eighteenth-century poetry, notably Thomson's very popular *The Seasons* (1730). The Priest's 'book' suggests the importance of human presences in the natural landscape, an attitude explicitly endorsed by Wordsworth in *Guide*, 132.

217 l. 273. *Like Roe-bucks*. Cf. 'Lines written . . . above Tintern Abbey', l. 68 and note (p. 341).

218 ll. 306–7. *great Gavel . . . Egremont*. Wordsworth's note accurately locates the mountain, now known as Great Gable, which he also described in *Guide*, 109–10. Egremont is a village to the south-west of Ennerdale, near the coast.

ll. 313–14. *the Moors . . . Barbary Coast*. The coast of North Africa, from Morocco to Tunisia, known during the seventeenth and eighteenth centuries as 'The Barbary Coast', was famous for slave markets where European slaves were bought and sold.

219 l. 363. *the Pillar*. Mountain at the head of Ennerdale, to the east of Ennerdale Water.

222 *Ellen Irwin*. Probably written in Germany, 1799. Traditional songs about 'Fair Helen' appeared in Herd's *Scottish Songs* (ii. 321) and Ritson (i. 145). Ritson includes the account recorded by Thomas Pennant, in his *Tour of Scotland* (ii. 101), which appears to be the source for Wordsworth's poem: 'In the burying-ground of Kirkonnel is the grave of fair Ellen Irvine, and that of her lover: she was daughter of the house of Kirkonnel; and was beloved by two gentlemen at the same time; the one vowed to sacrifice the successful rival to his resentment; and watched an opportunity while the happy pair were sitting on the banks of the Kirtle, that washes these grounds. Ellen perceived the desperate lover on the opposite side, and fondly thinking to save her favourite, interposed; and receiving the wound intended for her beloved, fell and expired in his arms. He instantly revenged her death; then fled to Spain, and served for some time against the infidels: on his return he visited the grave of his unfortunate mistress, stretched himself on it, and expiring on the spot, was interred by her side. A sword and a cross are engraven on the tomb-stone, with *hic jacet* Adam Fleming, the only memorial of this unhappy gentleman, except an ancient ballad of great merit, which records the tragical event.' Ritson includes Pennant's note that the events took place at 'either the latter end of the reign of James V. or the beginning of that of Mary' but adds his own sceptical comment that the 'infidels' were 'completely subdued many years before the reign of James V' (Ritson, i. 145). Wordsworth renamed Adam Fleming, 'Bruce', and called his rival 'Gordon', both very well-known surnames in the Scottish Borders and featuring in many traditional ballads. Wordsworth later commented that 'as there are Scotch poems on this subject in the simple ballad strain, I thought it would be both presumptuous and super-fluous to attempt treating it in the same way; and, accordingly, I chose

a construction of stanza quite new in our language; in fact the same as that of Burgher's *Leonora*, except that the first & third line do not, in my stanzas, rhyme. At the outset I threw out a classical image to prepare the reader for the style in which I meant to treat the story, and so to preclude all comparison' (*IF*, 26).

l. 2. *Braes of Kirtle*. Banks of the River Kirtle in Dumfriesshire. The 'Braes' of numerous rivers featured in traditional Scottish songs including many of those adapted or composed by Burns.

223 l. 40. *Moorish Crescent*. Probably referring to the battles associated with the decline of the Islamic occupation of Spain in the sixteenth century.

l. 51. *Kirkonnel*. A village in Dumfriesshire, close to the Solway.

l. 56. *HIC JACET*. Latin inscription common on tombstones meaning 'Here lies'.

Strange fits of passion. Composed in Germany in 1799. 'Lucy' was a name often given by poets to a lost love, as shown by Herman Hartman, 'Wordsworth's "Lucy" Poems: Notes and Marginalia', *PMLA* 49 (1934), 134–42. When Coleridge sent the 'most sublime epitaph' to Thomas Poole in 1799, he commented, 'whether it had any reality, I cannot say.—Most probably, in some gloomier moment he had fancied the moment in which his Sister might die' (*CL* i. 479).

224 *'She dwelt among th' untrodden ways'*. Composed in Germany in 1798. Dorothy sent an early, longer version to Coleridge on 14 or 21 December 1798.

l. 2. *Dove*. There are two rivers called the Dove in Yorkshire, one further south, near Barnsley, the other in the North Yorkshire Moors, not far from Sockburn, home of the Hutchinsons. The better known River Dove in Derbyshire, much visited by tourists, is an unlikely candidate for 'untrodden ways'. Wordsworth's choice may well be determined by the consonance with 'Love', a notoriously difficult word to rhyme.

l. 9. *liv'd*. Italicized in 1800, but not in 1802.

225 *'A slumber did my spirit seal'*. Composed in Germany in 1798.

The Waterfall and the Eglantine. Composed in 1800. Wordsworth later recalled that 'The Oak and the Broom' was 'suggested upon the mountain pathway that leads from Upper Rydal to Grasmere. The ponderous block of stone, which is mentioned in the poem, remains I believe to this day, a good way up Nab-Scar. Broom grows under it and in many places on the side of the precipice.' 'The Waterfall and the Eglantine' was 'suggested nearer to Grasmere on the same mountain track. The Eglantine remained many years afterwards, but is now gone' (*IF*, 11). Poetic dialogues between plants and other phenomena go back to Aesop, but were adapted in the eighteenth century by Langhorne, in *The Fables of Flora* (1771), and Cowper in poems such as 'The Lily and the Rose', 'The Pineapple and the Bee'. The voice of the waterfall may owe something to Burns's 'The Humble Petition of Bruar Water to the Noble Duke of Athole', the eglantine to the bryar in Spenser's February Eclogue, in *The Shepheardes Calendar*.

227 *The Oak and the Broom*. Composed in 1800. See note to the previous poem, and especially Aesop, fable 141, depicting the Reed, the Olive, and the storm. Spenser adapted the fable as 'the oake and the bryare' in the February Eclogue of *The Shepheardes Calendar*.

230 *The Complaint of a forsaken Indian Woman*. Moved into Volume II in 1802, perhaps to accommodate the expansion to the Preface in Volume I.

232 *Lucy Gray*. Composed in Germany in 1799. Wordsworth commented 'It was founded on a circumstance told me by my Sister, of a little girl, who not far from Halifax in Yorkshire was bewildered in a snow-storm. Her foot-steps were traced by her parents to the middle of a lock of a canal, and no other vestige of her, backward or forward, could be traced. The body how-ever was found in the canal. The way in which the incident was treated & the spiritualising of the character might furnish hints for contrasting the imaginative influences which I have endeavoured to throw over common life with Crabbe's matter of fact style of treating subjects of the same kind. This is not spoken in disparagement; far from it; but to direct the attention of thoughtful readers into whose hands these notes may fall to a comparison that may both enlarge the circle of their sensibilities and tend to produce in them a catholic judgment' (*IF*, 1–2). As Mason notes, 'Lucy Gray' was already a familiar name to many because of Robert Anderson's popular song, 'Lucy Gray of Allendale', published in 1794.

l. 2. *the Wild*. Cf. Burns, 'The Bonie Lass o' Ballochmyle', l. 20.

233 l. 27. *powd'ry snow*. Cf. Burns, 'A Winter Night', l. 90.

l. 30. *wander'd up and down*. Cf. 'The Children in the Wood' in Percy's *Reliques*, quoted by Wordsworth in the Preface to *Lyrical Ballads*.

l. 40. *furlong*. 220 yards or *c*.200 m.

234 *''Tis said that some have died for Love'*. Probably composed in Germany in 1799. Cf. *As You Like It*, IV. i. 96.

l. 8. *Helvellyn*. One of the highest mountains in the Lake District, towering above Thirlmere, 5 miles north of Grasmere. The mountain figured large in Wordsworth's imagination, featuring in some of the lines associated with, but not included in, 'Michael', and *Guide*, 110–12. See Butler and Green, 332–8 and McCracken, 52–62 .

l. 9. *pretty Barbara*. Not the same Barbara as that of 'The Pet-Lamb', though see the headnote to that poem, p. 359. Barbara was a name common in traditional ballads.

235 *The Idle Shepherd-Boys*. Composed Grasmere, 1800. Though the adjective may suggest disapproval, idleness is often presented very positively by

Wordsworth, see especially 'Lines written at a small distance from my House'. The different aspects of idleness or *otium* had been explored since the classical era and were integral to the pastoral tradition. The generic subtitle links the poem to the new title of *Lyrical Ballads*, and poems such as 'The Brothers' and 'Michael'. 'Industry', often set up as the contrary state in the eighteenth and nineteenth centuries, is similarly multifaceted, as evident in 'Michael' and 'The Old Cumberland Beggar'. Dungeon-Ghyll Force is in Langdale, west of Grasmere; Wordsworth commented that it 'could not be found without a guide, who may be taken up at one of the Cottages at the foot of the Mountain' (*Guide*, 151). He also related an anecdote about the poem to Isabella Fenwick: 'When Coleridge & Southey were walking together upon the Fells, Southey observed that, if I wished to be considered a faithful painter of rural manners, I ought not to have said that my Shepherd-boys trimmed their rushen hats as described in the poem. Just as the words had past his lips two boys appeared with the very plant entwined round their hats' (*IF*, 5).

236   l. 19. *Stag-horn, or Fox's Tail*. Stag's horn clubmoss, *Lycopodium clavatum*, is a wild plant common in the mountains of northern England and Scotland, whose green stems stand upright, resembling antlers. Foxtail is a common name for wild grasses with prickly heads, rather like barley.

l. 20. *rusty*. Old, worn-out, possibly also reddish brown in colour.

237   ll. 45–6. *'Now cross . . . lead'*. Revised from 1800, which read 'Till you have cross'd where I shall cross, | Say that you'll neither sleep nor eat'.

l. 48. *deed*. Read 'feat' in 1800.

l. 50. *If ever you to Langdale go*. Cf. 'Michael', 1–2. See headnote for Langdale and Wordsworth's advice on the need for a guide.

l. 70. *gulph profound*. *Paradise Lost*, ii. 592.

238   l. 79. *I ween*. I think, I believe. Used similarly parenthetically in traditional ballads such as 'The Not-Browne Maid', l. 332 (in Percy) and by Burns, 'Humble Petition of Bruar Water', l. 21. See also 'The Ancyent Marinere', l. 182.

Poor Susan. Composed 1798. Wordsworth recalled that the poem 'arose from my observation of the affecting music of these birds hanging in this way in the London Streets during the freshness and stillness of the Spring Morning' (*IF*, 14). The recollection of songbirds 'hanging' may suggest that Susan's thrush is in a birdcage. In *Poems*, 1815, the poem was called 'The Reverie of Poor Susan' and in his note on 'I wandered lonely as a cloud' Wordsworth emphasized that it was 'strictly a reverie'. William and Dorothy Wordsworth visited London in November–December 1797, though Wordsworth's vivid, retentive memory could have conjured up the image from earlier experience some years before. In 1800, the poem had an additional stanza at the end: 'Poor Outcast! Return—to receive thee once more | The house of thy Father will open its door, | And thou once again, in thy plain russet gown, | May'st hear the thrush sing from a tree of its own'. For Susan's situation, see Peter Manning, 'Placing Poor Susan: Wordsworth and the New Historicism', in *Reading Romantics: Text and Context* (Oxford, 1990), 300–20.

238 l. 1. *Wood-Street*. A street in the City of London.

239 ll. 7–8. *Lothbury . . . Cheapside*. London streets in the busy, commercial area around St Paul's Cathedral. Susan's vision may be compared with Leonard Ewbank's calenture in 'The Brothers', ll. 58–62.

Inscription for the Spot where the Hermitage stood. Composed 1800. The legend of St Herbert was part of local folklore, and featured in popular Guidebooks such as Thomas West's. It is also recorded in Bede's *Ecclesiastical History* of England. Wordsworth regarded Derwent Water as being 'distinguished from the other Lakes by being *surrounded* with sublimity' (*Guide*, 98). He also deemed the islands on Derwent Water as being the earliest parts of the Lake District to be adversely affected by tourism (*Guide*, 78). The poem may also be indebted to Burns's 'Written in Friar's Carse Hermitage'. For Wordsworth and 'Inscriptions', see Geoffrey Hartman, 'Wordworth, Inscriptions, and Romantic Nature Poetry', in F. W. Hilles and H. Bloom (eds.), *From Sensibility to Romanticism* (New York, 1965).

l. 13. *cataract of Lodore*. Celebrated waterfall at the end of Derwent Water.

240 *Lines written with a pencil*. Composed in 1799–1800. The title in 1800 was 'Inscription for the House (an Outhouse) on the Island at Grasmere'. The new title may have been inspired by Burns's 'Written with a Pencil Standing by the Falls of Fyers, near Loch Ness' and 'Verses written with a Pencil over the Chimney-Piece, in the Parlour of the Inn at Kenmore, Taymouth'. Such titles are usually indicative of spontaneous composition in response to immediate experience, but see note to previous poem.

l. 1. *Rude*. Unpolished, unsophisticated. A word that acquired positive connotations as anxieties about the effects of luxury increased, see, for example, 'Michael', l. 35. The 'rude forefathers' of Thomas Gray's 'Elegy written in a Country Churchyard', l. 16, lie in the background.

l. 7. *Vitruvius*. Roman architect M. Vitruvius Pollio, famous for classical symmetry and the Golden Mean. Cf. Gray's 'Elegy', ll. 57–60.

ll. 9–11. *red Morocco . . . Beauties yet unborn*. Architectural book of the largest size, bound in red leather, containing designs for new buildings.

ll. 11–12. *Box . . . Hermitage*. A small country house, probably a temporary residence for a gentleman during the hunting or shooting season, with additional features such as a coach-house and landscape garden. The decorative eighteenth-century hermitage contrasts with St Herbert's retreat at Derwent Water.

ll. 19–20. *(A lading . . . mountains)*. Parentheses added in 1802.

l. 22. *unshorn*. Revised in 1802 from 'unborn'.

To a Sexton. Composed in Germany, 1799. A sexton is employed to dig graves in a churchyard. Before the development of cemeteries, and latterly, crematoria, the bones were removed from churchyards after a period of time into an ossuary or 'bone-house', to make room for fresh committals.

241 *Andrew Jones.* Composed probably in 1800. Butler and Green suggest that the poem has strong connections, including in the choice of stanza, with *Peter Bell*, written in 1798–9 but not published until 1819.

l. 3. *press-gang or the drum.* Conscription was enforced during the war with France by the press gang. Cf. 'The Female Vagrant', ll. 93–4.

242 *Ruth.* Composed in Germany in 1799. Wordsworth later recalled that it was 'suggested by an account I had of a wanderer in Somersetshire' (*IF*, 14). Coleridge admired the poem greatly, writing to James Tobin, 17 September 1800, 'I think it the finest poem in the collection' (*CL* i. 623), though he admitted to Robert Southey that he was less impressed by the 'alterations' of 1802 (*CL* ii. 830). For full details of the revisions see Butler and Green, where both 1800 and 1802 versions are reprinted. The new stanzas added in 1802 are indicated below.

243 l. 8. *oaten Pipe.* A motif borrowed from classical and English pastoral, including Virgil, *Eclogues*, i; Spenser, *Shepheardes Calendar*, Prologue, 72, and December, 14; *Faerie Queene*, i. 4.

ll. 13–18. *Beneath . . . height.* Stanza added in 1802.

l. 19. *Georgia.* One of the southern states of America. As his note to l. 58 indicates, Wordsworth was drawing on William Bartram, *Travels Through North and South Carolina, Georgia, East and West Florida* (London, 1792, 1794). Bartram's description of Georgia begins in part III.

l. 20. *Casque.* Helmet. Bartram describes a Cherokee headdress as a woven, decorated band worn around the temples, 'embellished with a high waving plume, of crane or heron feathers' (*Travels*, 393).

l. 22. *Cherokees.* Native American people of the south-eastern states, described by Bartram in parts III and IV of his *Travels*. Other well-known accounts included James Adair, *The History of the American Indians; Particularly those Nations Adjoining the Mississippi, East and West Florida, Georgia, South and North Carolina, and Virginia* (London, 1775); and Henry Timberlake, *The Memoirs of Lieut. Henry Timberlake (Who Accompanied the Three Cherokee Indians to England in the Year 1762)* (London, 1765). See Fulford, *Romantic Indians.*

l. 28. *when America was free.* After the War of Independence, 1776–83. The Youth has been fighting in the British army and returned to Britain at the end of the war.

l. 31. *hues of genius.* If 'genius' retains its older meaning of characteristic disposition or inclination, this may refer to the Youth's skin, which has become tanned during his outdoor life in America. His eloquence suggests that, in Ruth's eyes at least, he possesses the kind of genius exalted from the later eighteenth century onwards—extraordinary innate power.

244 l. 44. *many tales*. Cf. *Othello*, I. iii. 129–50.

ll. 49–52. *Girls . . . all day long*. Recalling Bartram's account of the 'young, innocent Cherokee virgins' who offered the fresh strawberries they had been gathering to the party of Europeans (Bartram, *Travels*, 289–90).

ll. 55–7. *plants . . . hues*. Bartram, as a naturalist, included detailed descriptions of the exotic plants he encountered in America. The stanza recalls the long description of the *Gordonia lasianthus*, which 'may be said to change and renew its garments every morning throughout the year' (Bartram, *Travels*, 146).

245 ll. 61–102. *Of march and ambush . . . Of Lands where he had been*. Added in 1802.

l. 103. *Magnolia*. Magnolia grandiflora is mentioned frequently by Bartram, but this may recall the description of 'the sun-brightened tops of the lofty Cupressus disticha and Magnolia grandiflora' (Bartram, *Travels*, 89).

246 ll. 106–8. *flowers . . . fire*. Cf. Bartram's description of the 'splendid colours' of the 'fiery Azalea', whose 'blossoms cover the shrubs in such incredible profusion of the hill sides, that suddenly opening to view from dark shades, we are alarmed with the apprehension of the hill being set on fire' (*Travels*, 264).

l. 109. *Savannahs*. Treeless, grassy plains in tropical regions of America, described by Bartram: 'What a beautiful display of vegetation is here before me! Seemingly unlimited in extent and variety: how the dew-drops twinkle and play upon the sight, trembling on the tips of the lucid green savanna, sparkling as the gem that flames on the turban of the eastern prince' (*Travels*, 141–2).

l. 115. *How sweet it were*. See 'The Foster-Mother's Tale', l. 47.

l. 125. *world of woe*. Paradise Lost, ix. 11.

247 l. 156. *His name*. Ruth's desire to bear the Youth's name indicates her wish to be married. The Youth's name is never disclosed.

l. 168. Three stanzas dropped from 1800 version at this point.

248 l. 178. *without self-controul*. Cf. Burns, 'Bard's Epitaph', 29.

l. 186. *forlorn*. Abandoned, desolate. Cf. *Paradise Lost*, ix. 910.

249 l. 222. *Under the greenwood tree*. Shakespeare, *As You Like It*, II. v. 1. See also the refrain in 'The Not-Browne Maid' in Percy.

ll. 235–40. *The neighbours . . . and cold*. Added in 1802.

250 l. 250. *hemlock stalk*. The stalk of hemlock, a poisonous plant, contrasts with the innocent pastoral 'oaten pipe' of the opening stanza.

l. 252. *Quantock*. The hills in Somerset where Wordsworth and Coleridge often walked in 1797–8.

Lines written with a slate-pencil. Composed in 1800. See 'Lines written with a Pencil' and headnote. Rydale refers to Rydal Water, a small lake just east of Grasmere.

ll. 3–4. *Cairn . . . Chief.* Cairns are small heaps of stones constructed as memorials. Here the possibility of Celtic remains ('British' meaning a pre-Roman native) is raised and rejected, perhaps with reference to fashionable guides which directed visitors to antiquarian sites.

l. 8. *Sir William.* Sir William Fleming, owner of Rydal Hall, who died in 1736.

251 l. 22. *appertain'd.* Belonging by right or by nature (Johnson). See 'Michael', l. 18.

l. 31. *snow-white glory.* Wordsworth included a lengthy denunciation of the fashion for whitewashed houses in his *Guide*: 'The objections to white, as a colour, in large spots or masses in landscape, especially in a mountainous country, are insurmountable . . . I have seen a single white house materially impair the majesty of a mountain' (p. 85). Lady Holland, visiting the Lakes in 1807, thought white houses produced a cheerful effect, but reported that Wordsworth 'on the contrary, would brown, or even black-work them' (Woof, 257).

Lines written on a Tablet in a School. Composed in Goslar, 1798–9. A tablet is a wall-plaque. Wordsworth commented that 'poems connected with Matthew would not gain by a literal detail of facts. Like the Wanderer in The Excursion, the Schoolmaster was made up of several both of his class & men of other occupations. I do not ask pardon for what there is of untruth in such verses, considered strictly as matters of fact. It is enough, if, being true & consistent in spirit, they move & teach in a manner not unworthy of a poet's calling' (*IF*, 38). Speculation on the likely model for Matthew has nevertheless suggested William Taylor, Wordsworth's headteacher at Hawkshead School, who died in 1786 and whose grave at Cartmel is described in *The Prelude*, x. 490–9. Other candidates include John Harrison, Thomas Cowperthwaite, and John Gibson, who all lived and worked in Hawkshead during Wordsworth's childhood (*WH*, 151–90). Matthew's name, and some of his characteristics, may recall Burns's 'Elegy on Captain Matthew Henderson'.

l. 1. *If Nature . . . child.* Cf. *The Prelude*, i. 363–7. See also Burns, 'The Bonie Lass of Ballochmyle', 'There was a Lad', 'The Vision'.

252 l. 7. *hue.* Appearance, colour.

l. 24. *oil of gladness.* Hebrews 1: 9. Revised to 'dew' in 1815.

l. 31. *glittering gold.* Cf. Gray's 'Ode on the Death of a Favourite cat', l. 42. The two words of gold contrast with the unnamed graves discussed by the Priest in *The Brothers*, ll. 176–81. For extended meditation, see Wordsworth's *Essays Upon Epitaphs*.

252 *The Two April Mornings.* Composed in Germany, 1799. Companion to the previous poem, see headnote.

253 l. 5. *village Schoolmaster.* A recollection of Hawkshead school but also a literary motif, see Goldsmith, *The Deserted Village*, ll. 195–216.

l. 30. *Derwent's wave.* Probably the River Derwent, which flows through Cockermouth (see *The Prelude*, i. 271–304), rather than Derwent Water, where the Female Vagrant's father fished.

254 l. 60. *wilding.* Wild apple or crab apple, a common tree in Britain, with pale pink buds that open into a beautiful white blossom in late April.

The Fountain. Companion to the previous poems, see headnotes above. A fountain is a natural spring.

l. 5. *We lay . . . oak.* Recalling the classical pastoral of Virgil, *Eclogues*, i.

255 l. 11. *old Border-song.* The Scottish Borders were renowned for ballads and songs, many of which were reprinted by Percy, Herd, and Ritson. In 1802–3, Walter Scott published his influential collection of *Minstrelsy of the Scottish Borders.*

256 ll. 71–2. *crazy . . . chimes.* Thompson describes the old church clock at Hawkshead, 'one of whose many faults was striking the wrong hour' (*WH*, 173–5).

Nutting. Composed in Germany in 1798 and revised for *Lyrical Ballads* in 1800. Dorothy sent an early version to Coleridge on 14 or 21 December 1798 (*EY*, 241–2). Wordsworth later recalled, 'Like most of my school-fellows I was an impassioned nutter. For this pleasure the Vale of Esthwaite abounding in coppice-wood, furnished a very wide range. These verses arose out of the remembrance of feelings I had often had when a boy, and particularly in the extensive woods that still stretch from the side of Esthwaite Lake towards Graythwaite' (*IF*, 13). The woods are to the south of Esthwaite Water, 3–4 miles from Colthouse. See McCracken, 81–8.

257 l. 3. *our Cottage-door.* Wordsworth's note refers to the house where he boarded as a schoolboy, which was Ann Tyson's cottage at Colthouse, about half a mile from Hawkshead, recalled in *The Prelude*, iv. 30–83. For a full account of Hugh and Ann Tyson and their Boarders, see *WH*, 3–148.

l. 7. *Beggar's weeds.* Old clothes, to avoid unnecessary damage to smarter garments. Cf. Spenser, *Faerie Queene*, i. 2.

l. 9. *Dame.* Ann Tyson, remembered fondly in *The Prelude*, iv. 16–28, 207–21.

ll. 29–30. *violets . . . eye.* Cf. Gray's 'Elegy', ll. 55–6.

258 ll. 46–7. *unless . . . past.* An uncertainty explored in *The Prelude*, iv. 262–8, xi. 334–9.

Three years she grew. Composed in Germany, 1799. A companion to 'Strange fits of passion' and 'She dwelt beside th'untrodden ways'.

259 *The Pet-Lamb*. Composed 15 September 1800. Another of the pastoral poems, identified in the title. Wordsworth recalled in 1843 that 'Barbara Lewthwaite, now living at Ambleside though much changed as to beauty, was one of the two most lovely Sisters. Almost the first words my poor brother John said, when he visited us for the first time at Grasmere, were "Were these, two angels I have just seen?" and from his description, I have no doubt they were those two Sisters. The mother died in childbed; and one of our neighbours in Grasmere told me that the loveliest sight she had ever seen, was that mother as she lay in her coffin with her babe in her arm. I mention this to notice what I cannot but think a salutary custom, once universal in these vales. Every attendant on a funeral made it a duty to look at the corpse in the coffin before the lid was closed, which was never done . . . till a minute or two before the corpse was removed. Barbara Lewthwaite was not in fact the child whom I had seen and overheard as engaged in the poem' (*IF*, 5). Wordsworth later regretted his choice of name after learning of its effect on the vanity of the real Barbara Lewthwaite, who would claim to remember the incident in the poem. The Lewthwaite family were near neighbours, living in a cottage just outside Town End (*GJ*, 161).

260 l. 39. *yean*. Brought her into the world. The Dam was the ewe who gave birth to the lamb on the hillside.

262 *Written in Germany*. Composed in Germany in 1798–9. Wordsworth recollected, 'A bitter winter it was when these verses were composed, by the side of my Sister, in our lodgings at a draper's house in the romantic imperial town of Goslar, on the edge of the Hartz Forest. In this town the German emperors of the Franconian line were accustomed to keep their court, & it retains vestiges of ancient splendour. So severe was the cold of this winter, that when we past out of the parlour warmed by the stove, our cheeks were struck by the air as by cold iron. I slept in a room over the passage which was not ceiled. The people of the house used to say, rather unfeelingly, that they expected I should be frozen to death some night. With the protection of a pelisse lined with fur, & a dog's-skin bonnet such as was worn by the peasants, I walked daily on the ramparts, or in a sort of public ground or garden in which was a pond. Here, I had no companion but a Kings fisher, a beautiful creature, that used to glance by me. I consequently became much attached to it. During these walks I composed . . . *The Poet's Epitaph*' (*IF*, 38).

l. 9. *Glass stood low enough*. The reference is to a barometer, an instrument for measuring temperature, using mercury in a marked glass tube.

263 *The Childless Father*. Composed in Germany in 1799, revised in 1800. Wordsworth recalled that 'When I was a child in Cockermouth, no funeral took place without a basin filled with sprigs of boxwood being placed upon a table covered with a white cloth in front of the house. The huntings (on foot) which the Old Man is supposed to join as here described, were of

common, almost habitual, occurrence in our vales when I was a boy; & the people took much delight in them. They are now less frequent' (*IF*, 9–10). Boxwood is a native evergreen shrub.

263 l. 4. *Skiddaw*. One of the highest mountains in the Lake District, north of Keswick. Described in *Guide*, 109–10.

264 *The Old Cumberland Beggar*. Begun in 1796–7, continued in 1798, completed late 1799. Wordsworth recalled that the man was 'Observed & with great benefit to my own heart, when I was a child: written down at Race Down & Alfoxden in my 23rd year. The political economists were about that time beginning their war upon mendicity in all its forms & by implication, if not directly, on Alms-giving too. This heartless process has been carried as far as it can go by the AMENDED poor-law bill, tho' the inhumanity that prevails in this measure is somewhat disguised by the profession that one of its objects is to throw the poor upon the voluntary donations of their neighbours; that is, if rightly interpreted, to force them into a condition between relief in the union poor House & Alms robbed of their Christian grace & spirit, as being *forced* rather from the benevolent than given by them; while the avaricious & selfish & all in fact but the humane & charitable, are at liberty to keep all they possess from their distressed brethren' (*IF*, 56). As in 'The Female Vagrant' and 'The Last of the Flock', Wordsworth's concern about the topical issue of poor relief is a major impetus behind the poem. He was still writing about the plight of the poor and national policies on relief in 1834 when the Poor Law Amendment inspired a long postscript in *Yarrow Revisited* (1835).

265 l. 34. *wheel*. Spinning wheel.

l. 52. *Bowbent*. Mason notes a source in Bruce, 'Lochleven', 446.

l. 57. *Impress'd . . . line*. Wordsworth regarded this as 'the most dislocated line I know in my writing' (*EY*, 434).

266 l. 67. *Statesmen!*. Wordsworth's address recalls *The Deserted Village*, l. 265. Debate over Poor Relief was a major issue of the 1790s (see headnote to 'The Female Vagrant'). Thomas Malthus's *Essay on the Principles of Population* (1798), had emphasized the problems of a growing population and diminishing food supply.

267 l. 123. *respite*. Reprieve (Johnson).

268 l. 151. *scrip*. A small bag, especially one carried by pilgrims and shepherds, and already archaic or poetic in 1802.

l. 152. *Mendicant*. A beggar, but perhaps recalling the origins of the term, which was used to describe members of a Christian order who lived on alms, or itinerant holy men.

l. 168. *charter'd wind*. Cf. *As You Like It*, II. vii. 48.

269 *Rural Architecture*. Composed in Grasmere, September–October 1800. Wordsworth commented that 'these structures, as everyone knows, are

common among our hills, being built by shepherds as conspicuous marks, occasionally by boys in sport' (*IF*, 4–5).

l. 3. *Counsellor's bag*. Butler and Green note the practice common among barristers, of carrying their briefs in bags slung over their shoulders.

l. 12. *Magog . . . Legberthwaite*. In British folklore, Magog was a giant. Legberthwaite is small vale near the northern tip of Thirlmere, commended by Wordsworth for its 'noble view' (*Guide*, 34).

270 *A Poet's Epitaph*. See headnote on 'Written in Germany', p. 359. The poem is indebted to Burns's 'A Bard's Epitaph', published in *Poems, Chiefly in the Scottish Dialect*, 1786.

l. 11. *Doctor*. Clergyman or priest.

l. 18. *Philosopher*. Natural scientist.

l. 25. *Moralist*. Moral philosopher.

271 ll. 37–40. *But who . . . own*. Recalling various poems by Burns, notably the verse epistles 'To James Smith', ll. 32, 51–4, and 'To William Simson', ll. 53–60, 85–90; 'Written in Friar's Carse Hermitage', ll. 1–4. Wordsworth quoted these lines in the Preface to *Poems*, 1815.

ll. 57–60. *Come . . . this grave*. Cf. Burns's, 'A Bard's Epitaph', ll. 15–18.

A Fragment. Composed in Germany, 1799, and intended 'as a prelude to a ballad poem never written' (*IF*, 12). The title may owe something to the *Fragments of Ancient Poetry* published in 1760 by Macpherson as the first translations of Ossian. Wordsworth added a note in 1827, 'These stanzas were designed to introduce a Ballad upon the Story of a Danish Prince who had fled from Battle, and, for the sake of the valuables about him, was murdered by the inhabitant of a Cottage in which he had taken refuge. The House fell under a curse, and the Spirit of the Youth, it was believed, haunted the Valley where the crime had been committed' (Butler and Green, 397). Wordsworth emphasized the history of Danish influence in his *Guide*, 64–7.

273 *Poems on the Naming of Places*. Composed in December 1799–October 1800. Wordsworth's sequence of poems reflect his rediscovery of the Lake District and can be read, helpfully, in connection with 'Michael' and 'Home at Grasmere', the long poem he was writing, though did not publish, in 1800 (see Gill, 188–213). For thoughtful discussion of Wordsworth's acts of naming, see Jonathan Bate, *Romantic Ecology* (London and New York, 1991), 85–115.

I . . . It was an April morning. April 1800. Wordsworth recalled, 'This poem was suggested on the banks of the brook that runs through Easedale, which is in some parts of its course as wild & beautiful as brook can be. I have composed thousands of verses by the side of it' (*IF*, 18). Easedale runs westwards from Grasmere and the view from Easedale is beautifully described in the *Guide*, 47. See also McCracken, 107–14.

274 *II. To Joanna*. Joanna Hutchinson, younger sister of Wordsworth's wife, Mary, who had not grown up 'amid the smoke of cities'. McCracken emphasizes the absence of factual basis for many of the details in this poem (pp. 193–5). Wordsworth commented, 'The effect of her laugh is an extravagance; though the effect of the reverberation of voices in some parts of these mountains is very striking. There is in The Excursion the bleat of a lamb thus re-echoed, and described without any exaggeration, as I heard it on the side of Stickle Tarn from the precipice that stretches on to Langdale Pikes' (*IF*, 18).

275 l. 28. *Runic Priest*. Runic inscriptions were used for early Germanic and Scandinavian languages. The eighteenth-century antiquarian revival had created interest in Norse culture, in which runes were associated with the Gods.

l. 31. *Rotha . . . forest side*. As Wordsworth's note at the end of the poem indicates, the Rothay runs through Grasmere to Rydal Water, passing the area known as Forest Side, also mentioned in 'Michael'.

276 ll. 56–65. *That ancient woman . . . misty head*. As Wordsworth's note indicates, the lines refer to specific peaks, passes, gorges, and mountains in the Lake District. They are also indebted to Drayton, *Poly-Olbion* (1622), Song 30, ll. 155–64, as Coleridge pointed out, *BL* ii. 104.

277 *III . . . There is an Eminence*. 'It is not accurate that the eminence here alluded to could be seen from our orchard-seat. It arises above the road by the side of Grasmere Lake, towards Keswick, and its name is Stone-Arthur' (*IF*, 18).

l. 3. *Orchard-seat*. In the garden at Dove Cottage.

l. 15. *communion*. As Mason notes, the first recorded use of this word to mean intimate, personal companionship.

IV . . . A narrow girdle of rough stones. Wordsworth commented 'The character of the eastern shore of Grasmere Lake is quite changed since these verses were written, by the public road being carried along its side. The friends spoken of were Coleridge and my Sister, & the fact occurred strictly as recorded' (*IF*, 18–19). The walk, which probably took place in July, is recorded by Coleridge, Notebook entry 761.

278 ll. 35–6. *tall Fern . . . Osmunda*. Royal moonwort. Revised from 1800 which read 'tall Plant'.

279 *V. To M. H.* Mary Hutchinson. Wordsworth commented, 'Two years before our marriage. The pool alluded to is in Rydal Upper Park.' The Wordsworths married on 4 October 1802. Rydal lies to the east of Grasmere and became Wordsworth's home from 1815. In his *Guide*, Wordsworth noted that the best views of Rydal Water were from Rydal Park, but emphasized that the grounds were private (34). See McCracken, 114–26, for other poems relating to Rydal.

280 *Lines written when sailing in a Boat*. See 'Lines written near Richmond', 1798 and note (p. 337). In 1800, Wordsworth divided the earlier poem into two shorter pieces, which were then printed in Volume I. In 1802, both were moved into Volume II.

281 *Remembrance of Collins*. See note to the previous poem. In 1800, this poem retained the title 'Lines Written near Richmond', but in 1802 the revised title made its tribute to Collins more explicit.

282 *The Two Thieves*. Composed 1800. Wordsworth commented, 'This is described from the life as I was in the habit of observing when a boy at Hawkeskead School. Daniel was more than 80 years older than myself when he was daily thus occupied, under my notice, no book could so early taught me to think of the changes to which life is subject, & while looking at him I could not but say to myself we may, any of us I, or the happiest of my play mates, live to become still more the objects of pity than this old man, this half-doating pilferer' (*IF*, 57). See *WH*, 192–3, for the identity of Daniel.

ll. 1–2. *Bewick . . . Tyne*. Thomas Bewick (1755–1828), engraver from Cherryburn, near Newcastle-upon-Tyne, whose illustrated natural history books were very popular. The vignettes in his *British Birds* (1797) depicted various scenes of rural life, often comic or reflective.

l. 11. *Prodigal Son . . . Sheaves*. Well-known biblical stories, from Luke 15: 11–32 and Genesis 41: 22–53. The allusion underlines both Daniels' biblical name.

l. 13. *unbreech'd*. Not yet wearing trousers.

283 *'A whirl-blast from behind the Hill'*. Composed March 1798. Wordsworth commented, 'Observed in the holly grove at Alfoxden, where these verses were written' (*IF*, 11). Wordsworth's use of the Cumberland dialect word 'whirl-blast' for whirlwind is the first recorded use in the *OED*.

284 l. 21. *Robin Good-fellow*. Another name for Puck, the mischievous fairy from British folklore. See *A Midsummer Night's Dream*, II. i. 34.

Song for the Wandering Jew. Probably composed in Germany, 1799. The legend of the Jew who taunts Jesus on his last journey to the cross was well known from Percy, who included an account of the legend with the traditional ballad 'The Wandering Jew'. The figure fascinated Coleridge, who drew on the ballad for 'The Ancyent Marinere'. Lowes explored the sources, including the popular representations in the British theatres of the 1790s, in *The Road to Xanadu*, 242–54.

l. 6. *Chamois*. Alpine antelope.

285 *Michael*. Composed in Grasmere, October–December 1800. On Saturday 11 October, Dorothy Wordsworth recorded, 'After Dinner we walked up Greenhead Gill in search of a Sheepfold . . . The Colours of the Mountain soft & rich, with orange fern—The Cattle pasturing upon the hill-tops Kites sailing as in the sky above our heads—Sheep bleating & in lines and chains & patterns scattered over the mountains. They come down and feed

on the little green islands in the beds of the torrents & so may be swept away. The Sheepfold is falling away it is built nearly in the form of a heart' (*GJ*, 26). Wordsworth wrote several passages that were not part of the poem as published, including 'The Matron's Tale', later incorporated into *The Prelude*, viii. 222–311 (see Butler and Green, 319–38). In the first copies of 1800, ll. 202–16 were accidentally omitted. The importance to Wordsworth of 'Michael', and the passionate attachments of small farmers to their inherited lands depicted in the poem, is obvious from his letters to Charles James Fox (see Appendix 2) and to Thomas Poole, whose character was 'often before' his eyes during the composition of the poem (*EY*, 322–4). See also *Guide*, 74, where he describes the network of small, independent Lakeland sheep farmers as a 'perfect Republic of Shepherds and Agriculturalists', and his earlier, unpublished 'Letter to the Bishop of Llandaff' (1793). He later commented, 'The Sheepfold, on which so much of the poem turns, remains, or rather the ruins of it. The character & circumstances of Luke were taken from a family to whom had belonged, many years before, the house we lived in at Town-End, along with some fields and woodlands on the eastern shore of Grasmere. The name of the Evening Star was not in fact given to this house but to another on the same side of the valley more to the north' (*IF*, 10). Wordsworth's Endnotes are reprinted on p. 302.

285 l. 2. *Green-head Gill*. Stream near Grasmere, about 1 mile north of Dove Cottage.

l. 11. *kites*. Very large birds of prey, generally living on carrion.

l. 19. *ungarnish'd with events*. Unadorned. Cf. *Othello*, I. iii. 90.

286 l. 40. *Forest-side*. The area on the north-eastern side of Grasmere.

l. 75. *living Being*. The deep attachments of independent farmers to their small tracts of land are eloquently described in Wordsworth's letter to Fox.

287 ll. 84–6. *two wheels . . . flax*. Isabel spins wool and flax. Flax is a plant from which fibres can be harvested and spun. The first effective machine for spinning flax was developed in the early 1790s for the linen industry of North Yorkshire. For Wordsworth's concerns about traditional hand-spinning, see the note to p. 34, 'The Female Vagrant', l. 89.

l. 97. *industry*. The idealization of work, or industry, was traditionally part of the Georgic rather than pastoral tradition, but the Virgilian separation had already fused in eighteenth-century poems such as John Dyer's *The Fleece* (1757), as discussed by John Goodridge, *Rural Life in Eighteenth-Century English Poetry* (Cambridge, 1995). The modern associations of industry with heavy, mechanized labour were already current in 1800.

l. 113. *uncouth*. Unsophisticated, unpolished. The 'uncouth . . . style' may also have literary implications—see Spenser's prefatory epistle to 'E.K.' in *The Shepheardes Calendar*.

141. *Easedale . . . Dunmal-Raise*. Easedale runs out of Grasmere towards Langdale; Dunmail Raise is the pass on the road northwards to Thirlmere and Keswick.

l. 146. *EVENING STAR*. The name of Michael's cottage recalls Hesperus, and its appearance at the end of Virgil's *Eclogues*, x, though see also Wordsworth's comment, in the headnote above.

l. 149. *Help-mate*. Genesis 2: 18.

l. 150. *Son of his old age*. Genesis 21: 2, 37: 3.

289 l. 175. *old Oak*. Cf. Virgil, *Eclogues*, i.

290 ll. 202–16. *Though nought . . . his daily hope*. Lines omitted accidentally from 1800.

291 l. 256. *free as is the wind*. Michael wishes Luke to inherit the land without the heavy burden of a mortgage.

292 ll. 268–80. *Richard Bateman . . . lands*. Wordsworth's note on these lines appeared at the end of the volume (p. 302). Dorothy described the marble sent by Bateman in her journal, *GJ*, 132. The patterned marble floor remains in Ings Chapel, which is north-west of Kendal on the road to Windermere.

293 l. 340. *they had reach'd the place*. Genesis 22: 9.

295 ll. 417–20. *Be thy companions . . . pray that thou*. Revised from 1800: 'Be thy companions, let this Sheep-fold be | Thy anchor and thy shield; amid all fear | And all temptation let it be to thee | An emblem of the life thy Fathers liv'd'.

l. 425. *a covenant*. A solemn agreement, with powerful biblical associations. See Genesis 9: 12–17, 28: 12–15; Exodus 31: 12–17.

296 l. 454. *dissolute city*. Cf. Luke 15: 13. Unlike the Prodigal Son in the parable, Michael's son, Luke, does not return home to his father. Wordsworth's anxieties about the dangers posed by the great city to rural sons can be seen in *The Prelude*, vii.

298 *Appendix. 'What is usually called Poetic Diction'*. This 1802 addition sheds important light on Wordsworth's understanding of his new version of pastoral, as emphasized in the expanded title to the collection. Full annotation can be found in *Prose*, i. Wordsworth returned to the dangerous tendencies of certain kinds of language in the third *Essay upon Epitaphs*.

300 *'Turn on the prudent Ant . . . ambushed foe'*. Samuel Johnson, 'The Ant' (1766).

301 *'Religion! . . . never to see'*. Cowper, 'Verses supposed to be written by Alexander Selkirk', ll. 25–40.

INDEX OF TITLES AND FIRST LINES

Titles are in italics. Poems that appear in 1798 and 1802 are distinguished by the date of publication. Where first lines appear in 1798 and 1802, page references to both are included in chronological order.

American Literature

British and Irish Literature

Children's Literature

Classics and Ancient Literature

Colonial Literature

Eastern Literature

European Literature

Gothic Literature

History

Medieval Literature

Oxford English Drama

Philosophy

Poetry

Politics

Religion

The Oxford Shakespeare

A complete list of Oxford World's Classics, including Authors in Context, Oxford English Drama, and the Oxford Shakespeare, is available in the UK from the Marketing Services Department, Oxford University Press, Great Clarendon Street, Oxford OX2 6DP, or visit the website at www.oup.com/uk/worldsclassics.

In the USA, visit www.oup.com/us/owc for a complete title list.

Oxford World's Classics are available from all good bookshops. In case of difficulty, customers in the UK should contact Oxford University Press Bookshop, 116 High Street, Oxford OX1 4BR.

CHARLES DICKENS	A Tale of Two Cities
GEORGE DU MAURIER	Trilby
MARIA EDGEWORTH	Castle Rackrent
GEORGE ELIOT	Daniel Deronda
	The Lifted Veil and Brother Jacob
	Middlemarch
	The Mill on the Floss
	Silas Marner
SUSAN FERRIER	Marriage
ELIZABETH GASKELL	Cranford
	The Life of Charlotte Brontë
	Mary Barton
	North and South
	Wives and Daughters
GEORGE GISSING	New Grub Street
	The Odd Women
EDMUND GOSSE	Father and Son
THOMAS HARDY	Far from the Madding Crowd
	Jude the Obscure
	The Mayor of Casterbridge
	The Return of the Native
	Tess of the d'Urbervilles
	The Woodlanders
WILLIAM HAZLITT	Selected Writings
JAMES HOGG	The Private Memoirs and Confessions of a Justified Sinner
JOHN KEATS	The Major Works
	Selected Letters
CHARLES MATURIN	Melmoth the Wanderer
JOHN RUSKIN	Selected Writings
WALTER SCOTT	The Antiquary
	Ivanhoe